CLUE®

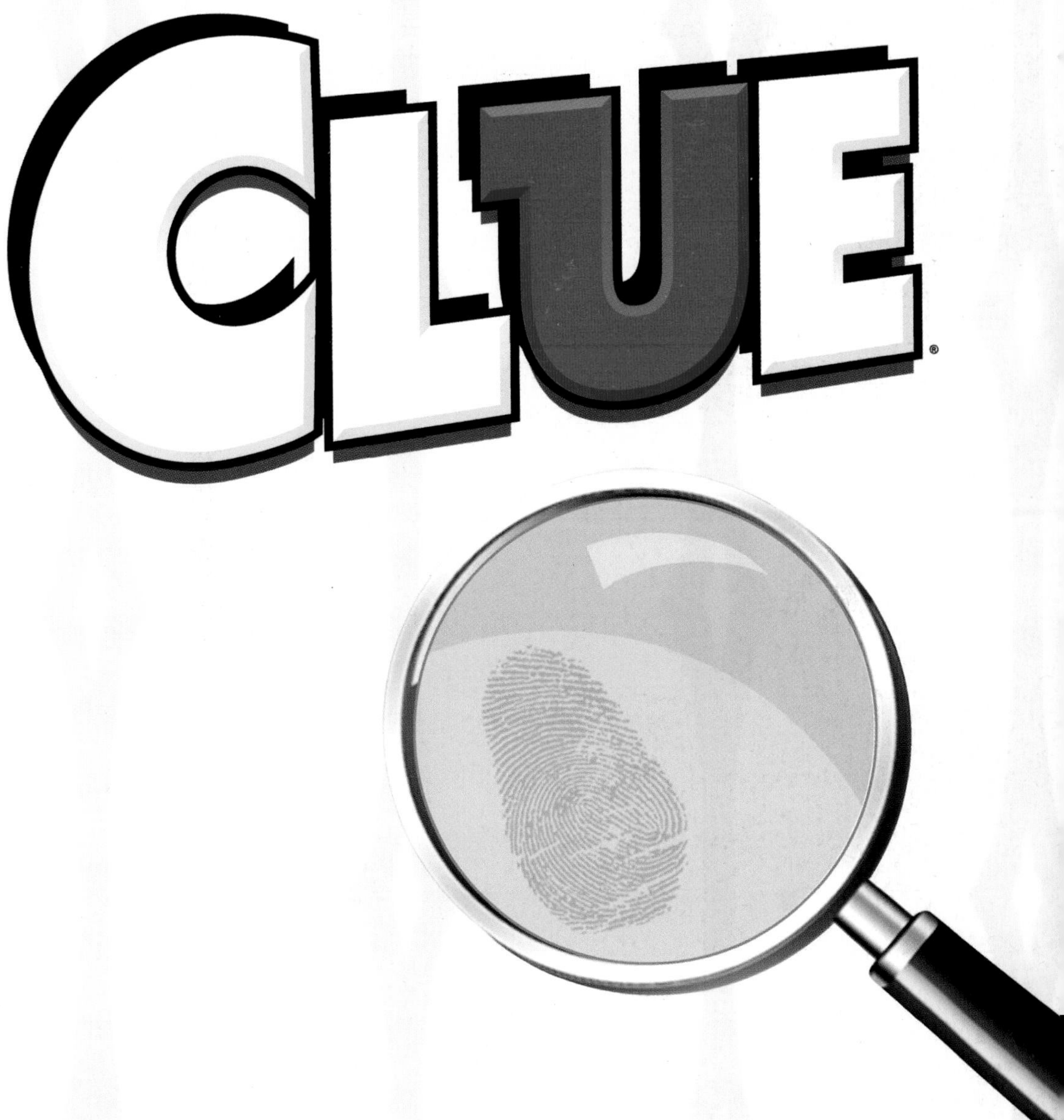

Become our fan on Facebook **facebook.com/idwpublishing**
Follow us on Twitter **@idwpublishing**
Subscribe to us on YouTube **youtube.com/idwpublishing**
See what's new on Tumblr **tumblr.idwpublishing.com**
Check us out on Instagram **instagram.com/idwpublishing**

IDW
www.IDWPUBLISHING.com

Licensed By:

Greg Goldstein, President & Publisher
Robbie Robbins, EVP/Sr. Art Director
Chris Ryall, Chief Creative Officer & Editor-in-Chief
Matthew Ruzicka, CPA, Chief Financial Officer
David Hedgecock, Associate Publisher
Laurie Windrow, Senior Vice President of Sales & Marketing
Lorelei Bunjes, VP of Digital Services
Eric Moss, Sr. Director, Licensing & Business Development

Ted Adams, Founder & CEO of IDW Media Holdings

ISBN: 978-1-68405-118-2   21 20 19 18   1 2 3 4

Originally published as CLUE issues #1–6.

Special thanks to Nate Fernando, Nikki Kennamer, Ed Lane, Beth Artale, and Michael Kelly.

For international rights, contact licensing@idwpublishing.com

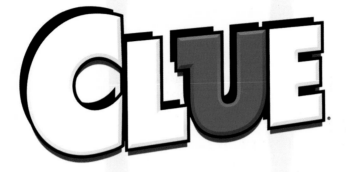

WRITTEN BY
PAUL ALLOR

ART BY
NELSON DANIEL

LETTERS BY
NEIL UYETAKE AND **GILBERTO LAZCANO**

SERIES EDITS BY
CARLOS GUZMAN

COLLECTION EDITS BY
JUSTIN EISINGER AND **ALONZO SIMON**

COLLECTION DESIGN BY
CLAUDIA CHONG

PUBLISHER
GREG GOLDSTEIN

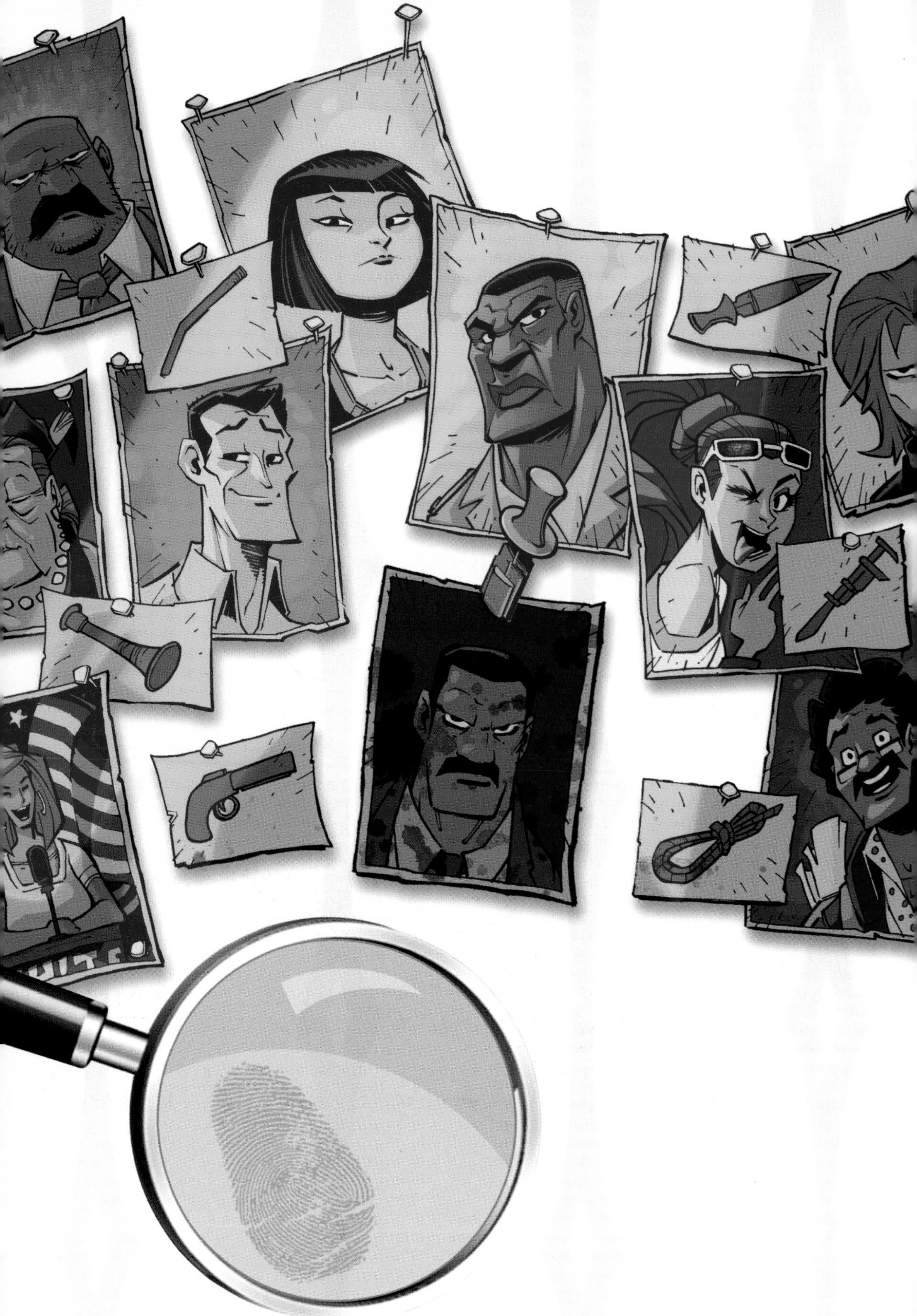

Roll Call

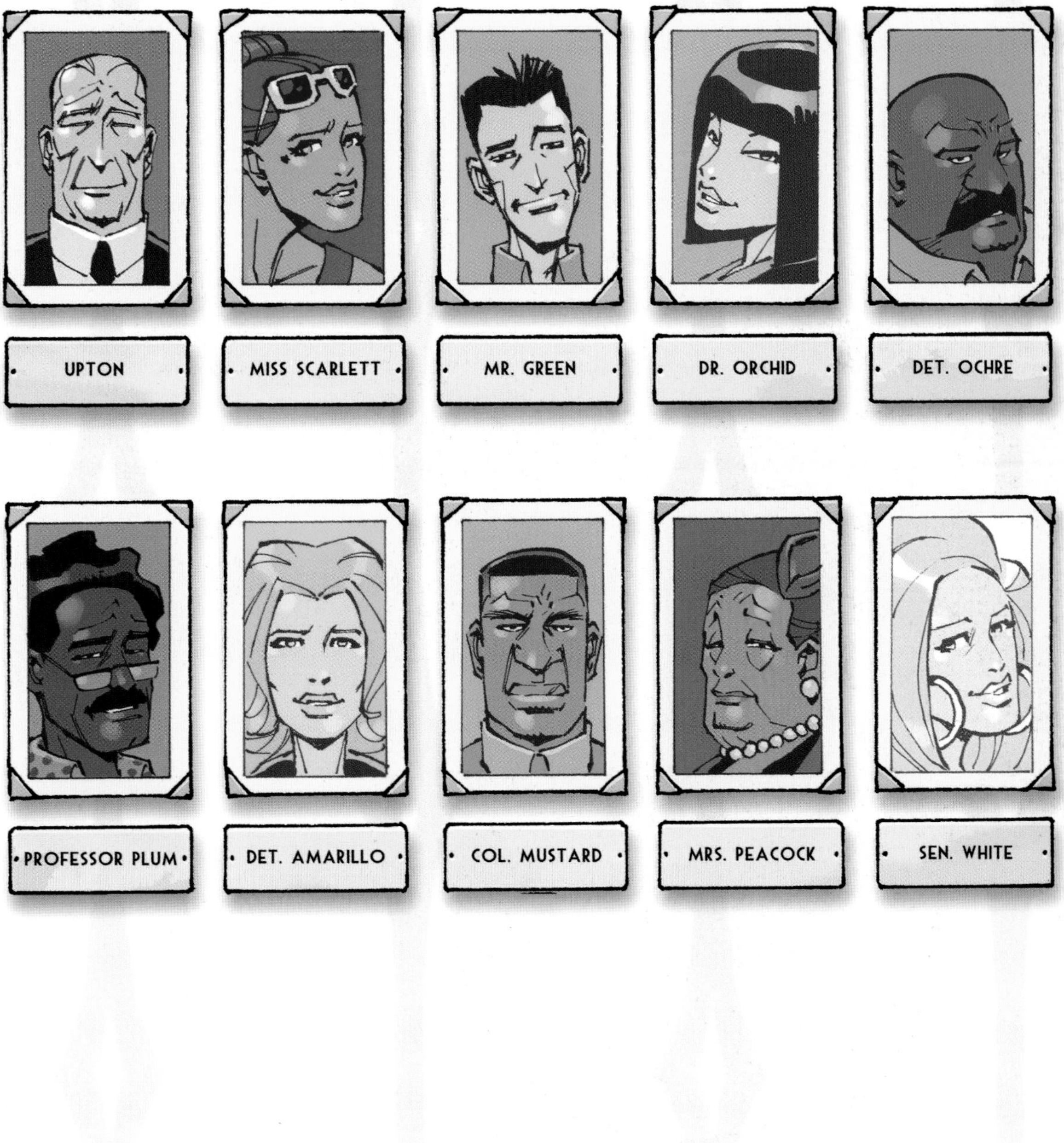
UPTON
MISS SCARLETT
MR. GREEN
DR. ORCHID
DET. OCHRE
PROFESSOR PLUM
DET. AMARILLO
COL. MUSTARD
MRS. PEACOCK
SEN. WHITE

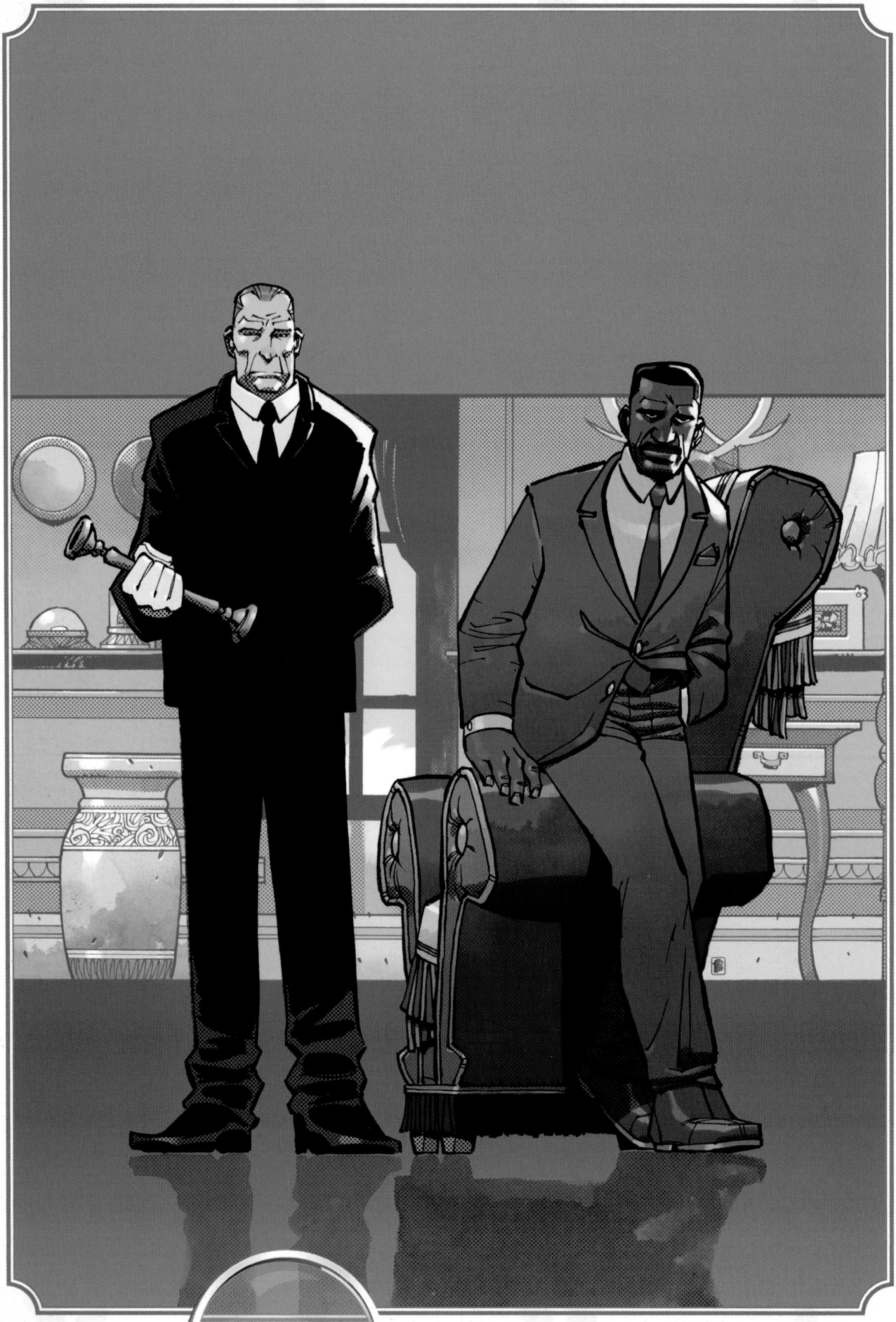

COVER ART BY
NELSON DANIEL

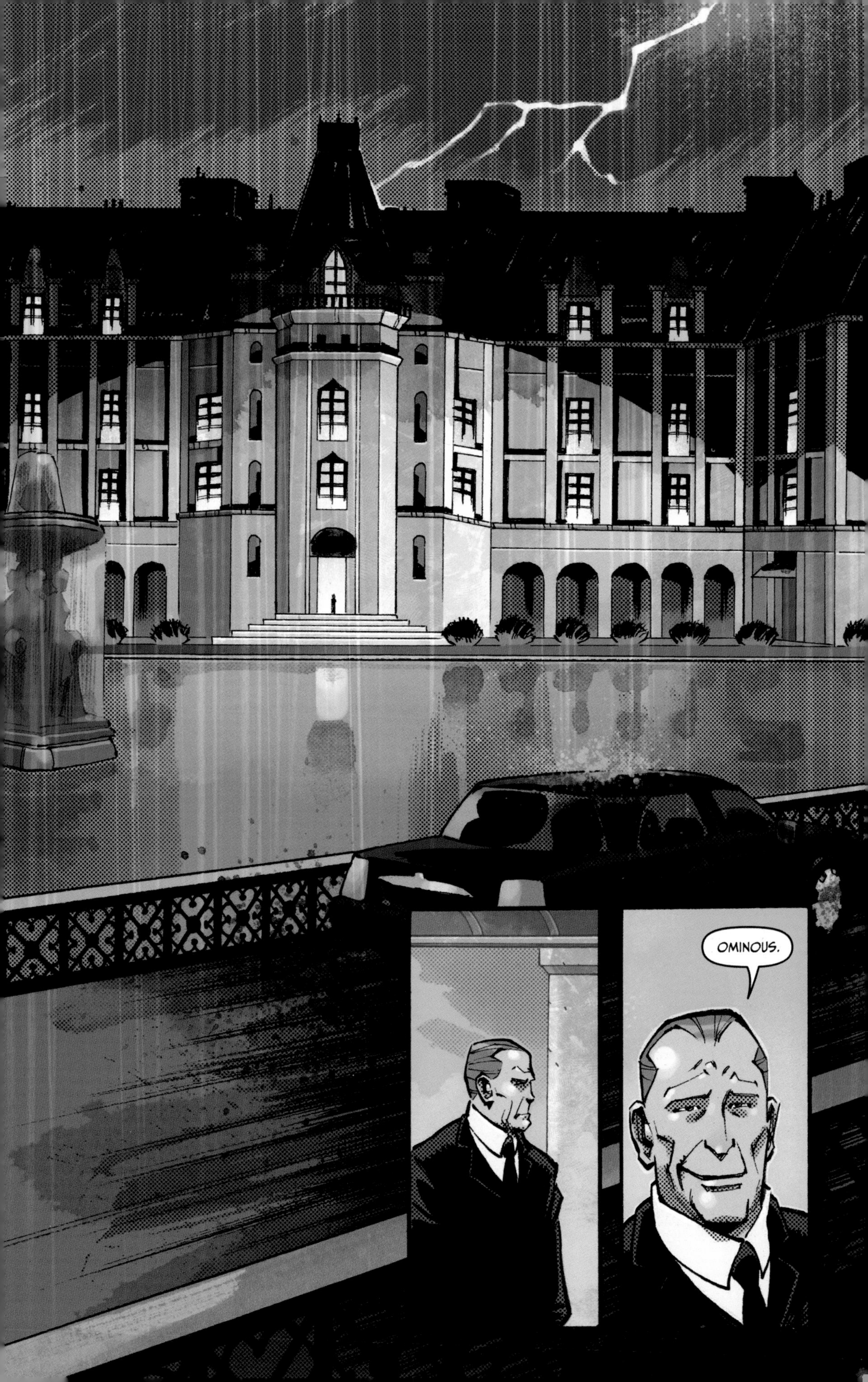
OMINOUS.

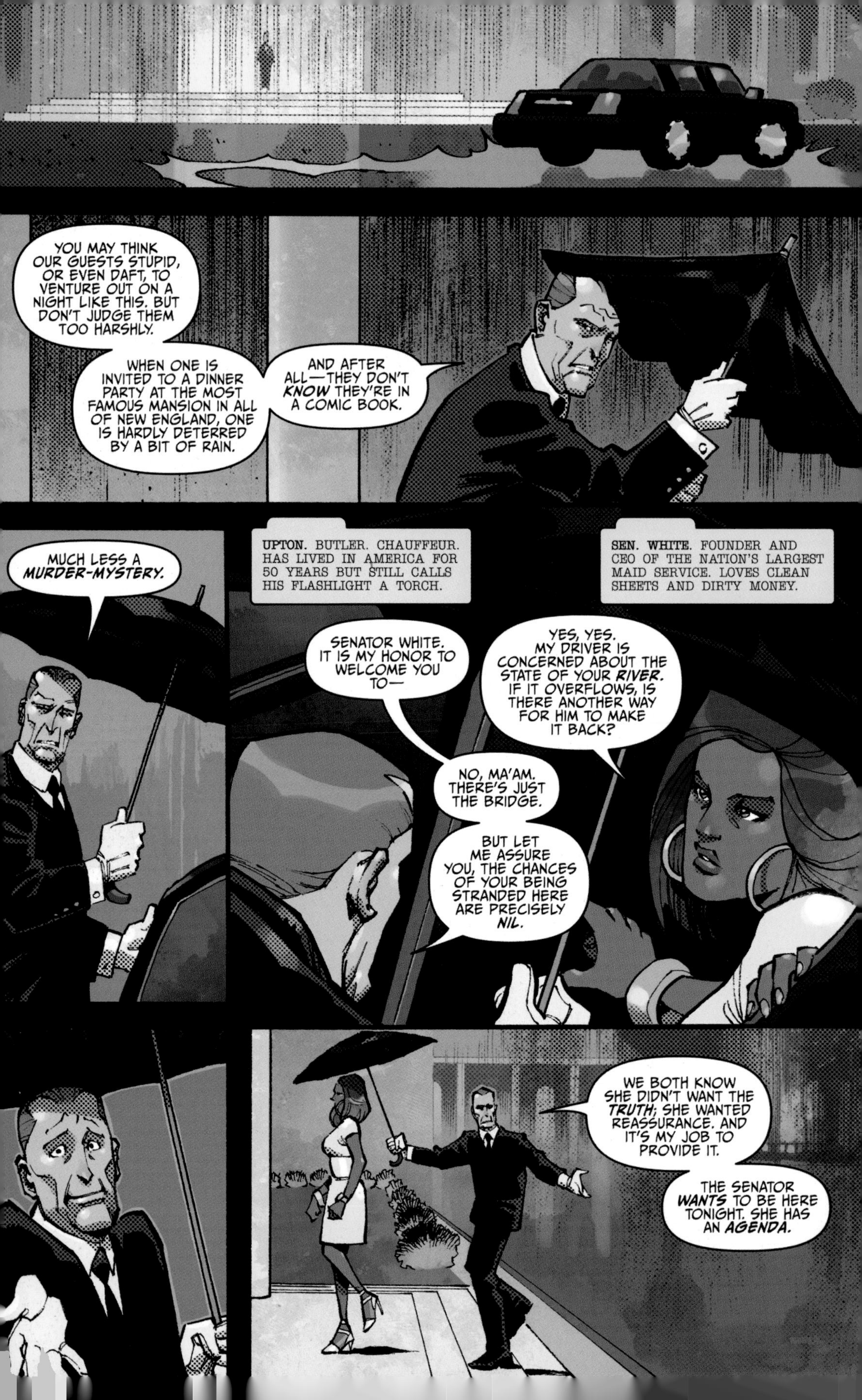
YOU MAY THINK OUR GUESTS STUPID, OR EVEN DAFT, TO VENTURE OUT ON A NIGHT LIKE THIS. BUT DON'T JUDGE THEM TOO HARSHLY.
WHEN ONE IS INVITED TO A DINNER PARTY AT THE MOST FAMOUS MANSION IN ALL OF NEW ENGLAND, ONE IS HARDLY DETERRED BY A BIT OF RAIN.
AND AFTER ALL—THEY DON'T KNOW THEY'RE IN A COMIC BOOK.
MUCH LESS A MURDER-MYSTERY.
UPTON. BUTLER. CHAUFFEUR. HAS LIVED IN AMERICA FOR 50 YEARS BUT STILL CALLS HIS FLASHLIGHT A TORCH.
SEN. WHITE. FOUNDER AND CEO OF THE NATION'S LARGEST MAID SERVICE. LOVES CLEAN SHEETS AND DIRTY MONEY.
SENATOR WHITE. IT IS MY HONOR TO WELCOME YOU TO—
YES, YES. MY DRIVER IS CONCERNED ABOUT THE STATE OF YOUR RIVER. IF IT OVERFLOWS, IS THERE ANOTHER WAY FOR HIM TO MAKE IT BACK?
NO, MA'AM. THERE'S JUST THE BRIDGE.
BUT LET ME ASSURE YOU, THE CHANCES OF YOUR BEING STRANDED HERE ARE PRECISELY NIL.
WE BOTH KNOW SHE DIDN'T WANT THE TRUTH; SHE WANTED REASSURANCE. AND IT'S MY JOB TO PROVIDE IT.
THE SENATOR WANTS TO BE HERE TONIGHT. SHE HAS AN AGENDA.

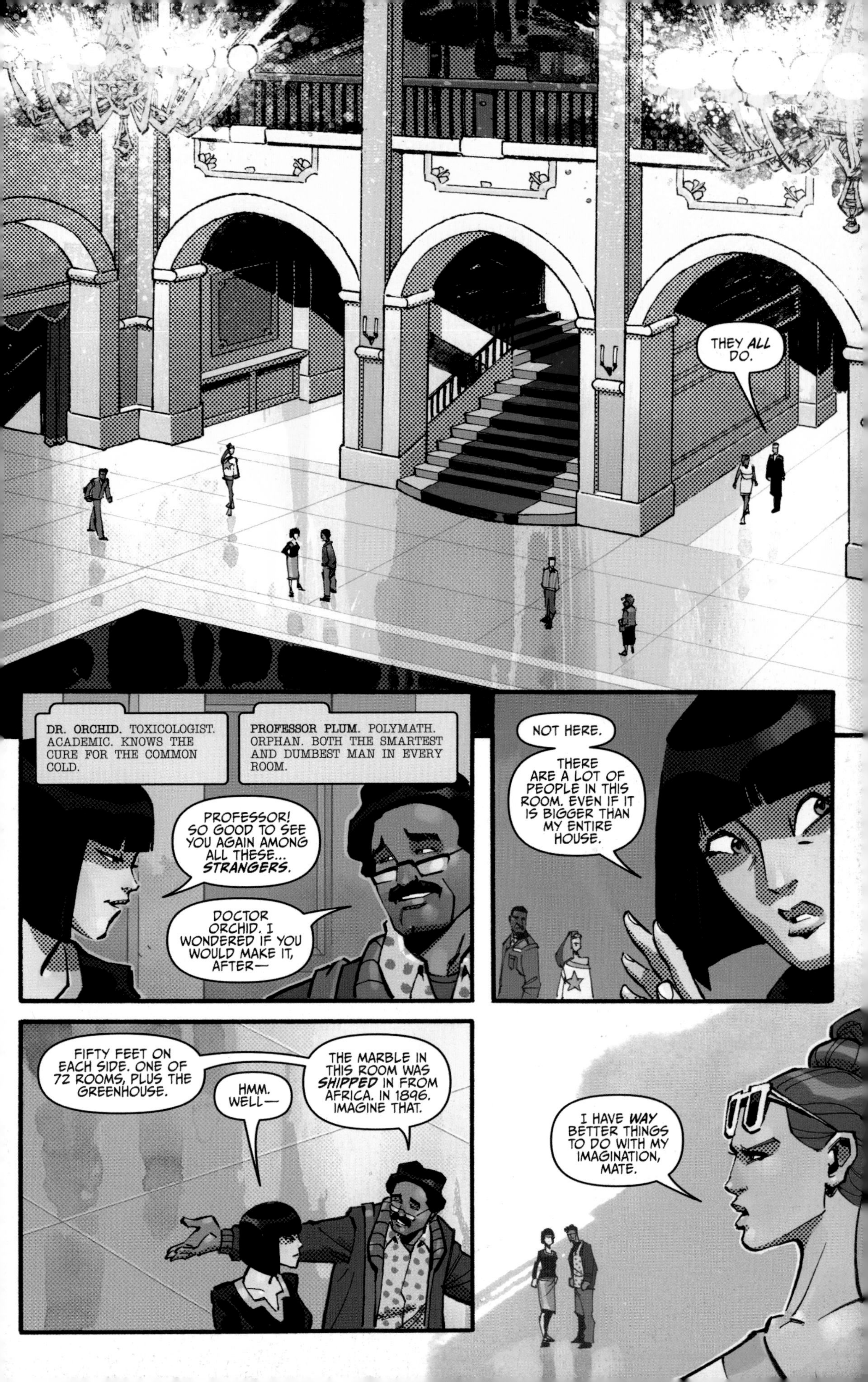
THEY ALL DO.
DR. ORCHID. TOXICOLOGIST. ACADEMIC. KNOWS THE CURE FOR THE COMMON COLD.
PROFESSOR PLUM. POLYMATH. ORPHAN. BOTH THE SMARTEST AND DUMBEST MAN IN EVERY ROOM.
PROFESSOR! SO GOOD TO SEE YOU AGAIN AMONG ALL THESE... STRANGERS.
DOCTOR ORCHID. I WONDERED IF YOU WOULD MAKE IT, AFTER—
NOT HERE.
THERE ARE A LOT OF PEOPLE IN THIS ROOM. EVEN IF IT IS BIGGER THAN MY ENTIRE HOUSE.
FIFTY FEET ON EACH SIDE. ONE OF 72 ROOMS, PLUS THE GREENHOUSE.
HMM. WELL—
THE MARBLE IN THIS ROOM WAS SHIPPED IN FROM AFRICA. IN 1896. IMAGINE THAT.
I HAVE WAY BETTER THINGS TO DO WITH MY IMAGINATION, MATE.

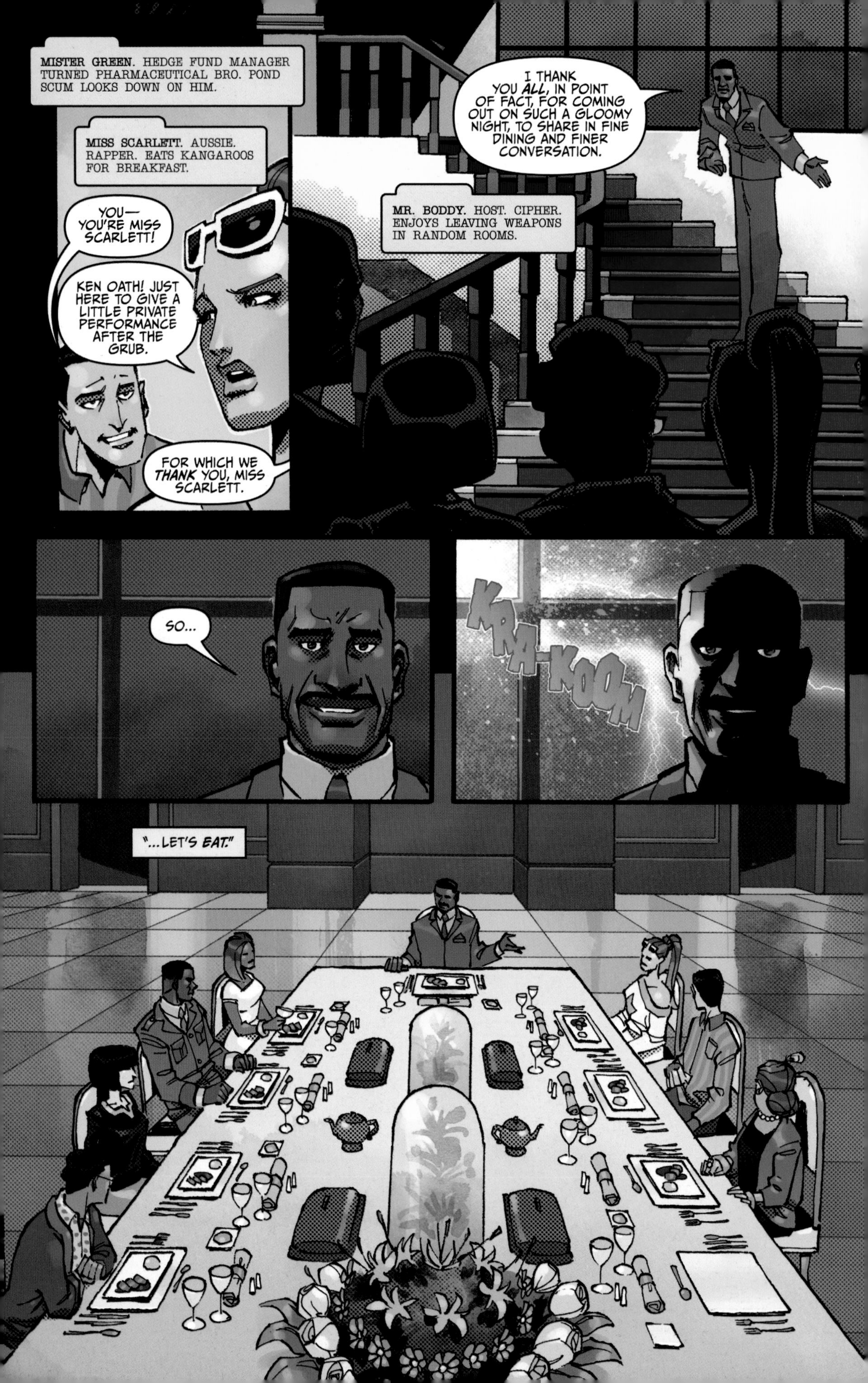
MISTER GREEN. HEDGE FUND MANAGER TURNED PHARMACEUTICAL BRO. POND SCUM LOOKS DOWN ON HIM.
MISS SCARLETT. AUSSIE. RAPPER. EATS KANGAROOS FOR BREAKFAST.
YOU— YOU'RE MISS SCARLETT!
KEN OATH! JUST HERE TO GIVE A LITTLE PRIVATE PERFORMANCE AFTER THE GRUB.
FOR WHICH WE THANK YOU, MISS SCARLETT.
I THANK YOU ALL, IN POINT OF FACT, FOR COMING OUT ON SUCH A GLOOMY NIGHT, TO SHARE IN FINE DINING AND FINER CONVERSATION.
MR. BODDY. HOST. CIPHER. ENJOYS LEAVING WEAPONS IN RANDOM ROOMS.
SO...
KRA-KOOM
"...LET'S EAT."

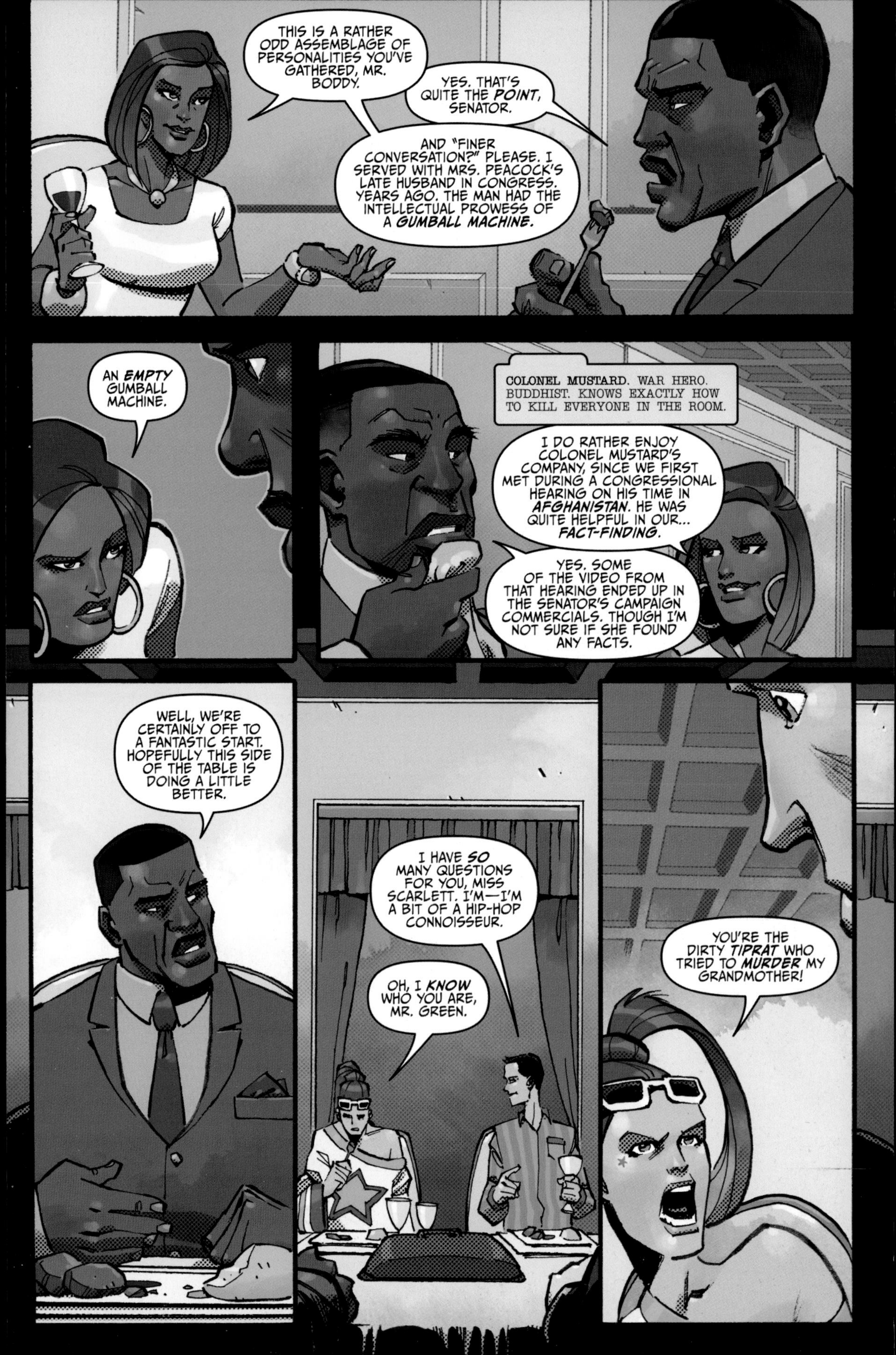
THIS IS A RATHER ODD ASSEMBLAGE OF PERSONALITIES YOU'VE GATHERED, MR. BODDY.
YES. THAT'S QUITE THE POINT, SENATOR.
AND "FINER CONVERSATION?" PLEASE. I SERVED WITH MRS. PEACOCK'S LATE HUSBAND IN CONGRESS. YEARS AGO. THE MAN HAD THE INTELLECTUAL PROWESS OF A GUMBALL MACHINE.
AN EMPTY GUMBALL MACHINE.
COLONEL MUSTARD. WAR HERO. BUDDHIST. KNOWS EXACTLY HOW TO KILL EVERYONE IN THE ROOM.
I DO RATHER ENJOY COLONEL MUSTARD'S COMPANY, SINCE WE FIRST MET DURING A CONGRESSIONAL HEARING ON HIS TIME IN AFGHANISTAN. HE WAS QUITE HELPFUL IN OUR... FACT-FINDING.
YES. SOME OF THE VIDEO FROM THAT HEARING ENDED UP IN THE SENATOR'S CAMPAIGN COMMERCIALS. THOUGH I'M NOT SURE IF SHE FOUND ANY FACTS.
WELL, WE'RE CERTAINLY OFF TO A FANTASTIC START. HOPEFULLY THIS SIDE OF THE TABLE IS DOING A LITTLE BETTER.
I HAVE SO MANY QUESTIONS FOR YOU, MISS SCARLETT. I'M—I'M A BIT OF A HIP-HOP CONNOISSEUR.
OH, I KNOW WHO YOU ARE, MR. GREEN.
YOU'RE THE DIRTY TIPRAT WHO TRIED TO MURDER MY GRANDMOTHER!

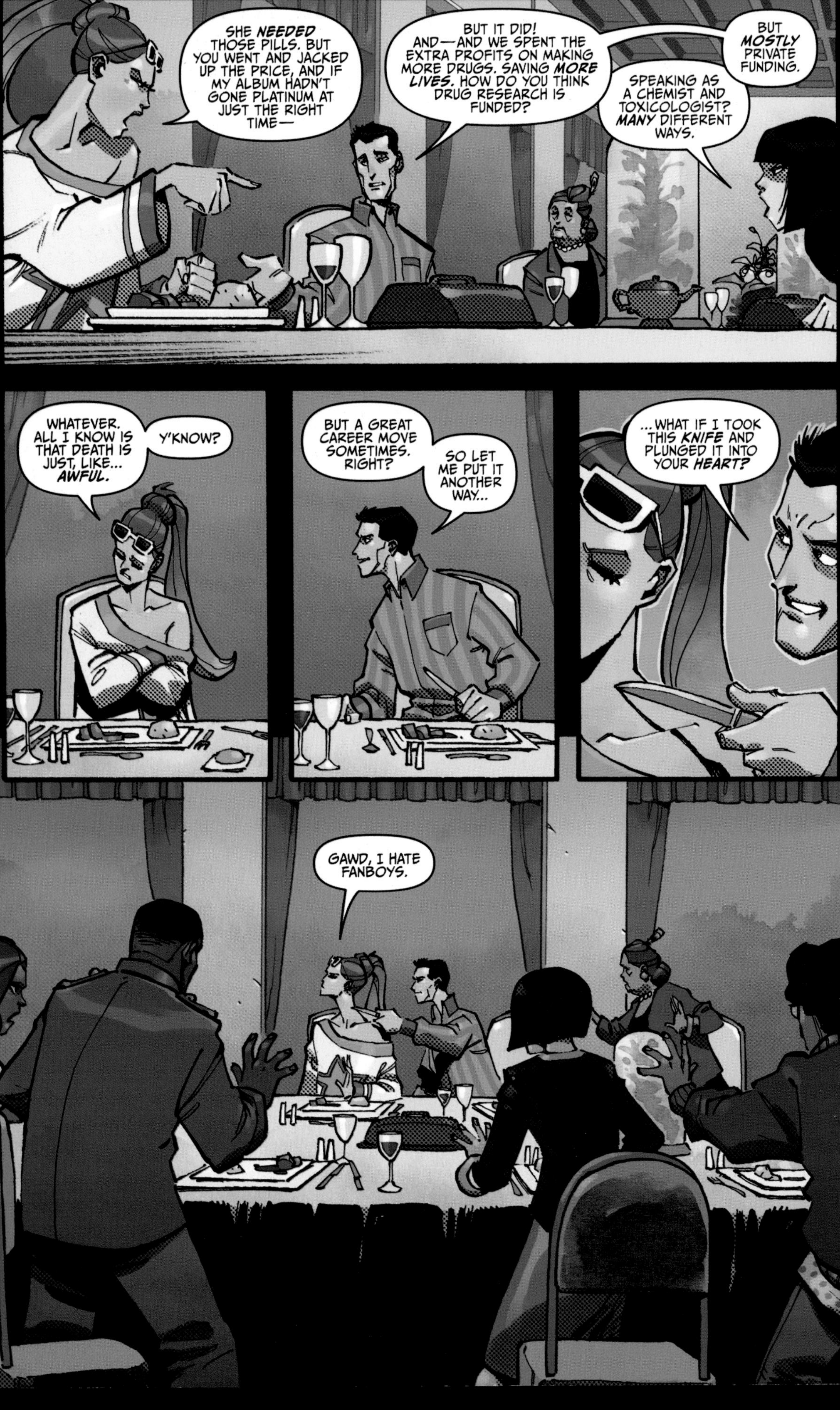
SHE NEEDED THOSE PILLS. BUT YOU WENT AND JACKED UP THE PRICE, AND IF MY ALBUM HADN'T GONE PLATINUM AT JUST THE RIGHT TIME—
BUT IT DID! AND—AND WE SPENT THE EXTRA PROFITS ON MAKING MORE DRUGS. SAVING MORE LIVES. HOW DO YOU THINK DRUG RESEARCH IS FUNDED?
SPEAKING AS A CHEMIST AND TOXICOLOGIST? MANY DIFFERENT WAYS.
BUT MOSTLY PRIVATE FUNDING.
WHATEVER. ALL I KNOW IS THAT DEATH IS JUST, LIKE... AWFUL.
Y'KNOW?
BUT A GREAT CAREER MOVE SOMETIMES. RIGHT?
SO LET ME PUT IT ANOTHER WAY...
...WHAT IF I TOOK THIS KNIFE AND PLUNGED IT INTO YOUR HEART?
GAWD, I HATE FANBOYS.

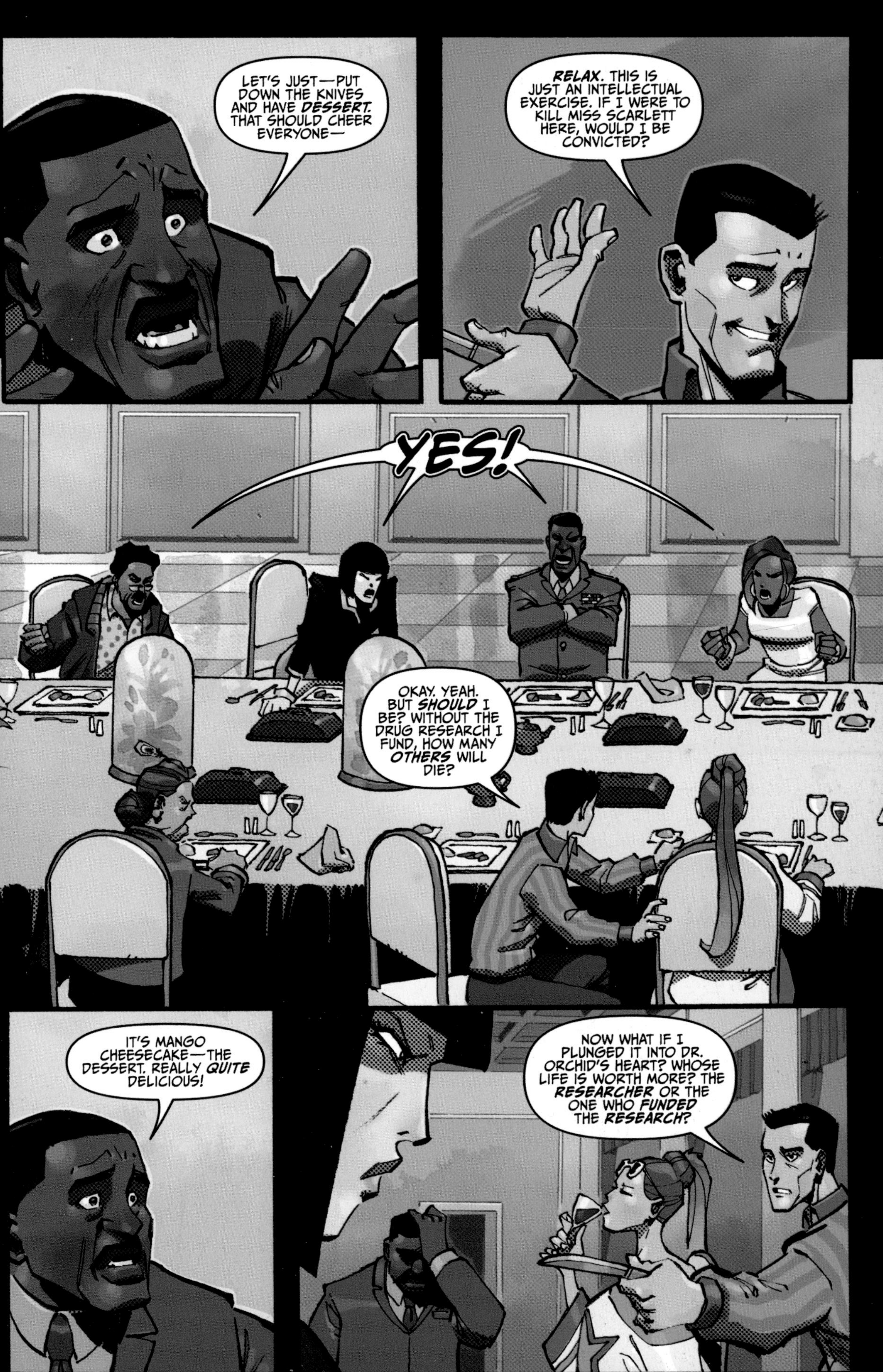
LET'S JUST—PUT DOWN THE KNIVES AND HAVE DESSERT. THAT SHOULD CHEER EVERYONE—
RELAX. THIS IS JUST AN INTELLECTUAL EXERCISE. IF I WERE TO KILL MISS SCARLETT HERE, WOULD I BE CONVICTED?
YES!
OKAY. YEAH. BUT SHOULD I BE? WITHOUT THE DRUG RESEARCH I FUND, HOW MANY OTHERS WILL DIE?
IT'S MANGO CHEESECAKE—THE DESSERT. REALLY QUITE DELICIOUS!
NOW WHAT IF I PLUNGED IT INTO DR. ORCHID'S HEART? WHOSE LIFE IS WORTH MORE? THE RESEARCHER OR THE ONE WHO FUNDED THE RESEARCH?

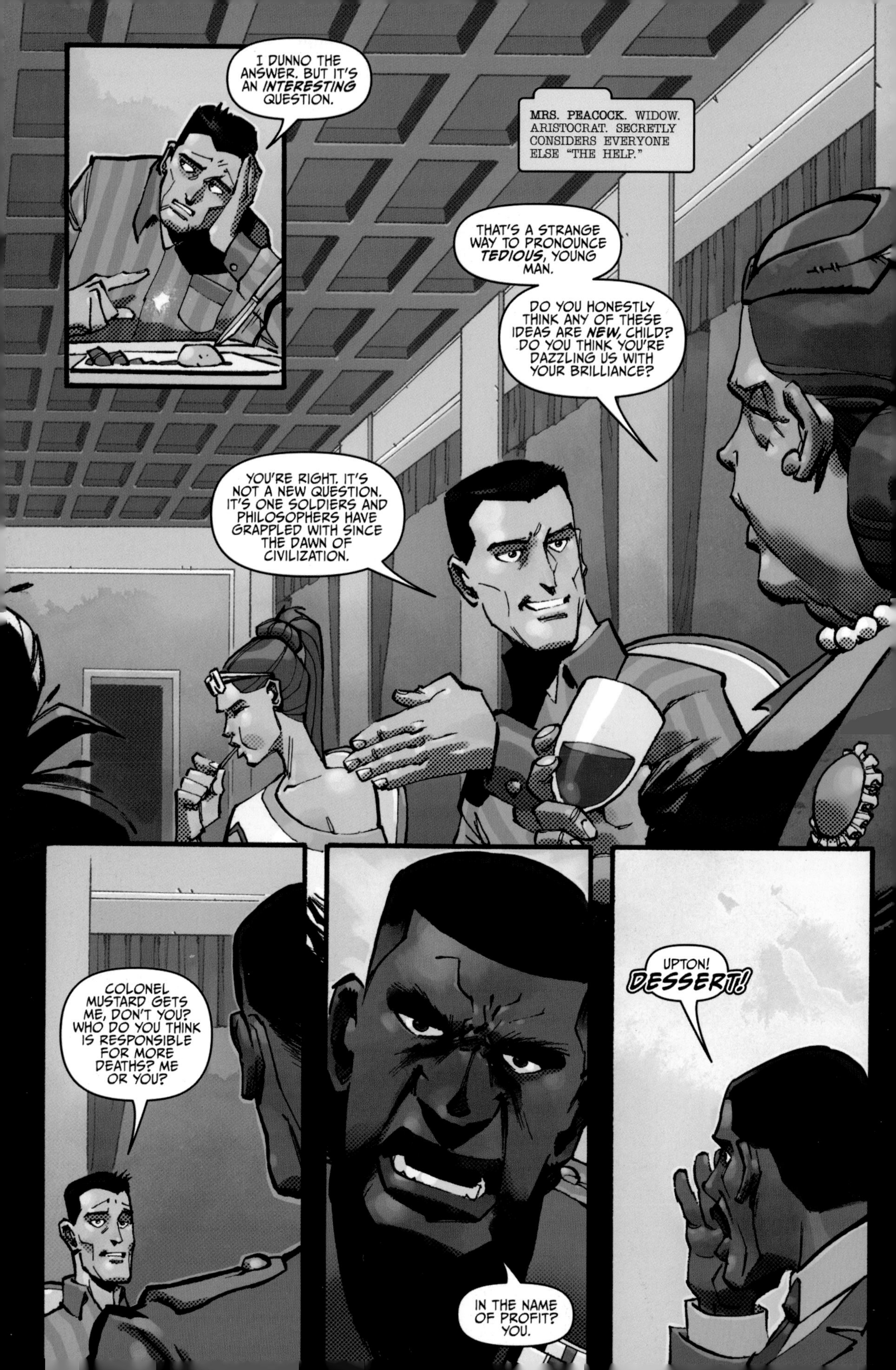
I DUNNO THE ANSWER. BUT IT'S AN *INTERESTING* QUESTION.
MRS. PEACOCK. WIDOW. ARISTOCRAT. SECRETLY CONSIDERS EVERYONE ELSE "THE HELP."
THAT'S A STRANGE WAY TO PRONOUNCE *TEDIOUS*, YOUNG MAN.
DO YOU HONESTLY THINK ANY OF THESE IDEAS ARE *NEW*, CHILD? DO YOU THINK YOU'RE DAZZLING US WITH YOUR BRILLIANCE?
YOU'RE RIGHT. IT'S NOT A NEW QUESTION. IT'S ONE SOLDIERS AND PHILOSOPHERS HAVE GRAPPLED WITH SINCE THE DAWN OF CIVILIZATION.
COLONEL MUSTARD GETS ME, DON'T YOU? WHO DO YOU THINK IS RESPONSIBLE FOR MORE DEATHS? ME OR YOU?
IN THE NAME OF PROFIT? YOU.
UPTON! DESSERT!

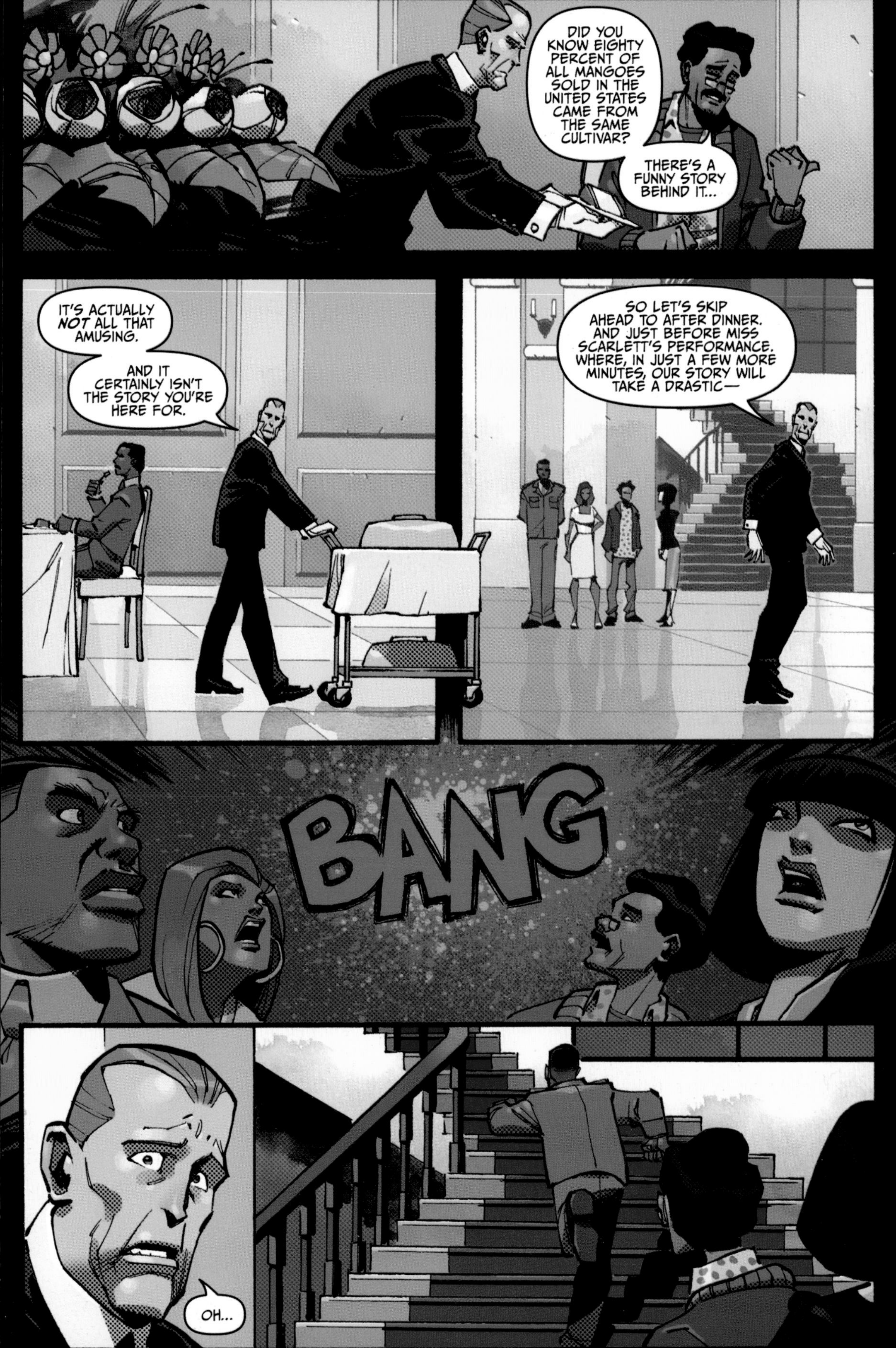
DID YOU KNOW EIGHTY PERCENT OF ALL MANGOES SOLD IN THE UNITED STATES CAME FROM THE SAME CULTIVAR?
THERE'S A FUNNY STORY BEHIND IT...
IT'S ACTUALLY NOT ALL THAT AMUSING.
AND IT CERTAINLY ISN'T THE STORY YOU'RE HERE FOR.
SO LET'S SKIP AHEAD TO AFTER DINNER. AND JUST BEFORE MISS SCARLETT'S PERFORMANCE. WHERE, IN JUST A FEW MORE MINUTES, OUR STORY WILL TAKE A DRASTIC—
BANG
OH...

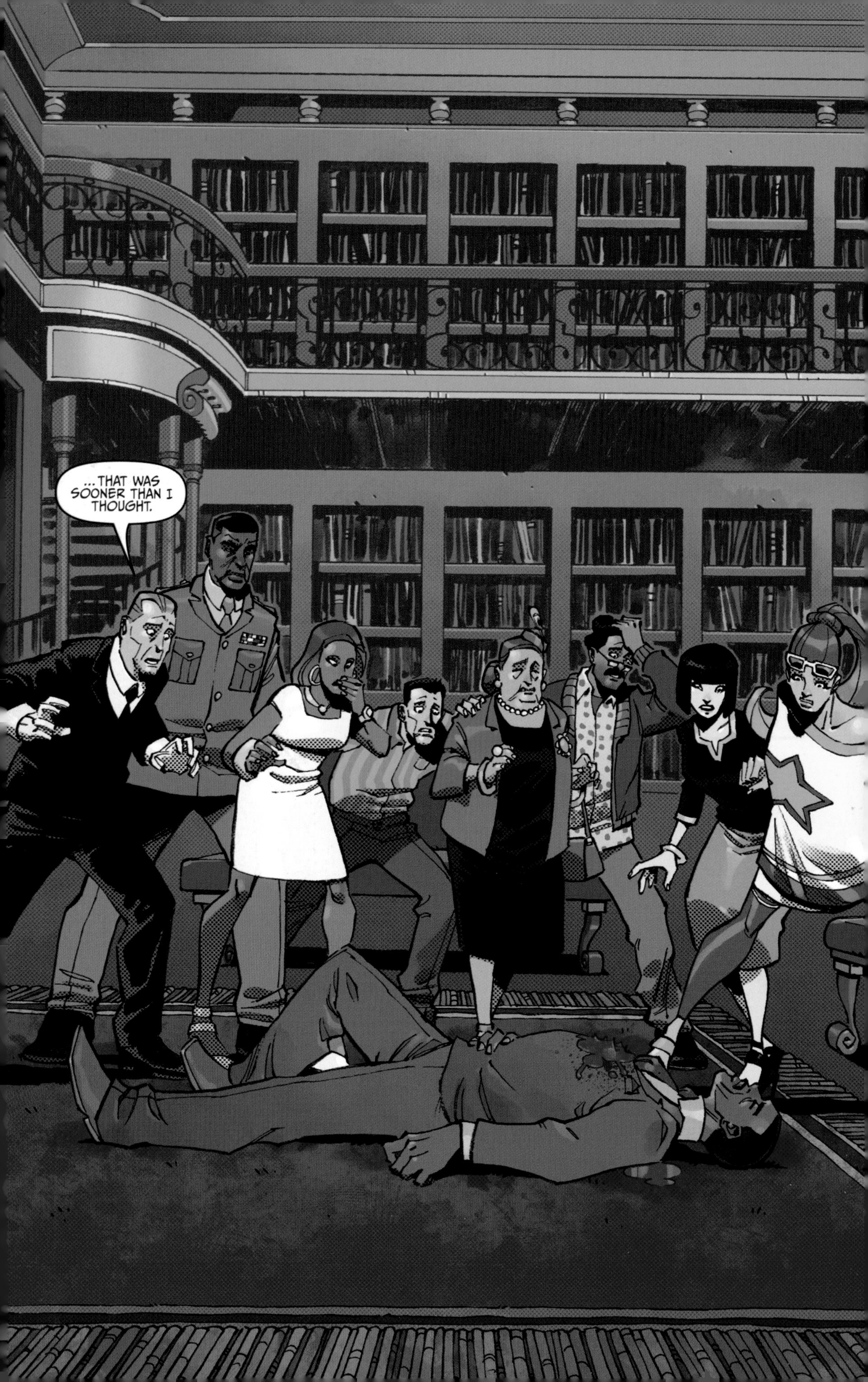
...THAT WAS SOONER THAN I THOUGHT.

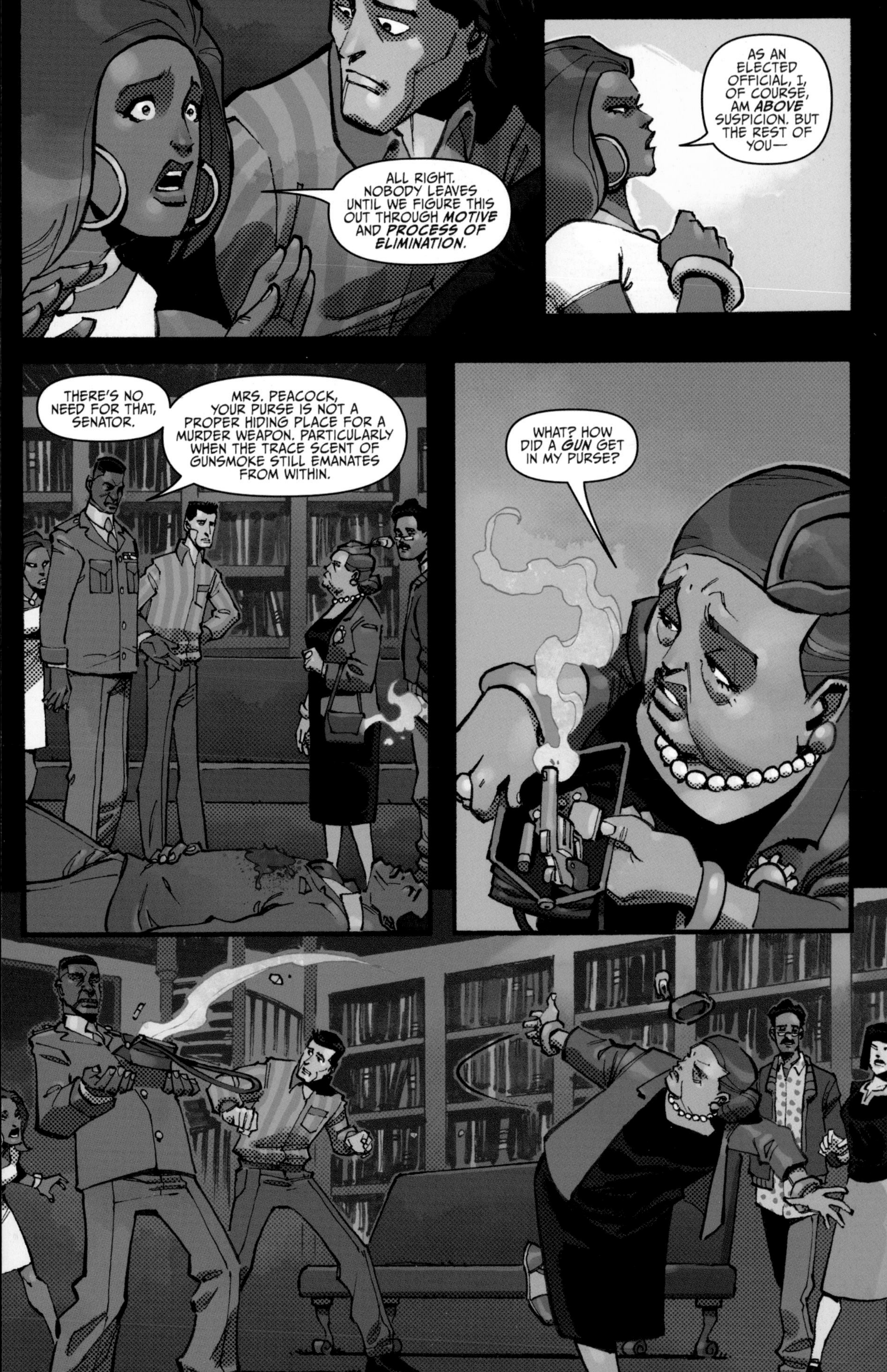
ALL RIGHT. NOBODY LEAVES UNTIL WE FIGURE THIS OUT THROUGH *MOTIVE* AND *PROCESS OF ELIMINATION.*
AS AN ELECTED OFFICIAL, I, OF COURSE, AM *ABOVE* SUSPICION. BUT THE REST OF YOU—
THERE'S NO NEED FOR THAT, SENATOR.
MRS. PEACOCK, YOUR PURSE IS NOT A PROPER HIDING PLACE FOR A MURDER WEAPON. PARTICULARLY WHEN THE TRACE SCENT OF GUNSMOKE STILL EMANATES FROM WITHIN.
WHAT? HOW DID A *GUN* GET IN MY PURSE?

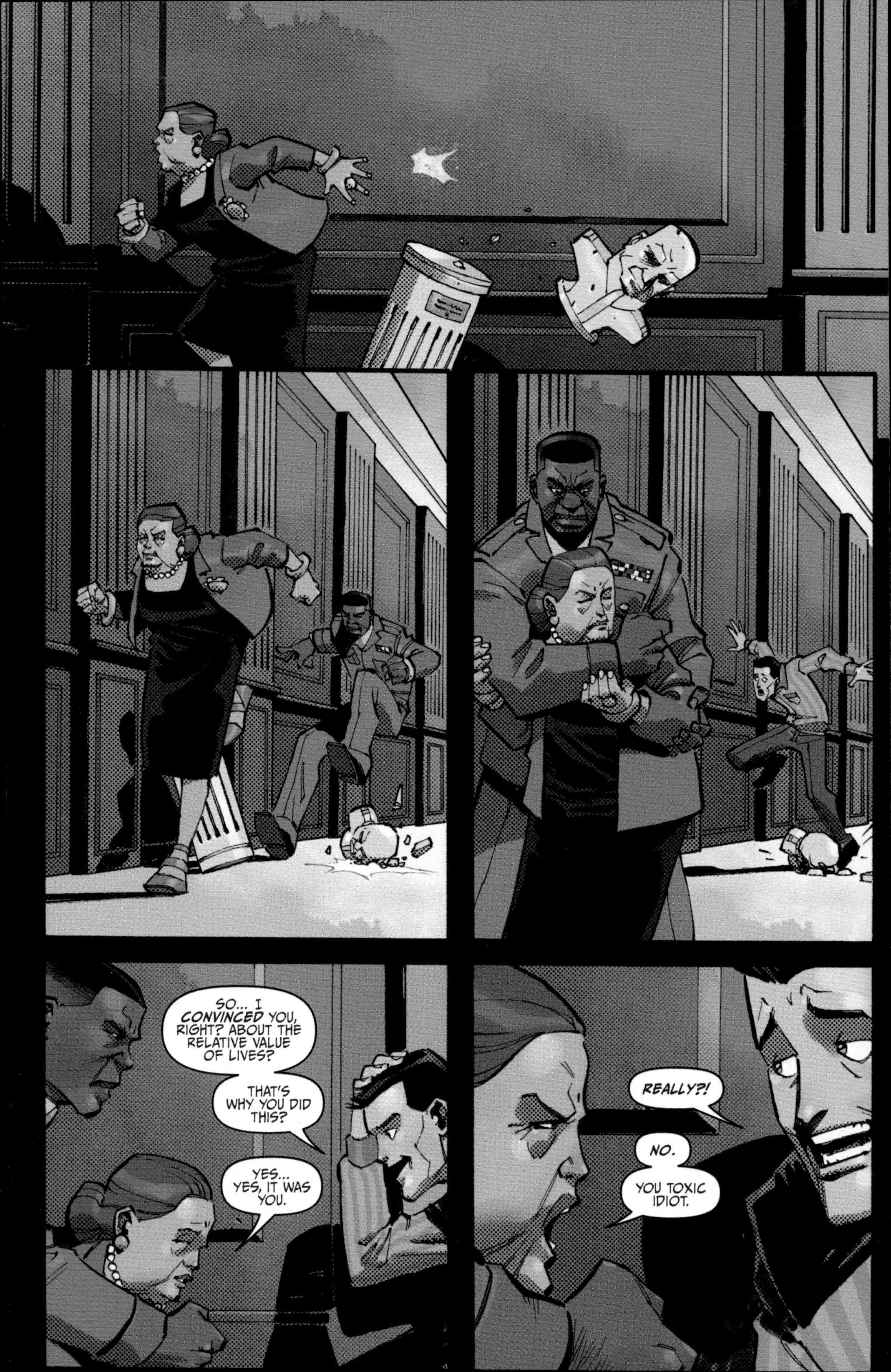
SO... I CONVINCED YOU, RIGHT? ABOUT THE RELATIVE VALUE OF LIVES?
THAT'S WHY YOU DID THIS?
YES... YES, IT WAS YOU.
REALLY?!
NO.
YOU TOXIC IDIOT.

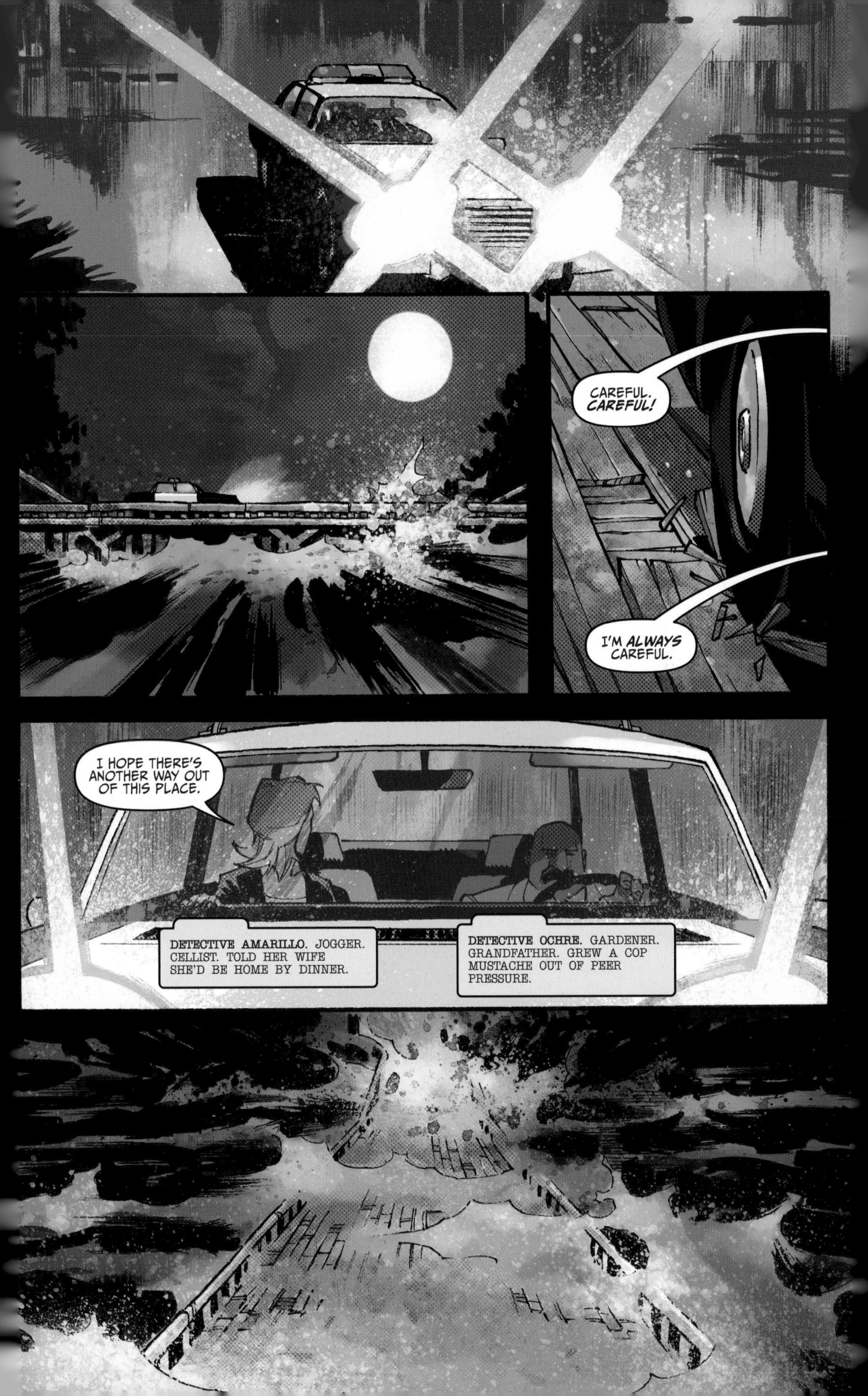
CAREFUL. *CAREFUL!*
I'M *ALWAYS* CAREFUL.
I HOPE THERE'S ANOTHER WAY OUT OF THIS PLACE.
DETECTIVE AMARILLO. JOGGER. CELLIST. TOLD HER WIFE SHE'D BE HOME BY DINNER.
DETECTIVE OCHRE. GARDENER. GRANDFATHER. GREW A COP MUSTACHE OUT OF PEER PRESSURE.

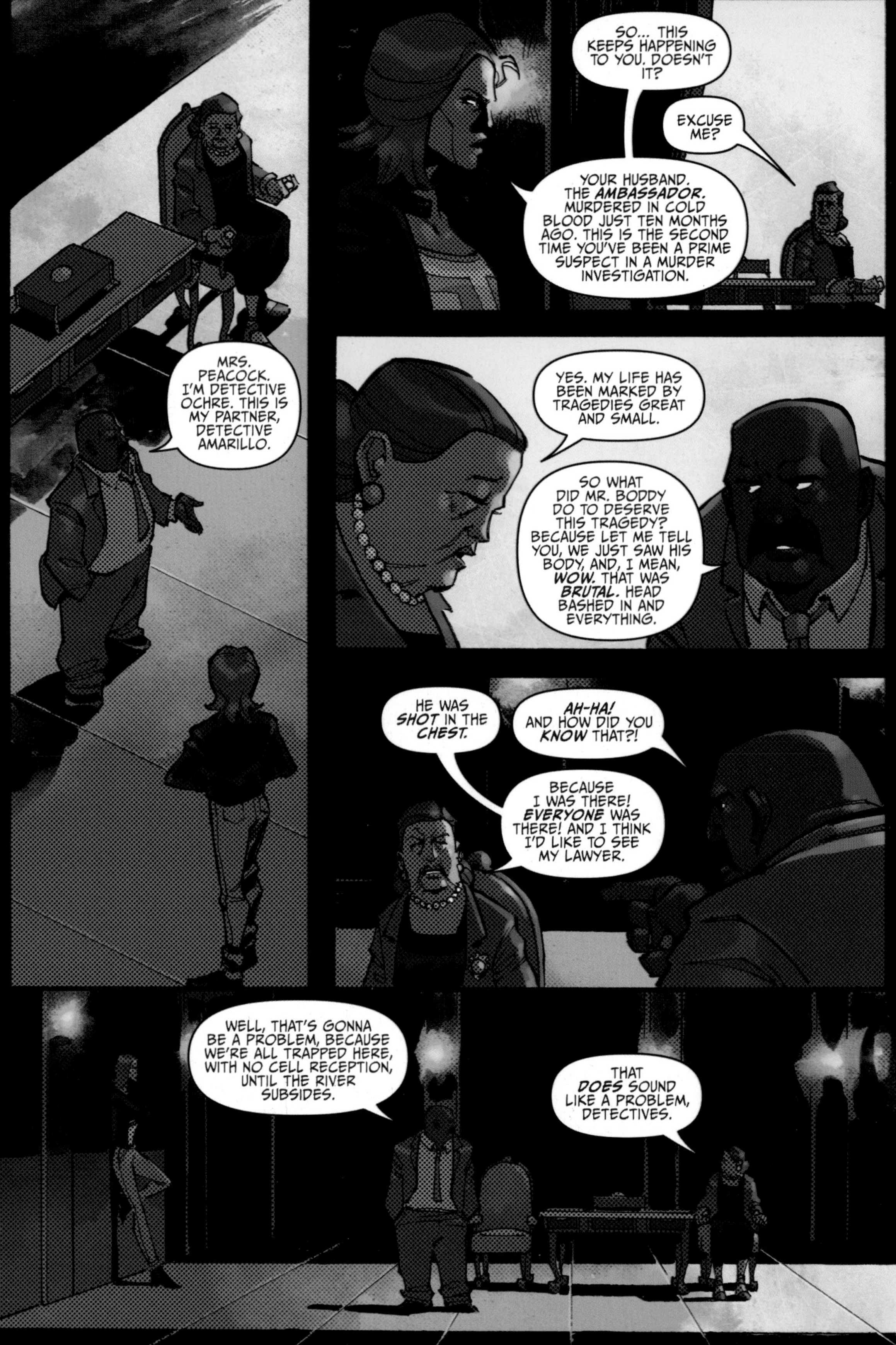

MRS. PEACOCK. I'M DETECTIVE OCHRE. THIS IS MY PARTNER, DETECTIVE AMARILLO.
SO... THIS KEEPS HAPPENING TO YOU. DOESN'T IT?
EXCUSE ME?
YOUR HUSBAND. THE AMBASSADOR. MURDERED IN COLD BLOOD JUST TEN MONTHS AGO. THIS IS THE SECOND TIME YOU'VE BEEN A PRIME SUSPECT IN A MURDER INVESTIGATION.
YES. MY LIFE HAS BEEN MARKED BY TRAGEDIES GREAT AND SMALL.
SO WHAT DID MR. BODDY DO TO DESERVE THIS TRAGEDY? BECAUSE LET ME TELL YOU, WE JUST SAW HIS BODY, AND, I MEAN, WOW. THAT WAS BRUTAL. HEAD BASHED IN AND EVERYTHING.
HE WAS SHOT IN THE CHEST.
AH-HA! AND HOW DID YOU KNOW THAT?!
BECAUSE I WAS THERE! EVERYONE WAS THERE! AND I THINK I'D LIKE TO SEE MY LAWYER.
WELL, THAT'S GONNA BE A PROBLEM, BECAUSE WE'RE ALL TRAPPED HERE, WITH NO CELL RECEPTION, UNTIL THE RIVER SUBSIDES.
THAT DOES SOUND LIKE A PROBLEM, DETECTIVES.

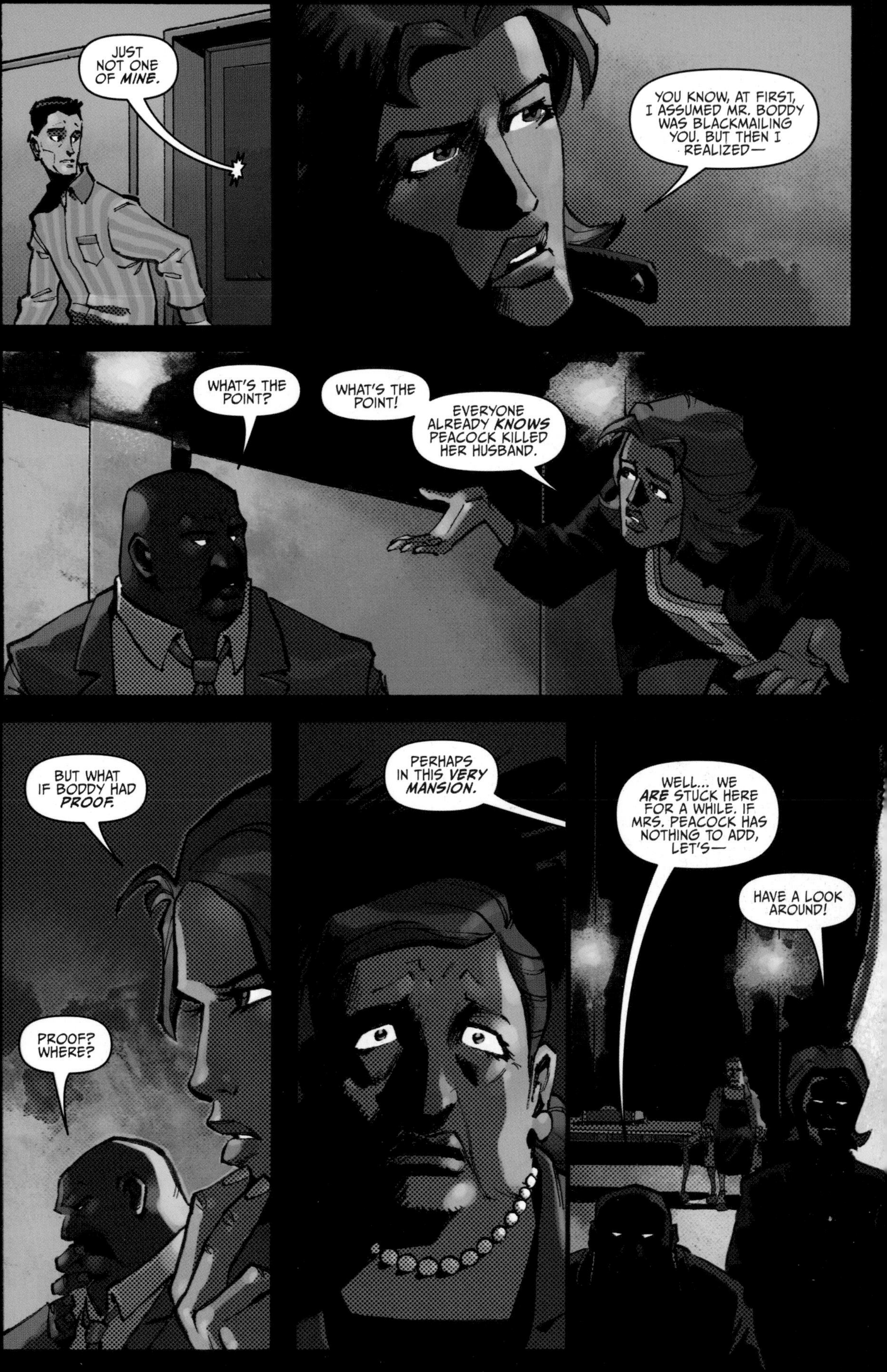

JUST NOT ONE OF *MINE.*
YOU KNOW, AT FIRST, I ASSUMED MR. BODDY WAS BLACKMAILING YOU. BUT THEN I REALIZED—
WHAT'S THE POINT?
WHAT'S THE POINT!
EVERYONE ALREADY ***KNOWS*** PEACOCK KILLED HER HUSBAND.
BUT WHAT IF BODDY HAD ***PROOF.***
PROOF? WHERE?
PERHAPS IN THIS ***VERY MANSION.***
WELL... WE ***ARE*** STUCK HERE FOR A WHILE. IF MRS. PEACOCK HAS NOTHING TO ADD, LET'S—
HAVE A LOOK AROUND!

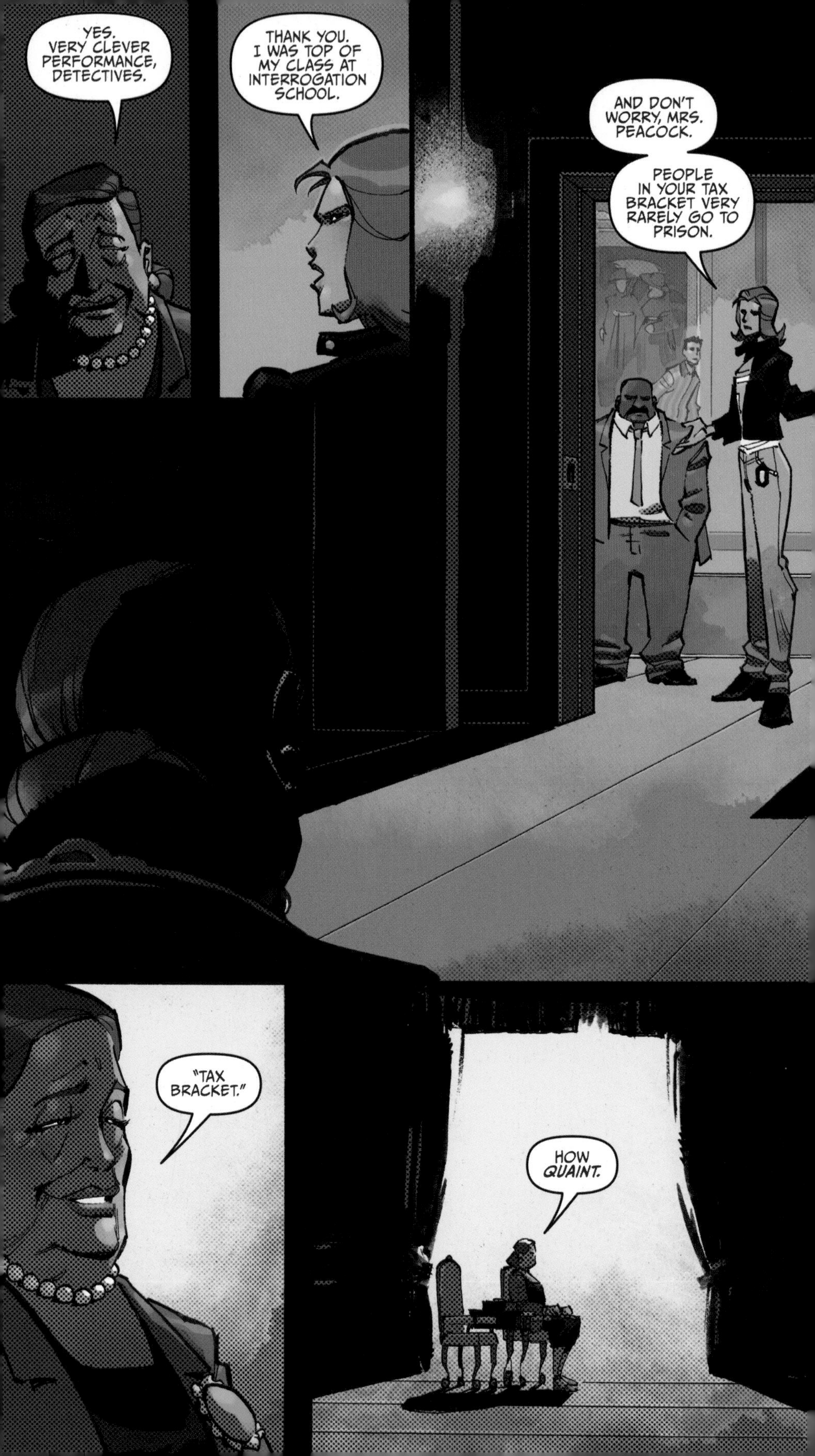
YES. VERY CLEVER PERFORMANCE, DETECTIVES.
THANK YOU. I WAS TOP OF MY CLASS AT INTERROGATION SCHOOL.
AND DON'T WORRY, MRS. PEACOCK.
PEOPLE IN YOUR TAX BRACKET VERY RARELY GO TO PRISON.
"TAX BRACKET."
HOW QUAINT.

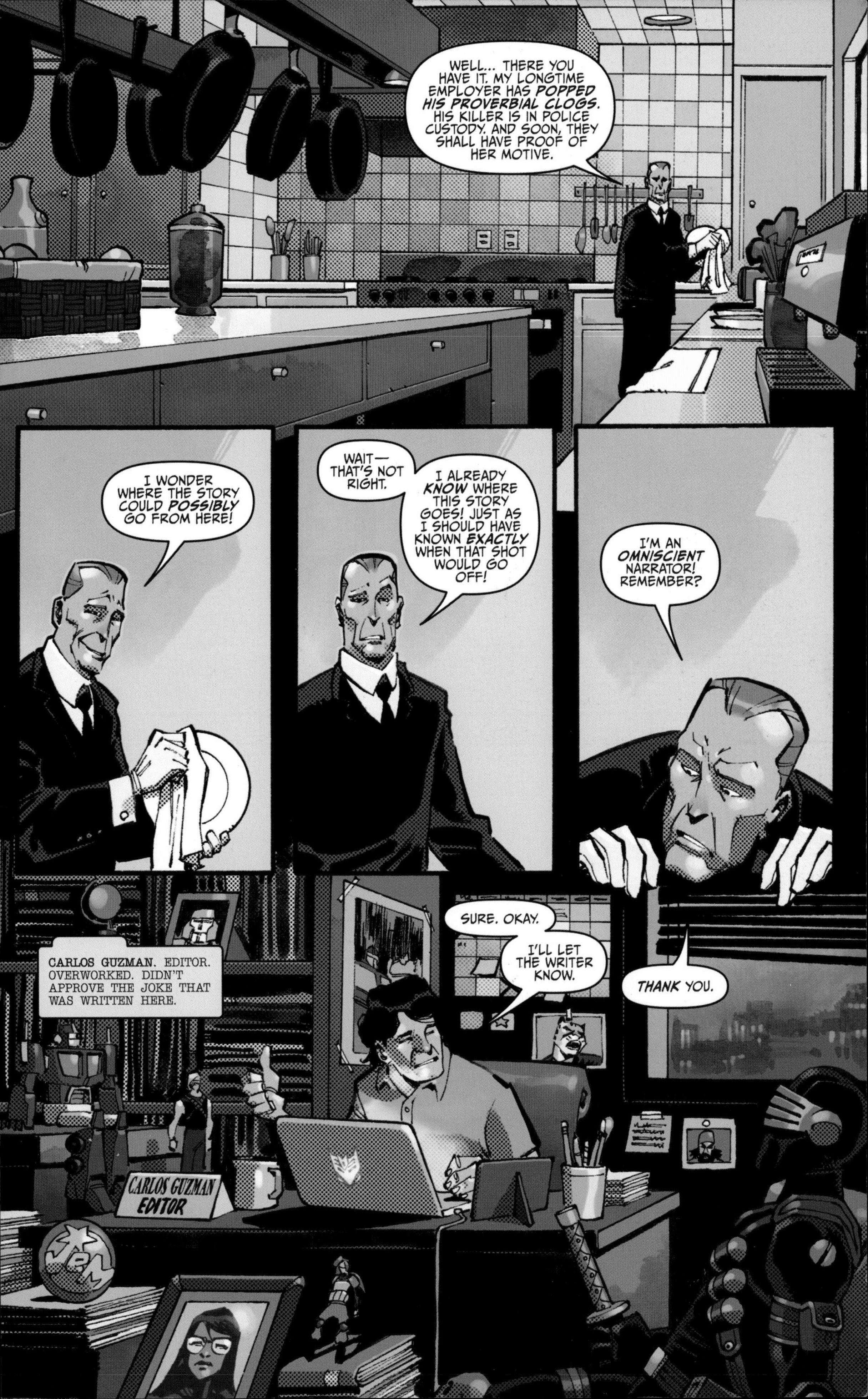
WELL... THERE YOU HAVE IT. MY LONGTIME EMPLOYER HAS POPPED HIS PROVERBIAL CLOGS. HIS KILLER IS IN POLICE CUSTODY. AND SOON, THEY SHALL HAVE PROOF OF HER MOTIVE.
I WONDER WHERE THE STORY COULD POSSIBLY GO FROM HERE!
WAIT—THAT'S NOT RIGHT.
I ALREADY KNOW WHERE THIS STORY GOES! JUST AS I SHOULD HAVE KNOWN EXACTLY WHEN THAT SHOT WOULD GO OFF!
I'M AN OMNISCIENT NARRATOR! REMEMBER?
CARLOS GUZMAN. EDITOR. OVERWORKED. DIDN'T APPROVE THE JOKE THAT WAS WRITTEN HERE.
SURE. OKAY.
I'LL LET THE WRITER KNOW.
THANK YOU.
CARLOS GUZMAN
EDITOR

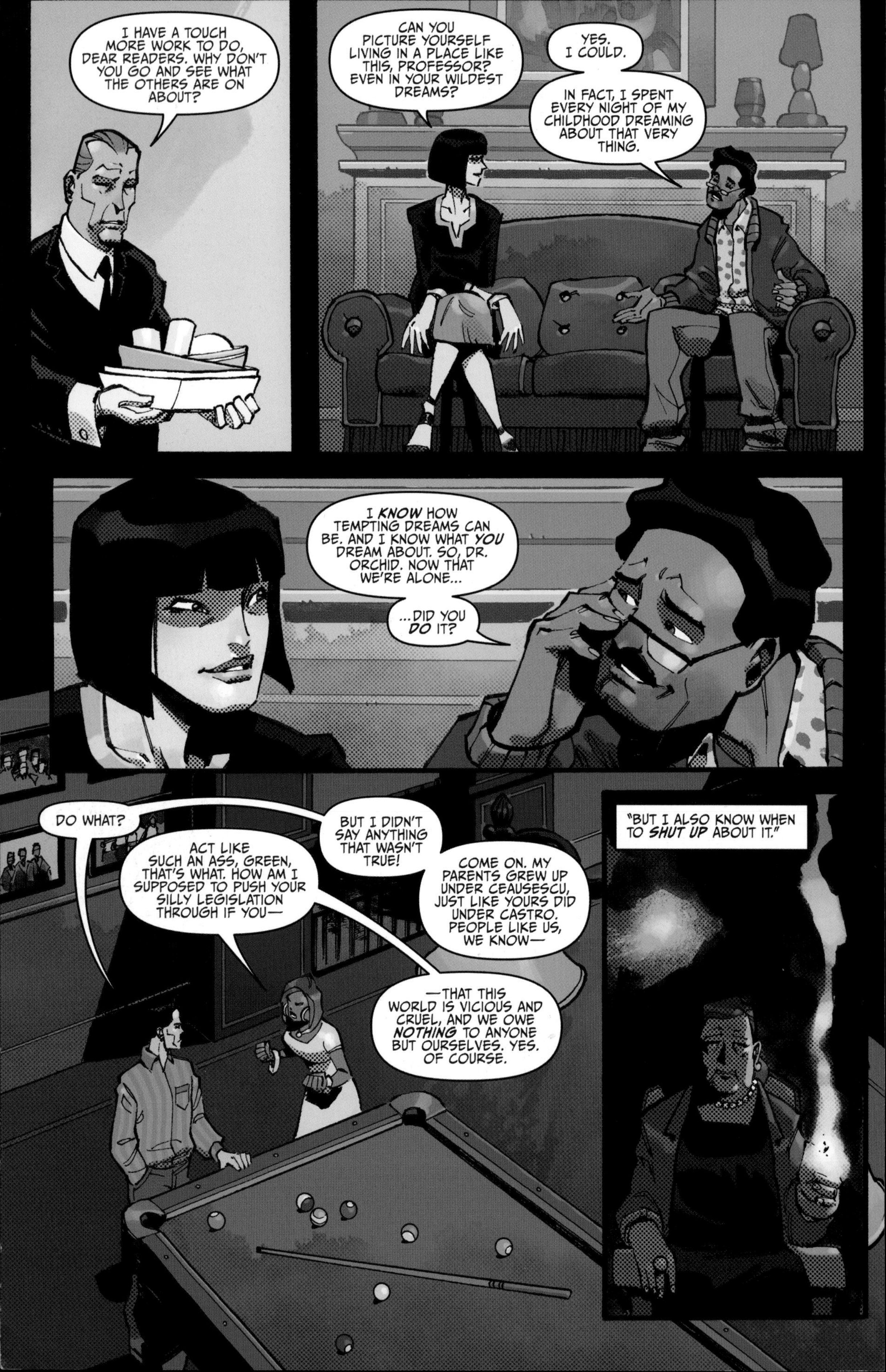
I HAVE A TOUCH MORE WORK TO DO, DEAR READERS. WHY DON'T YOU GO AND SEE WHAT THE OTHERS ARE ON ABOUT?
CAN YOU PICTURE YOURSELF LIVING IN A PLACE LIKE THIS, PROFESSOR? EVEN IN YOUR WILDEST DREAMS?
YES. I COULD.
IN FACT, I SPENT EVERY NIGHT OF MY CHILDHOOD DREAMING ABOUT THAT VERY THING.
I KNOW HOW TEMPTING DREAMS CAN BE. AND I KNOW WHAT YOU DREAM ABOUT. SO, DR. ORCHID. NOW THAT WE'RE ALONE...
...DID YOU DO IT?
DO WHAT?
ACT LIKE SUCH AN ASS, GREEN, THAT'S WHAT. HOW AM I SUPPOSED TO PUSH YOUR SILLY LEGISLATION THROUGH IF YOU—
BUT I DIDN'T SAY ANYTHING THAT WASN'T TRUE!
COME ON. MY PARENTS GREW UP UNDER CEAUSESCU, JUST LIKE YOURS DID UNDER CASTRO. PEOPLE LIKE US, WE KNOW—
—THAT THIS WORLD IS VICIOUS AND CRUEL, AND WE OWE NOTHING TO ANYONE BUT OURSELVES. YES. OF COURSE.
"BUT I ALSO KNOW WHEN TO SHUT UP ABOUT IT."

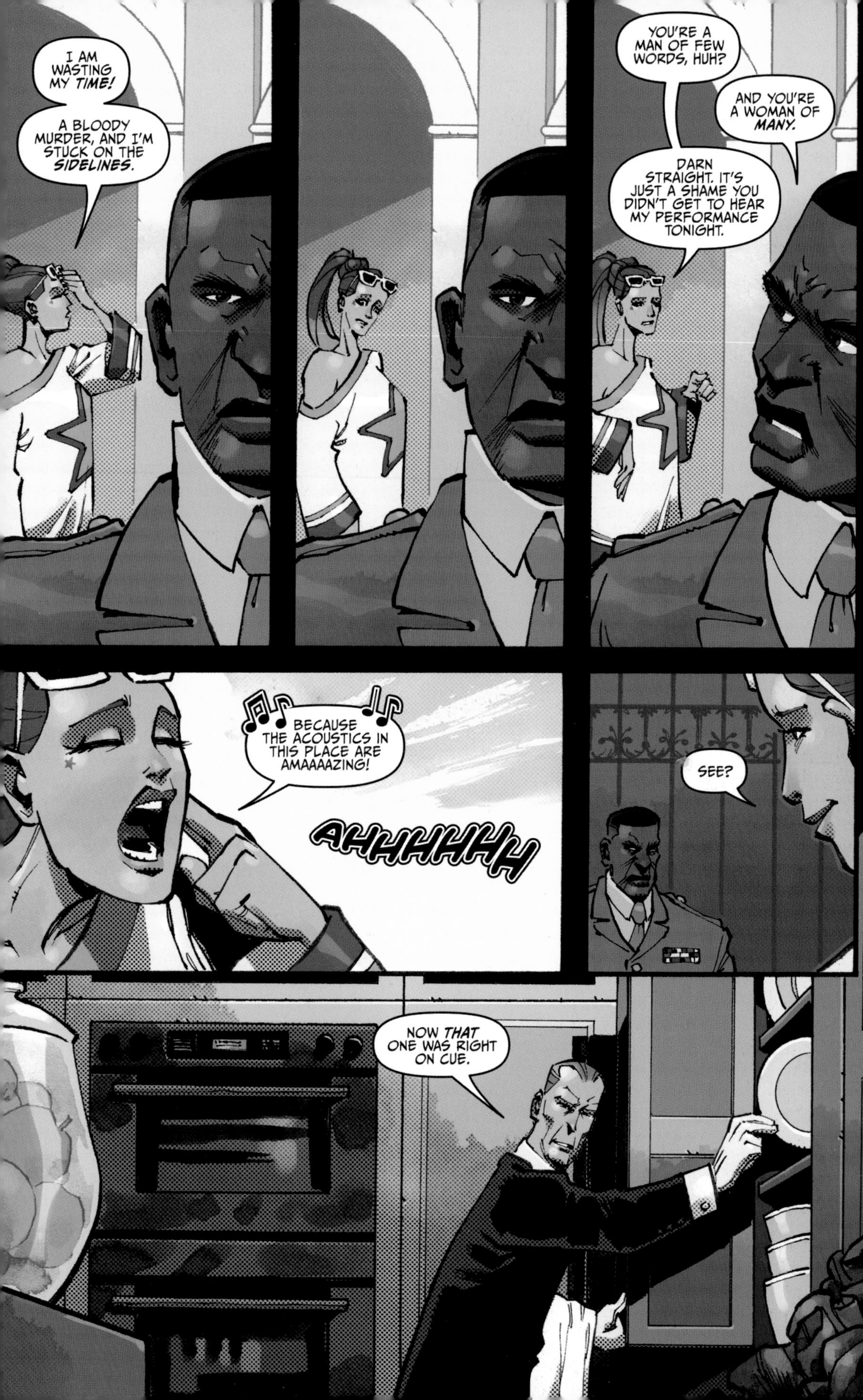
I AM WASTING MY TIME!
A BLOODY MURDER, AND I'M STUCK ON THE SIDELINES.
YOU'RE A MAN OF FEW WORDS, HUH?
AND YOU'RE A WOMAN OF MANY.
DARN STRAIGHT. IT'S JUST A SHAME YOU DIDN'T GET TO HEAR MY PERFORMANCE TONIGHT.
BECAUSE THE ACOUSTICS IN THIS PLACE ARE AMAAAAZING!
AHHHHHH
SEE?
NOW THAT ONE WAS RIGHT ON CUE.

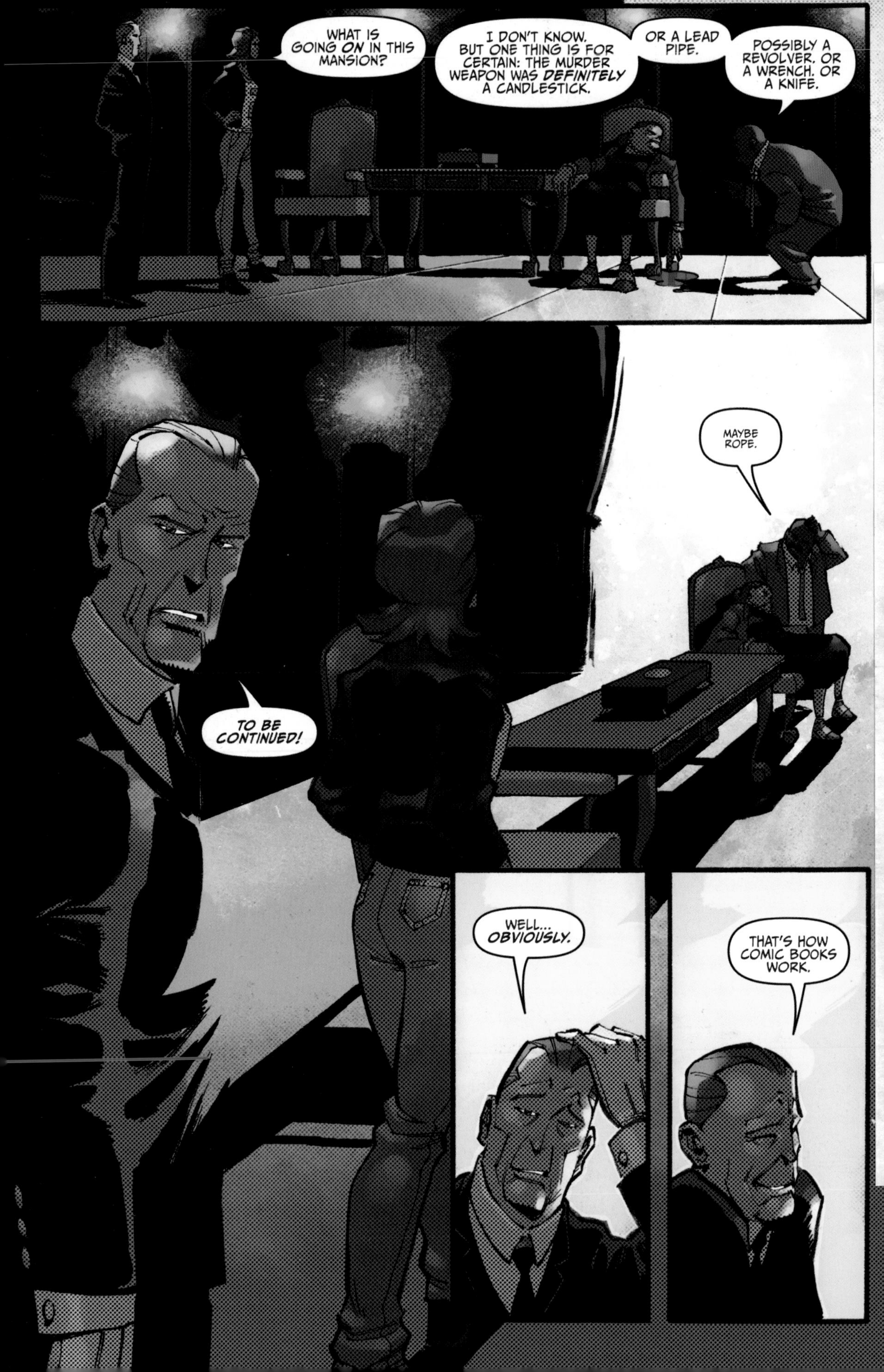
WHAT IS GOING ON IN THIS MANSION?
I DON'T KNOW. BUT ONE THING IS FOR CERTAIN: THE MURDER WEAPON WAS DEFINITELY A CANDLESTICK.
OR A LEAD PIPE.
POSSIBLY A REVOLVER. OR A WRENCH. OR A KNIFE.
MAYBE ROPE.
TO BE CONTINUED!
WELL... OBVIOUSLY.
THAT'S HOW COMIC BOOKS WORK.

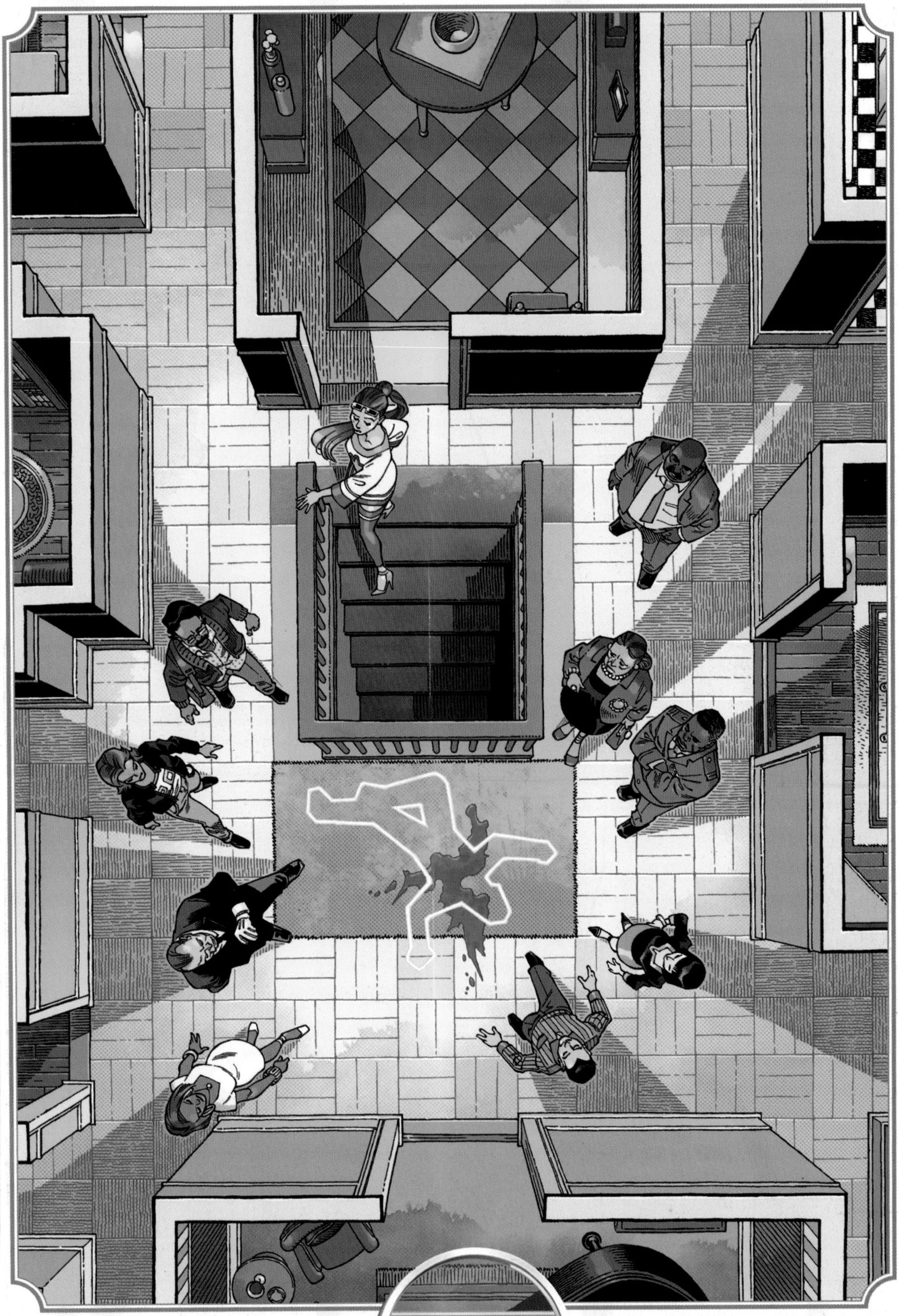

COVER ART BY
GABRIEL RODRIGUEZ

COLORS BY
NELSON DANIEL

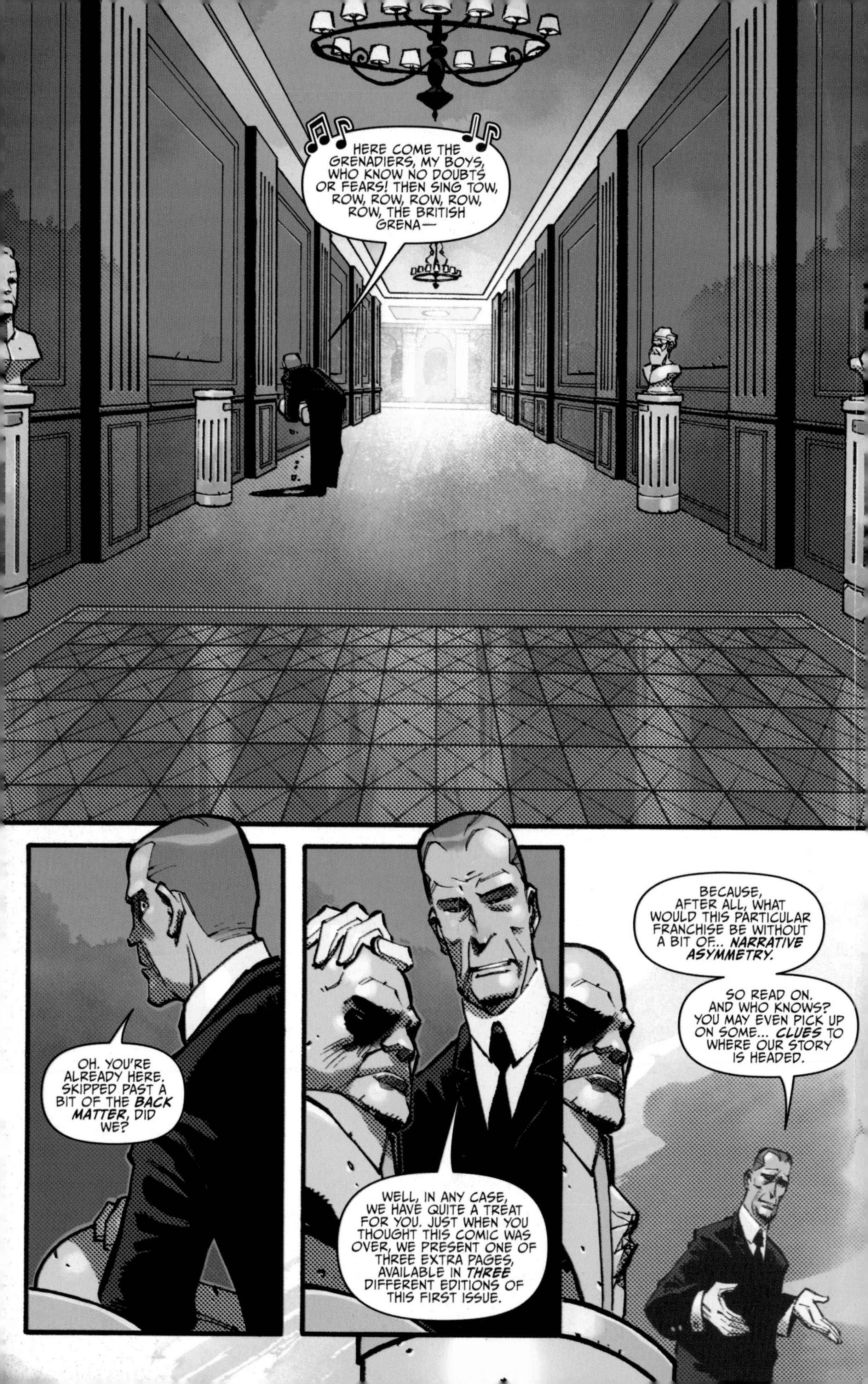
HERE COME THE GRENADIERS, MY BOYS, WHO KNOW NO DOUBTS OR FEARS! THEN SING TOW, ROW, ROW, ROW, ROW, ROW, THE BRITISH GRENA—
OH. YOU'RE ALREADY HERE. SKIPPED PAST A BIT OF THE **BACK MATTER**, DID WE?
WELL, IN ANY CASE, WE HAVE QUITE A TREAT FOR YOU. JUST WHEN YOU THOUGHT THIS COMIC WAS OVER, WE PRESENT ONE OF THREE EXTRA PAGES, AVAILABLE IN ***THREE*** DIFFERENT EDITIONS OF THIS FIRST ISSUE.
BECAUSE, AFTER ALL, WHAT WOULD THIS PARTICULAR FRANCHISE BE WITHOUT A BIT OF... ***NARRATIVE ASYMMETRY.***
SO READ ON. AND WHO KNOWS? YOU MAY EVEN PICK UP ON SOME... ***CLUES*** TO WHERE OUR STORY IS HEADED.

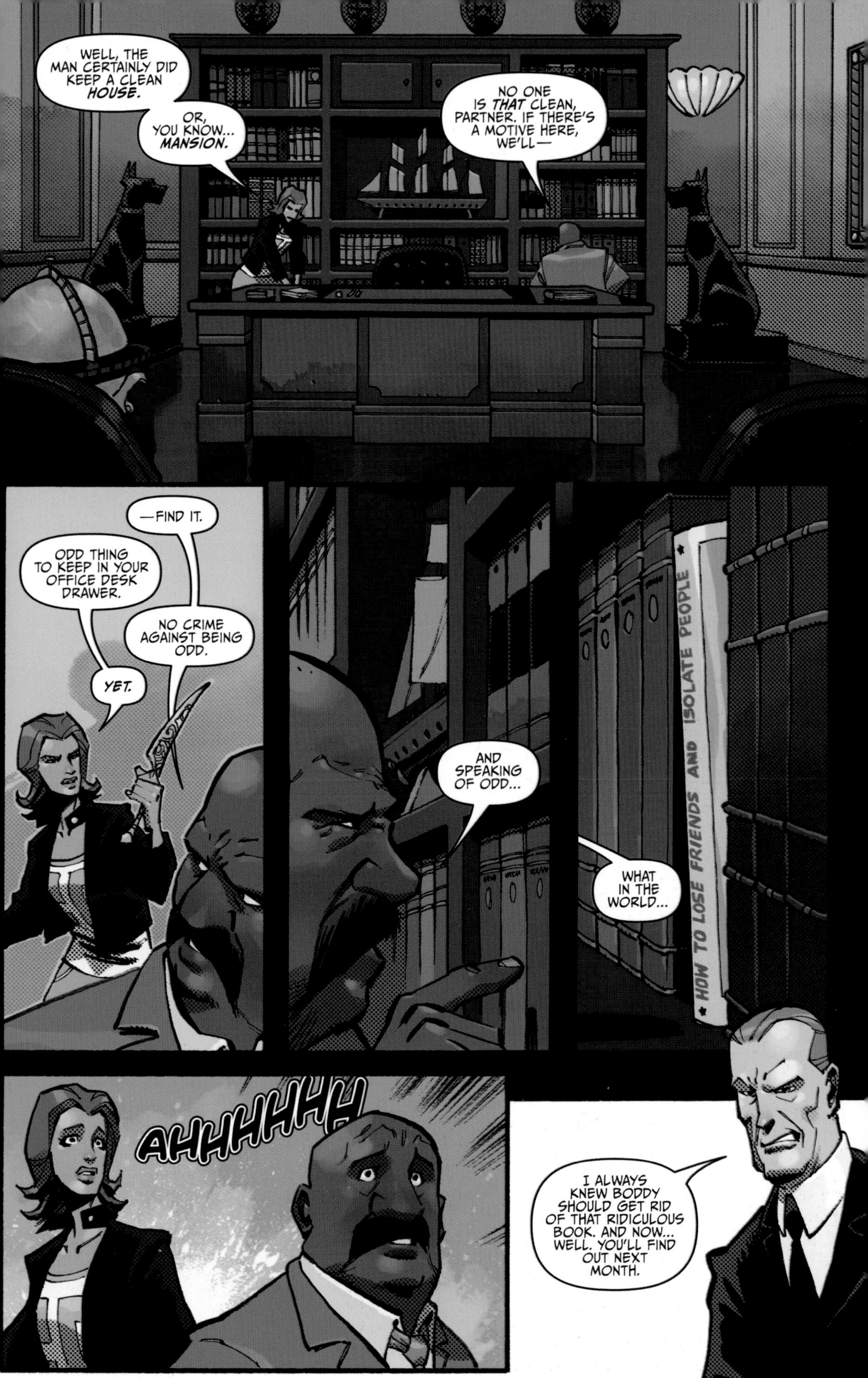
WELL, THE MAN CERTAINLY DID KEEP A CLEAN HOUSE.
OR, YOU KNOW... MANSION.
NO ONE IS THAT CLEAN, PARTNER. IF THERE'S A MOTIVE HERE, WE'LL—
—FIND IT.
ODD THING TO KEEP IN YOUR OFFICE DESK DRAWER.
NO CRIME AGAINST BEING ODD.
YET.
AND SPEAKING OF ODD...
WHAT IN THE WORLD...
HOW TO LOSE FRIENDS AND ISOLATE PEOPLE
AHHHHHHH
I ALWAYS KNEW BODDY SHOULD GET RID OF THAT RIDICULOUS BOOK. AND NOW... WELL. YOU'LL FIND OUT NEXT MONTH.

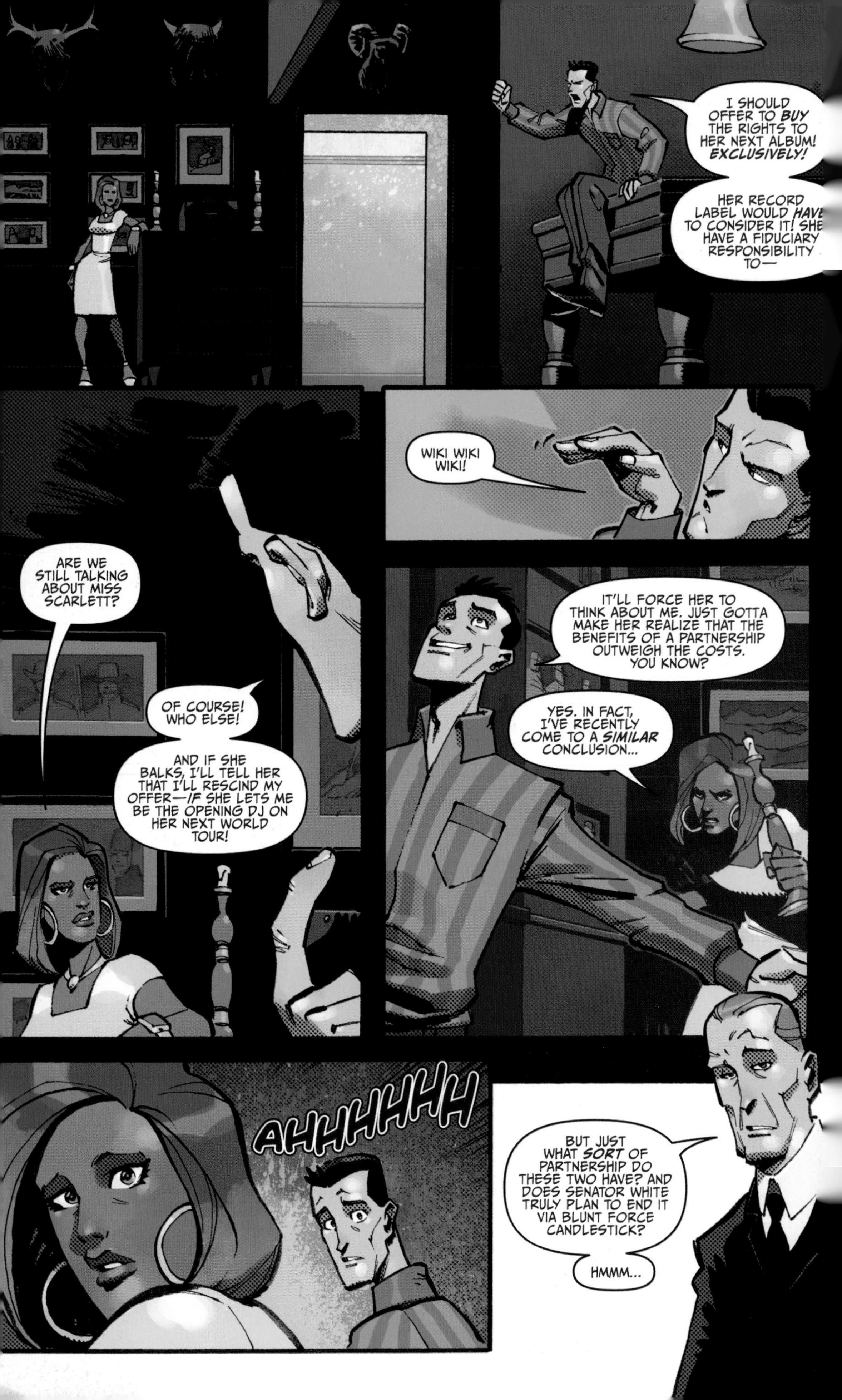
I SHOULD OFFER TO BUY THE RIGHTS TO HER NEXT ALBUM! EXCLUSIVELY!
HER RECORD LABEL WOULD HAVE TO CONSIDER IT! SHE HAVE A FIDUCIARY RESPONSIBILITY TO—
WIKI WIKI WIKI!
ARE WE STILL TALKING ABOUT MISS SCARLETT?
OF COURSE! WHO ELSE!
AND IF SHE BALKS, I'LL TELL HER THAT I'LL RESCIND MY OFFER—IF SHE LETS ME BE THE OPENING DJ ON HER NEXT WORLD TOUR!
IT'LL FORCE HER TO THINK ABOUT ME. JUST GOTTA MAKE HER REALIZE THAT THE BENEFITS OF A PARTNERSHIP OUTWEIGH THE COSTS. YOU KNOW?
YES. IN FACT, I'VE RECENTLY COME TO A SIMILAR CONCLUSION...
AHHHHHH
BUT JUST WHAT SORT OF PARTNERSHIP DO THESE TWO HAVE? AND DOES SENATOR WHITE TRULY PLAN TO END IT VIA BLUNT FORCE CANDLESTICK?
HMMM...

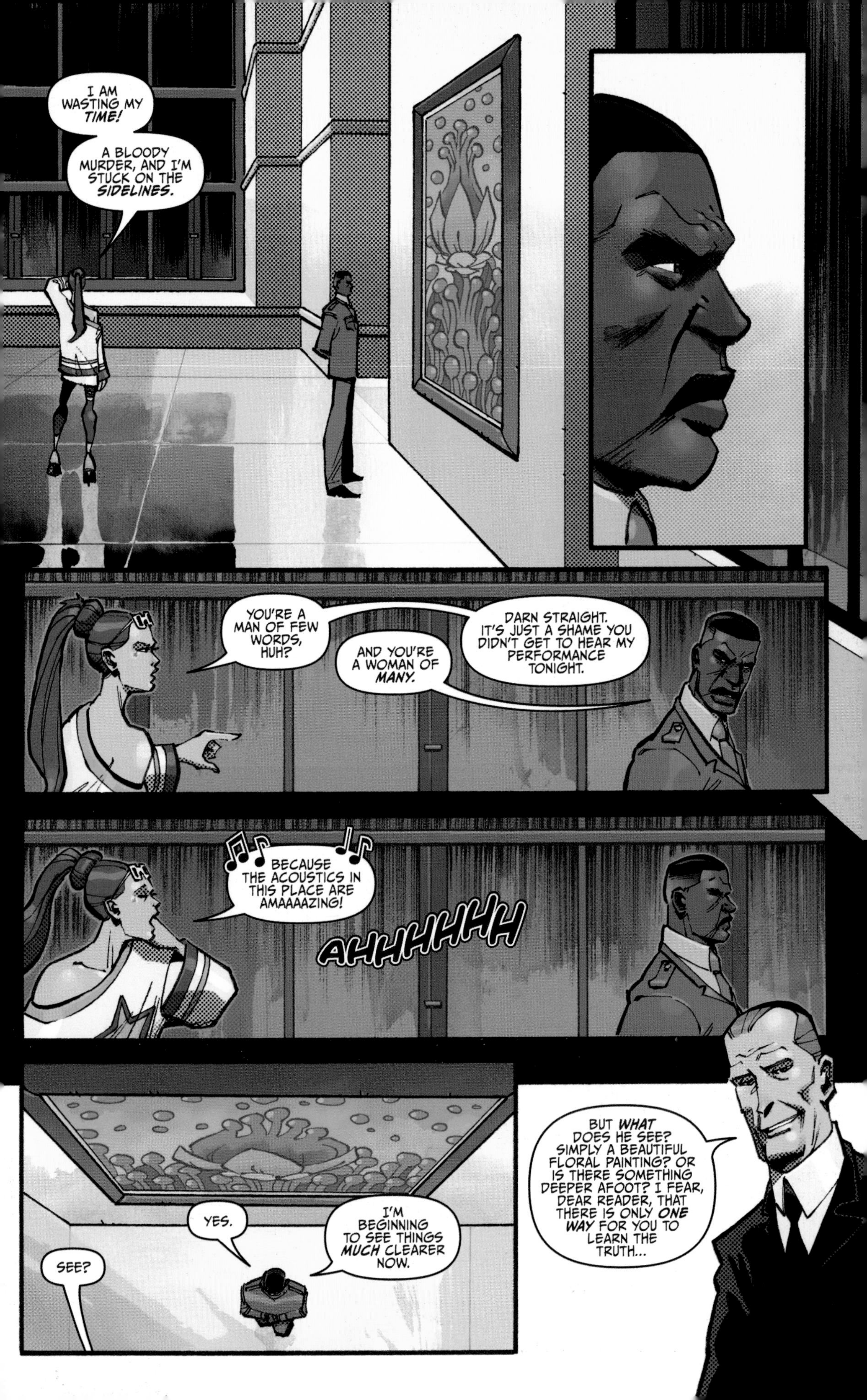
I AM WASTING MY TIME!
A BLOODY MURDER, AND I'M STUCK ON THE SIDELINES.
YOU'RE A MAN OF FEW WORDS, HUH?
AND YOU'RE A WOMAN OF MANY.
DARN STRAIGHT. IT'S JUST A SHAME YOU DIDN'T GET TO HEAR MY PERFORMANCE TONIGHT.
BECAUSE THE ACOUSTICS IN THIS PLACE ARE AMAAAAZING!
AHHHHHH
SEE?
YES.
I'M BEGINNING TO SEE THINGS MUCH CLEARER NOW.
BUT WHAT DOES HE SEE? SIMPLY A BEAUTIFUL FLORAL PAINTING? OR IS THERE SOMETHING DEEPER AFOOT? I FEAR, DEAR READER, THAT THERE IS ONLY ONE WAY FOR YOU TO LEARN THE TRUTH...

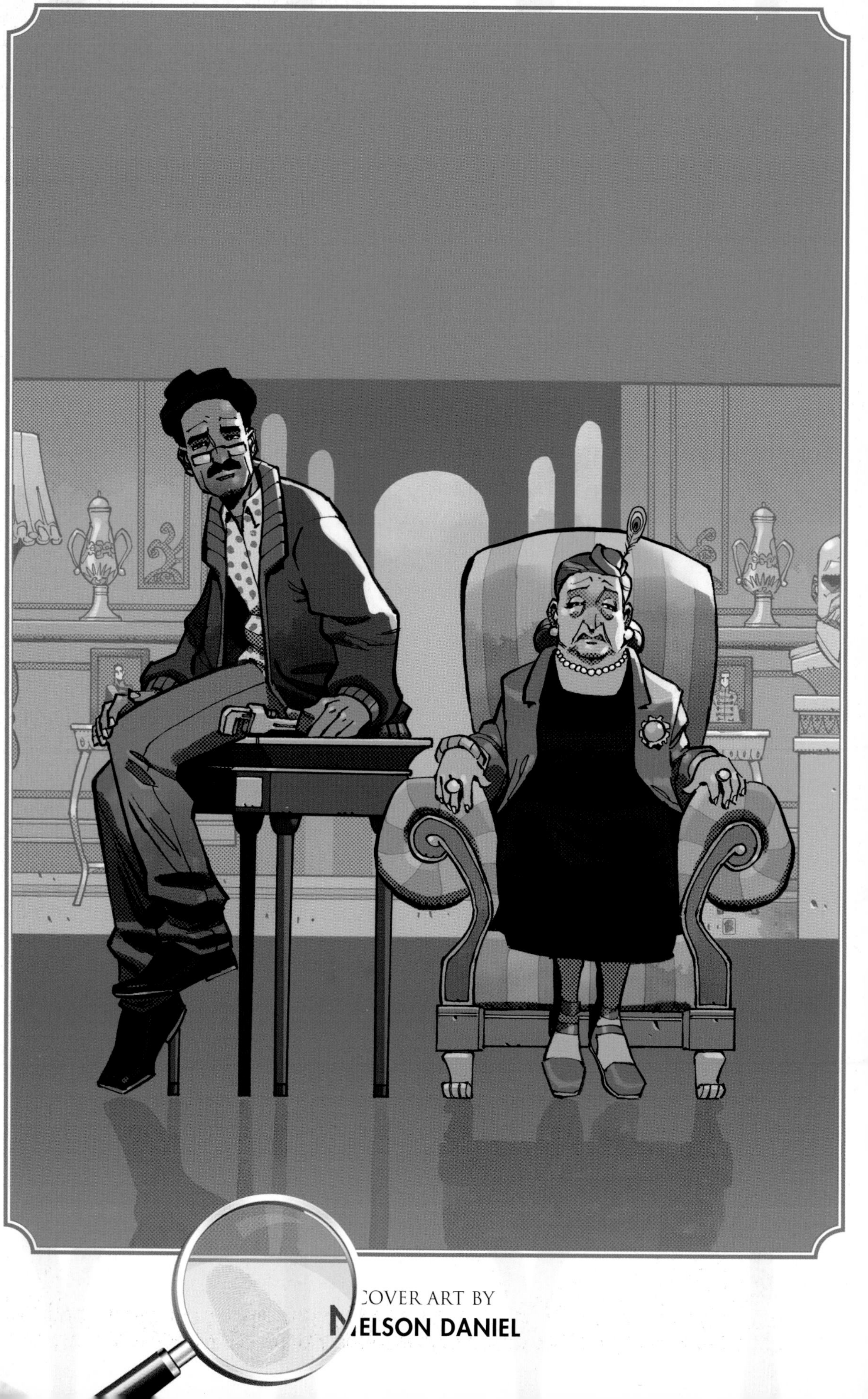

COVER ART BY
NELSON DANIEL

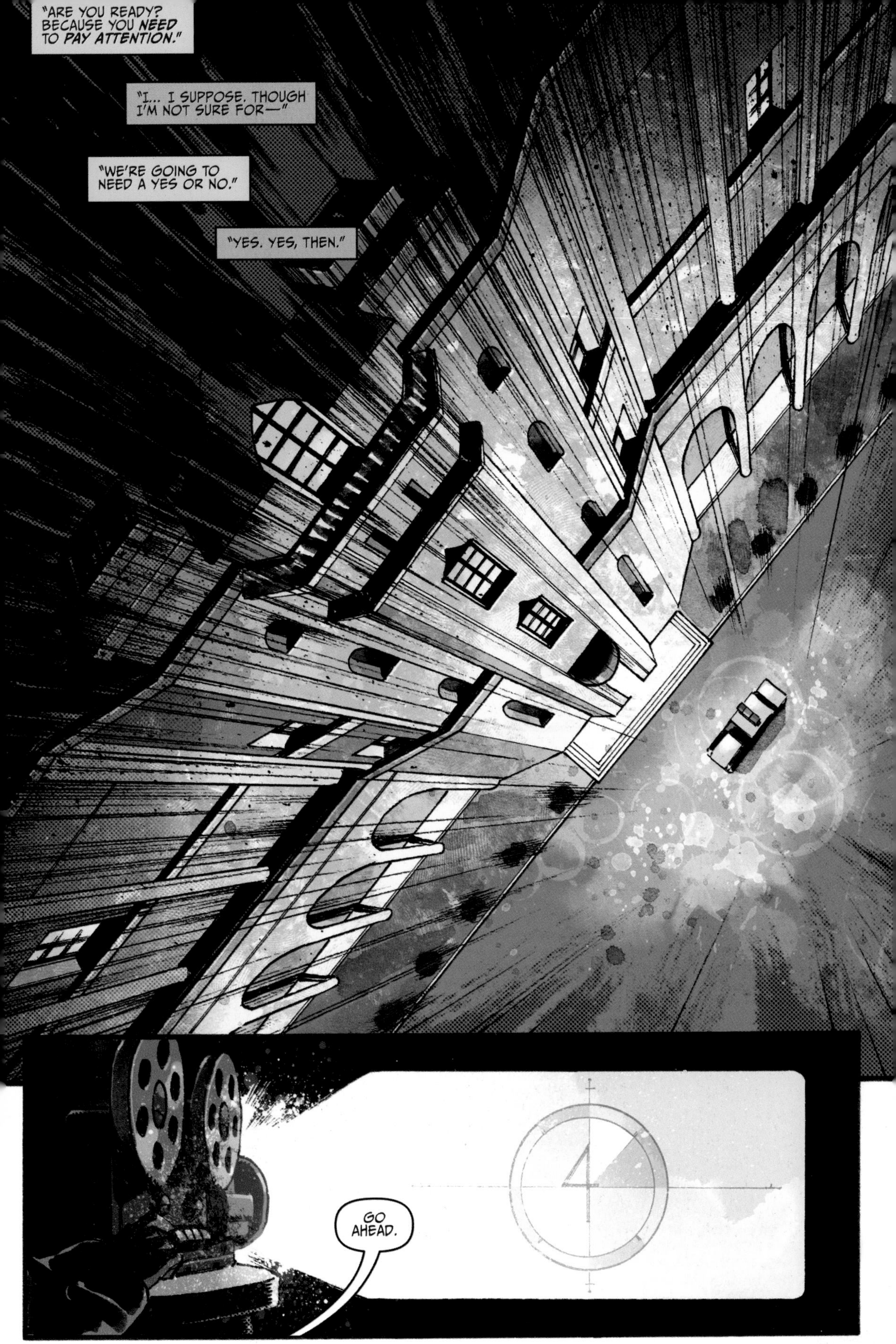
"ARE YOU READY? BECAUSE YOU NEED TO PAY ATTENTION."
"I... I SUPPOSE. THOUGH I'M NOT SURE FOR—"
"WE'RE GOING TO NEED A YES OR NO."
"YES. YES, THEN."
GO AHEAD.

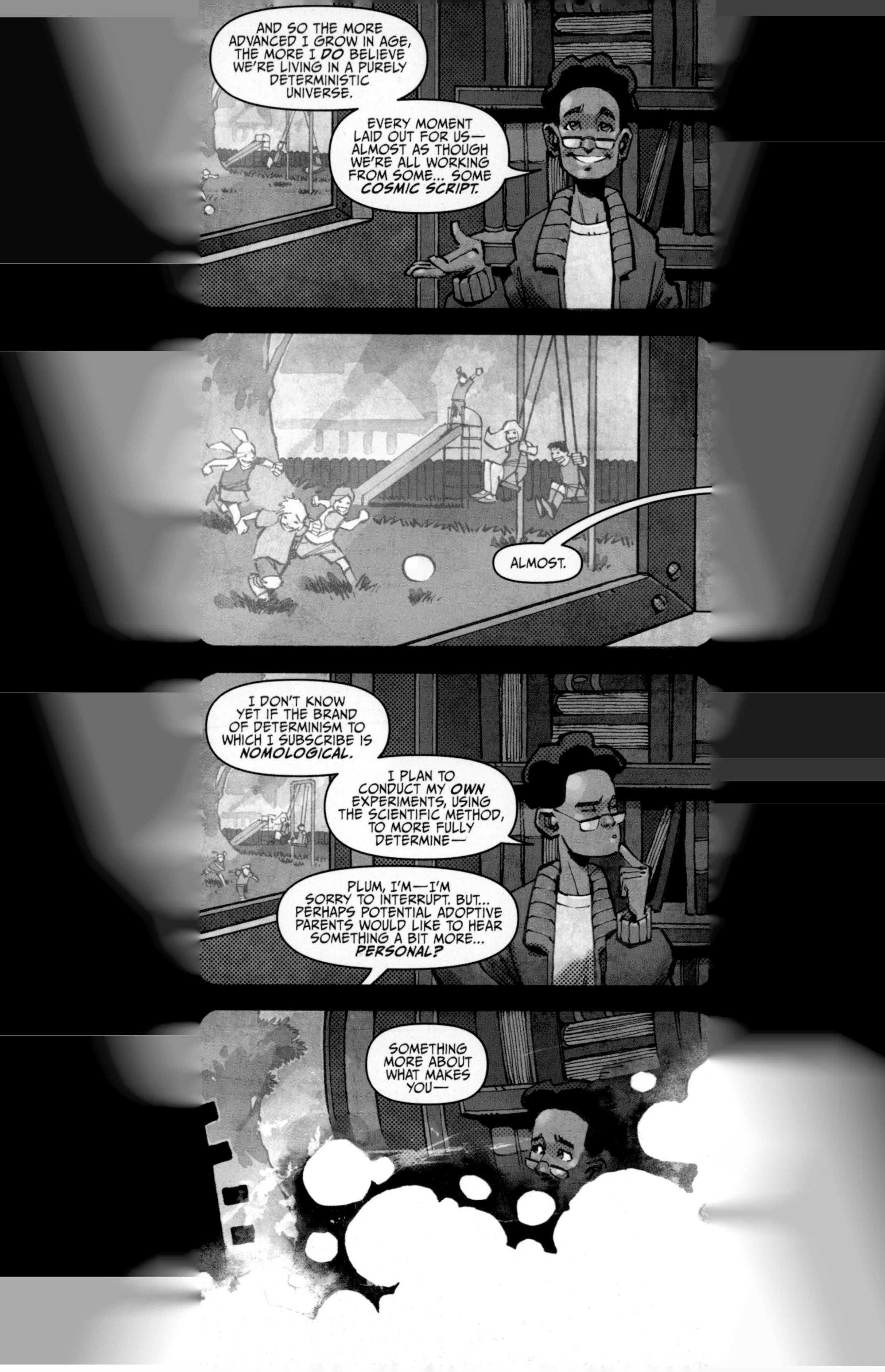
AND SO THE MORE ADVANCED I GROW IN AGE, THE MORE I DO BELIEVE WE'RE LIVING IN A PURELY DETERMINISTIC UNIVERSE.
EVERY MOMENT LAID OUT FOR US— ALMOST AS THOUGH WE'RE ALL WORKING FROM SOME... SOME COSMIC SCRIPT.
ALMOST.
I DON'T KNOW YET IF THE BRAND OF DETERMINISM TO WHICH I SUBSCRIBE IS NOMOLOGICAL.
I PLAN TO CONDUCT MY OWN EXPERIMENTS, USING THE SCIENTIFIC METHOD, TO MORE FULLY DETERMINE—
PLUM, I'M—I'M SORRY TO INTERRUPT. BUT... PERHAPS POTENTIAL ADOPTIVE PARENTS WOULD LIKE TO HEAR SOMETHING A BIT MORE... PERSONAL?
SOMETHING MORE ABOUT WHAT MAKES YOU—

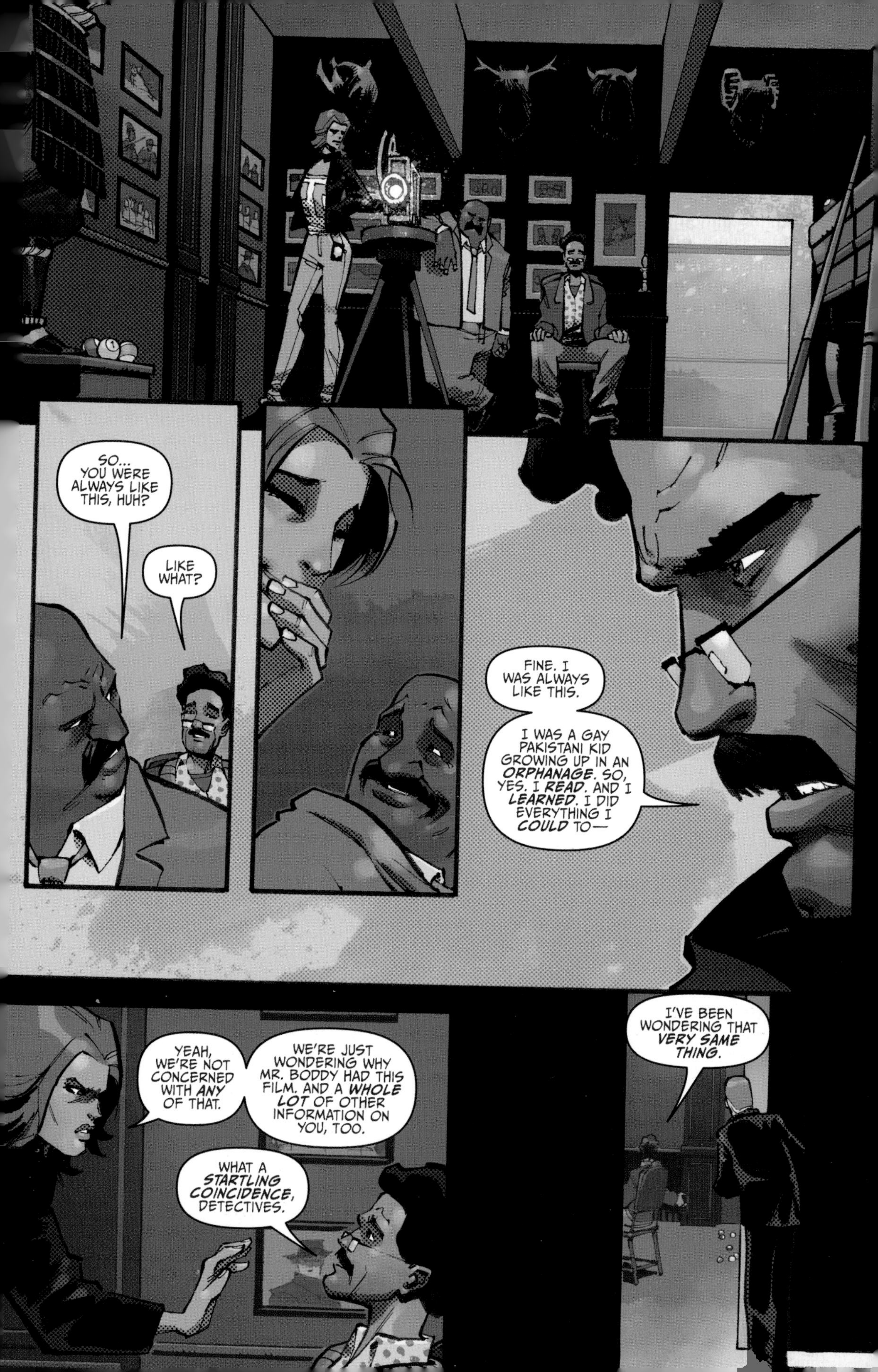
SO... YOU WERE ALWAYS LIKE THIS, HUH?
LIKE WHAT?
FINE. I WAS ALWAYS LIKE THIS.
I WAS A GAY PAKISTANI KID GROWING UP IN AN ORPHANAGE. SO, YES. I READ. AND I LEARNED. I DID EVERYTHING I COULD TO—
YEAH, WE'RE NOT CONCERNED WITH ANY OF THAT.
WE'RE JUST WONDERING WHY MR. BODDY HAD THIS FILM. AND A WHOLE LOT OF OTHER INFORMATION ON YOU, TOO.
WHAT A STARTLING COINCIDENCE, DETECTIVES.
I'VE BEEN WONDERING THAT VERY SAME THING.

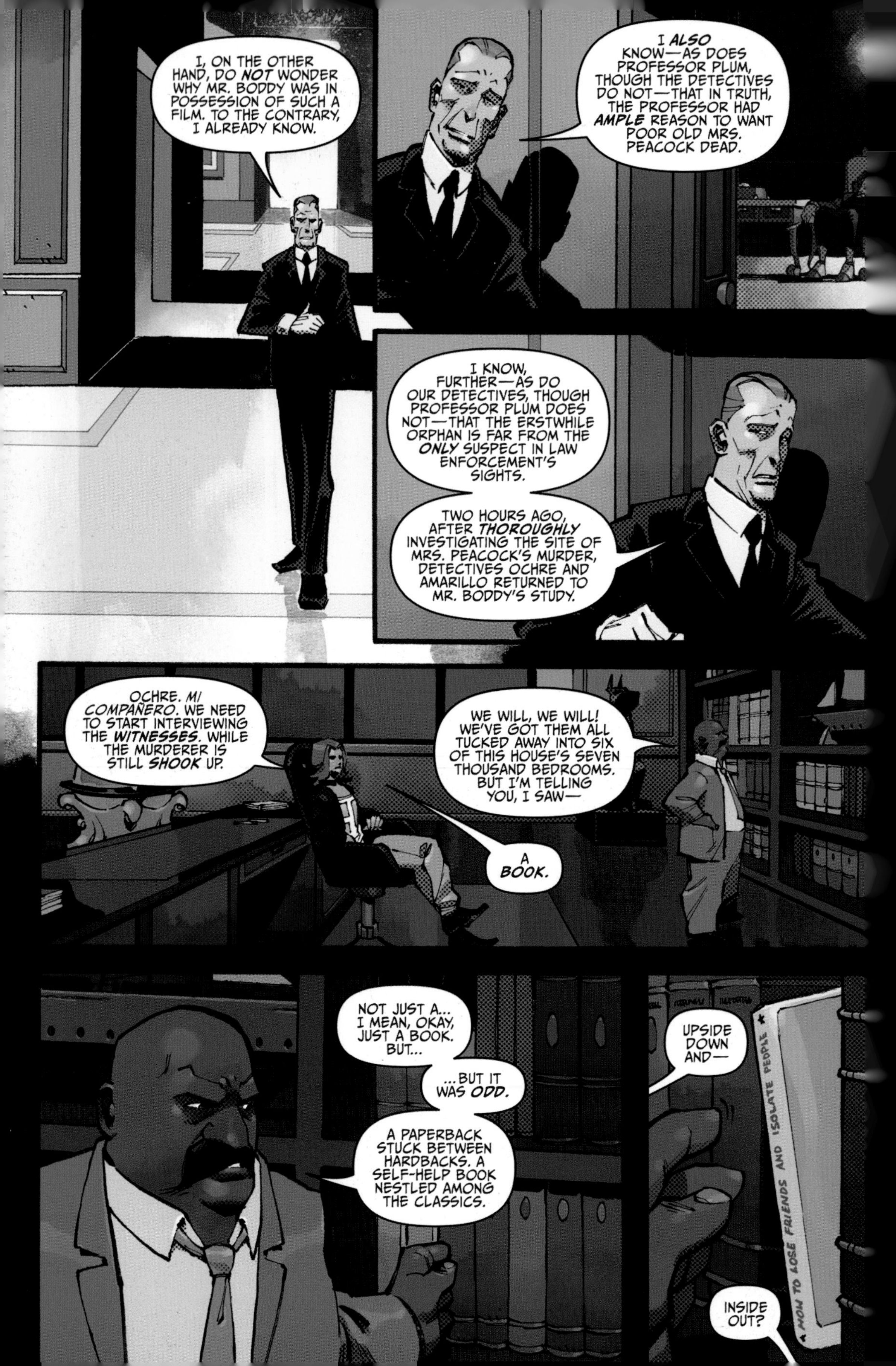
I, ON THE OTHER HAND, DO NOT WONDER WHY MR. BODDY WAS IN POSSESSION OF SUCH A FILM. TO THE CONTRARY, I ALREADY KNOW.
I ALSO KNOW—AS DOES PROFESSOR PLUM, THOUGH THE DETECTIVES DO NOT—THAT IN TRUTH, THE PROFESSOR HAD AMPLE REASON TO WANT POOR OLD MRS. PEACOCK DEAD.
I KNOW, FURTHER—AS DO OUR DETECTIVES, THOUGH PROFESSOR PLUM DOES NOT—THAT THE ERSTWHILE ORPHAN IS FAR FROM THE ONLY SUSPECT IN LAW ENFORCEMENT'S SIGHTS.
TWO HOURS AGO, AFTER THOROUGHLY INVESTIGATING THE SITE OF MRS. PEACOCK'S MURDER, DETECTIVES OCHRE AND AMARILLO RETURNED TO MR. BODDY'S STUDY.
OCHRE. MI COMPAÑERO. WE NEED TO START INTERVIEWING THE WITNESSES. WHILE THE MURDERER IS STILL SHOOK UP.
WE WILL, WE WILL! WE'VE GOT THEM ALL TUCKED AWAY INTO SIX OF THIS HOUSE'S SEVEN THOUSAND BEDROOMS. BUT I'M TELLING YOU, I SAW—
A BOOK.
NOT JUST A... I MEAN, OKAY, JUST A BOOK. BUT...
...BUT IT WAS ODD.
A PAPERBACK STUCK BETWEEN HARDBACKS. A SELF-HELP BOOK NESTLED AMONG THE CLASSICS.
UPSIDE DOWN AND—
HOW TO LOSE FRIENDS AND ISOLATE PEOPLE
INSIDE OUT?

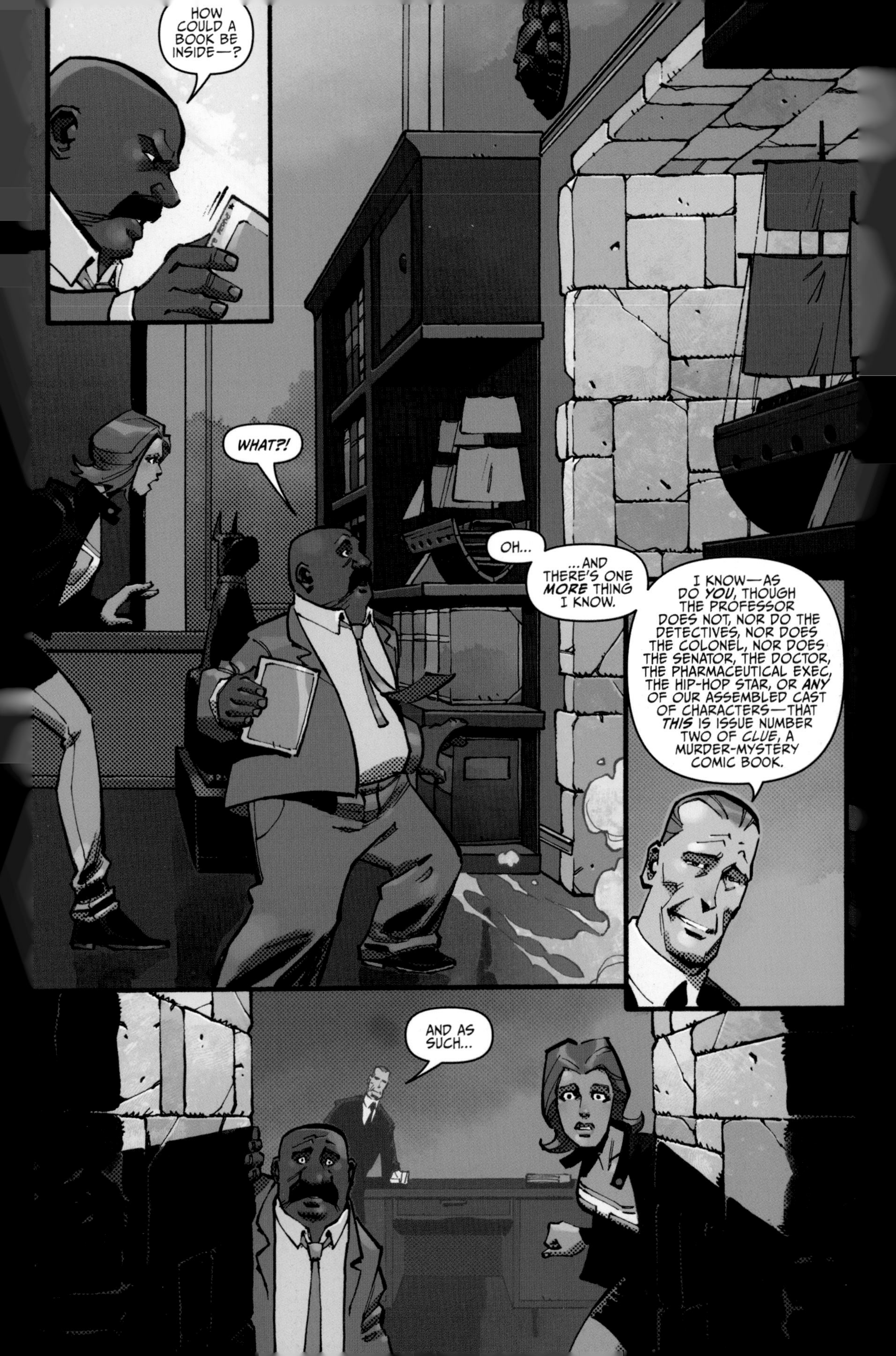

HOW COULD A BOOK BE INSIDE—?
WHAT?!
OH...
...AND THERE'S ONE MORE THING I KNOW.
I KNOW—AS DO YOU, THOUGH THE PROFESSOR DOES NOT, NOR DO THE DETECTIVES, NOR DOES THE COLONEL, NOR DOES THE SENATOR, THE DOCTOR, THE PHARMACEUTICAL EXEC, THE HIP-HOP STAR, OR ANY OF OUR ASSEMBLED CAST OF CHARACTERS—THAT THIS IS ISSUE NUMBER TWO OF CLUE, A MURDER-MYSTERY COMIC BOOK.
AND AS SUCH...

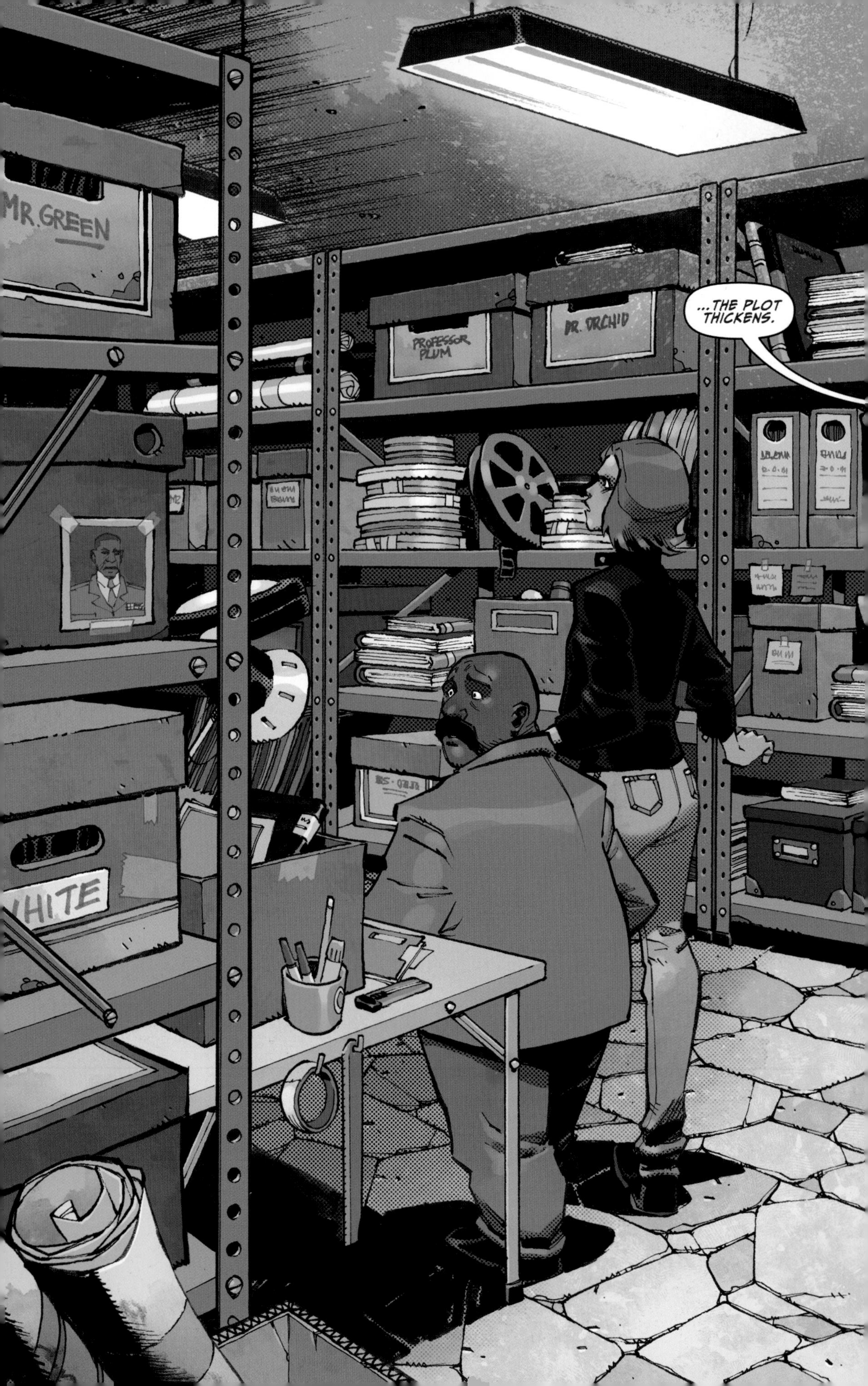

MR. GREEN
PROFESSOR PLUM
DR. ORCHID
...THE PLOT THICKENS.
WHITE

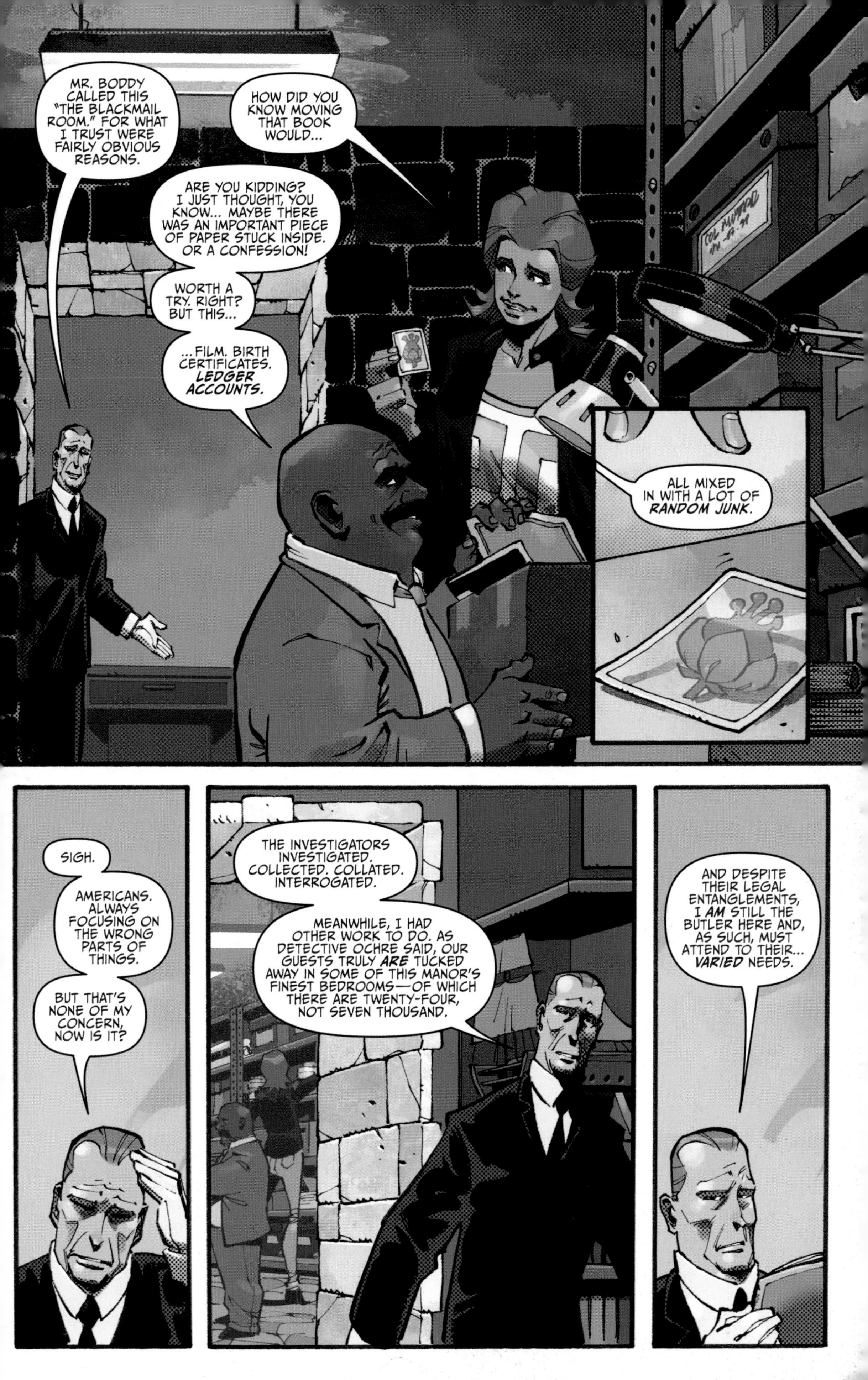
MR. BODDY CALLED THIS "THE BLACKMAIL ROOM." FOR WHAT I TRUST WERE FAIRLY OBVIOUS REASONS.
HOW DID YOU KNOW MOVING THAT BOOK WOULD...
ARE YOU KIDDING? I JUST THOUGHT, YOU KNOW... MAYBE THERE WAS AN IMPORTANT PIECE OF PAPER STUCK INSIDE. OR A CONFESSION!
WORTH A TRY. RIGHT? BUT THIS...
...FILM. BIRTH CERTIFICATES. LEDGER ACCOUNTS.
ALL MIXED IN WITH A LOT OF RANDOM JUNK.
SIGH.
AMERICANS. ALWAYS FOCUSING ON THE WRONG PARTS OF THINGS.
BUT THAT'S NONE OF MY CONCERN, NOW IS IT?
THE INVESTIGATORS INVESTIGATED. COLLECTED. COLLATED. INTERROGATED.
MEANWHILE, I HAD OTHER WORK TO DO. AS DETECTIVE OCHRE SAID, OUR GUESTS TRULY ARE TUCKED AWAY IN SOME OF THIS MANOR'S FINEST BEDROOMS—OF WHICH THERE ARE TWENTY-FOUR, NOT SEVEN THOUSAND.
AND DESPITE THEIR LEGAL ENTANGLEMENTS, I AM STILL THE BUTLER HERE AND, AS SUCH, MUST ATTEND TO THEIR... VARIED NEEDS.

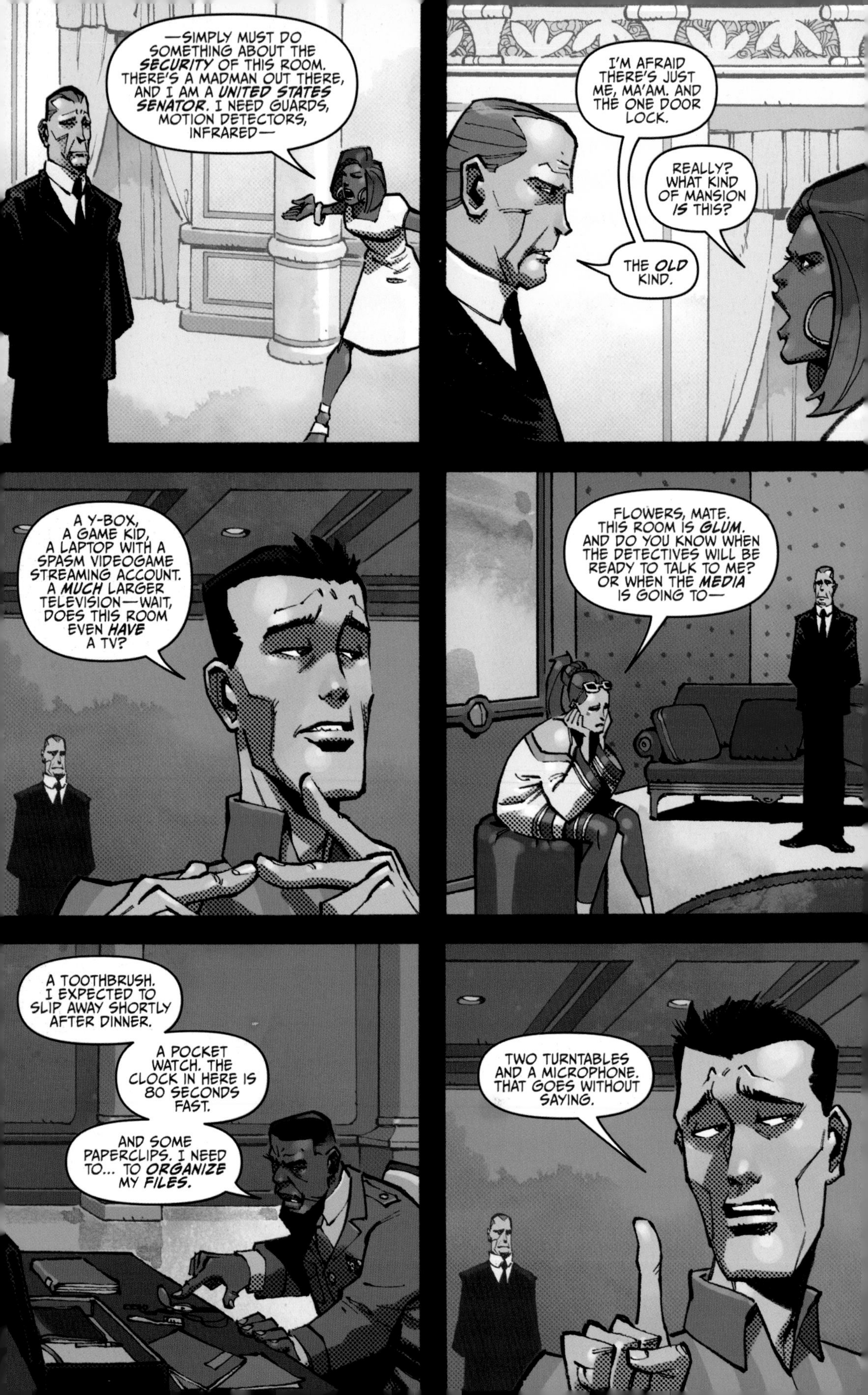
—SIMPLY MUST DO SOMETHING ABOUT THE *SECURITY* OF THIS ROOM. THERE'S A MADMAN OUT THERE, AND I AM A *UNITED STATES SENATOR*. I NEED GUARDS, MOTION DETECTORS, INFRARED—
I'M AFRAID THERE'S JUST ME, MA'AM. AND THE ONE DOOR LOCK.
REALLY? WHAT KIND OF MANSION *IS* THIS?
THE *OLD* KIND.
A Y-BOX, A GAME KID, A LAPTOP WITH A SPASM VIDEOGAME STREAMING ACCOUNT. A *MUCH* LARGER TELEVISION—WAIT, DOES THIS ROOM EVEN *HAVE* A TV?
FLOWERS, MATE. THIS ROOM IS *GLUM*. AND DO YOU KNOW WHEN THE DETECTIVES WILL BE READY TO TALK TO ME? OR WHEN THE *MEDIA* IS GOING TO—
A TOOTHBRUSH. I EXPECTED TO SLIP AWAY SHORTLY AFTER DINNER.
A POCKET WATCH. THE CLOCK IN HERE IS 80 SECONDS FAST.
AND SOME PAPERCLIPS. I NEED TO... TO *ORGANIZE* MY *FILES*.
TWO TURNTABLES AND A MICROPHONE. THAT GOES WITHOUT SAYING.

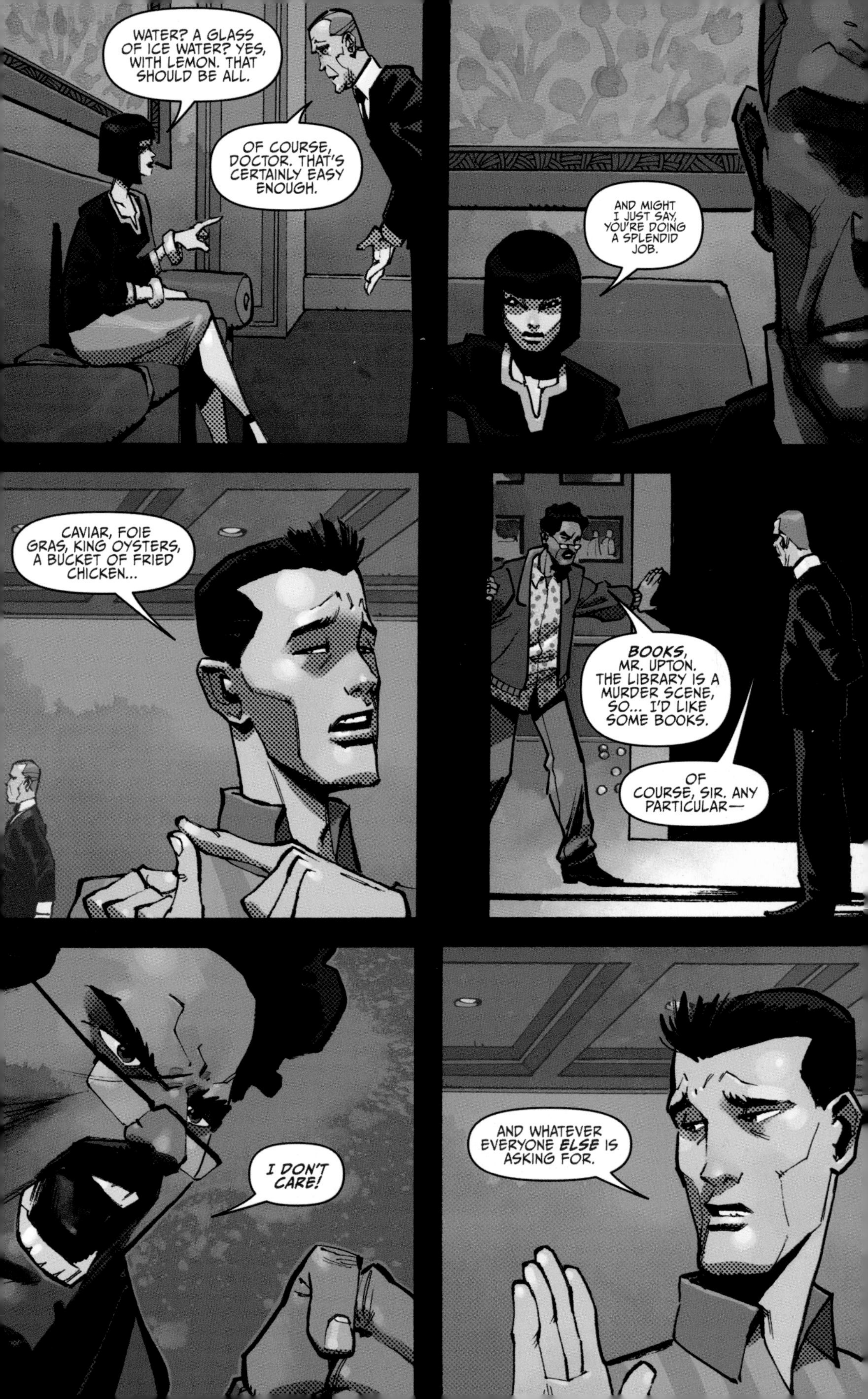
WATER? A GLASS OF ICE WATER? YES, WITH LEMON. THAT SHOULD BE ALL.
OF COURSE, DOCTOR. THAT'S CERTAINLY EASY ENOUGH.
AND MIGHT I JUST SAY, YOU'RE DOING A SPLENDID JOB.
CAVIAR, FOIE GRAS, KING OYSTERS, A BUCKET OF FRIED CHICKEN...
BOOKS, MR. UPTON. THE LIBRARY IS A MURDER SCENE, SO... I'D LIKE SOME BOOKS.
OF COURSE, SIR. ANY PARTICULAR—
I DON'T CARE!
AND WHATEVER EVERYONE ELSE IS ASKING FOR.

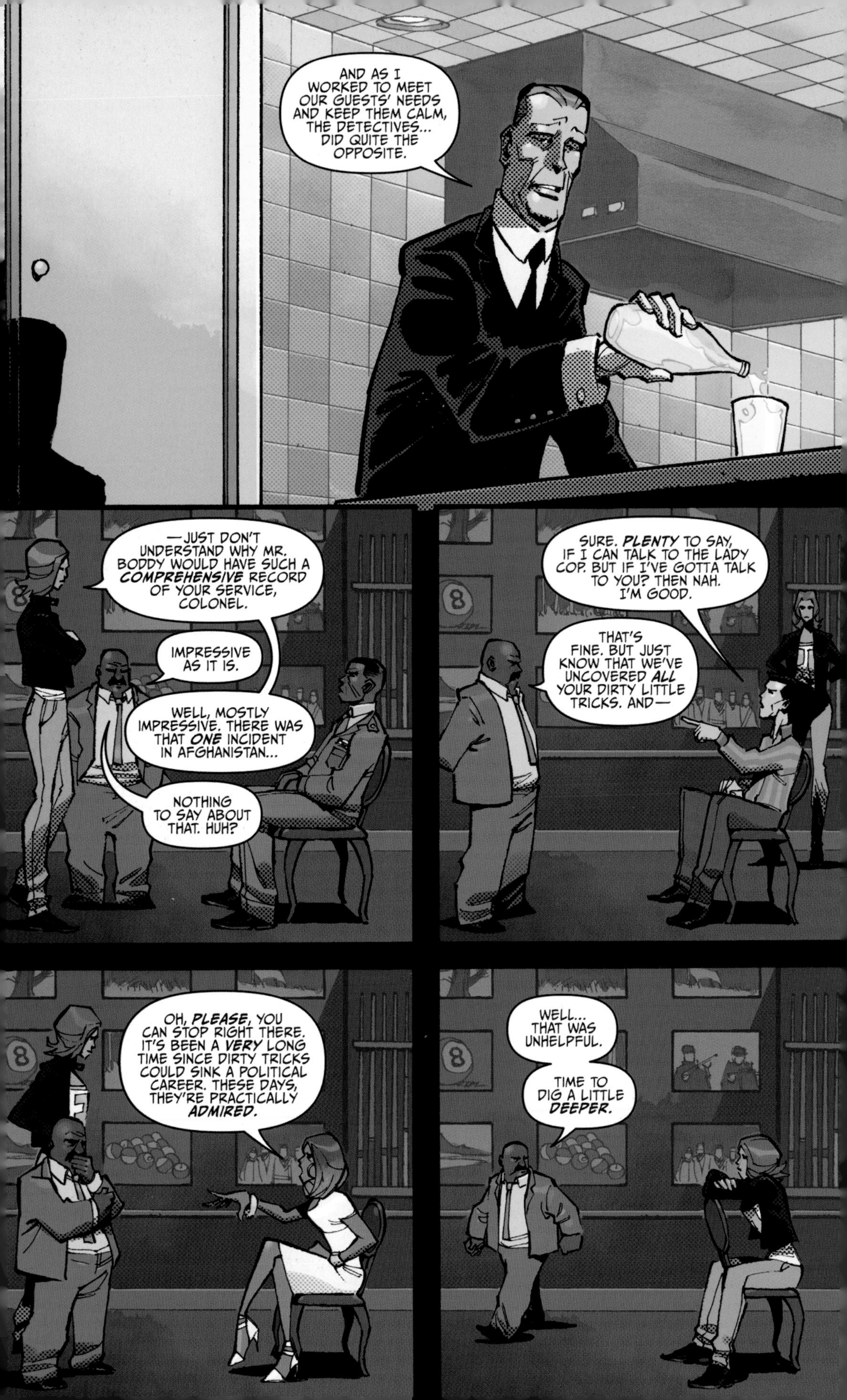
AND AS I WORKED TO MEET OUR GUESTS' NEEDS AND KEEP THEM CALM, THE DETECTIVES... DID QUITE THE OPPOSITE.
—JUST DON'T UNDERSTAND WHY MR. BODDY WOULD HAVE SUCH A COMPREHENSIVE RECORD OF YOUR SERVICE, COLONEL.
IMPRESSIVE AS IT IS.
WELL, MOSTLY IMPRESSIVE. THERE WAS THAT ONE INCIDENT IN AFGHANISTAN...
NOTHING TO SAY ABOUT THAT. HUH?
SURE. PLENTY TO SAY, IF I CAN TALK TO THE LADY COP. BUT IF I'VE GOTTA TALK TO YOU? THEN NAH. I'M GOOD.
THAT'S FINE. BUT JUST KNOW THAT WE'VE UNCOVERED ALL YOUR DIRTY LITTLE TRICKS. AND—
OH, PLEASE, YOU CAN STOP RIGHT THERE. IT'S BEEN A VERY LONG TIME SINCE DIRTY TRICKS COULD SINK A POLITICAL CAREER. THESE DAYS, THEY'RE PRACTICALLY ADMIRED.
WELL... THAT WAS UNHELPFUL.
TIME TO DIG A LITTLE DEEPER.

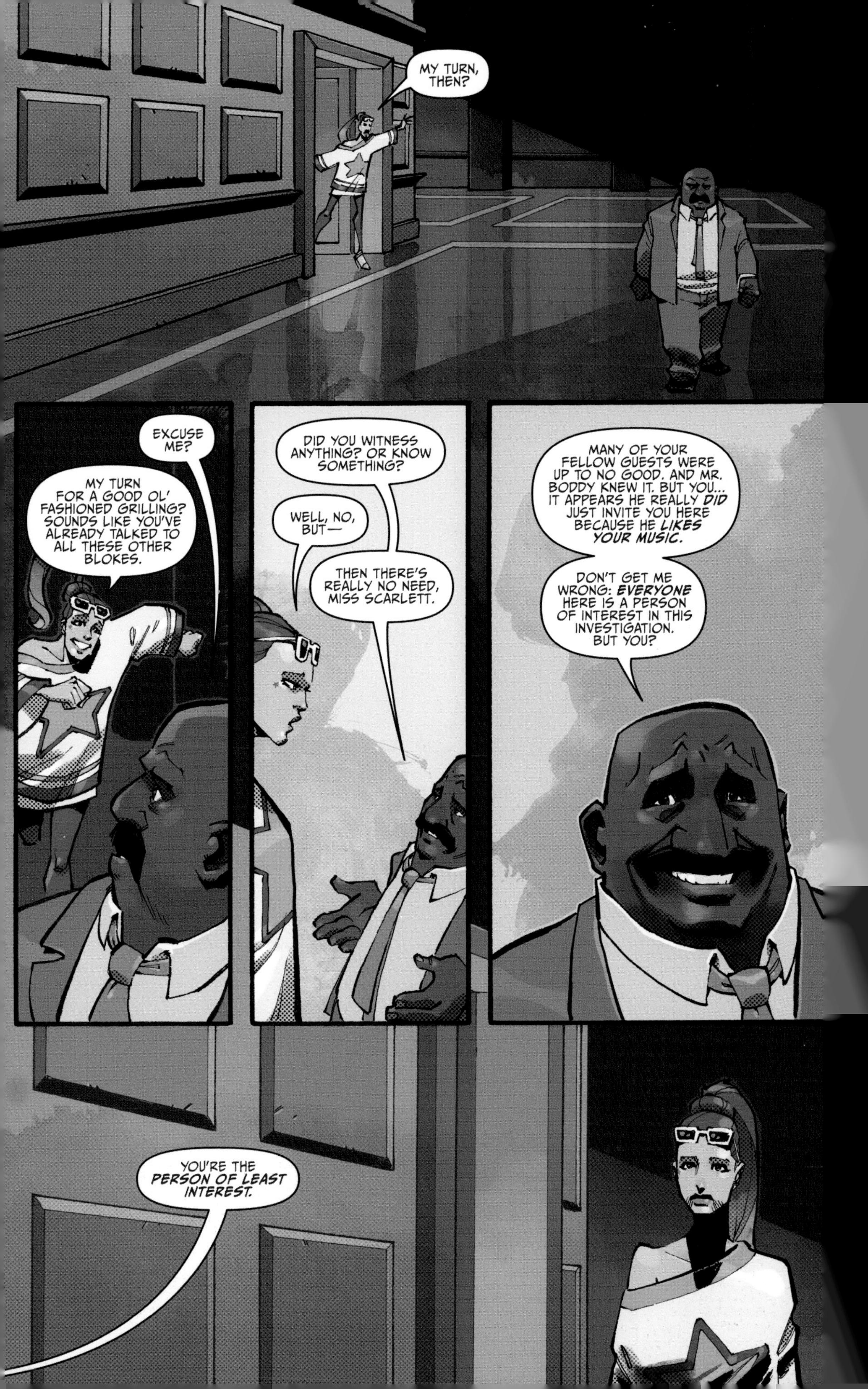
MY TURN, THEN?
EXCUSE ME?
MY TURN FOR A GOOD OL' FASHIONED GRILLING? SOUNDS LIKE YOU'VE ALREADY TALKED TO ALL THESE OTHER BLOKES.
DID YOU WITNESS ANYTHING? OR KNOW SOMETHING?
WELL, NO, BUT—
THEN THERE'S REALLY NO NEED, MISS SCARLETT.
MANY OF YOUR FELLOW GUESTS WERE UP TO NO GOOD. AND MR. BODDY KNEW IT. BUT YOU... IT APPEARS HE REALLY *DID* JUST INVITE YOU HERE BECAUSE HE *LIKES YOUR MUSIC.*
DON'T GET ME WRONG: *EVERYONE* HERE IS A PERSON OF INTEREST IN THIS INVESTIGATION. BUT YOU?
YOU'RE THE *PERSON OF LEAST INTEREST.*

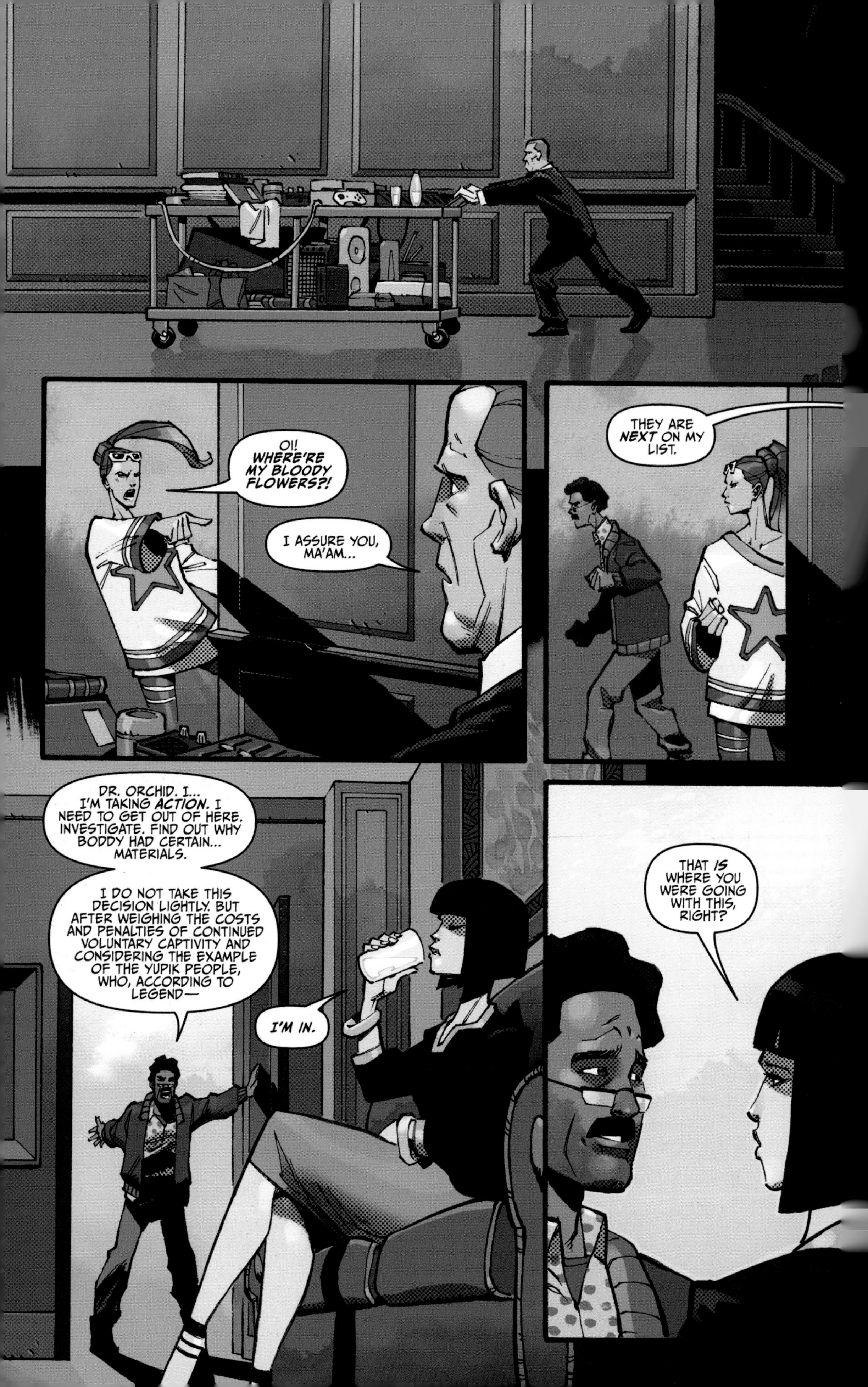
OI! WHERE'RE MY BLOODY FLOWERS?!
I ASSURE YOU, MA'AM...
THEY ARE NEXT ON MY LIST.
DR. ORCHID. I... I'M TAKING ACTION. I NEED TO GET OUT OF HERE. INVESTIGATE. FIND OUT WHY BODDY HAD CERTAIN... MATERIALS.
I DO NOT TAKE THIS DECISION LIGHTLY. BUT AFTER WEIGHING THE COSTS AND PENALTIES OF CONTINUED VOLUNTARY CAPTIVITY AND CONSIDERING THE EXAMPLE OF THE YUPIK PEOPLE, WHO, ACCORDING TO LEGEND—
I'M IN.
THAT IS WHERE YOU WERE GOING WITH THIS, RIGHT?

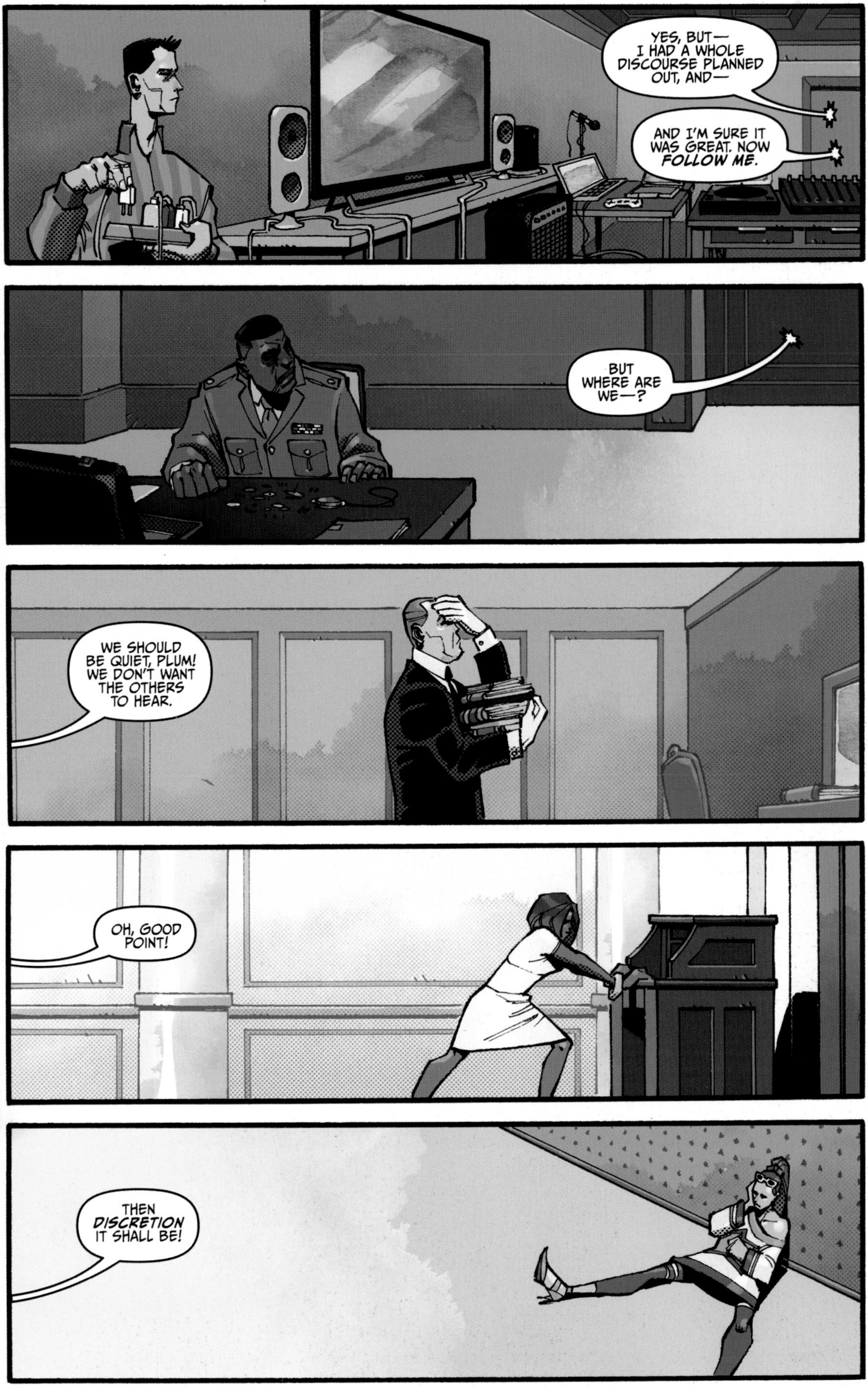
YES, BUT— I HAD A WHOLE DISCOURSE PLANNED OUT, AND—
AND I'M SURE IT WAS GREAT. NOW *FOLLOW ME.*
BUT WHERE ARE WE—?
WE SHOULD BE QUIET, PLUM! WE DON'T WANT THE OTHERS TO HEAR.
OH, GOOD POINT!
THEN *DISCRETION* IT SHALL BE!

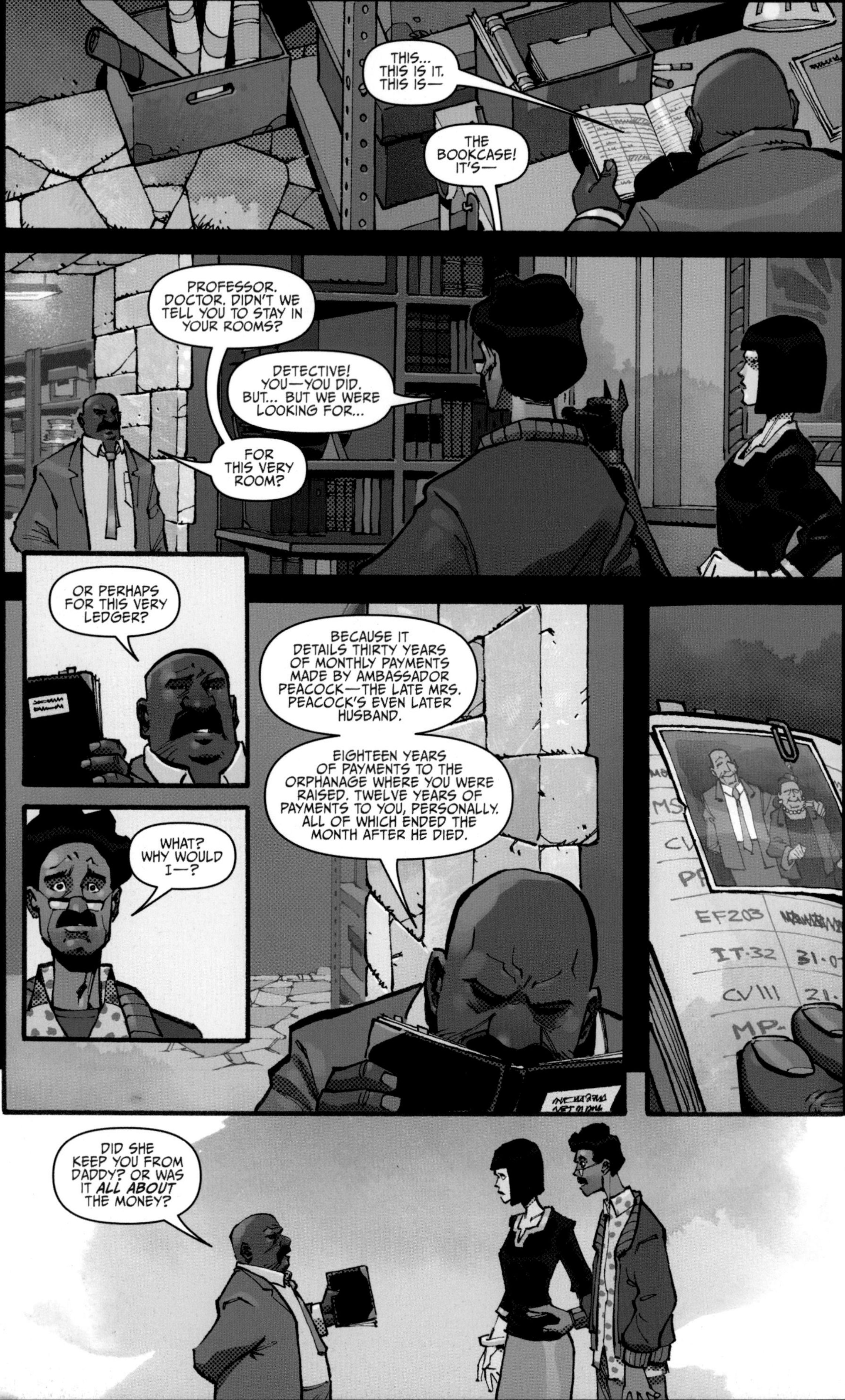
THIS... THIS IS IT. THIS IS—
THE BOOKCASE! IT'S—
PROFESSOR. DOCTOR. DIDN'T WE TELL YOU TO STAY IN YOUR ROOMS?
DETECTIVE! YOU—YOU DID. BUT... BUT WE WERE LOOKING FOR...
FOR THIS VERY ROOM?
OR PERHAPS FOR THIS VERY LEDGER?
WHAT? WHY WOULD I—?
BECAUSE IT DETAILS THIRTY YEARS OF MONTHLY PAYMENTS MADE BY AMBASSADOR PEACOCK—THE LATE MRS. PEACOCK'S EVEN LATER HUSBAND.
EIGHTEEN YEARS OF PAYMENTS TO THE ORPHANAGE WHERE YOU WERE RAISED. TWELVE YEARS OF PAYMENTS TO YOU, PERSONALLY. ALL OF WHICH ENDED THE MONTH AFTER HE DIED.
EF203
IT-32
CV111
DID SHE KEEP YOU FROM DADDY? OR WAS IT ***ALL ABOUT*** THE MONEY?

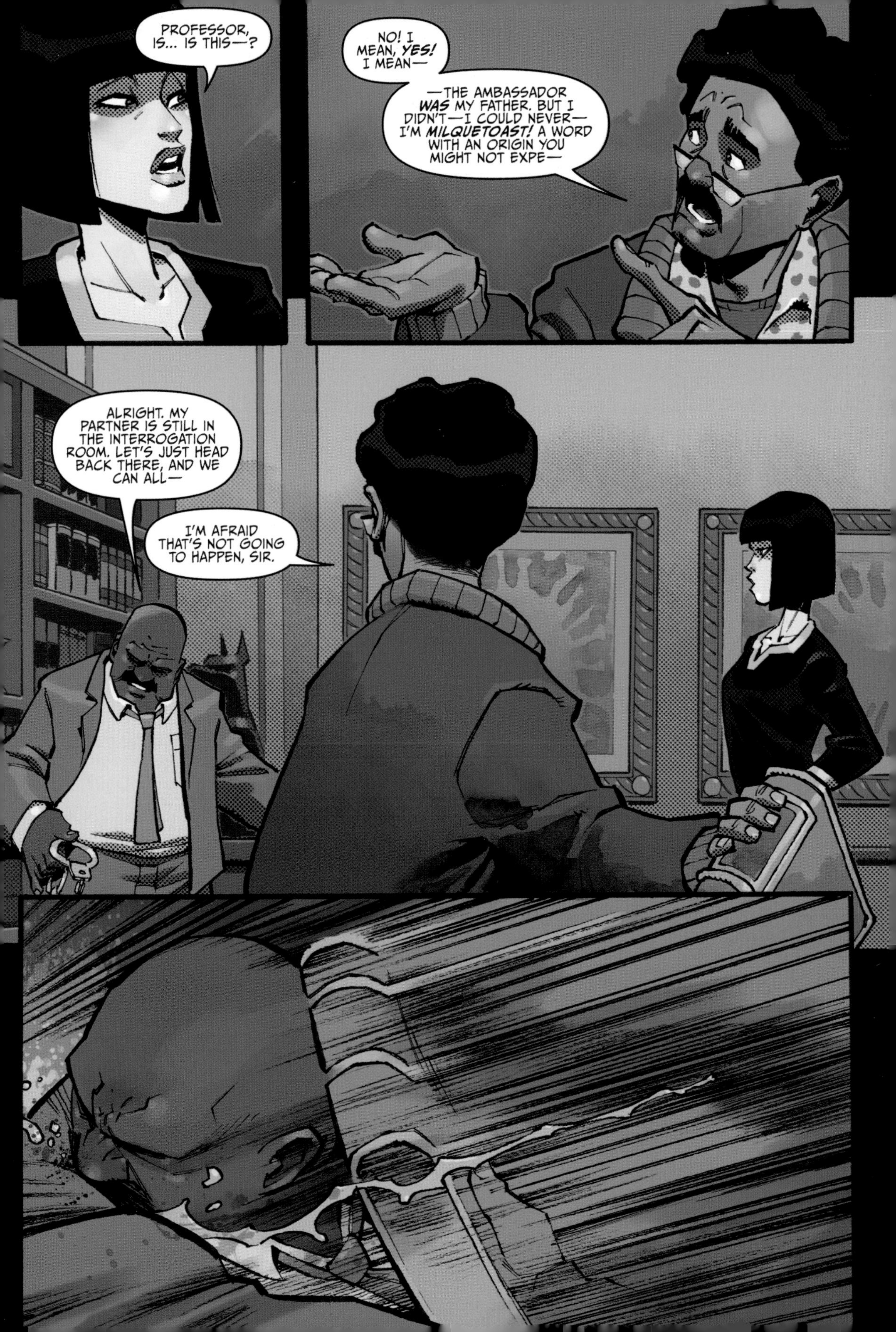
PROFESSOR, IS... IS THIS—?
NO! I MEAN, YES! I MEAN—
—THE AMBASSADOR WAS MY FATHER. BUT I DIDN'T—I COULD NEVER—I'M MILQUETOAST! A WORD WITH AN ORIGIN YOU MIGHT NOT EXPE—
ALRIGHT. MY PARTNER IS STILL IN THE INTERROGATION ROOM. LET'S JUST HEAD BACK THERE, AND WE CAN ALL—
I'M AFRAID THAT'S NOT GOING TO HAPPEN, SIR.

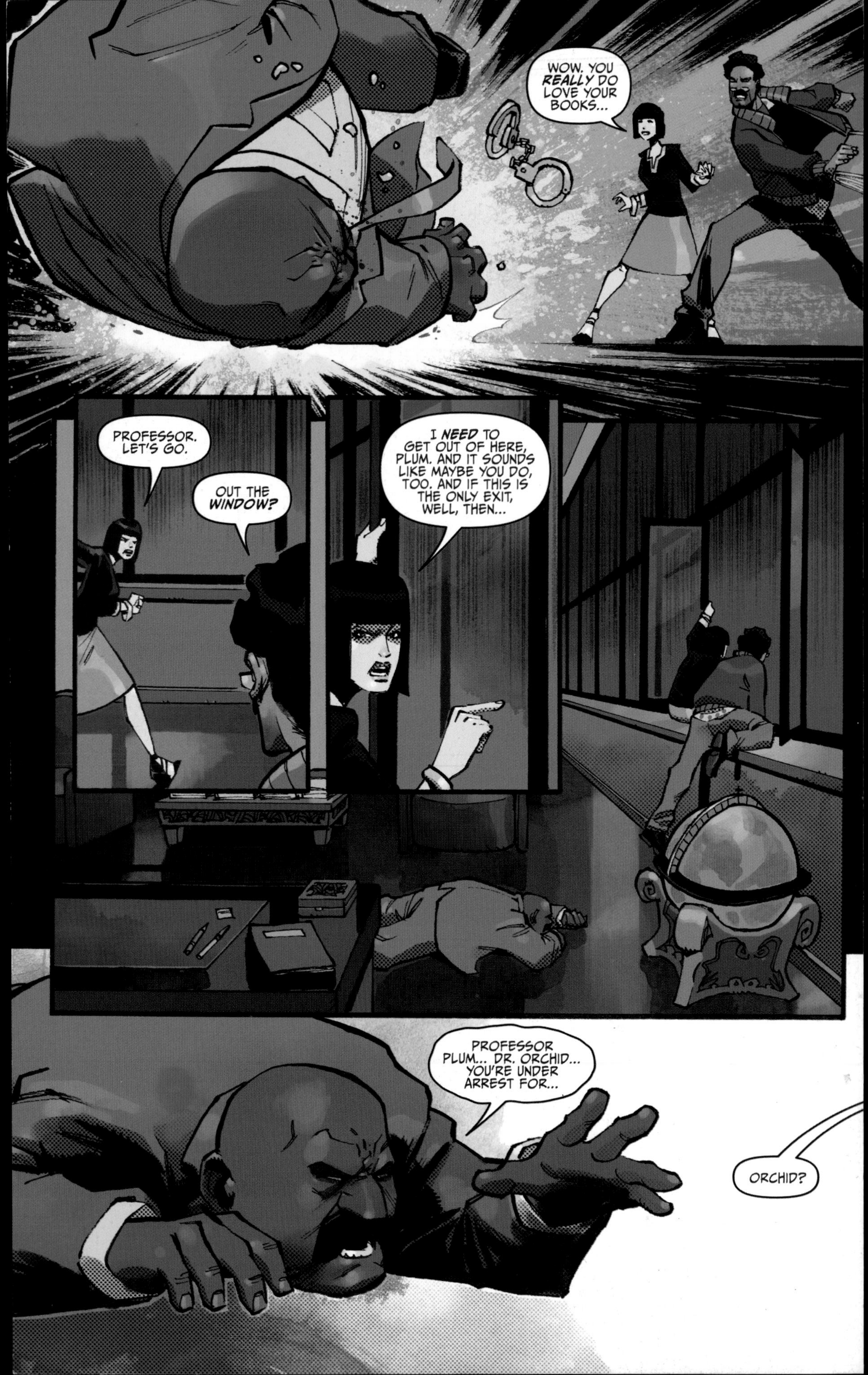
WOW. YOU REALLY DO LOVE YOUR BOOKS...
PROFESSOR. LET'S GO.
OUT THE WINDOW?
I NEED TO GET OUT OF HERE, PLUM. AND IT SOUNDS LIKE MAYBE YOU DO, TOO. AND IF THIS IS THE ONLY EXIT, WELL, THEN...
PROFESSOR PLUM... DR. ORCHID... YOU'RE UNDER ARREST FOR...
ORCHID?

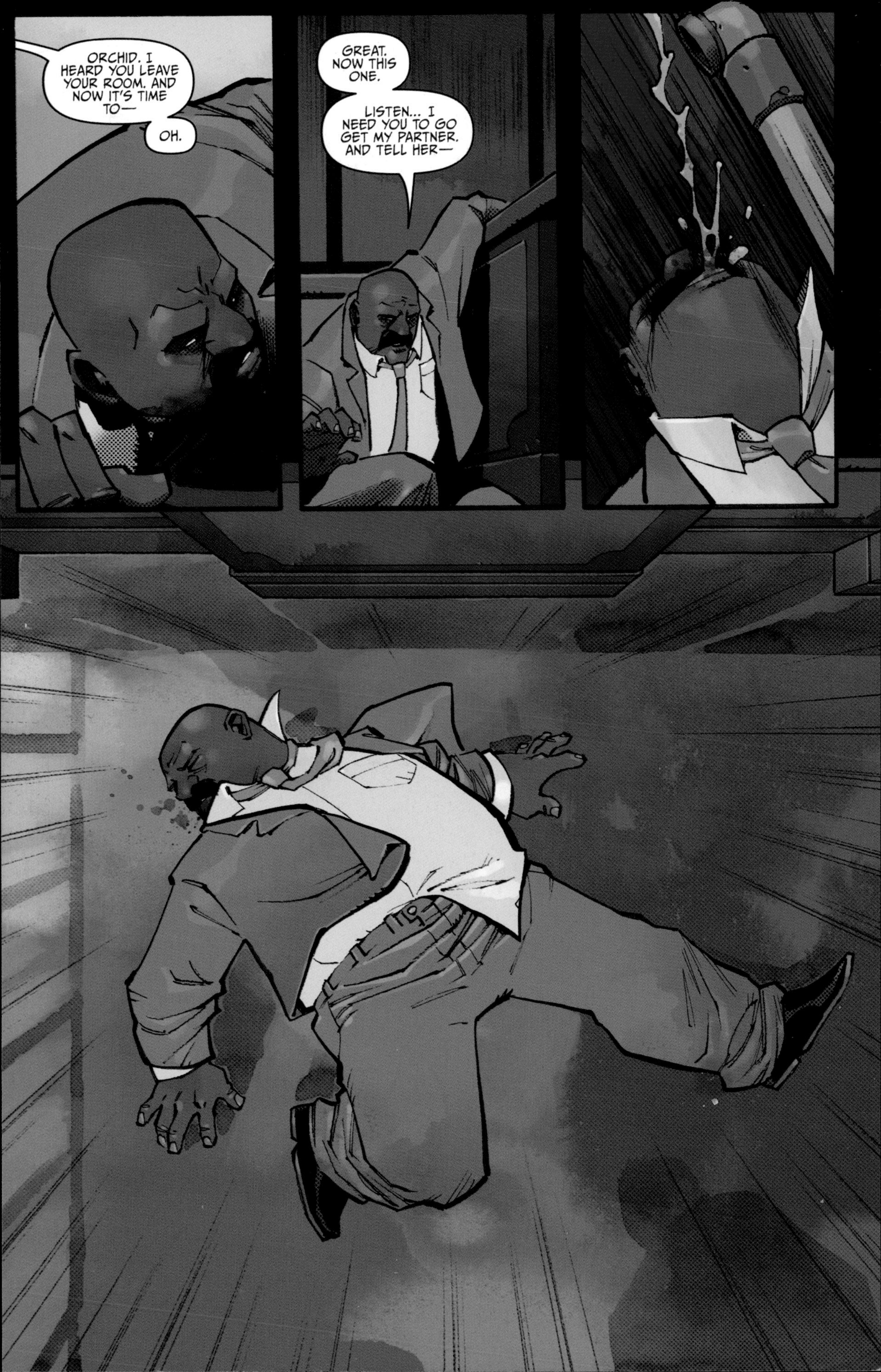
ORCHID. I HEARD YOU LEAVE YOUR ROOM. AND NOW IT'S TIME TO—
OH.
GREAT. NOW THIS ONE.
LISTEN... I NEED YOU TO GO GET MY PARTNER. AND TELL HER—

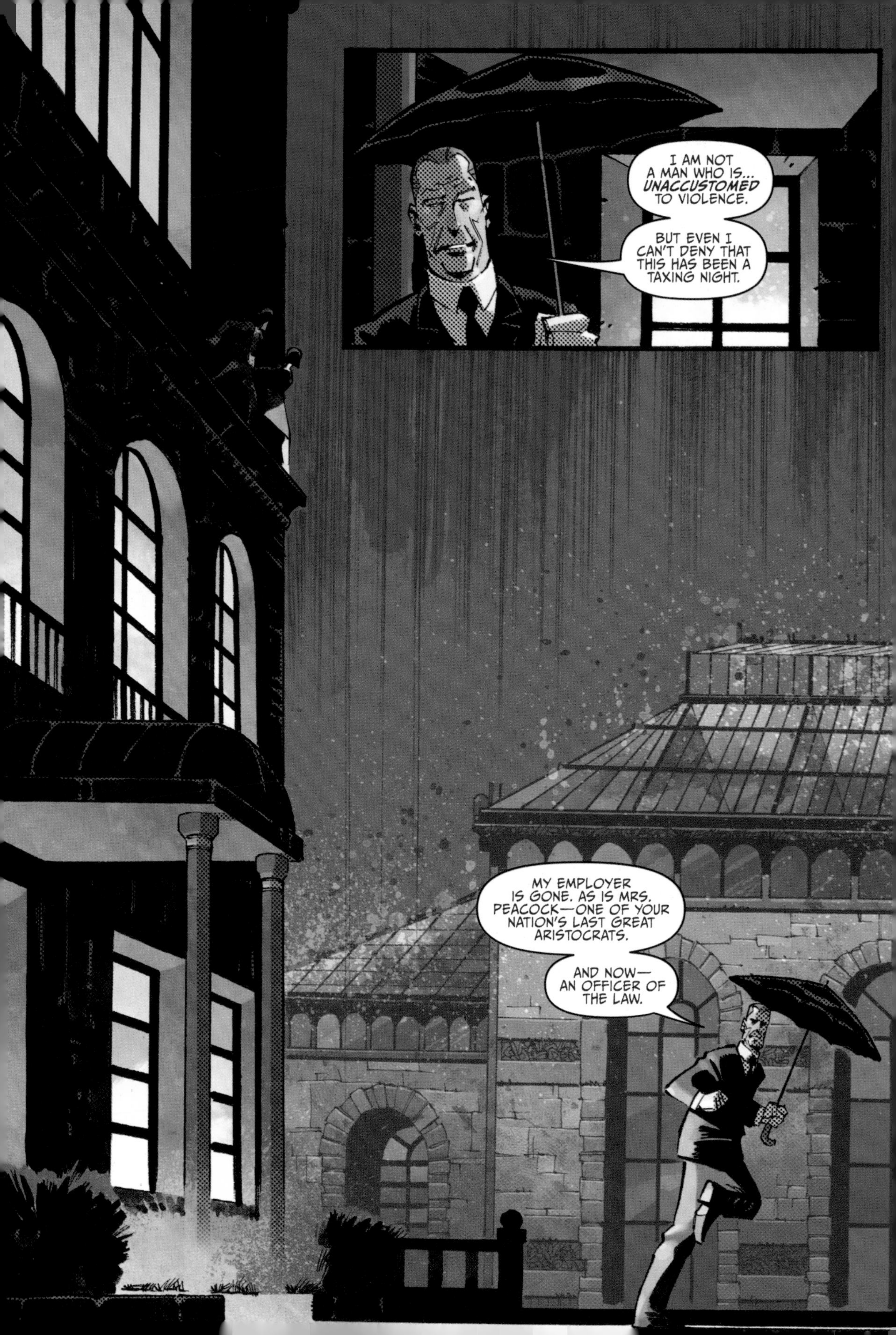
I AM NOT A MAN WHO IS... *UNACCUSTOMED* TO VIOLENCE.
BUT EVEN I CAN'T DENY THAT THIS HAS BEEN A TAXING NIGHT.
MY EMPLOYER IS GONE. AS IS MRS. PEACOCK—ONE OF YOUR NATION'S LAST GREAT ARISTOCRATS.
AND NOW— AN OFFICER OF THE LAW.

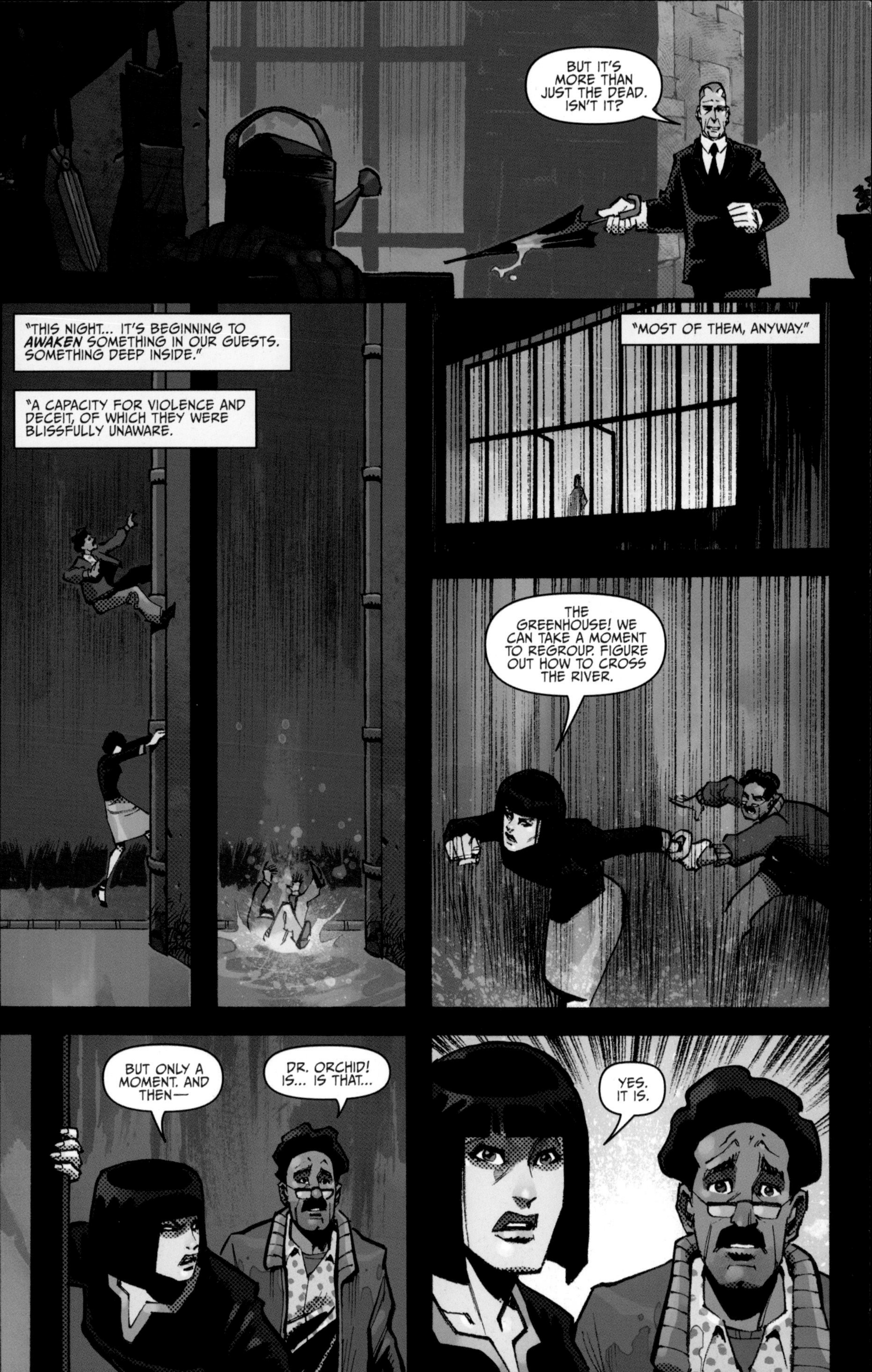
BUT IT'S MORE THAN JUST THE DEAD. ISN'T IT?
"THIS NIGHT... IT'S BEGINNING TO AWAKEN SOMETHING IN OUR GUESTS. SOMETHING DEEP INSIDE."
"A CAPACITY FOR VIOLENCE AND DECEIT, OF WHICH THEY WERE BLISSFULLY UNAWARE.
"MOST OF THEM, ANYWAY."
THE GREENHOUSE! WE CAN TAKE A MOMENT TO REGROUP. FIGURE OUT HOW TO CROSS THE RIVER.
BUT ONLY A MOMENT. AND THEN—
DR. ORCHID! IS... IS THAT...
YES. IT IS.

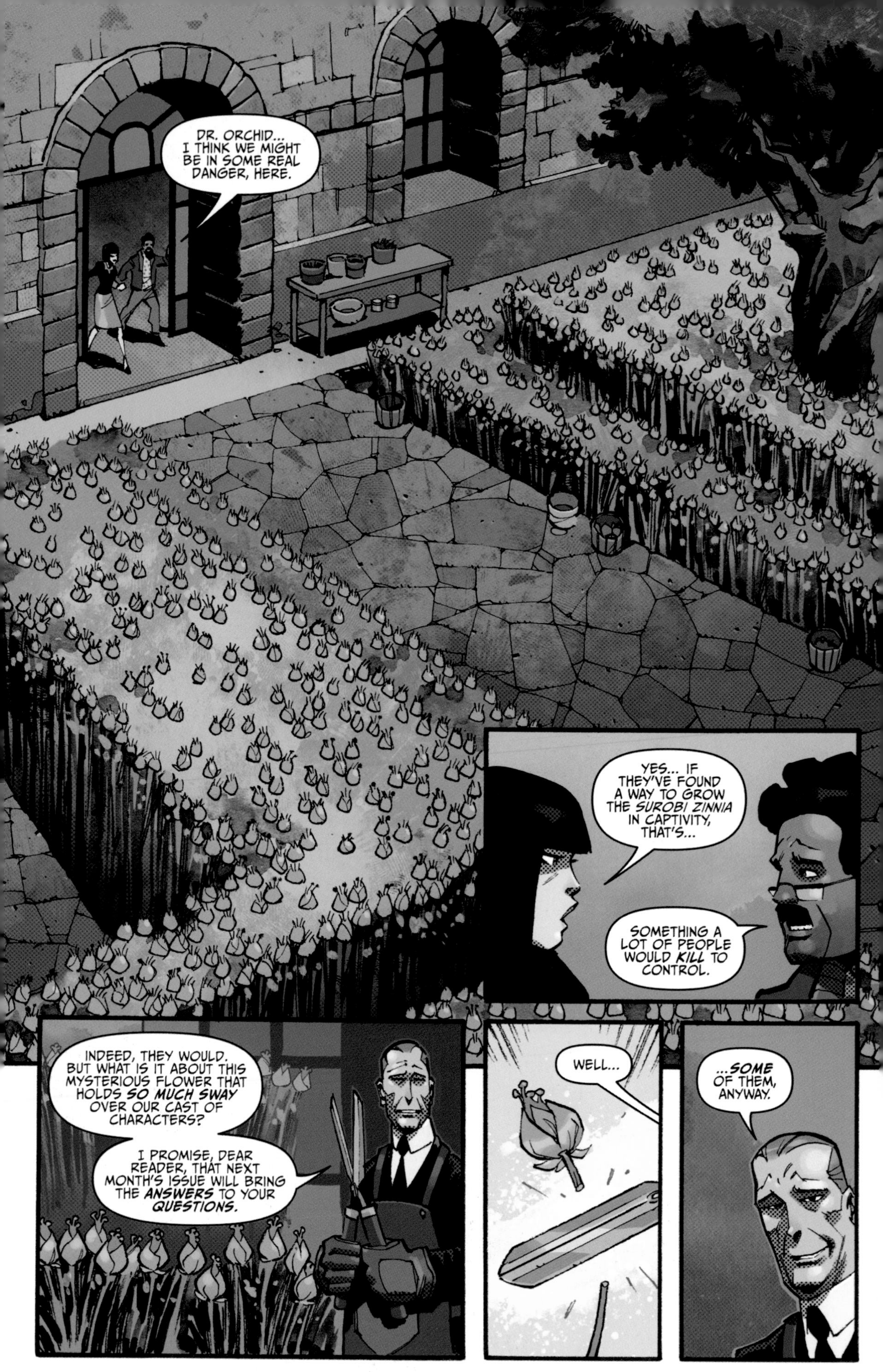
DR. ORCHID... I THINK WE MIGHT BE IN SOME REAL DANGER, HERE.
YES... IF THEY'VE FOUND A WAY TO GROW THE *SUROBI ZINNIA* IN CAPTIVITY, THAT'S...
SOMETHING A LOT OF PEOPLE WOULD ***KILL*** TO CONTROL.
INDEED, THEY WOULD. BUT WHAT IS IT ABOUT THIS MYSTERIOUS FLOWER THAT HOLDS ***SO MUCH SWAY*** OVER OUR CAST OF CHARACTERS?
I PROMISE, DEAR READER, THAT NEXT MONTH'S ISSUE WILL BRING THE ***ANSWERS*** TO YOUR ***QUESTIONS.***
WELL...
...***SOME*** OF THEM, ANYWAY.

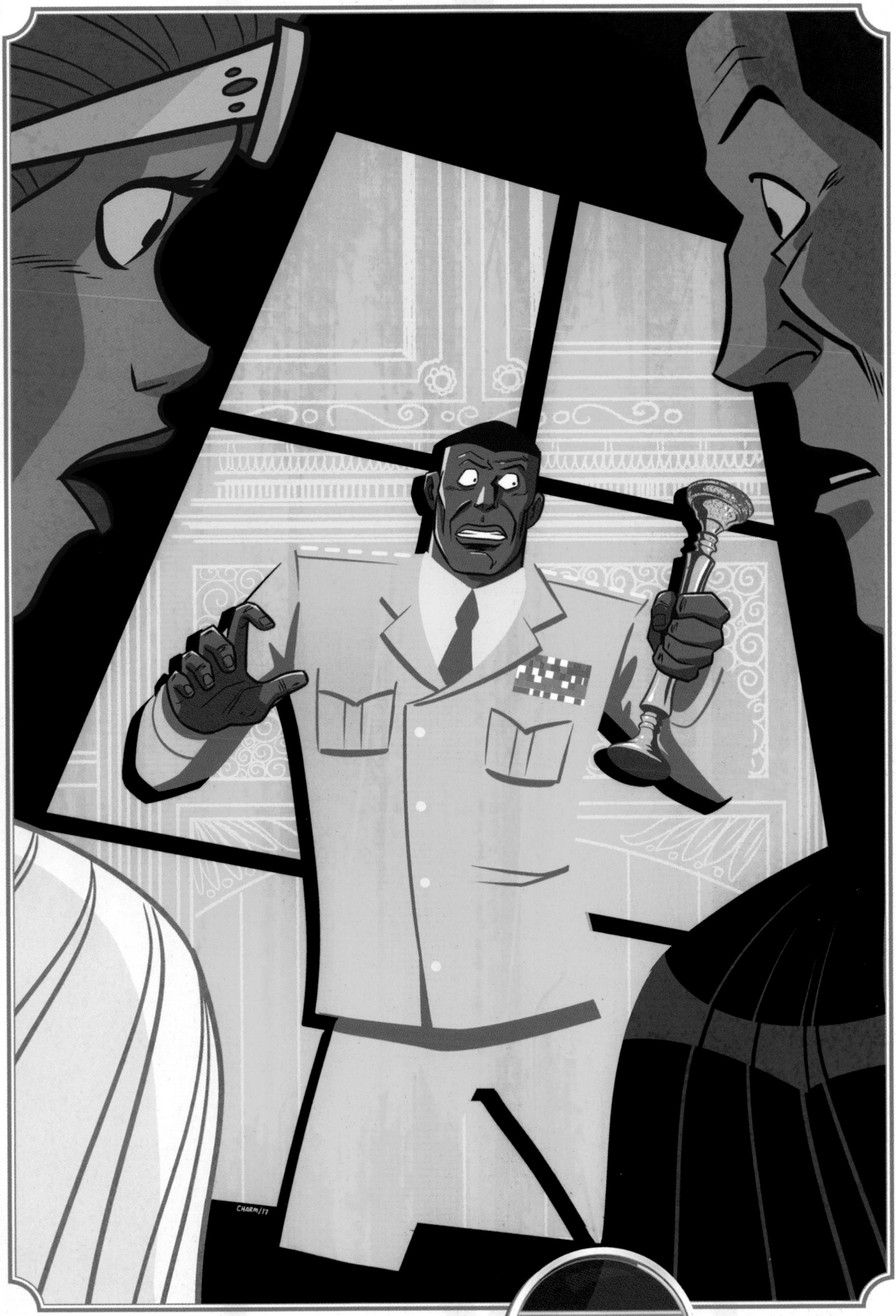
CHARM/17

COVER ART BY
DEREK CHARM

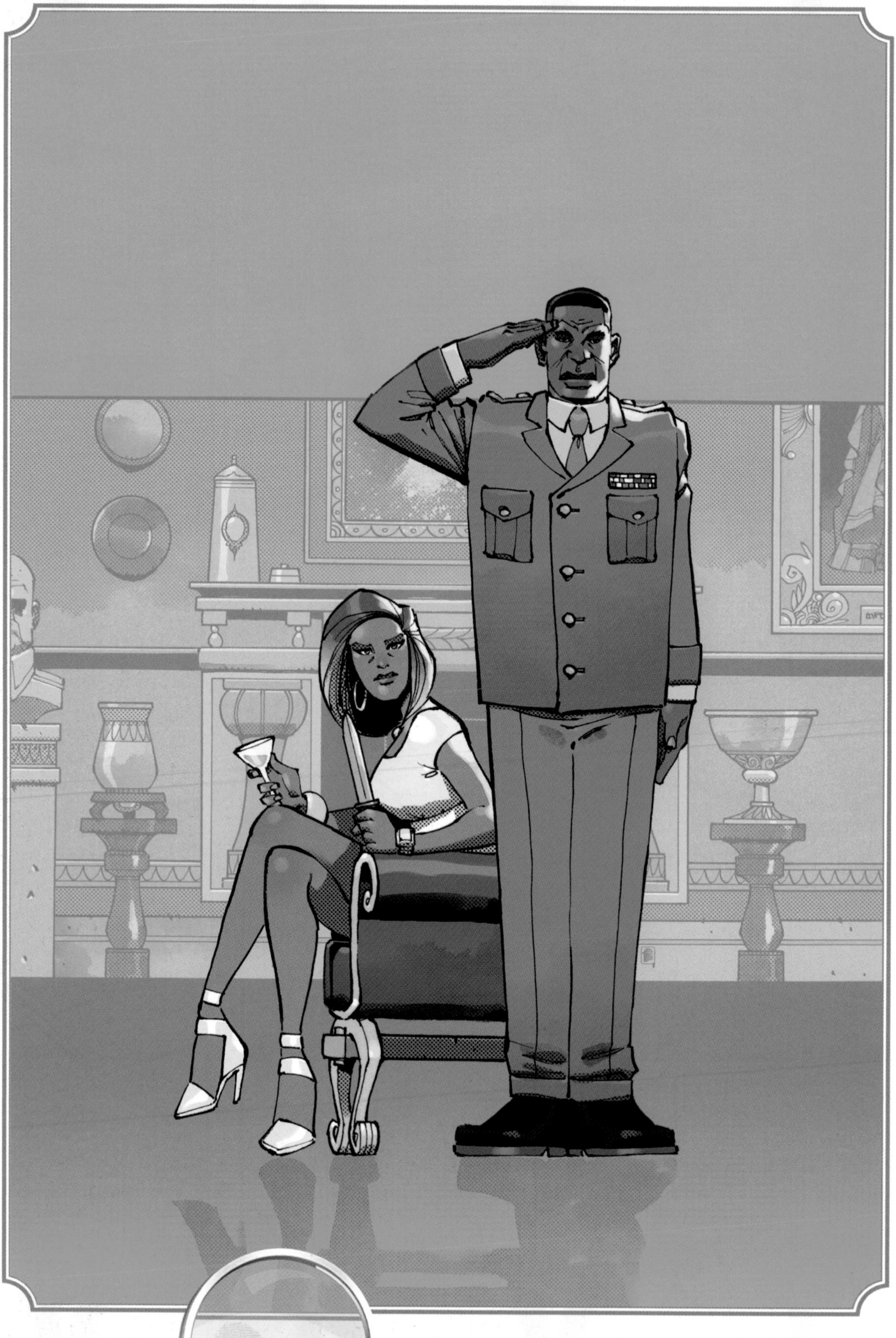

COVER ART BY
NELSON DANIEL

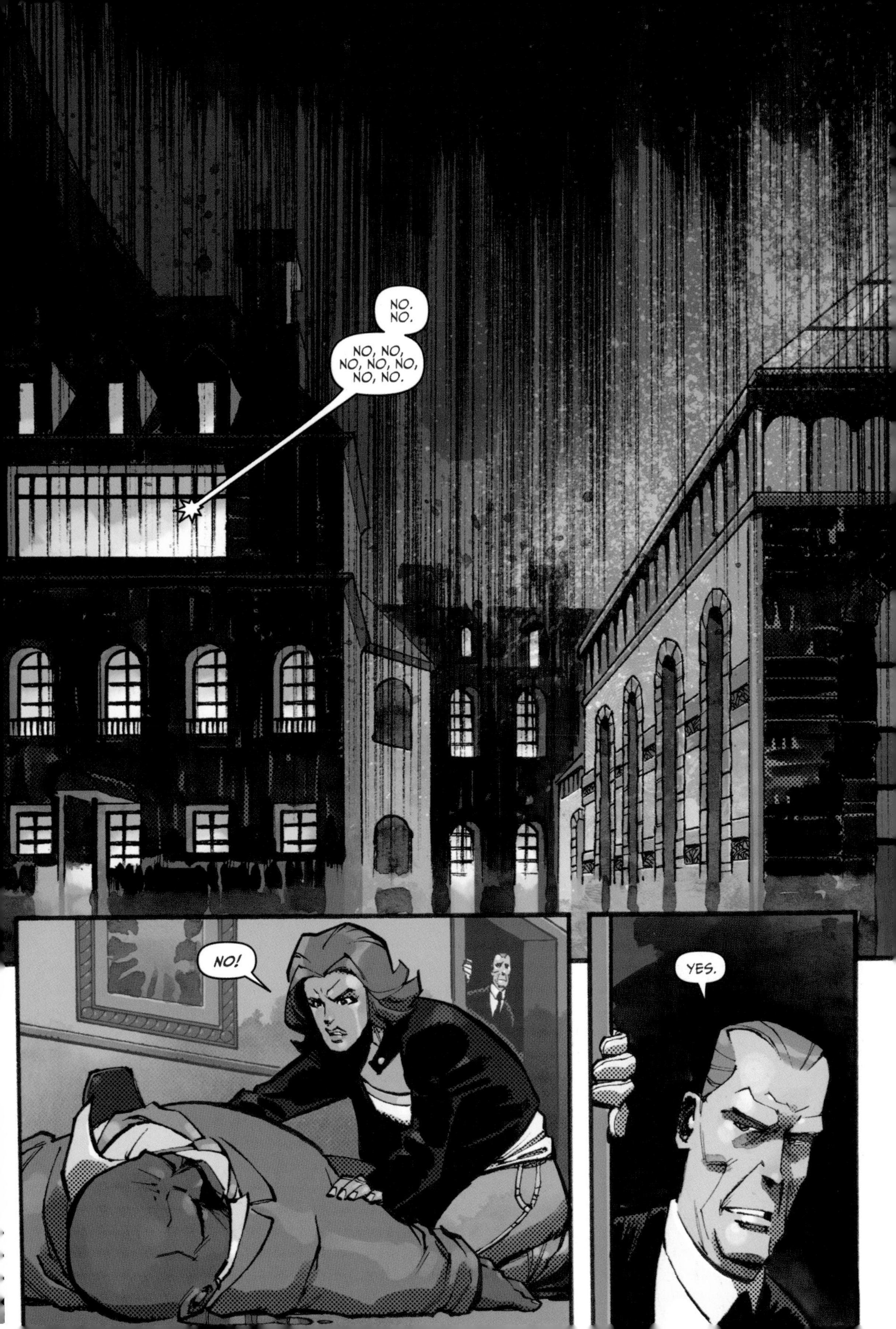
NO.
NO.
NO, NO,
NO, NO, NO,
NO, NO.
NO!
YES.

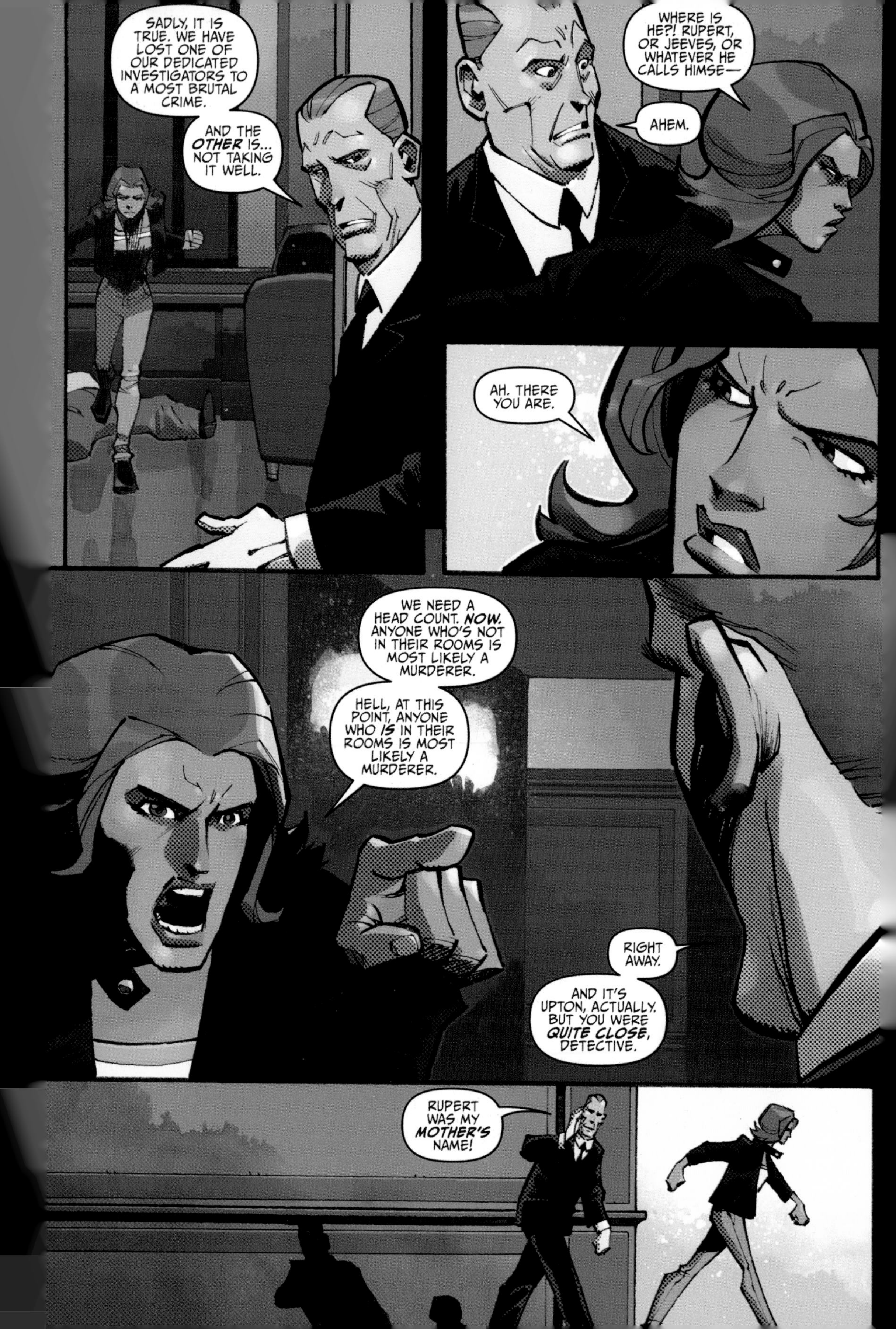
SADLY, IT IS TRUE. WE HAVE LOST ONE OF OUR DEDICATED INVESTIGATORS TO A MOST BRUTAL CRIME.
AND THE OTHER IS... NOT TAKING IT WELL.
WHERE IS HE?! RUPERT, OR JEEVES, OR WHATEVER HE CALLS HIMSE—
AHEM.
AH. THERE YOU ARE.
WE NEED A HEAD COUNT. NOW. ANYONE WHO'S NOT IN THEIR ROOMS IS MOST LIKELY A MURDERER.
HELL, AT THIS POINT, ANYONE WHO IS IN THEIR ROOMS IS MOST LIKELY A MURDERER.
RIGHT AWAY.
AND IT'S UPTON, ACTUALLY. BUT YOU WERE QUITE CLOSE, DETECTIVE.
RUPERT WAS MY MOTHER'S NAME!

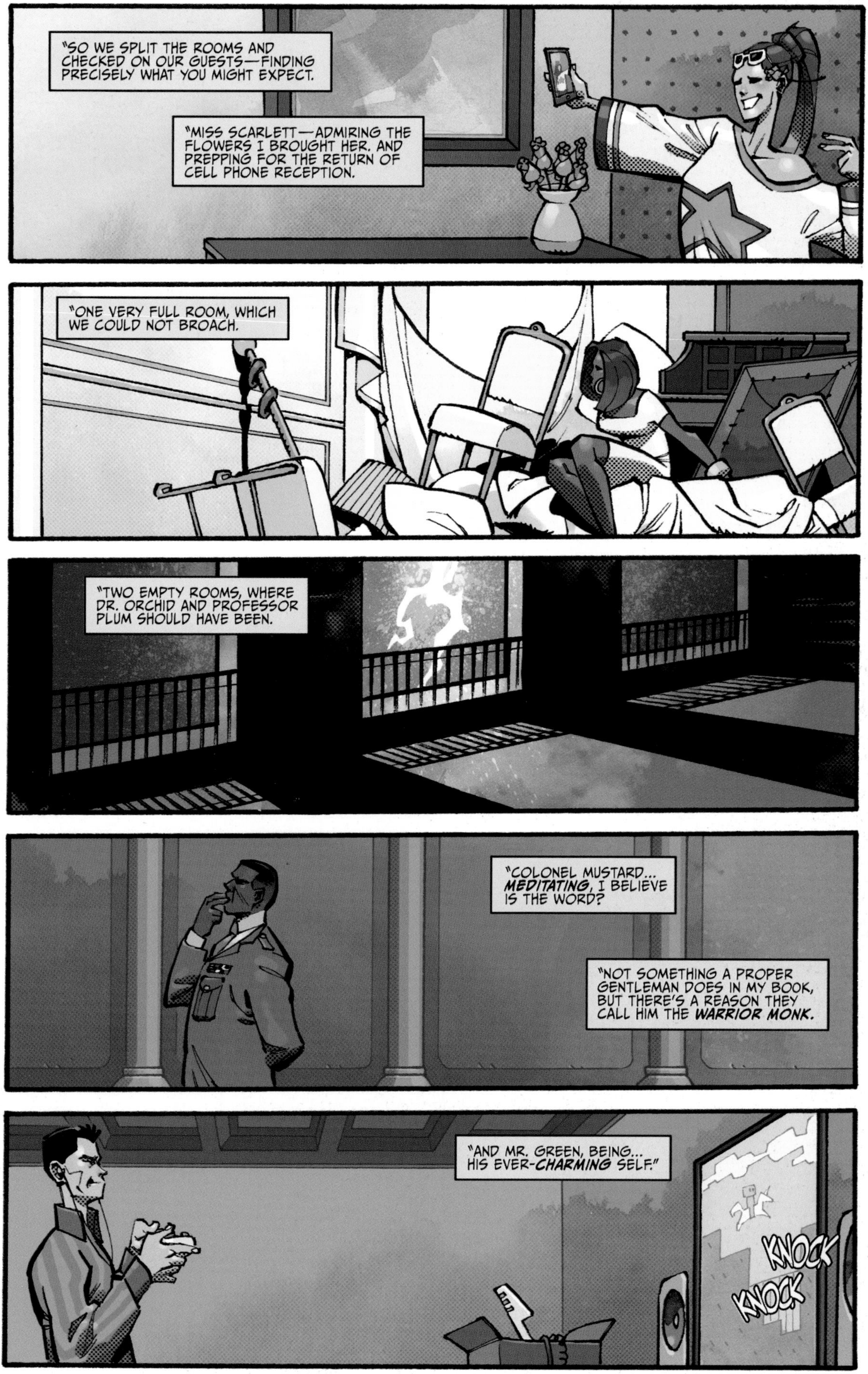
"SO WE SPLIT THE ROOMS AND CHECKED ON OUR GUESTS—FINDING PRECISELY WHAT YOU MIGHT EXPECT.
"MISS SCARLETT—ADMIRING THE FLOWERS I BROUGHT HER. AND PREPPING FOR THE RETURN OF CELL PHONE RECEPTION.
"ONE VERY FULL ROOM, WHICH WE COULD NOT BROACH.
"TWO EMPTY ROOMS, WHERE DR. ORCHID AND PROFESSOR PLUM SHOULD HAVE BEEN.
"COLONEL MUSTARD... MEDITATING, I BELIEVE IS THE WORD?
"NOT SOMETHING A PROPER GENTLEMAN DOES IN MY BOOK, BUT THERE'S A REASON THEY CALL HIM THE WARRIOR MONK.
"AND MR. GREEN, BEING... HIS EVER-CHARMING SELF."
KNOCK
KNOCK

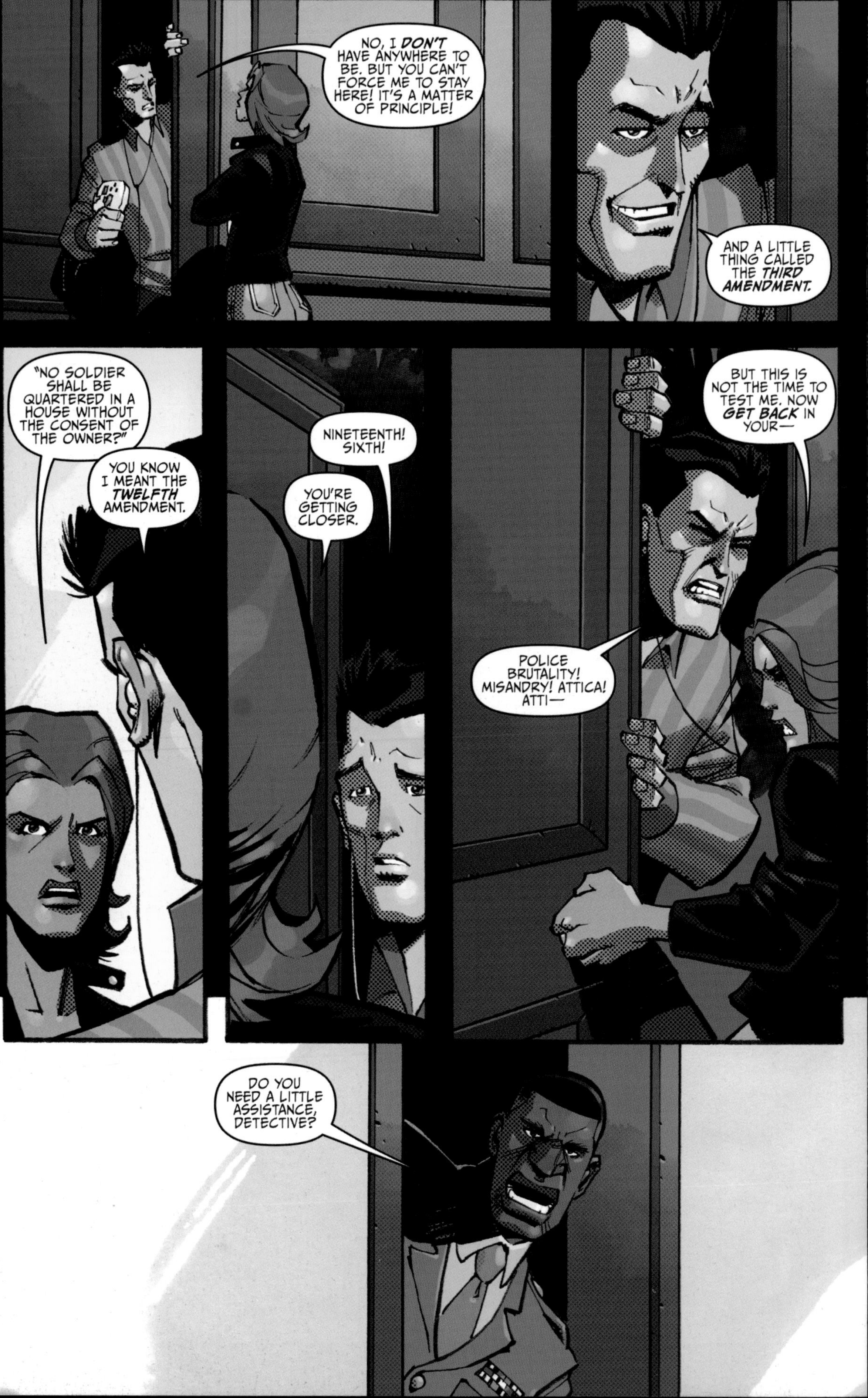
NO, I DON'T HAVE ANYWHERE TO BE. BUT YOU CAN'T FORCE ME TO STAY HERE! IT'S A MATTER OF PRINCIPLE!
AND A LITTLE THING CALLED THE THIRD AMENDMENT.
"NO SOLDIER SHALL BE QUARTERED IN A HOUSE WITHOUT THE CONSENT OF THE OWNER?"
YOU KNOW I MEANT THE TWELFTH AMENDMENT.
NINETEENTH! SIXTH!
YOU'RE GETTING CLOSER.
BUT THIS IS NOT THE TIME TO TEST ME. NOW GET BACK IN YOUR—
POLICE BRUTALITY! MISANDRY! ATTICA! ATTI—
DO YOU NEED A LITTLE ASSISTANCE, DETECTIVE?

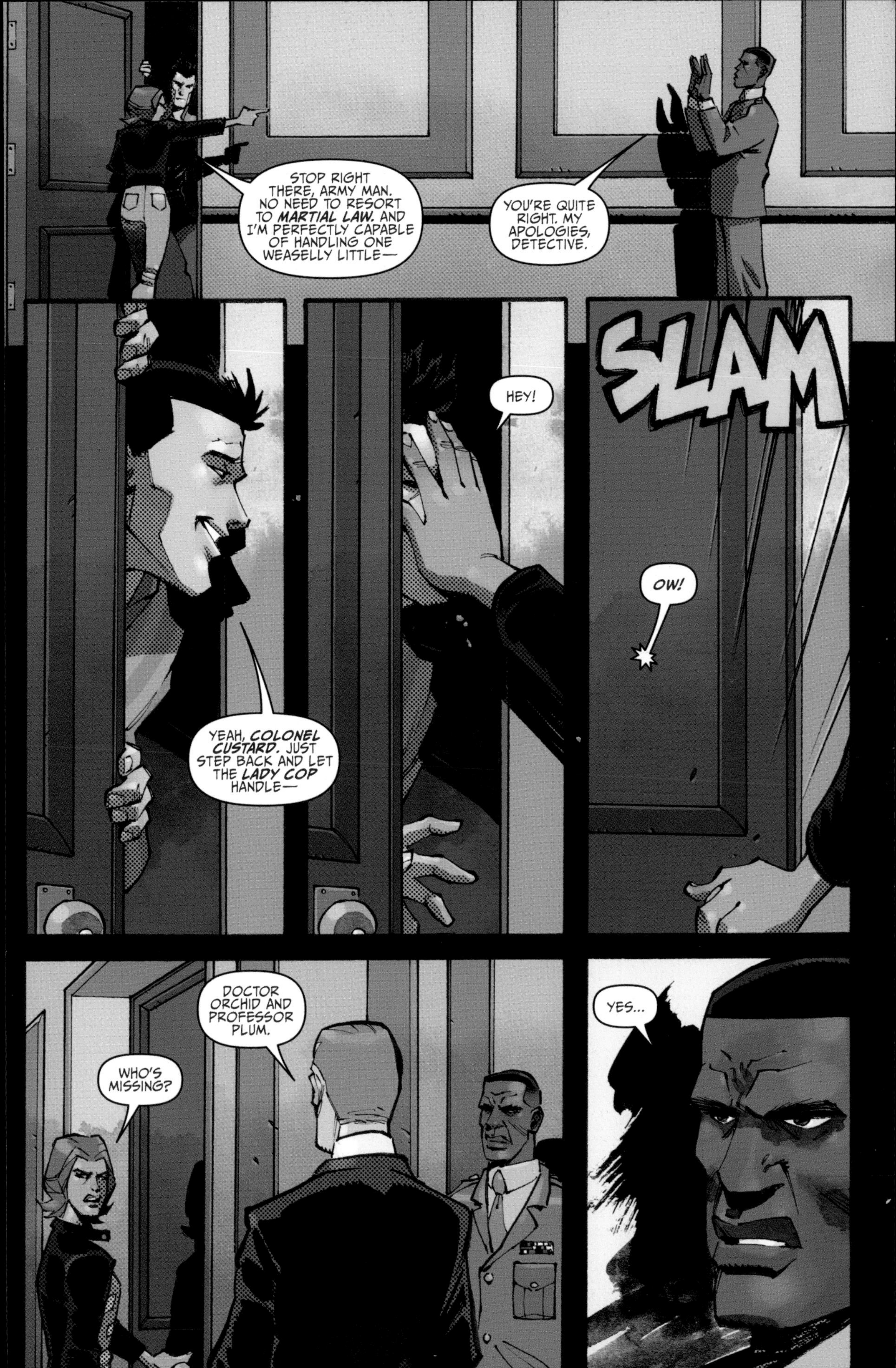
STOP RIGHT THERE, ARMY MAN. NO NEED TO RESORT TO MARTIAL LAW. AND I'M PERFECTLY CAPABLE OF HANDLING ONE WEASELLY LITTLE—
YOU'RE QUITE RIGHT. MY APOLOGIES, DETECTIVE.
YEAH, COLONEL CUSTARD. JUST STEP BACK AND LET THE LADY COP HANDLE—
HEY!
SLAM
OW!
WHO'S MISSING?
DOCTOR ORCHID AND PROFESSOR PLUM.
YES...

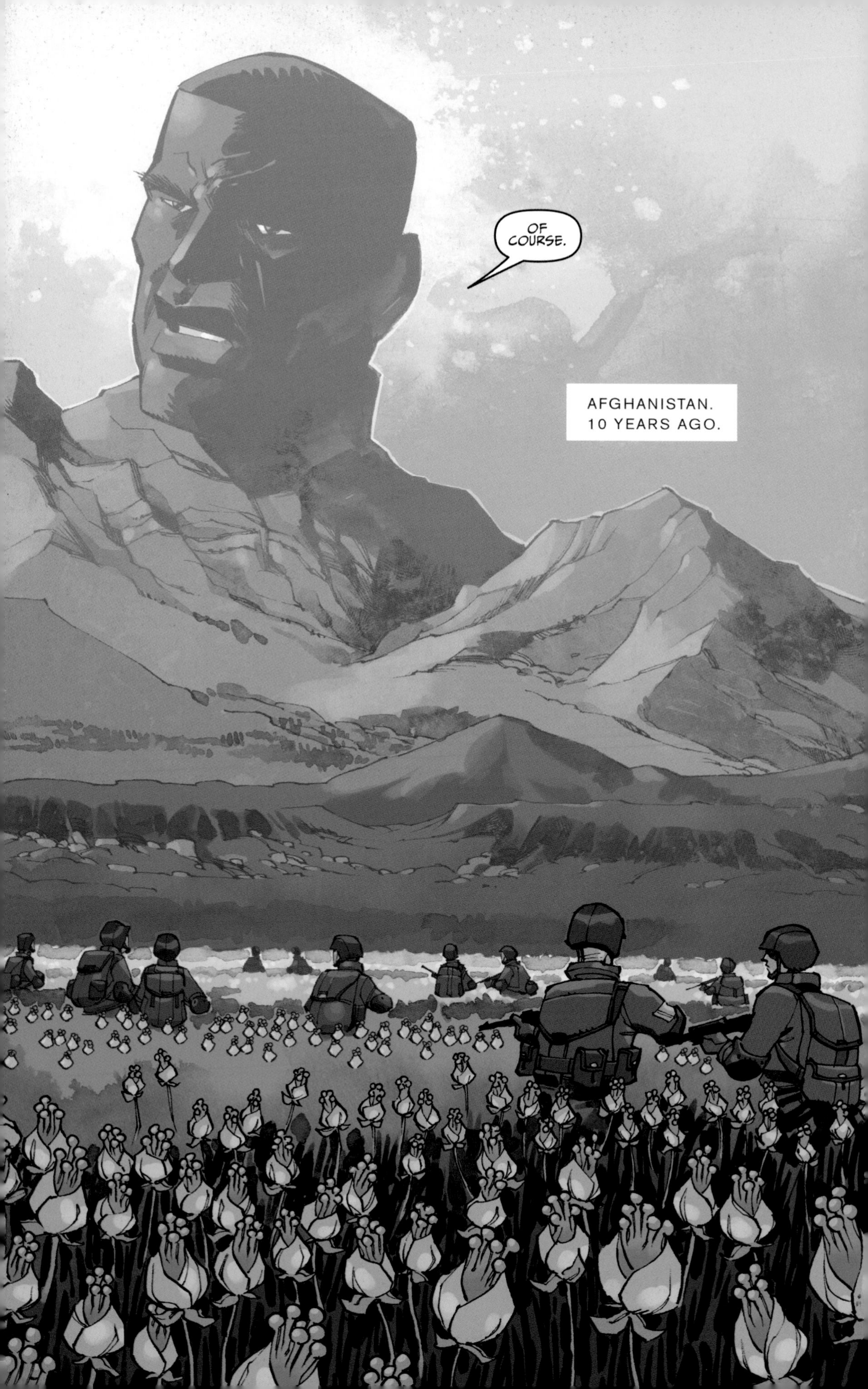
OF COURSE.
AFGHANISTAN. 10 YEARS AGO.

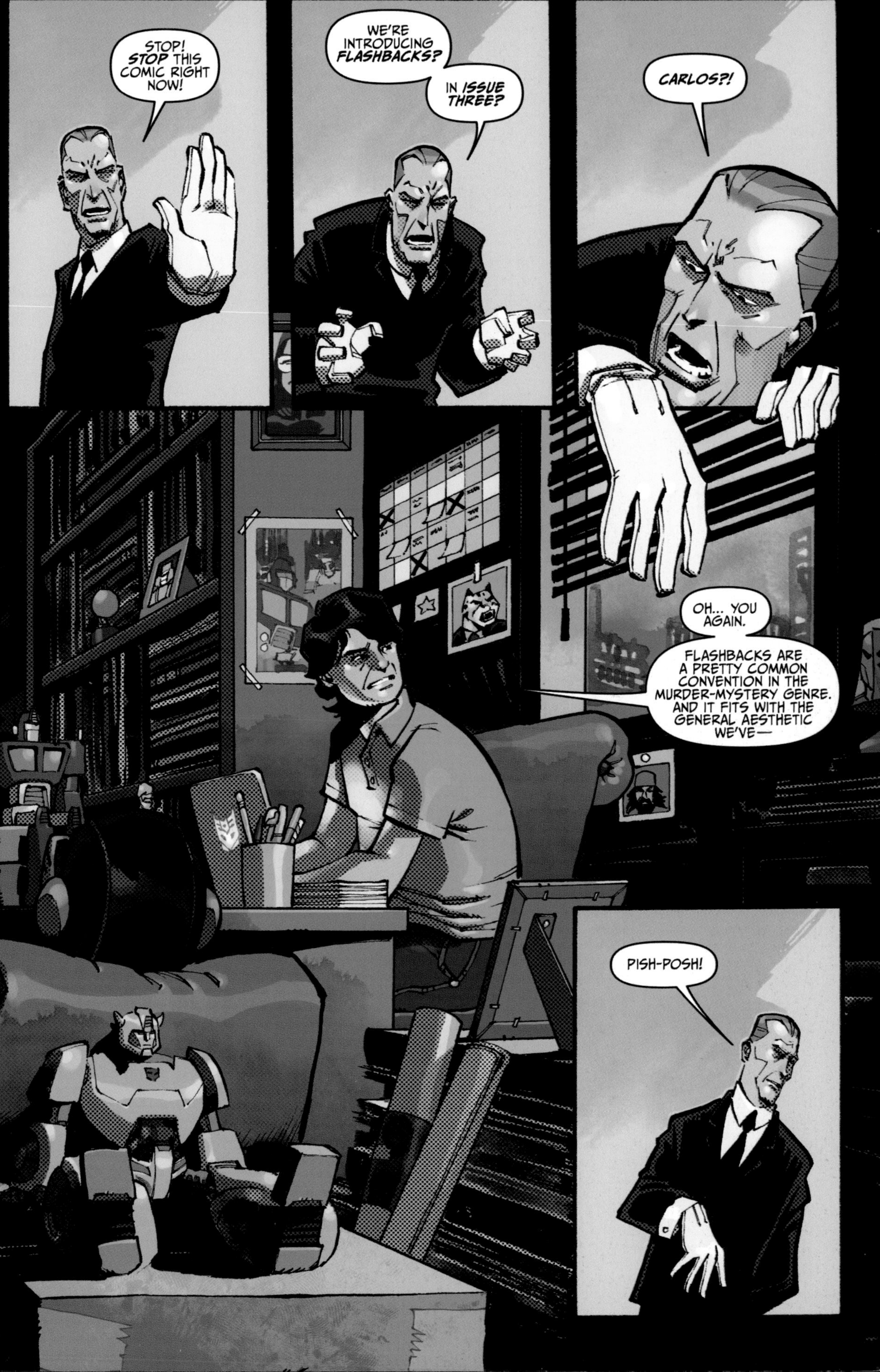
STOP! STOP THIS COMIC RIGHT NOW!
WE'RE INTRODUCING FLASHBACKS?
IN ISSUE THREE?
CARLOS?!
OH... YOU AGAIN.
FLASHBACKS ARE A PRETTY COMMON CONVENTION IN THE MURDER-MYSTERY GENRE. AND IT FITS WITH THE GENERAL AESTHETIC WE'VE—
PISH-POSH!

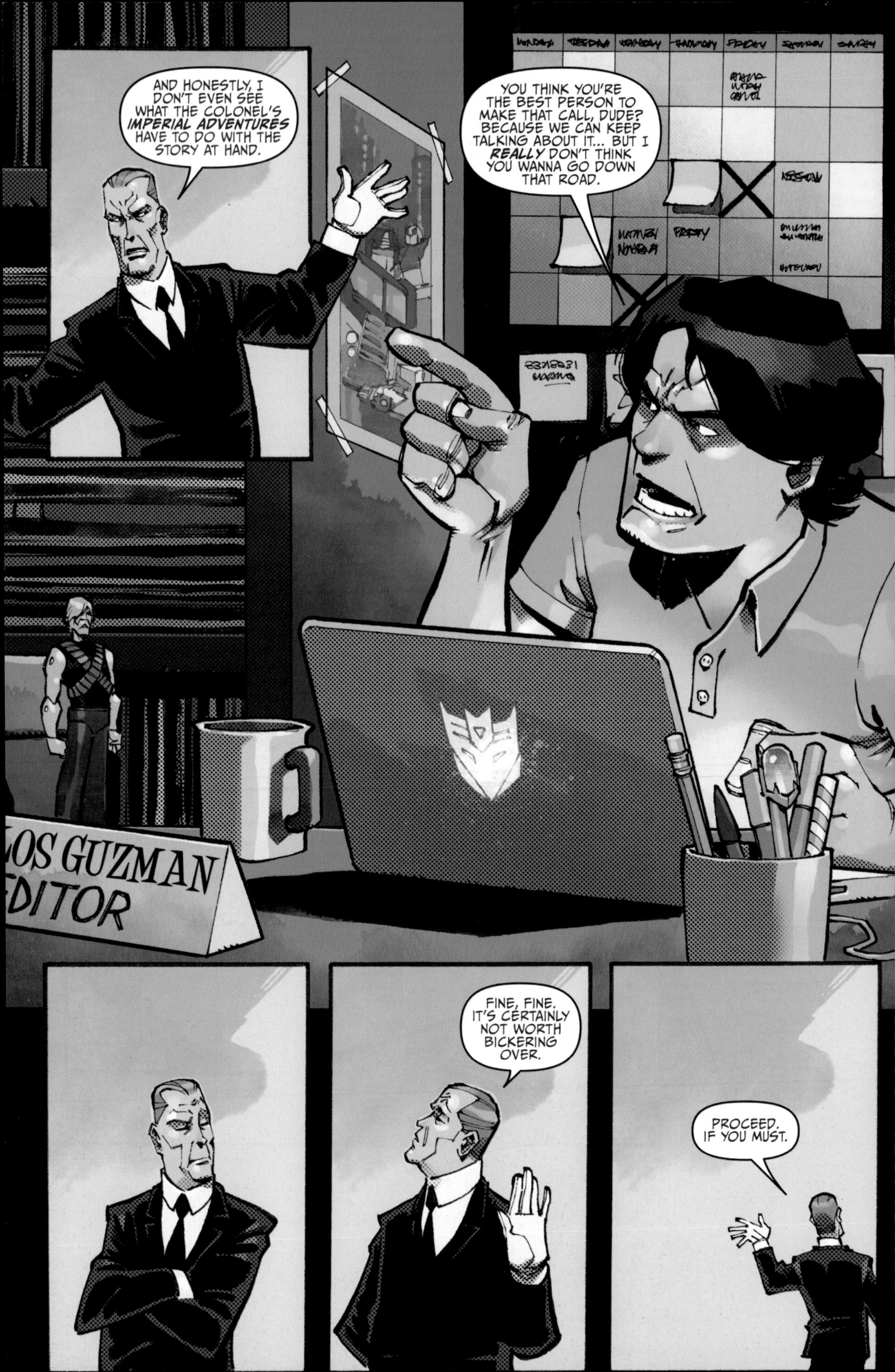
AND HONESTLY, I DON'T EVEN SEE WHAT THE COLONEL'S IMPERIAL ADVENTURES HAVE TO DO WITH THE STORY AT HAND.
YOU THINK YOU'RE THE BEST PERSON TO MAKE THAT CALL, DUDE? BECAUSE WE CAN KEEP TALKING ABOUT IT... BUT I REALLY DON'T THINK YOU WANNA GO DOWN THAT ROAD.
LOS GUZMAN
EDITOR
FINE, FINE. IT'S CERTAINLY NOT WORTH BICKERING OVER.
PROCEED. IF YOU MUST.

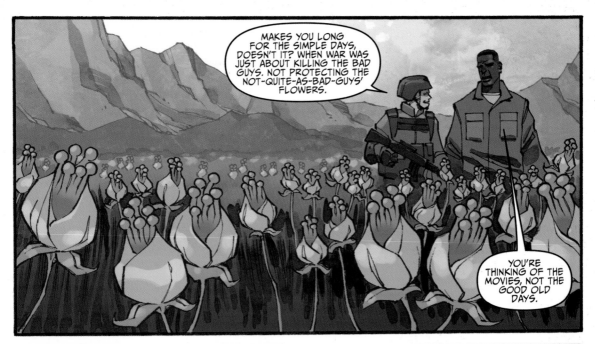

MAKES YOU LONG FOR THE SIMPLE DAYS, DOESN'T IT? WHEN WAR WAS JUST ABOUT KILLING THE BAD GUYS. NOT PROTECTING THE NOT-QUITE-AS-BAD-GUYS' FLOWERS.

YOU'RE THINKING OF THE MOVIES, NOT THE GOOD OLD DAYS.

AND THESE AREN'T JUST FLOWERS, PRIVATE.

THEY'RE *SUROBI ZINNIAS.*

WHAT'S THE DIFFERENCE?

WHAT'S THE DIFFERENCE BETWEEN A HORSE AND A PEGASUS?

SO, *NATO* HAS US GUARDING A FLOWER FIELD BECAUSE IT'S... MAGICAL?

NO. NOT MAGICAL...

...JUST A *MIRACLE.*

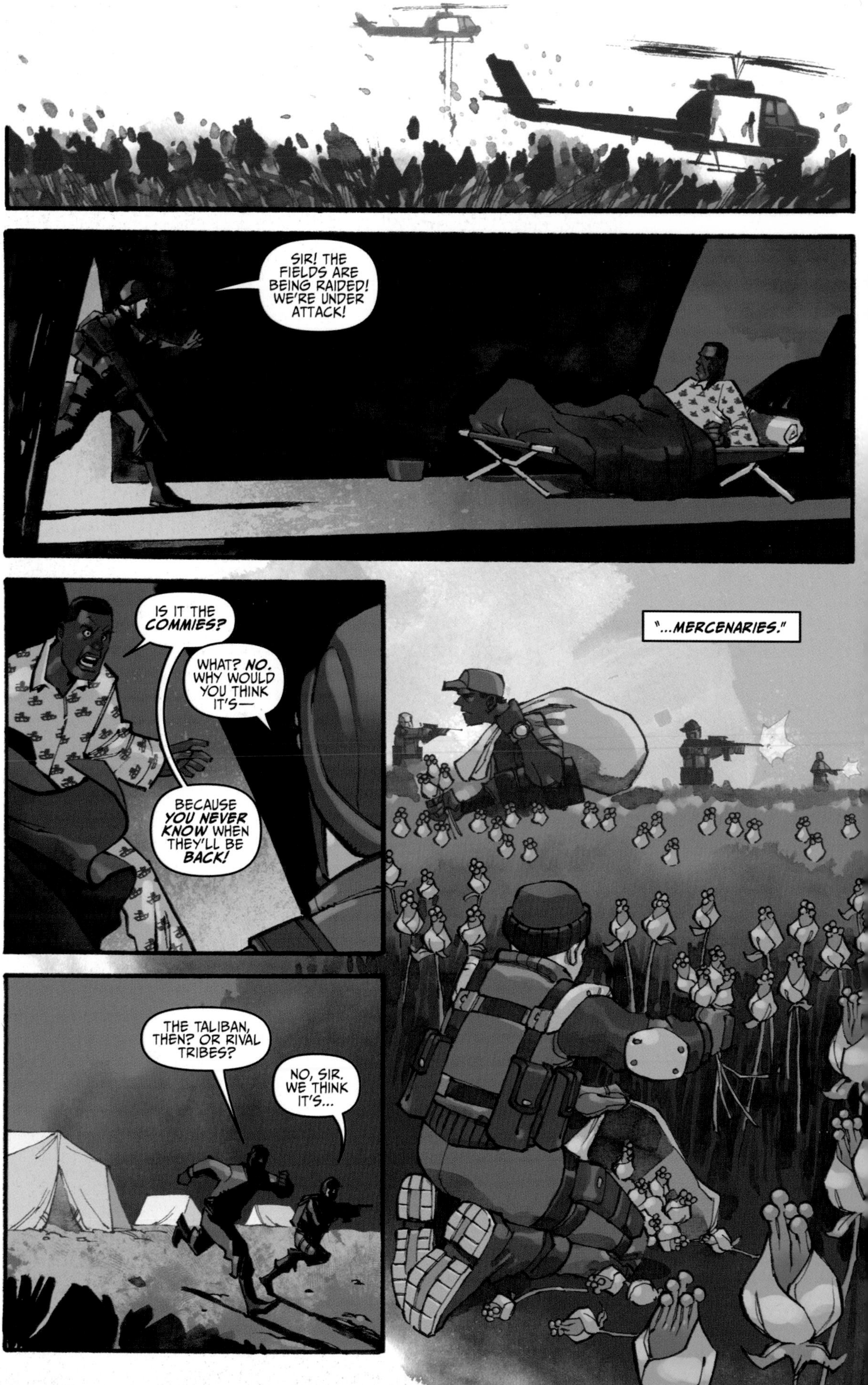
SIR! THE FIELDS ARE BEING RAIDED! WE'RE UNDER ATTACK!
IS IT THE COMMIES?
WHAT? NO. WHY WOULD YOU THINK IT'S—
BECAUSE YOU NEVER KNOW WHEN THEY'LL BE BACK!
THE TALIBAN, THEN? OR RIVAL TRIBES?
NO, SIR. WE THINK IT'S...
"...MERCENARIES."

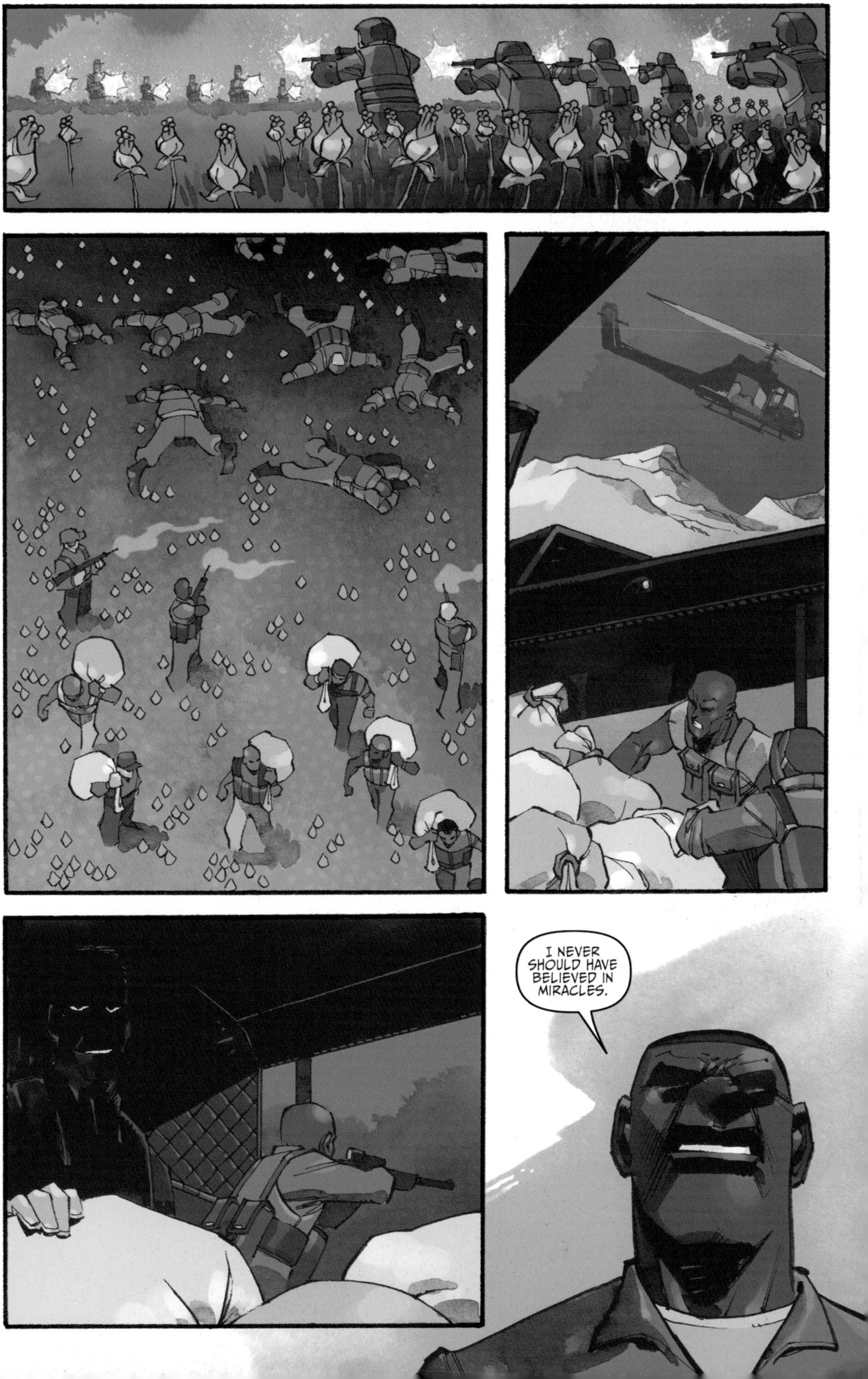
I NEVER SHOULD HAVE BELIEVED IN MIRACLES.

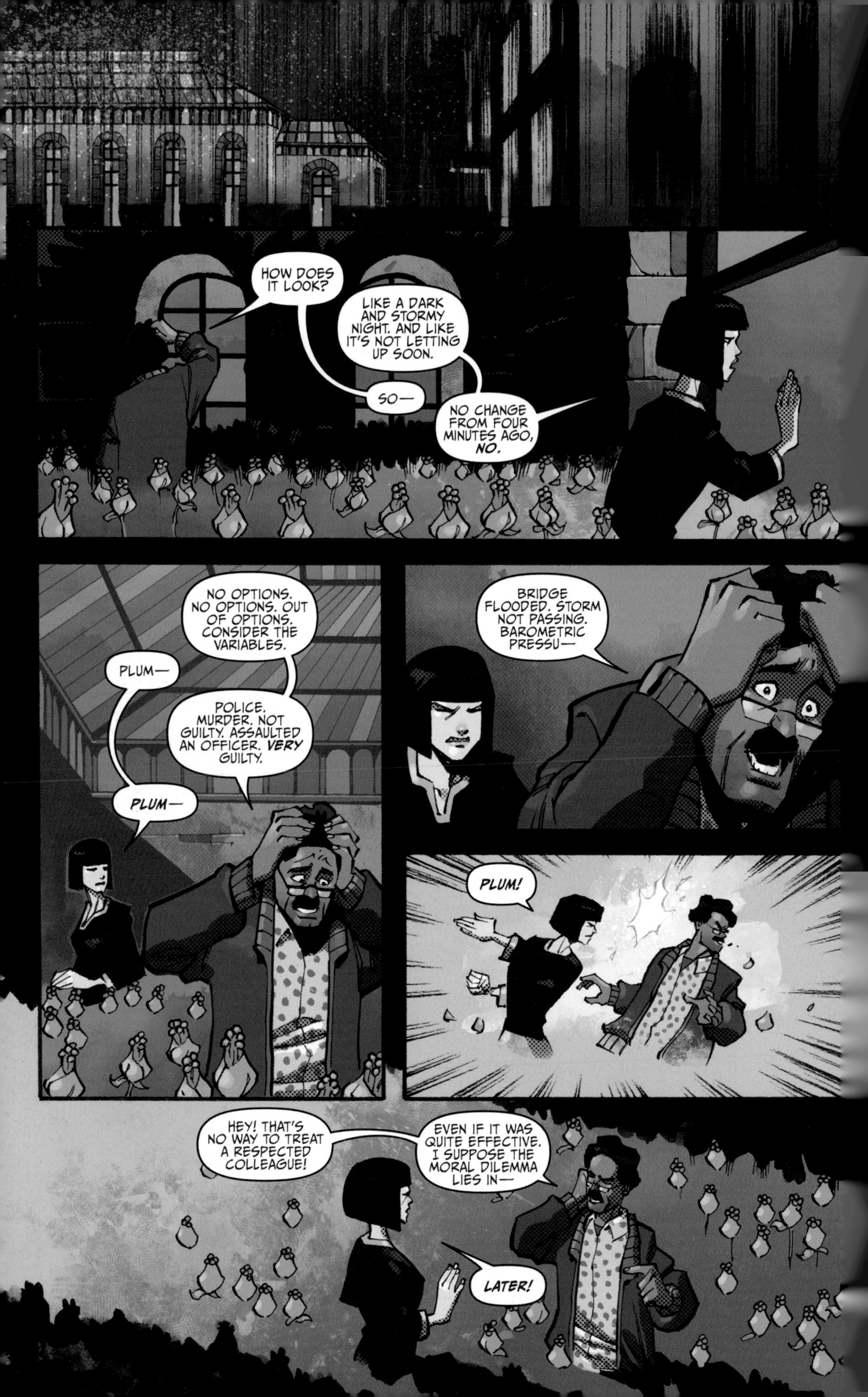
HOW DOES IT LOOK?
LIKE A DARK AND STORMY NIGHT. AND LIKE IT'S NOT LETTING UP SOON.
SO—
NO CHANGE FROM FOUR MINUTES AGO, NO.
NO OPTIONS. NO OPTIONS. OUT OF OPTIONS. CONSIDER THE VARIABLES.
PLUM—
POLICE. MURDER. NOT GUILTY. ASSAULTED AN OFFICER. VERY GUILTY.
PLUM—
BRIDGE FLOODED. STORM NOT PASSING. BAROMETRIC PRESSU—
PLUM!
HEY! THAT'S NO WAY TO TREAT A RESPECTED COLLEAGUE!
EVEN IF IT WAS QUITE EFFECTIVE. I SUPPOSE THE MORAL DILEMMA LIES IN—
LATER!

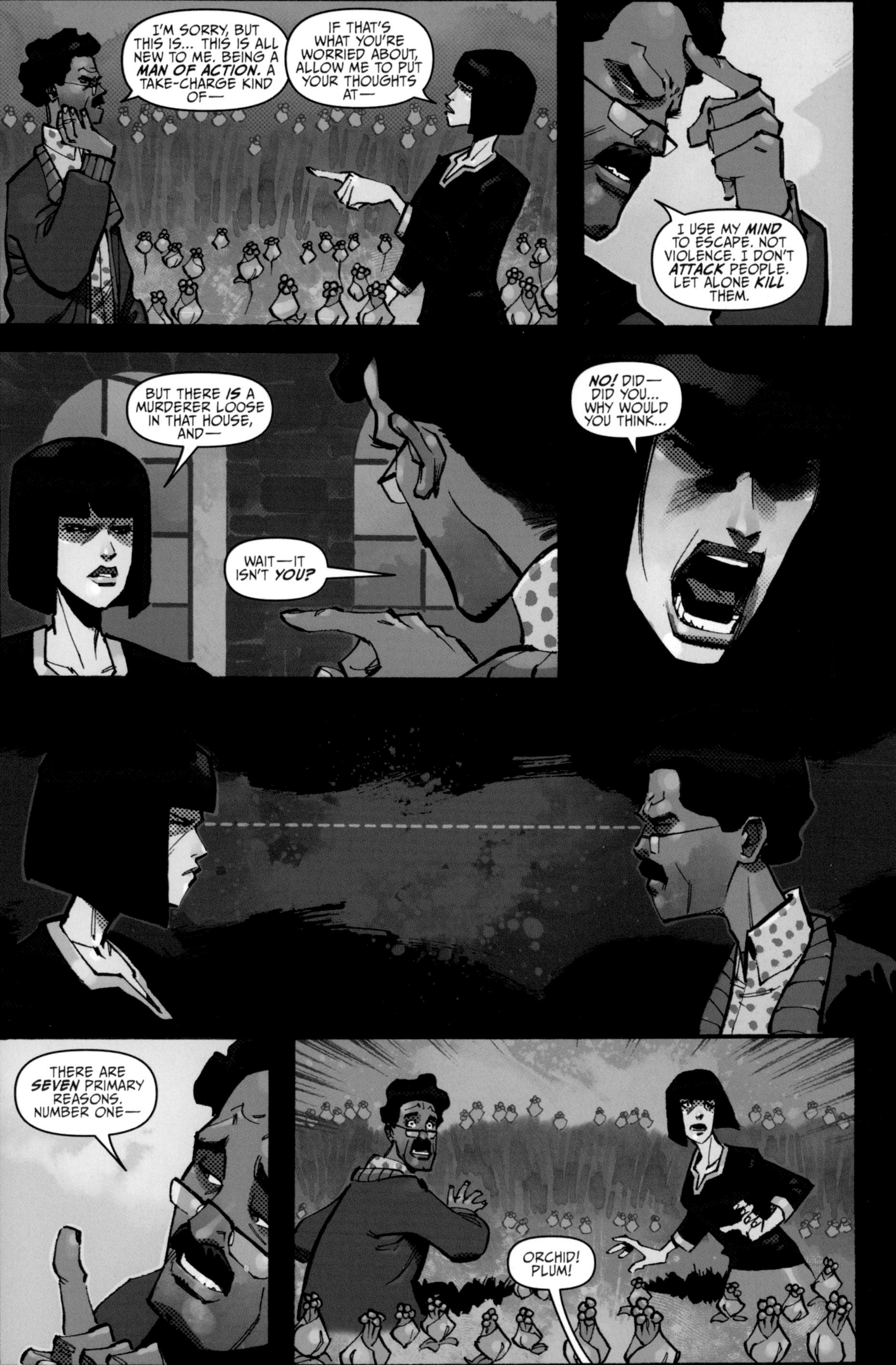
I'M SORRY, BUT THIS IS... THIS IS ALL NEW TO ME. BEING A MAN OF ACTION. A TAKE-CHARGE KIND OF—
IF THAT'S WHAT YOU'RE WORRIED ABOUT, ALLOW ME TO PUT YOUR THOUGHTS AT—
I USE MY MIND TO ESCAPE. NOT VIOLENCE. I DON'T ATTACK PEOPLE. LET ALONE KILL THEM.
BUT THERE IS A MURDERER LOOSE IN THAT HOUSE, AND—
WAIT—IT ISN'T YOU?
NO! DID— DID YOU... WHY WOULD YOU THINK...
THERE ARE SEVEN PRIMARY REASONS. NUMBER ONE—
ORCHID! PLUM!

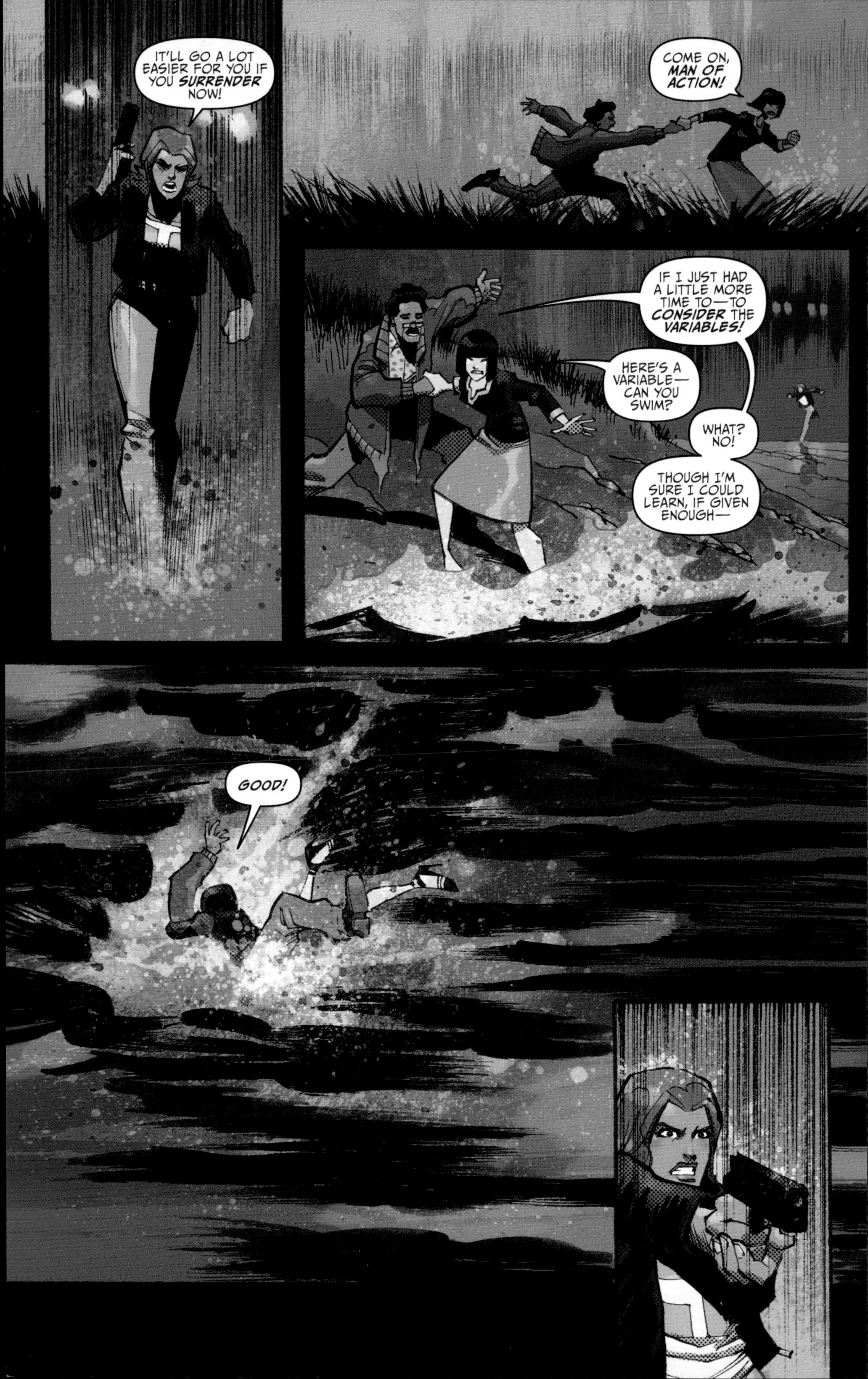

IT'LL GO A LOT EASIER FOR YOU IF YOU SURRENDER NOW!
COME ON, MAN OF ACTION!
IF I JUST HAD A LITTLE MORE TIME TO—TO CONSIDER THE VARIABLES!
HERE'S A VARIABLE—CAN YOU SWIM?
WHAT? NO!
THOUGH I'M SURE I COULD LEARN, IF GIVEN ENOUGH—
GOOD!

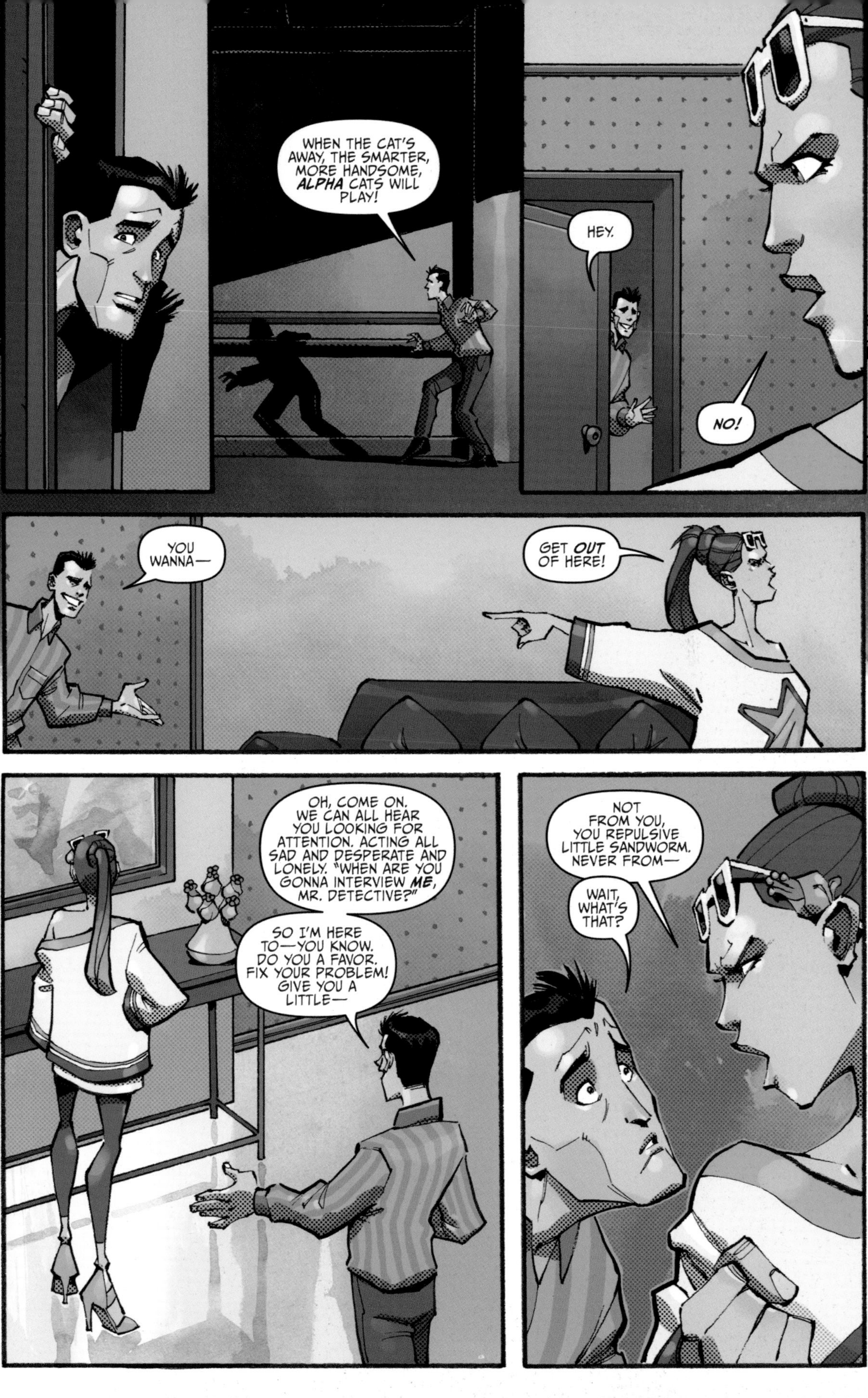
WHEN THE CAT'S AWAY, THE SMARTER, MORE HANDSOME, ALPHA CATS WILL PLAY!
HEY.
NO!
YOU WANNA—
GET OUT OF HERE!
OH, COME ON. WE CAN ALL HEAR YOU LOOKING FOR ATTENTION. ACTING ALL SAD AND DESPERATE AND LONELY. "WHEN ARE YOU GONNA INTERVIEW ME, MR. DETECTIVE?"
SO I'M HERE TO—YOU KNOW. DO YOU A FAVOR. FIX YOUR PROBLEM! GIVE YOU A LITTLE—
NOT FROM YOU, YOU REPULSIVE LITTLE SANDWORM. NEVER FROM—
WAIT, WHAT'S THAT?

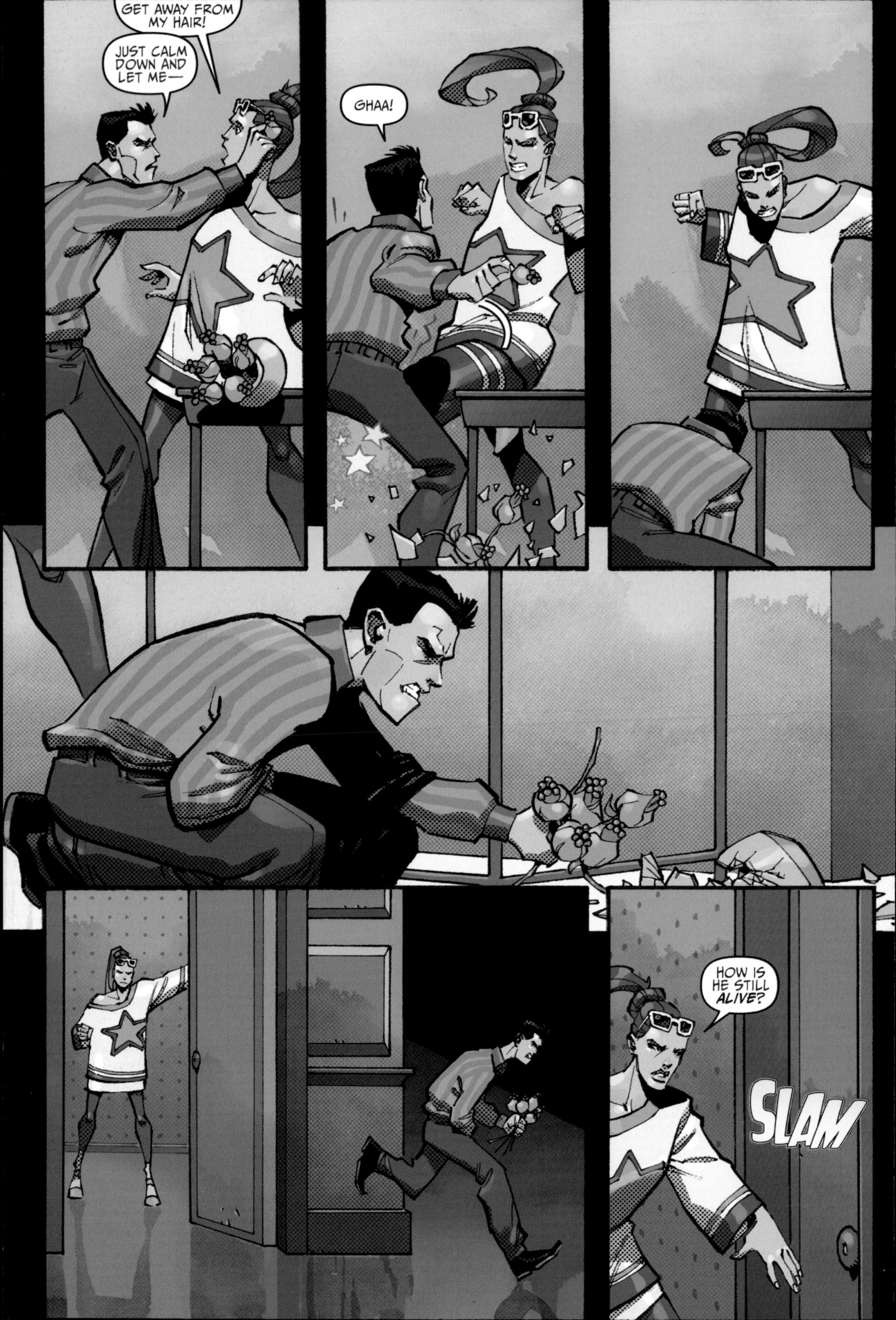

GET AWAY FROM MY HAIR!
JUST CALM DOWN AND LET ME—
GHAA!
HOW IS HE STILL *ALIVE*?
SLAM

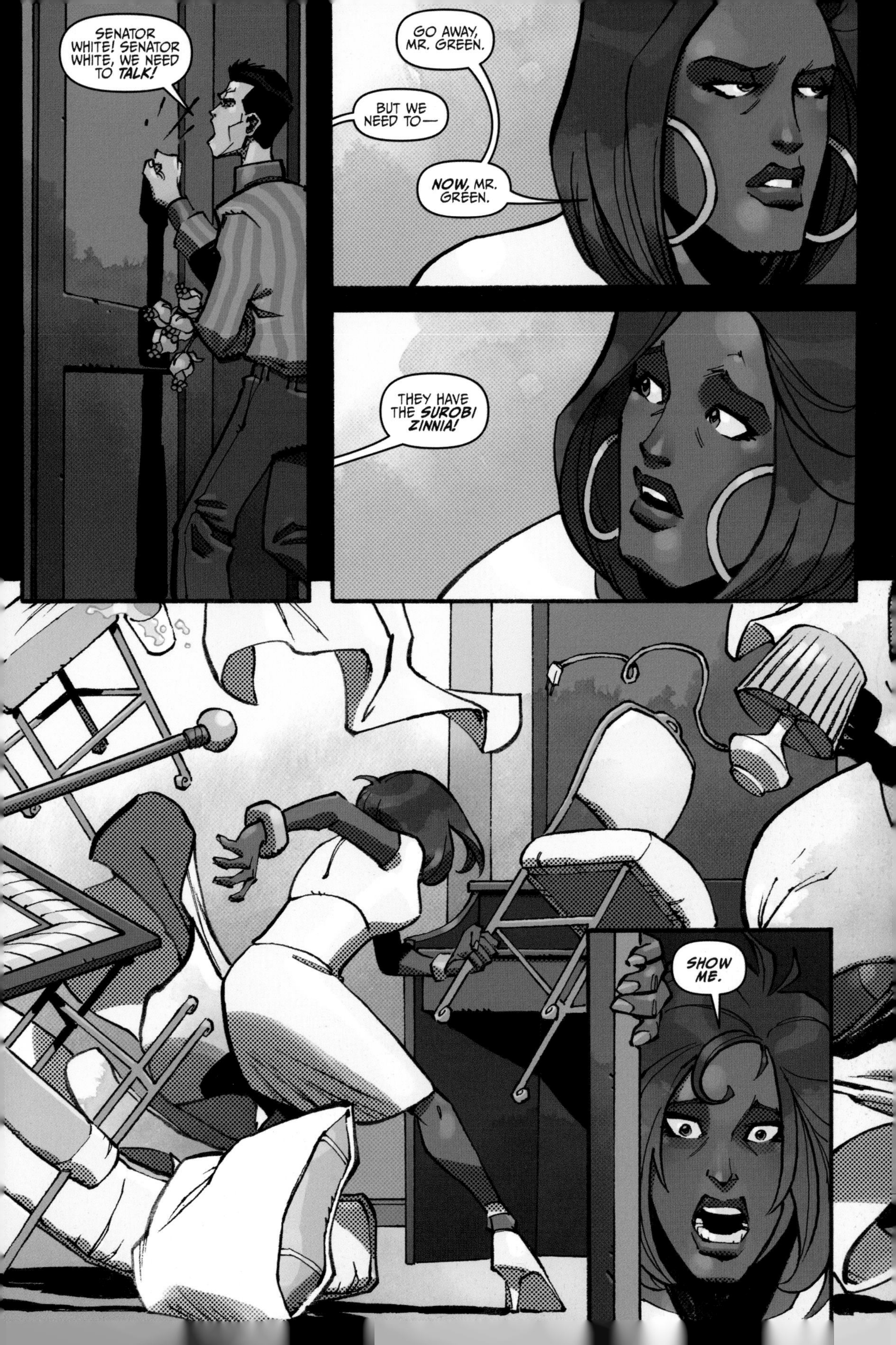
SENATOR WHITE! SENATOR WHITE, WE NEED TO TALK!
GO AWAY, MR. GREEN.
BUT WE NEED TO—
NOW, MR. GREEN.
THEY HAVE THE SUROBI ZINNIA!
SHOW ME.

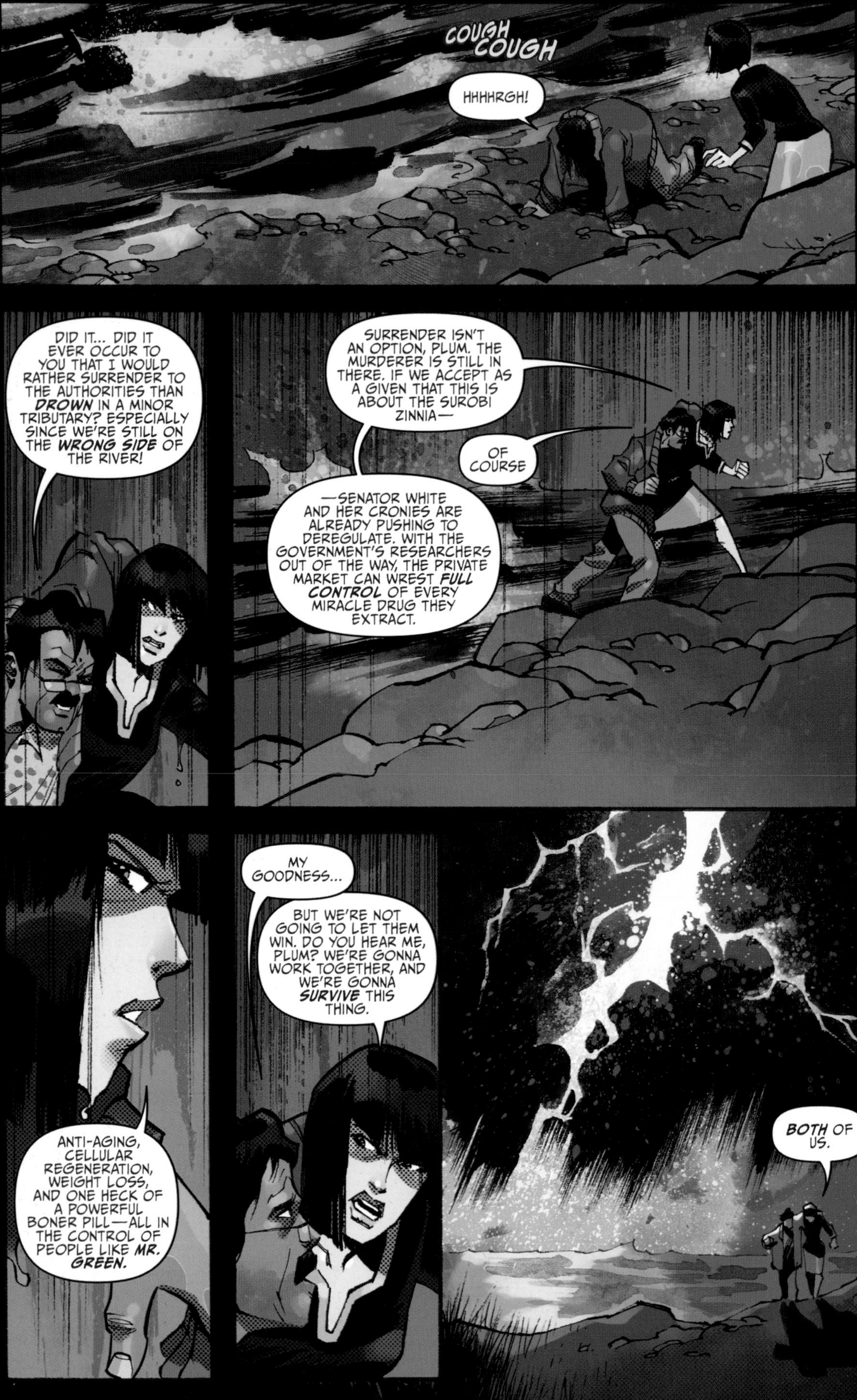
COUGH COUGH
HHHHRGH!
DID IT... DID IT EVER OCCUR TO YOU THAT I WOULD RATHER SURRENDER TO THE AUTHORITIES THAN DROWN IN A MINOR TRIBUTARY? ESPECIALLY SINCE WE'RE STILL ON THE WRONG SIDE OF THE RIVER!
SURRENDER ISN'T AN OPTION, PLUM. THE MURDERER IS STILL IN THERE. IF WE ACCEPT AS A GIVEN THAT THIS IS ABOUT THE SUROBI ZINNIA—
OF COURSE
—SENATOR WHITE AND HER CRONIES ARE ALREADY PUSHING TO DEREGULATE. WITH THE GOVERNMENT'S RESEARCHERS OUT OF THE WAY, THE PRIVATE MARKET CAN WREST FULL CONTROL OF EVERY MIRACLE DRUG THEY EXTRACT.
ANTI-AGING, CELLULAR REGENERATION, WEIGHT LOSS, AND ONE HECK OF A POWERFUL BONER PILL—ALL IN THE CONTROL OF PEOPLE LIKE MR. GREEN.
MY GOODNESS...
BUT WE'RE NOT GOING TO LET THEM WIN. DO YOU HEAR ME, PLUM? WE'RE GONNA WORK TOGETHER, AND WE'RE GONNA SURVIVE THIS THING.
BOTH OF US.

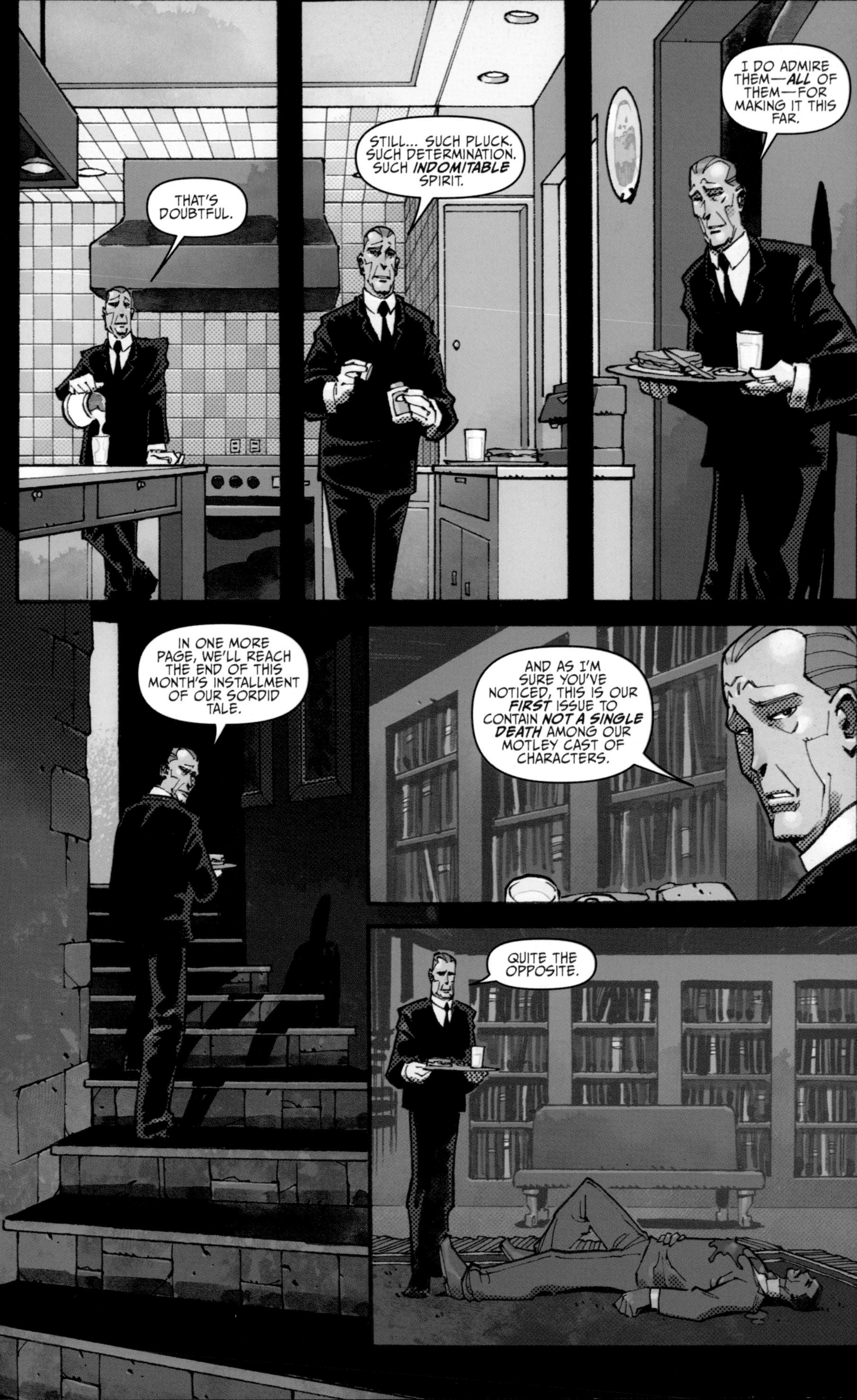
THAT'S DOUBTFUL.
STILL... SUCH PLUCK. SUCH DETERMINATION. SUCH INDOMITABLE SPIRIT.
I DO ADMIRE THEM—ALL OF THEM—FOR MAKING IT THIS FAR.
IN ONE MORE PAGE, WE'LL REACH THE END OF THIS MONTH'S INSTALLMENT OF OUR SORDID TALE.
AND AS I'M SURE YOU'VE NOTICED, THIS IS OUR FIRST ISSUE TO CONTAIN NOT A SINGLE DEATH AMONG OUR MOTLEY CAST OF CHARACTERS.
QUITE THE OPPOSITE.

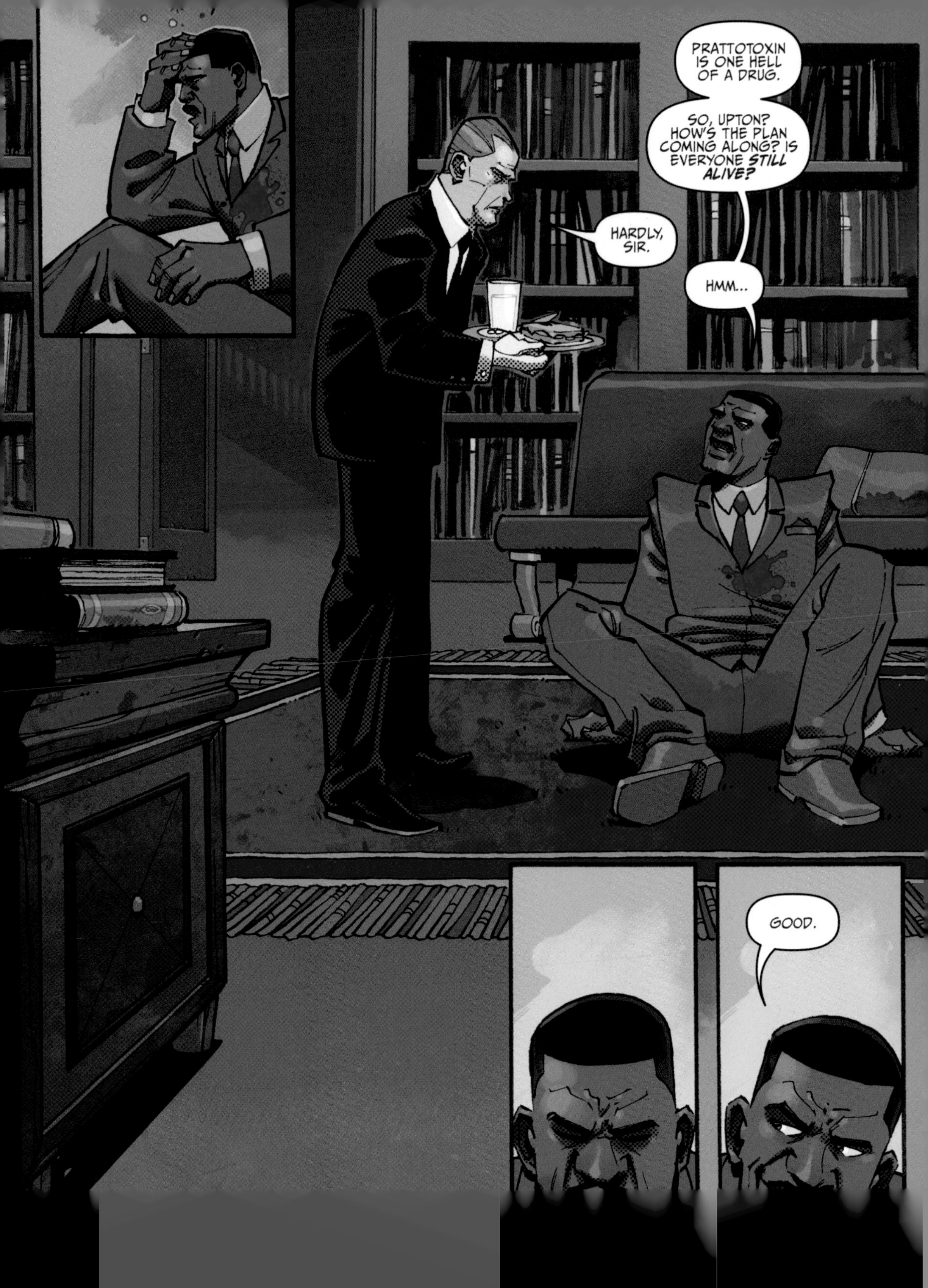
PRATTOTOXIN IS ONE HELL OF A DRUG.
SO, UPTON? HOW'S THE PLAN COMING ALONG? IS EVERYONE **STILL ALIVE?**
HARDLY, SIR.
HMM...
GOOD.

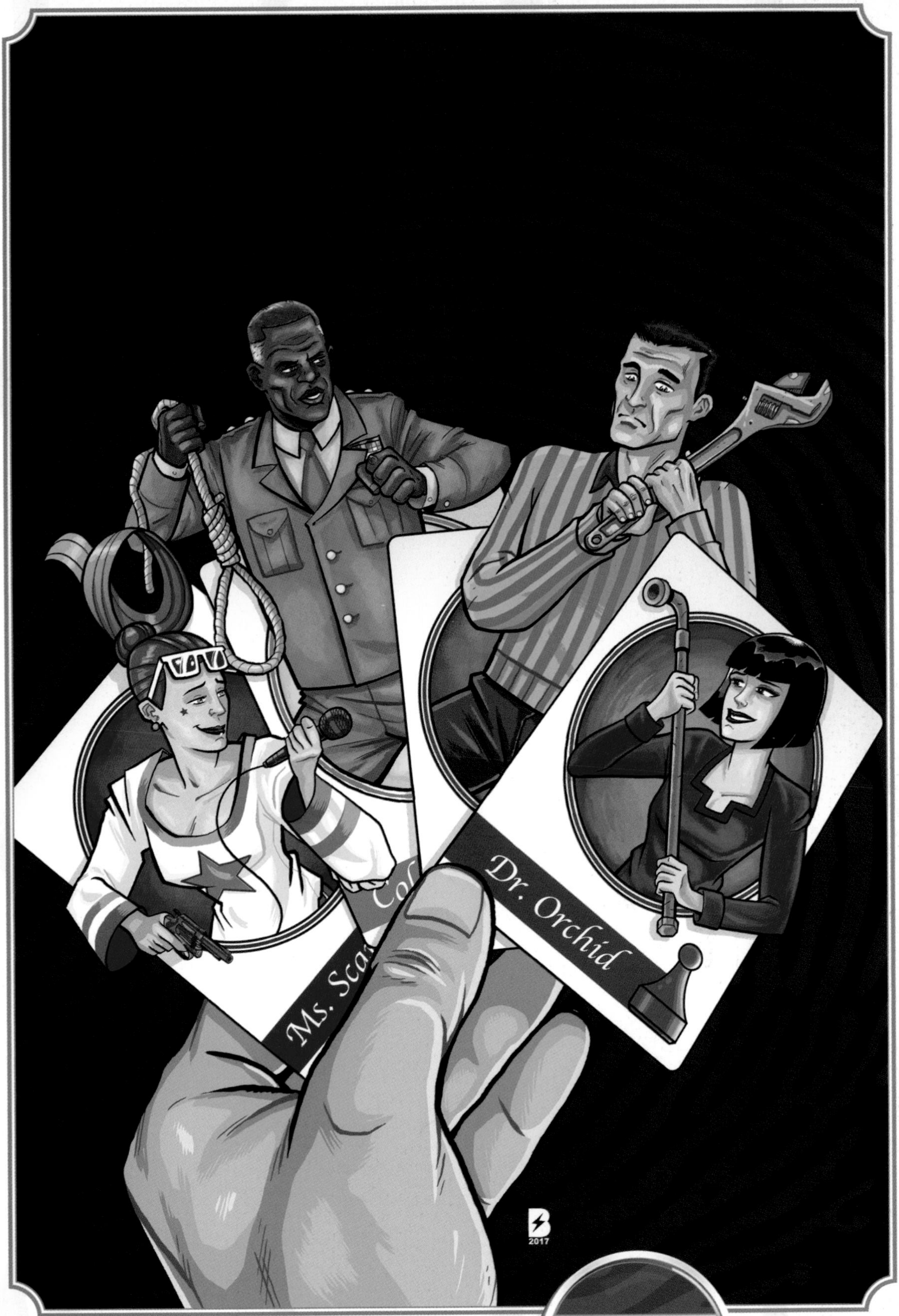
Dr. Orchid
2017

COVER ART BY
BRENT SCHOONOVER

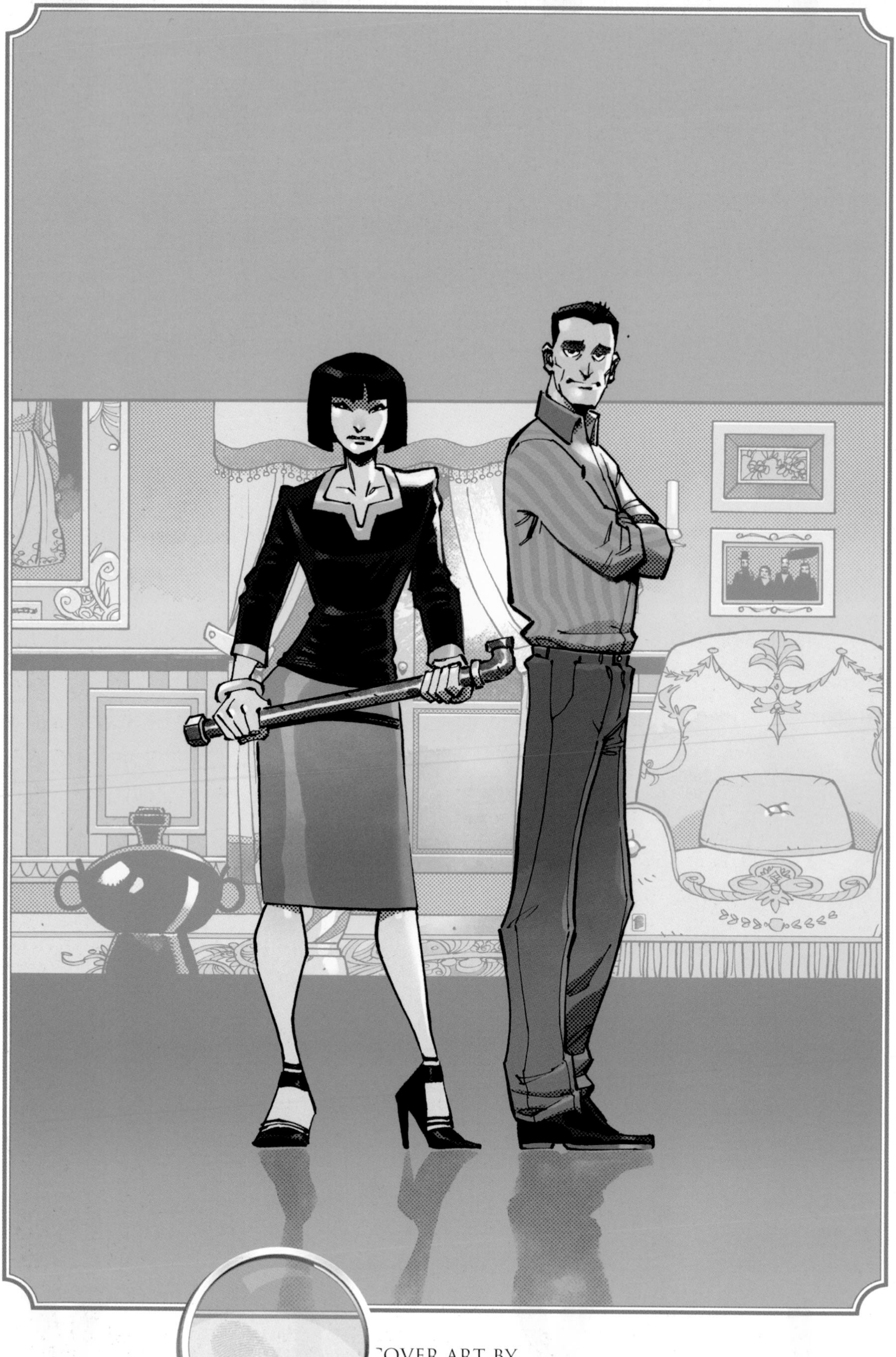

COVER ART BY
NELSON DANIEL

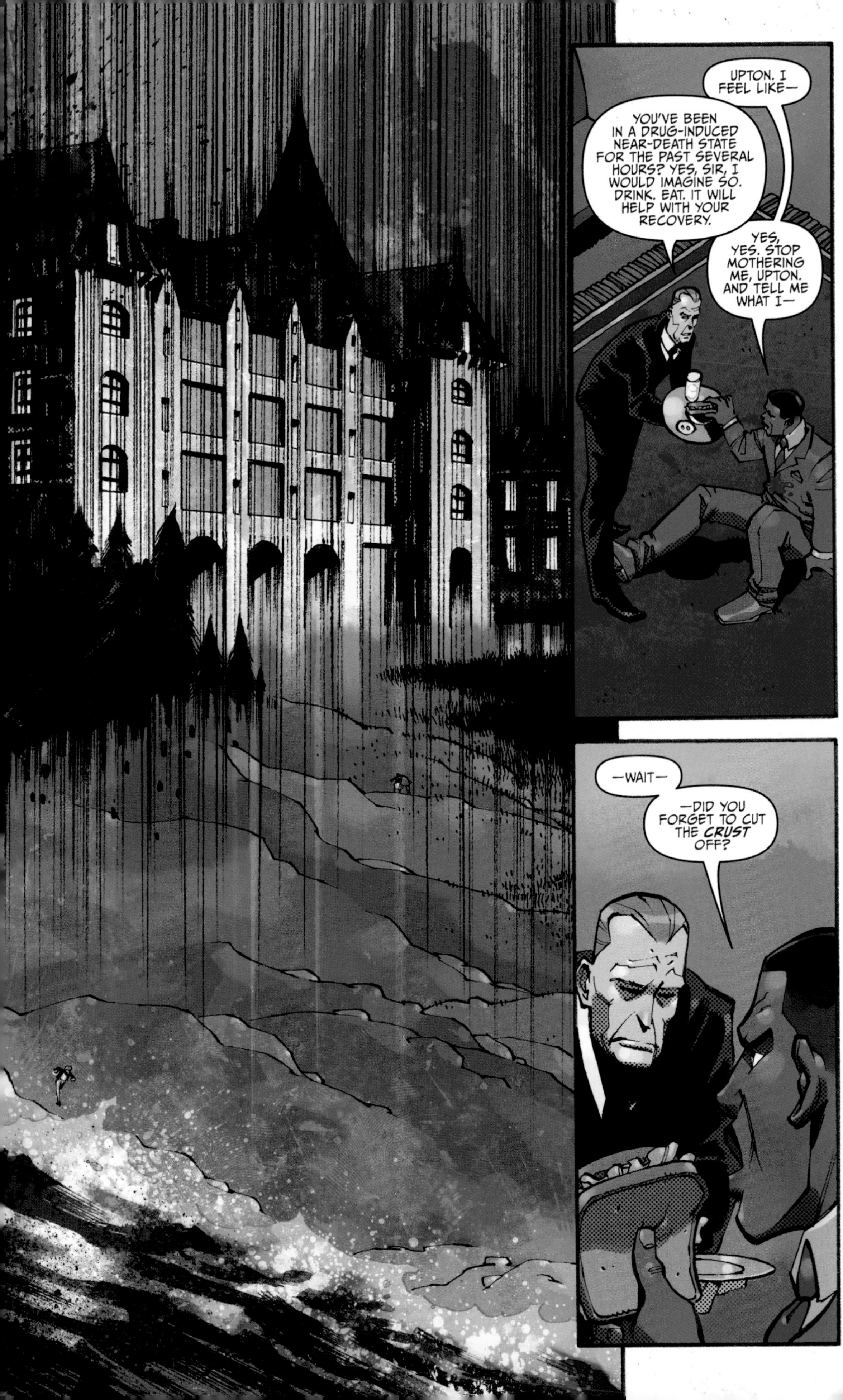
UPTON. I FEEL LIKE—
YOU'VE BEEN IN A DRUG-INDUCED NEAR-DEATH STATE FOR THE PAST SEVERAL HOURS? YES, SIR, I WOULD IMAGINE SO. DRINK. EAT. IT WILL HELP WITH YOUR RECOVERY.
YES, YES. STOP MOTHERING ME, UPTON. AND TELL ME WHAT I—
—WAIT—
—DID YOU FORGET TO CUT THE *CRUST* OFF?

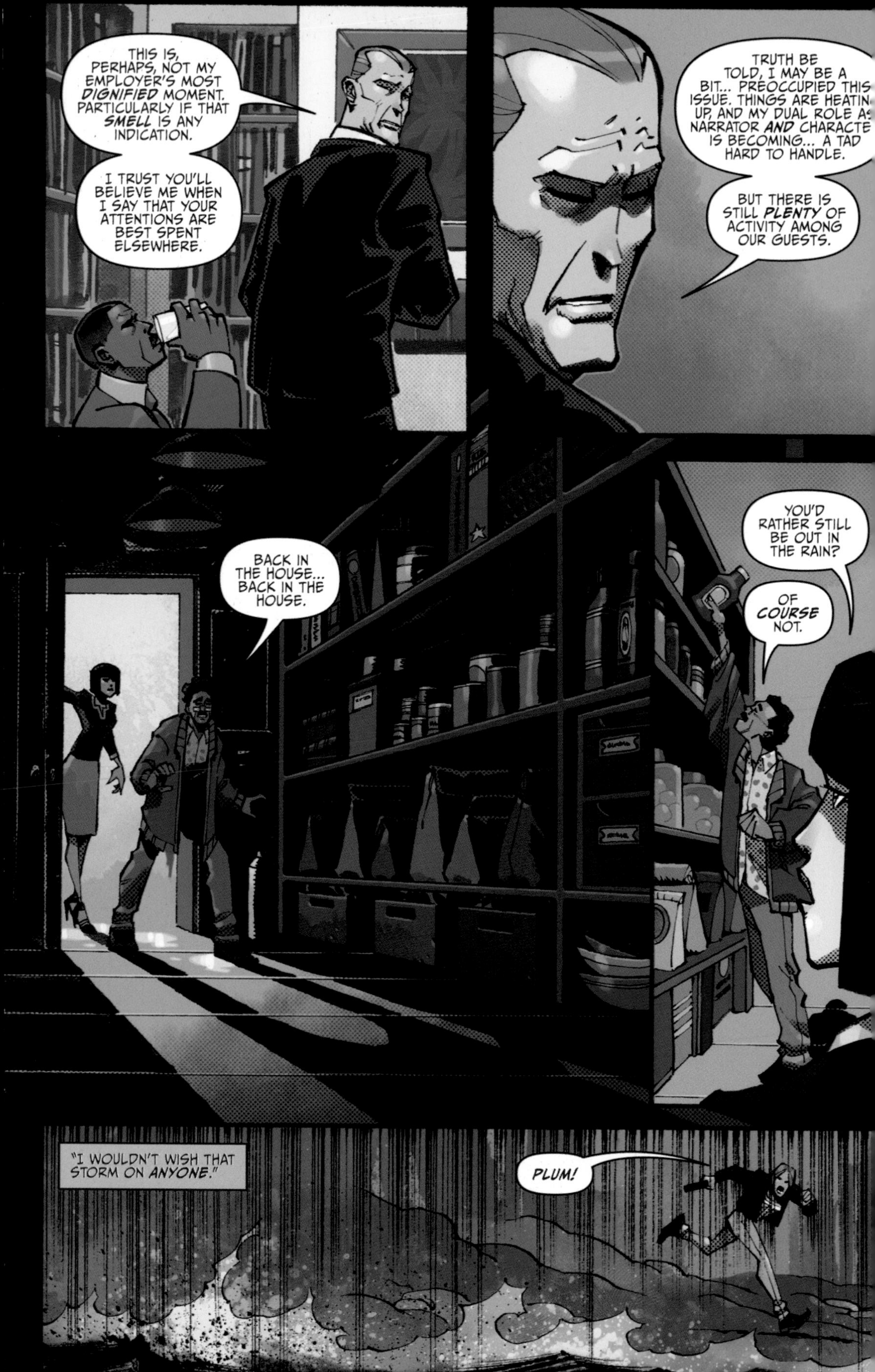
THIS IS, PERHAPS, NOT MY EMPLOYER'S MOST DIGNIFIED MOMENT. PARTICULARLY IF THAT SMELL IS ANY INDICATION.
I TRUST YOU'LL BELIEVE ME WHEN I SAY THAT YOUR ATTENTIONS ARE BEST SPENT ELSEWHERE.
TRUTH BE TOLD, I MAY BE A BIT... PREOCCUPIED THIS ISSUE. THINGS ARE HEATIN UP, AND MY DUAL ROLE A NARRATOR AND CHARACTE IS BECOMING... A TAD HARD TO HANDLE.
BUT THERE IS STILL PLENTY OF ACTIVITY AMONG OUR GUESTS.
BACK IN THE HOUSE... BACK IN THE HOUSE.
YOU'D RATHER STILL BE OUT IN THE RAIN?
OF COURSE NOT.
"I WOULDN'T WISH THAT STORM ON ANYONE."
PLUM!

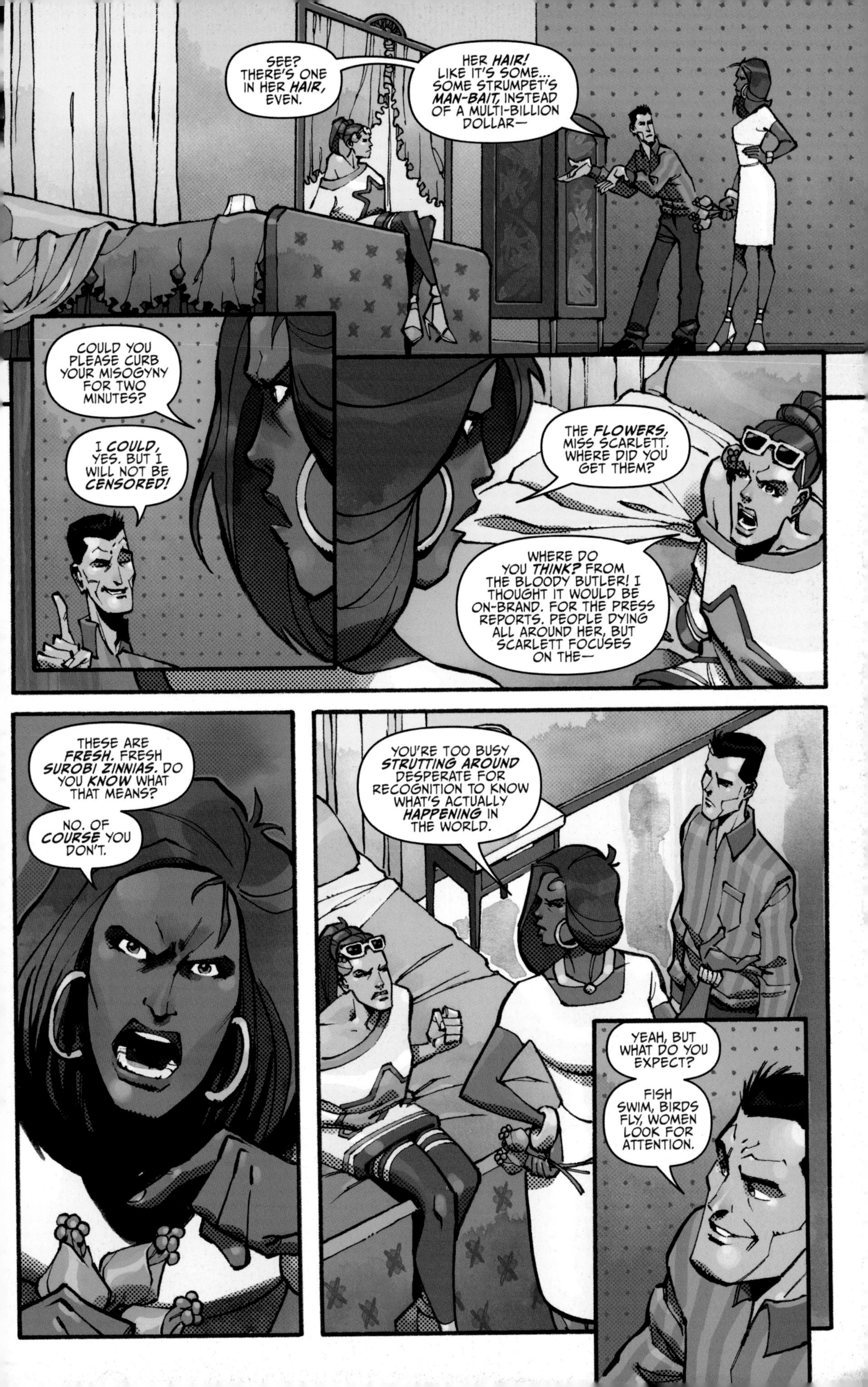

SEE? THERE'S ONE IN HER HAIR, EVEN.
HER HAIR! LIKE IT'S SOME... SOME STRUMPET'S MAN-BAIT, INSTEAD OF A MULTI-BILLION DOLLAR—
COULD YOU PLEASE CURB YOUR MISOGYNY FOR TWO MINUTES?
I COULD, YES. BUT I WILL NOT BE CENSORED!
THE FLOWERS, MISS SCARLETT. WHERE DID YOU GET THEM?
WHERE DO YOU THINK? FROM THE BLOODY BUTLER! I THOUGHT IT WOULD BE ON-BRAND. FOR THE PRESS REPORTS. PEOPLE DYING ALL AROUND HER, BUT SCARLETT FOCUSES ON THE—
THESE ARE FRESH. FRESH SUROBI ZINNIAS. DO YOU KNOW WHAT THAT MEANS?
NO. OF COURSE YOU DON'T.
YOU'RE TOO BUSY STRUTTING AROUND DESPERATE FOR RECOGNITION TO KNOW WHAT'S ACTUALLY HAPPENING IN THE WORLD.
YEAH, BUT WHAT DO YOU EXPECT?
FISH SWIM, BIRDS FLY, WOMEN LOOK FOR ATTENTION.

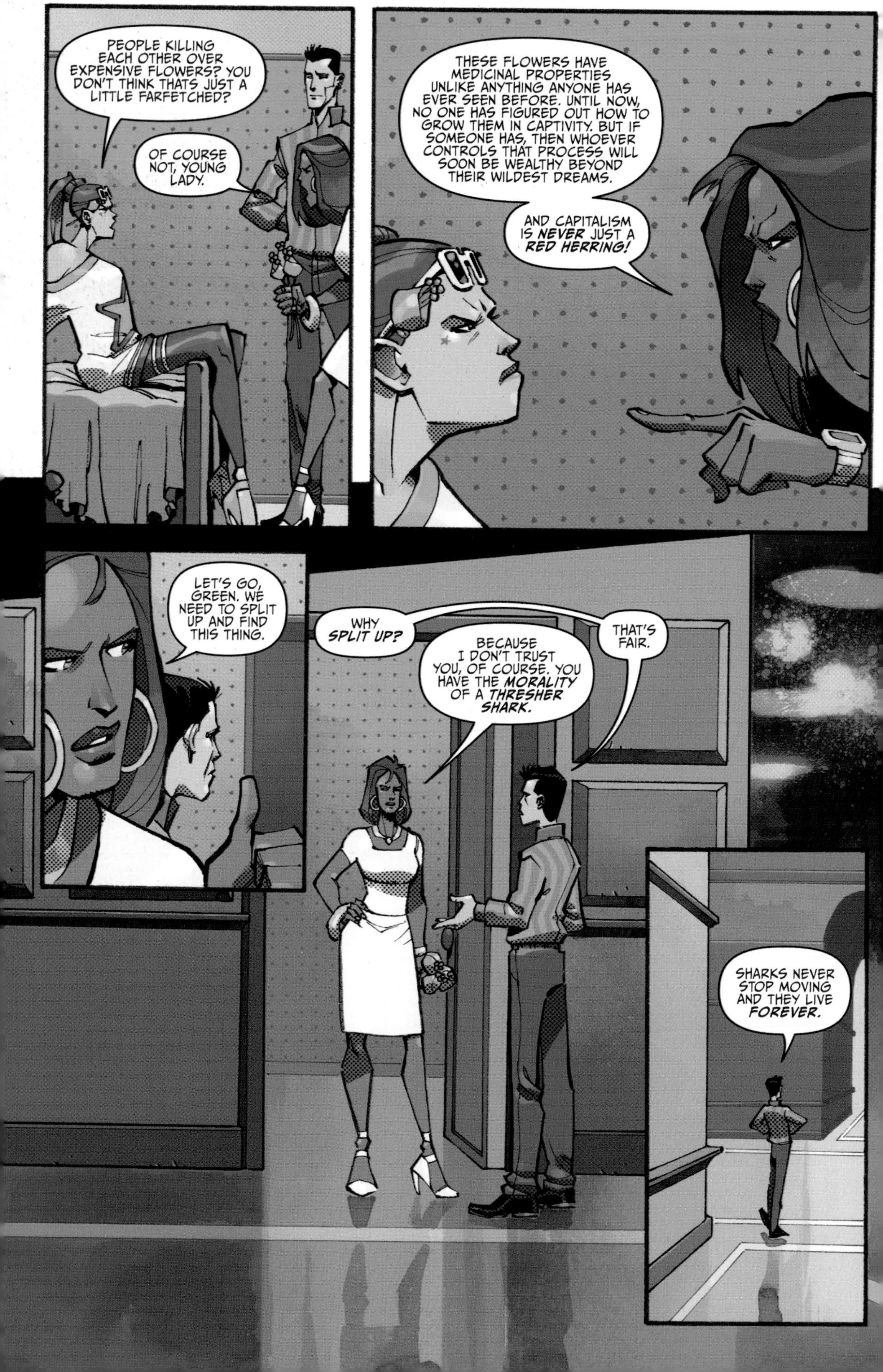
PEOPLE KILLING EACH OTHER OVER EXPENSIVE FLOWERS? YOU DON'T THINK THATS JUST A LITTLE FARFETCHED?
OF COURSE NOT, YOUNG LADY.
THESE FLOWERS HAVE MEDICINAL PROPERTIES UNLIKE ANYTHING ANYONE HAS EVER SEEN BEFORE. UNTIL NOW, NO ONE HAS FIGURED OUT HOW TO GROW THEM IN CAPTIVITY. BUT IF SOMEONE HAS, THEN WHOEVER CONTROLS THAT PROCESS WILL SOON BE WEALTHY BEYOND THEIR WILDEST DREAMS.
AND CAPITALISM IS ***NEVER*** JUST A ***RED HERRING!***
LET'S GO, GREEN. WE NEED TO SPLIT UP AND FIND THIS THING.
WHY ***SPLIT UP?***
BECAUSE I DON'T TRUST YOU, OF COURSE. YOU HAVE THE ***MORALITY*** OF A ***THRESHER SHARK.***
THAT'S FAIR.
SHARKS NEVER STOP MOVING AND THEY LIVE ***FOREVER.***

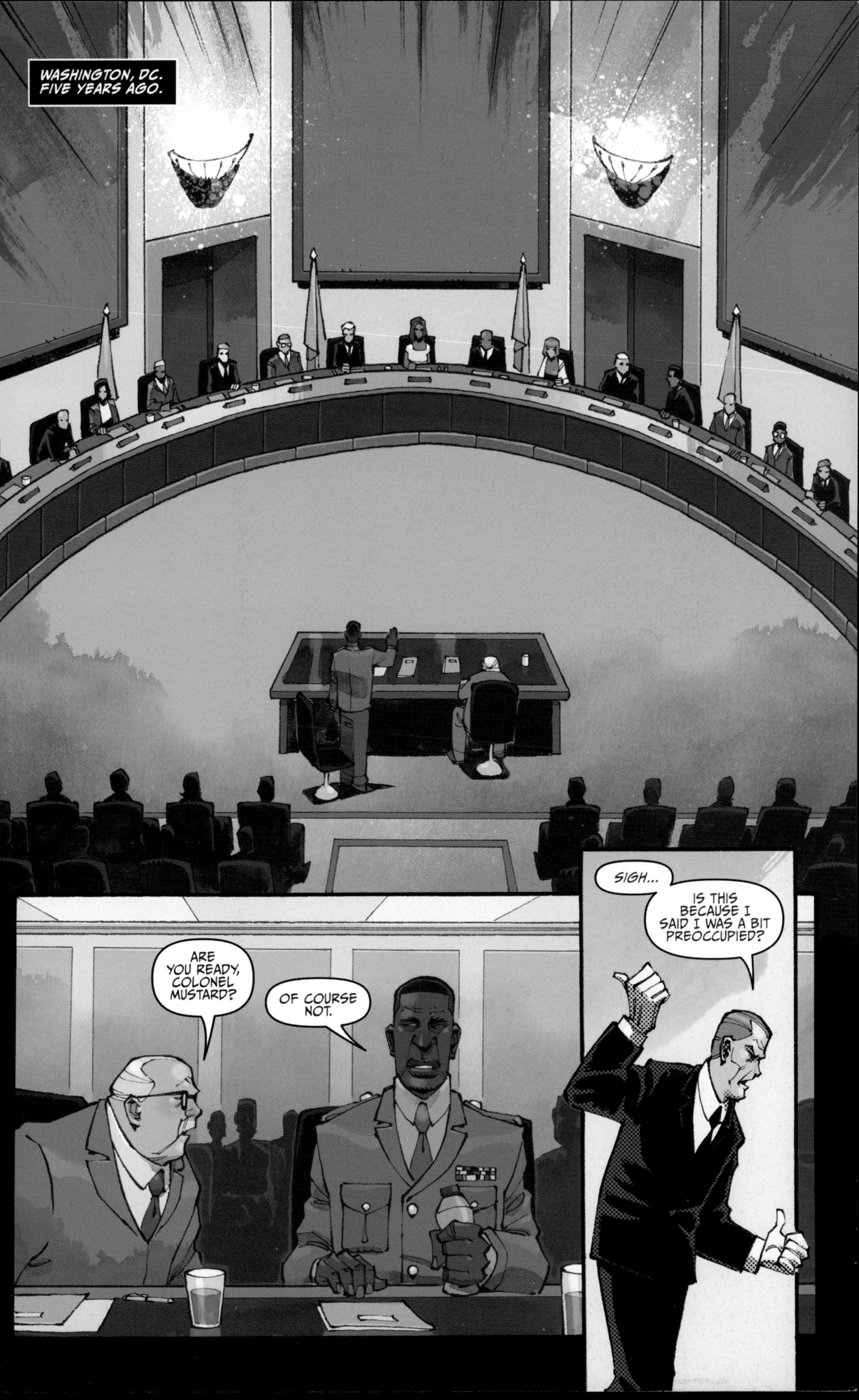
WASHINGTON, DC.
FIVE YEARS AGO.
ARE YOU READY, COLONEL MUSTARD?
OF COURSE NOT.
SIGH...
IS THIS BECAUSE I SAID I WAS A BIT PREOCCUPIED?

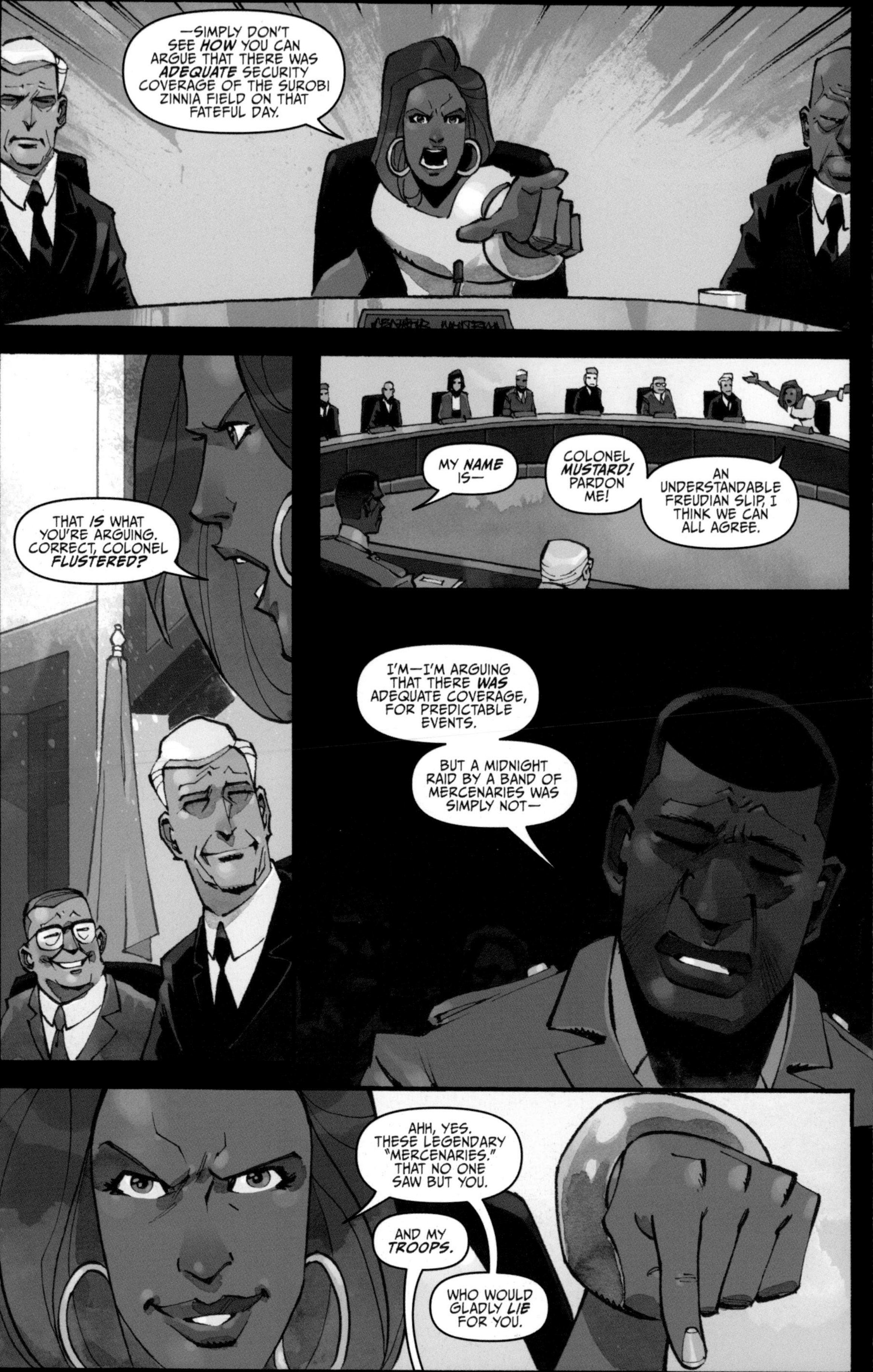
—SIMPLY DON'T SEE HOW YOU CAN ARGUE THAT THERE WAS ADEQUATE SECURITY COVERAGE OF THE SUROBI ZINNIA FIELD ON THAT FATEFUL DAY.
THAT IS WHAT YOU'RE ARGUING. CORRECT, COLONEL FLUSTERED?
MY NAME IS—
COLONEL MUSTARD! PARDON ME!
AN UNDERSTANDABLE FREUDIAN SLIP, I THINK WE CAN ALL AGREE.
I'M—I'M ARGUING THAT THERE WAS ADEQUATE COVERAGE, FOR PREDICTABLE EVENTS.
BUT A MIDNIGHT RAID BY A BAND OF MERCENARIES WAS SIMPLY NOT—
AHH, YES. THESE LEGENDARY "MERCENARIES." THAT NO ONE SAW BUT YOU.
AND MY TROOPS.
WHO WOULD GLADLY LIE FOR YOU.

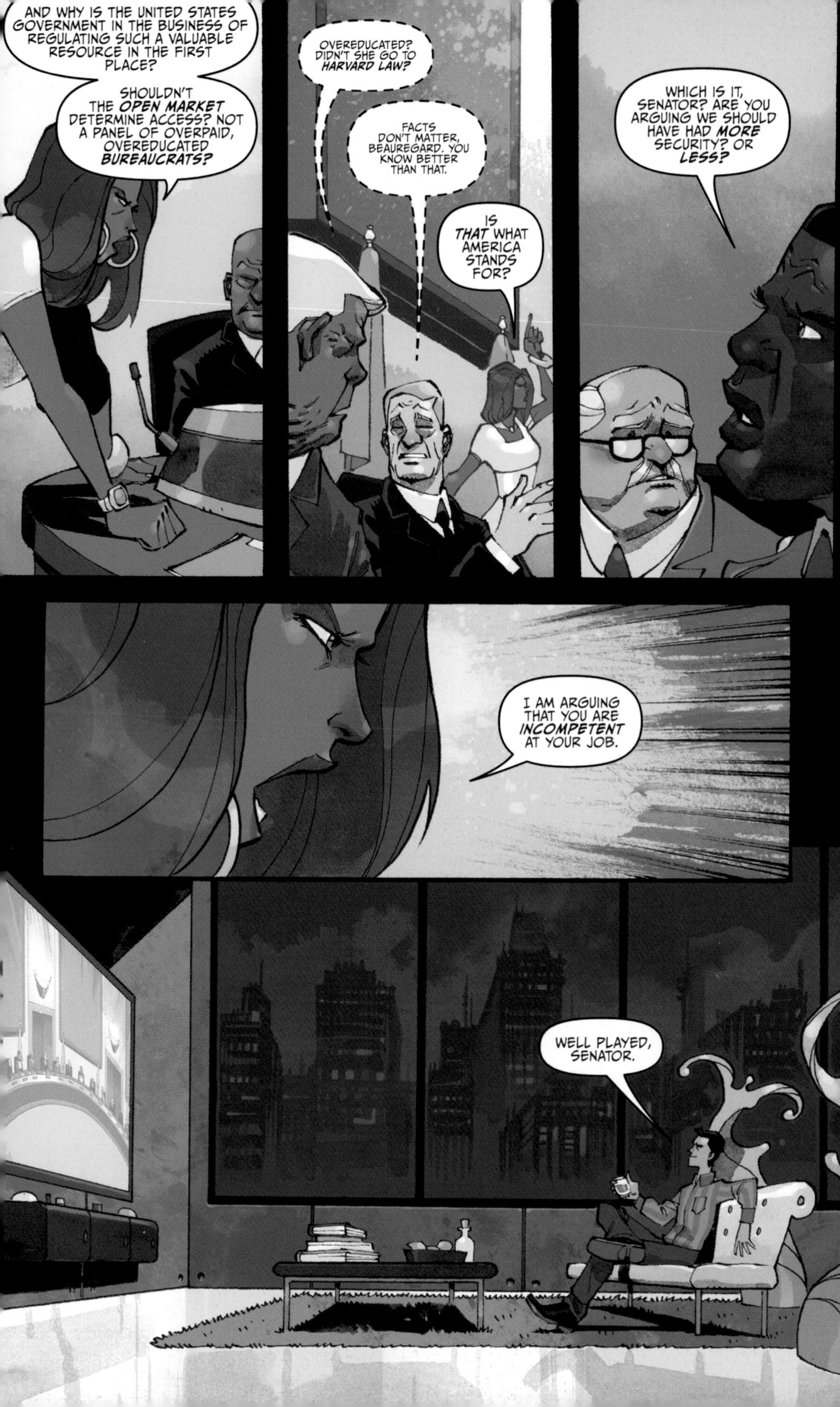
AND WHY IS THE UNITED STATES GOVERNMENT IN THE BUSINESS OF REGULATING SUCH A VALUABLE RESOURCE IN THE FIRST PLACE?
SHOULDN'T THE OPEN MARKET DETERMINE ACCESS? NOT A PANEL OF OVERPAID, OVEREDUCATED BUREAUCRATS?
OVEREDUCATED? DIDN'T SHE GO TO HARVARD LAW?
FACTS DON'T MATTER, BEAUREGARD. YOU KNOW BETTER THAN THAT.
IS THAT WHAT AMERICA STANDS FOR?
WHICH IS IT, SENATOR? ARE YOU ARGUING WE SHOULD HAVE HAD MORE SECURITY? OR LESS?
I AM ARGUING THAT YOU ARE INCOMPETENT AT YOUR JOB.
WELL PLAYED, SENATOR.

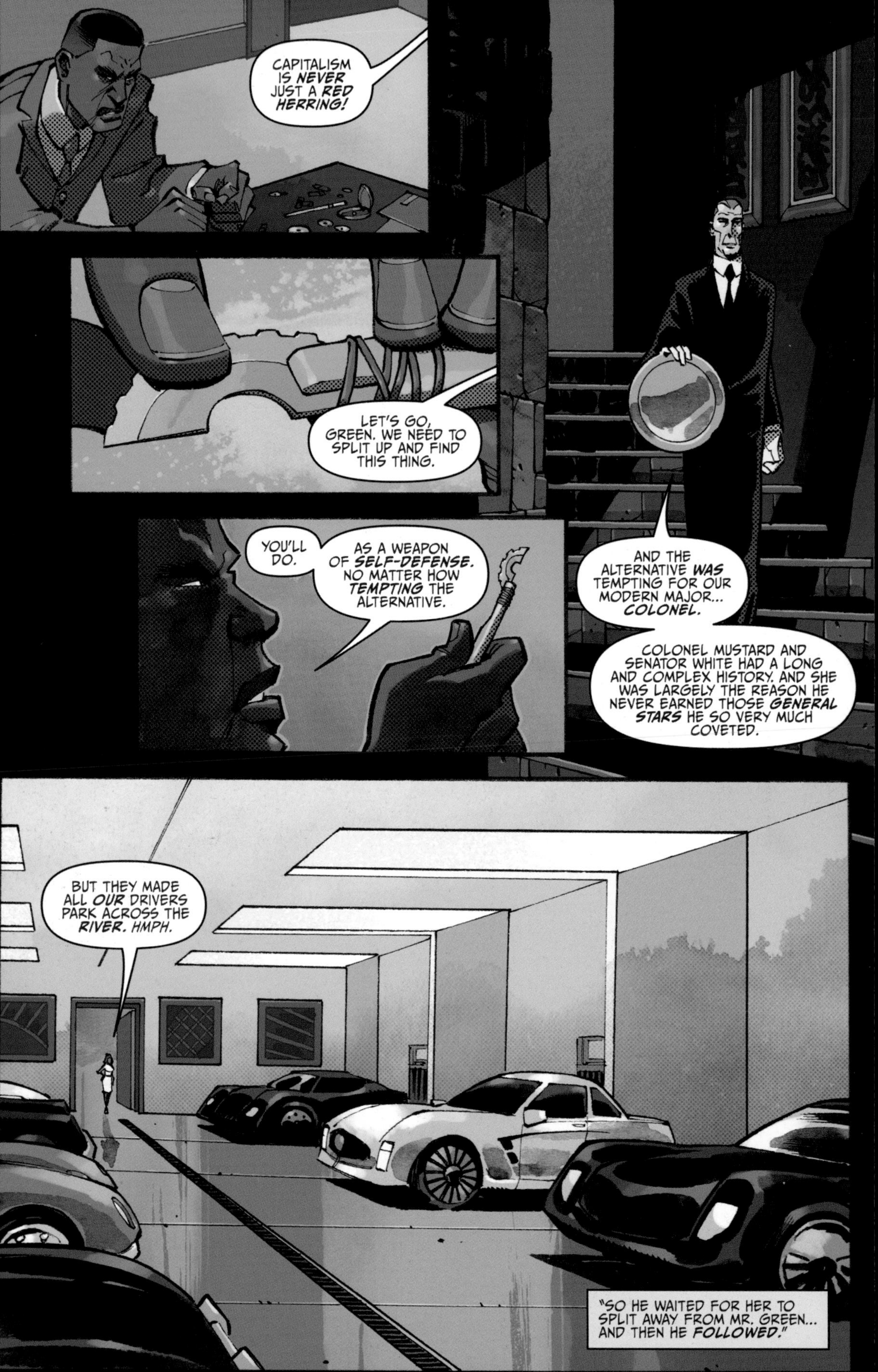
CAPITALISM IS NEVER JUST A RED HERRING!
LET'S GO, GREEN. WE NEED TO SPLIT UP AND FIND THIS THING.
YOU'LL DO.
AS A WEAPON OF SELF-DEFENSE. NO MATTER HOW TEMPTING THE ALTERNATIVE.
AND THE ALTERNATIVE WAS TEMPTING FOR OUR MODERN MAJOR... COLONEL.
COLONEL MUSTARD AND SENATOR WHITE HAD A LONG AND COMPLEX HISTORY. AND SHE WAS LARGELY THE REASON HE NEVER EARNED THOSE GENERAL STARS HE SO VERY MUCH COVETED.
BUT THEY MADE ALL OUR DRIVERS PARK ACROSS THE RIVER. HMPH.
"SO HE WAITED FOR HER TO SPLIT AWAY FROM MR. GREEN... AND THEN HE FOLLOWED."

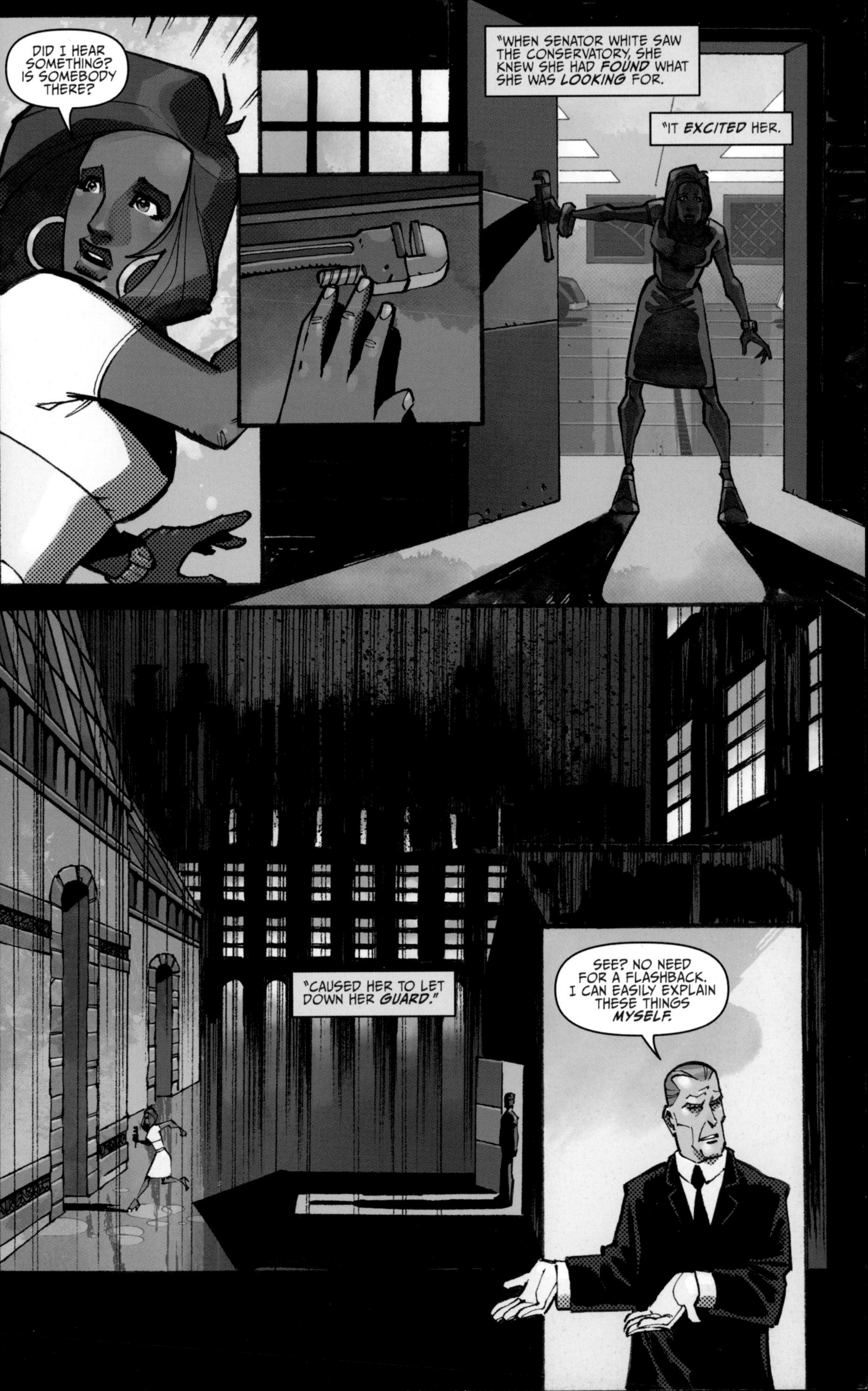
DID I HEAR SOMETHING? IS SOMEBODY THERE?
"WHEN SENATOR WHITE SAW THE CONSERVATORY, SHE KNEW SHE HAD FOUND WHAT SHE WAS LOOKING FOR.
"IT EXCITED HER.
"CAUSED HER TO LET DOWN HER GUARD."
SEE? NO NEED FOR A FLASHBACK. I CAN EASILY EXPLAIN THESE THINGS MYSELF.

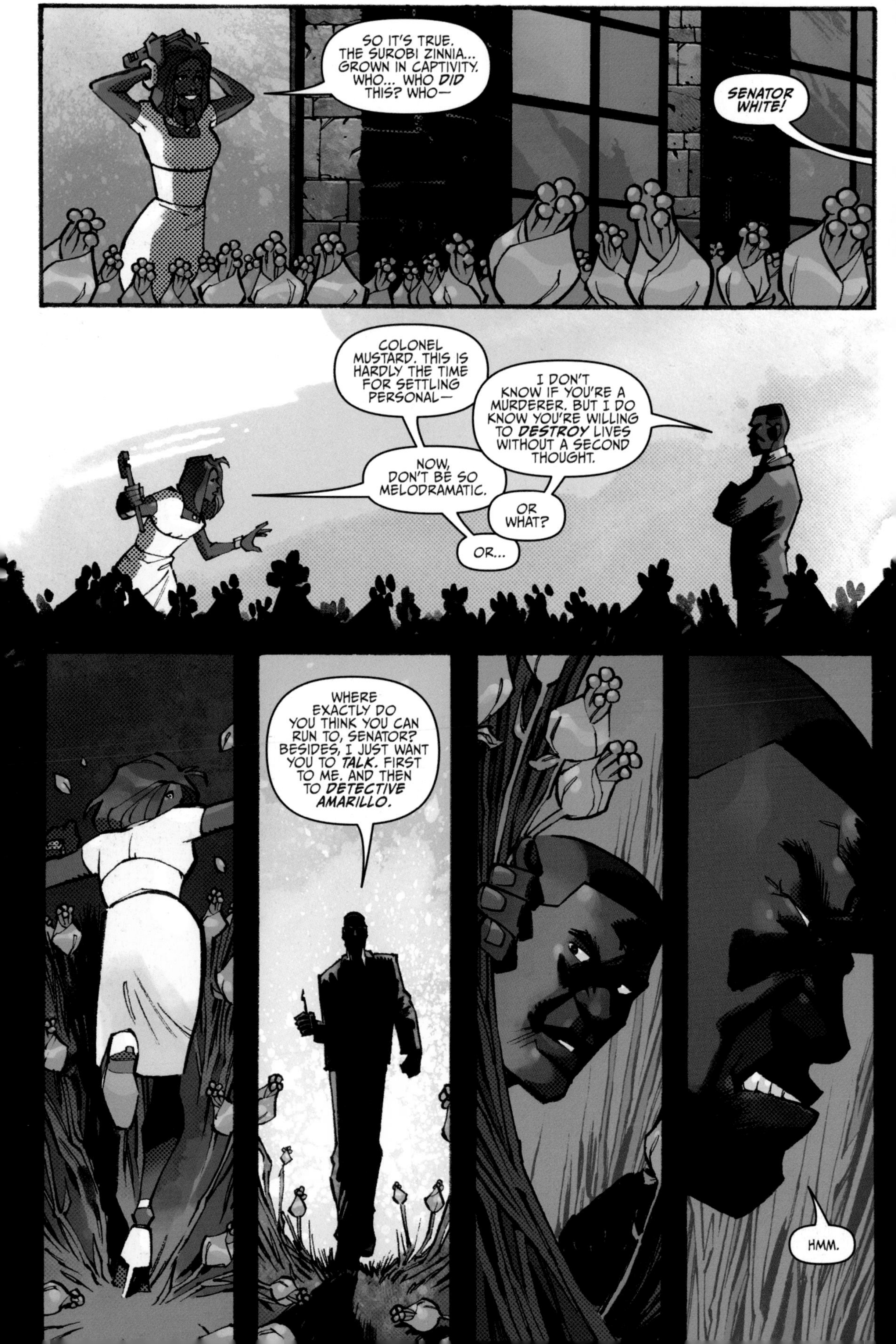

SO IT'S TRUE. THE SUROBI ZINNIA... GROWN IN CAPTIVITY. WHO... WHO DID THIS? WHO—
SENATOR WHITE!
COLONEL MUSTARD. THIS IS HARDLY THE TIME FOR SETTLING PERSONAL—
I DON'T KNOW IF YOU'RE A MURDERER. BUT I DO KNOW YOU'RE WILLING TO DESTROY LIVES WITHOUT A SECOND THOUGHT.
NOW, DON'T BE SO MELODRAMATIC.
OR WHAT?
OR...
WHERE EXACTLY DO YOU THINK YOU CAN RUN TO, SENATOR? BESIDES, I JUST WANT YOU TO TALK. FIRST TO ME. AND THEN TO DETECTIVE AMARILLO.
HMM.

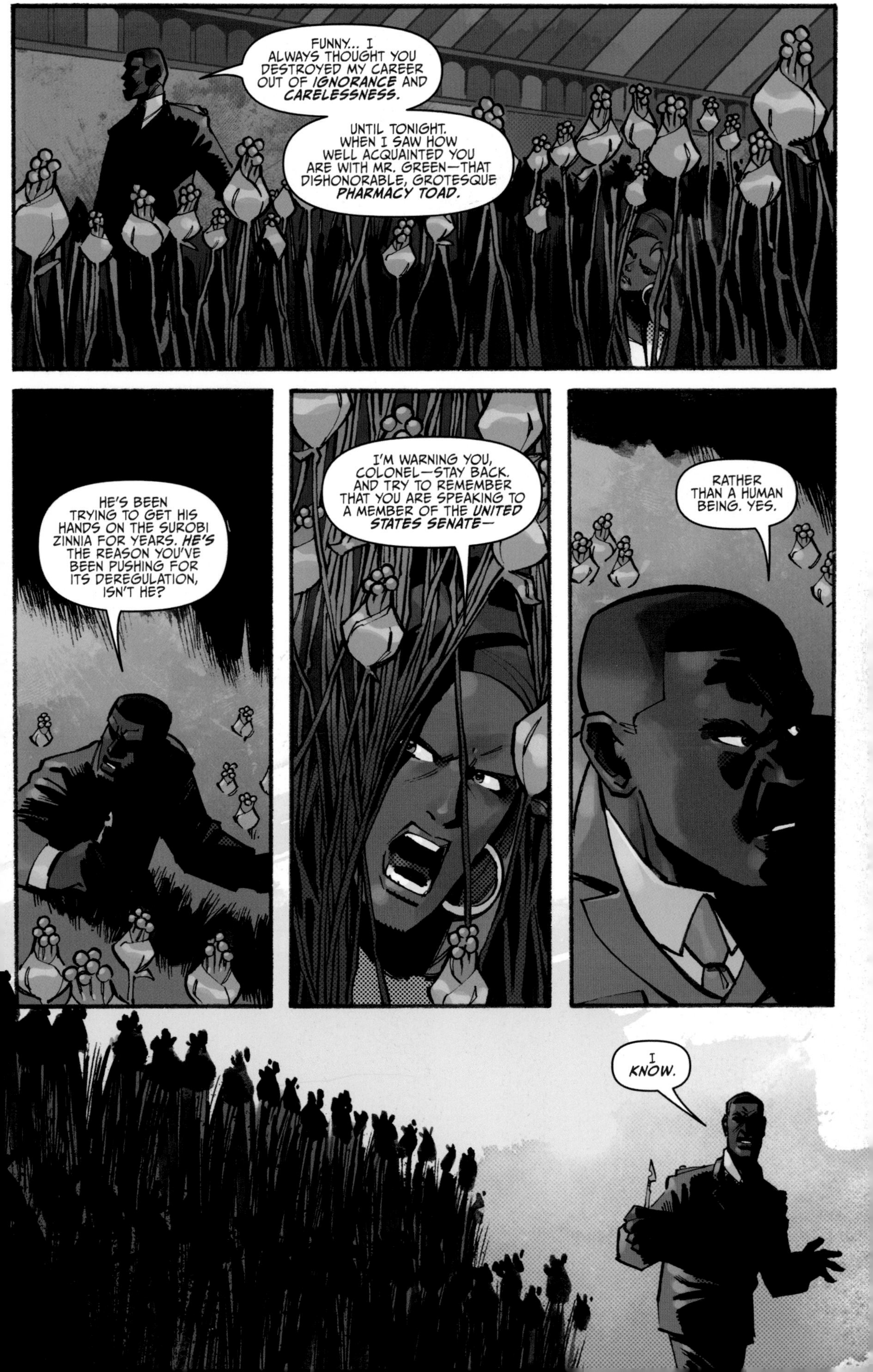
FUNNY... I ALWAYS THOUGHT YOU DESTROYED MY CAREER OUT OF IGNORANCE AND CARELESSNESS.
UNTIL TONIGHT. WHEN I SAW HOW WELL ACQUAINTED YOU ARE WITH MR. GREEN—THAT DISHONORABLE, GROTESQUE PHARMACY TOAD.
HE'S BEEN TRYING TO GET HIS HANDS ON THE SUROBI ZINNIA FOR YEARS. HE'S THE REASON YOU'VE BEEN PUSHING FOR ITS DEREGULATION, ISN'T HE?
I'M WARNING YOU, COLONEL—STAY BACK. AND TRY TO REMEMBER THAT YOU ARE SPEAKING TO A MEMBER OF THE UNITED STATES SENATE—
RATHER THAN A HUMAN BEING. YES.
I KNOW.

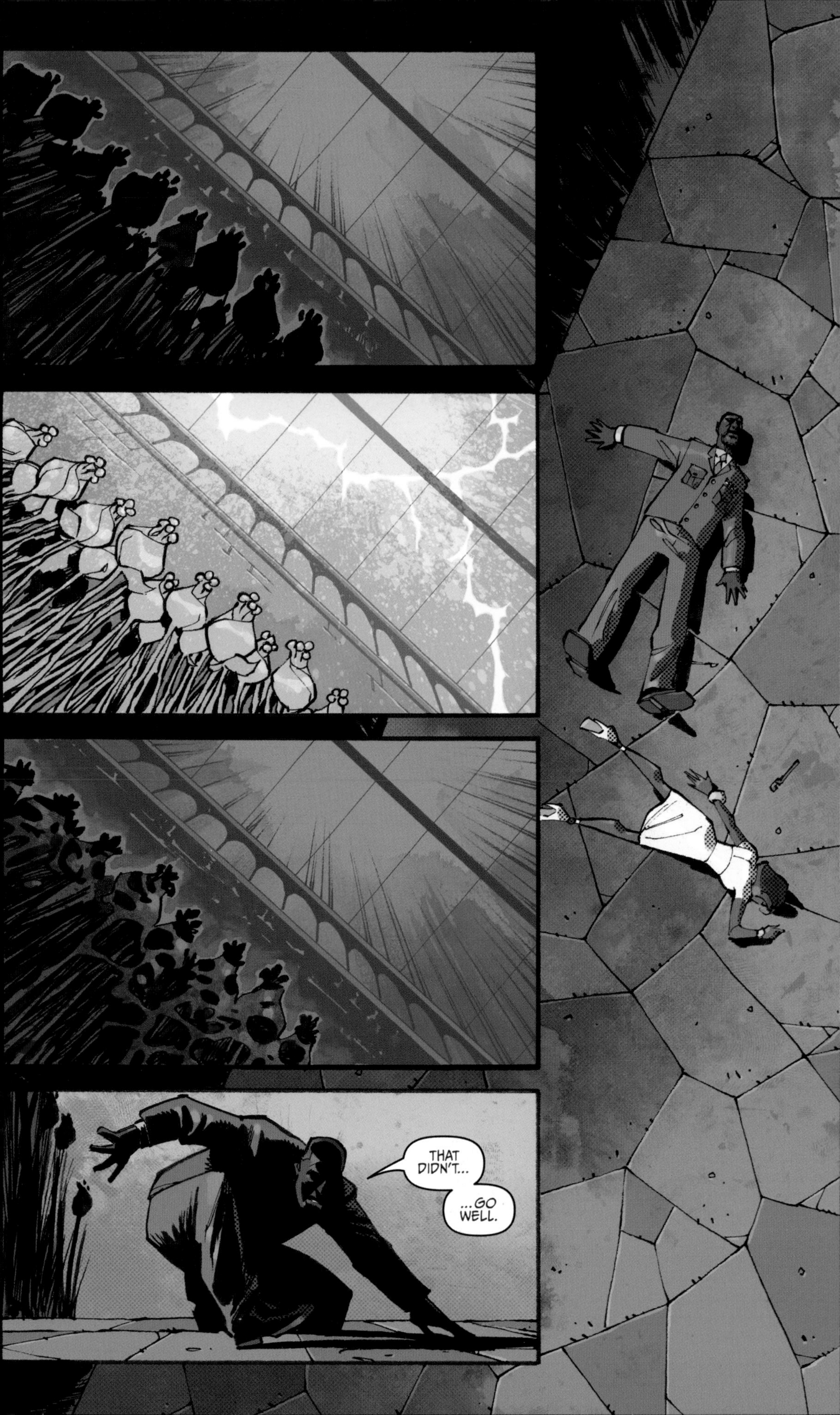
THAT DIDN'T...
...GO WELL.

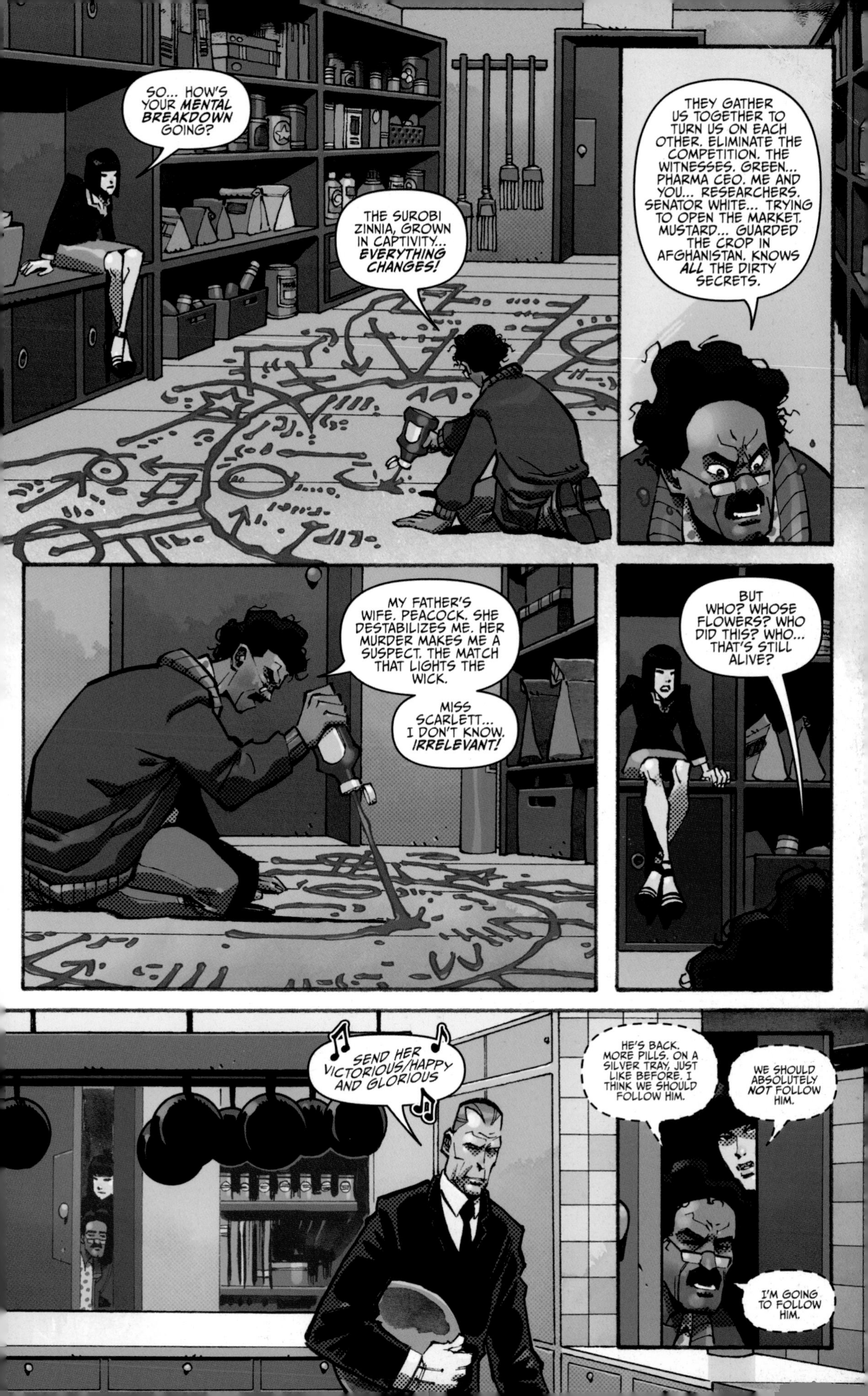
SO... HOW'S YOUR **MENTAL BREAKDOWN** GOING?
THE SUROBI ZINNIA, GROWN IN CAPTIVITY... **EVERYTHING CHANGES!**
THEY GATHER US TOGETHER TO TURN US ON EACH OTHER. ELIMINATE THE COMPETITION. THE WITNESSES. GREEN... PHARMA CEO. ME AND YOU... RESEARCHERS. SENATOR WHITE... TRYING TO OPEN THE MARKET. MUSTARD... GUARDED THE CROP IN AFGHANISTAN. KNOWS **ALL** THE DIRTY SECRETS.
MY FATHER'S WIFE. PEACOCK. SHE DESTABILIZES ME. HER MURDER MAKES ME A SUSPECT. THE MATCH THAT LIGHTS THE WICK.
MISS SCARLETT... I DON'T KNOW. **IRRELEVANT!**
BUT WHO? WHOSE FLOWERS? WHO DID THIS? WHO... THAT'S STILL ALIVE?
SEND HER VICTORIOUS/HAPPY AND GLORIOUS
HE'S BACK. MORE PILLS. ON A SILVER TRAY, JUST LIKE BEFORE. I THINK WE SHOULD FOLLOW HIM.
WE SHOULD ABSOLUTELY **NOT** FOLLOW HIM.
I'M GOING TO FOLLOW HIM.

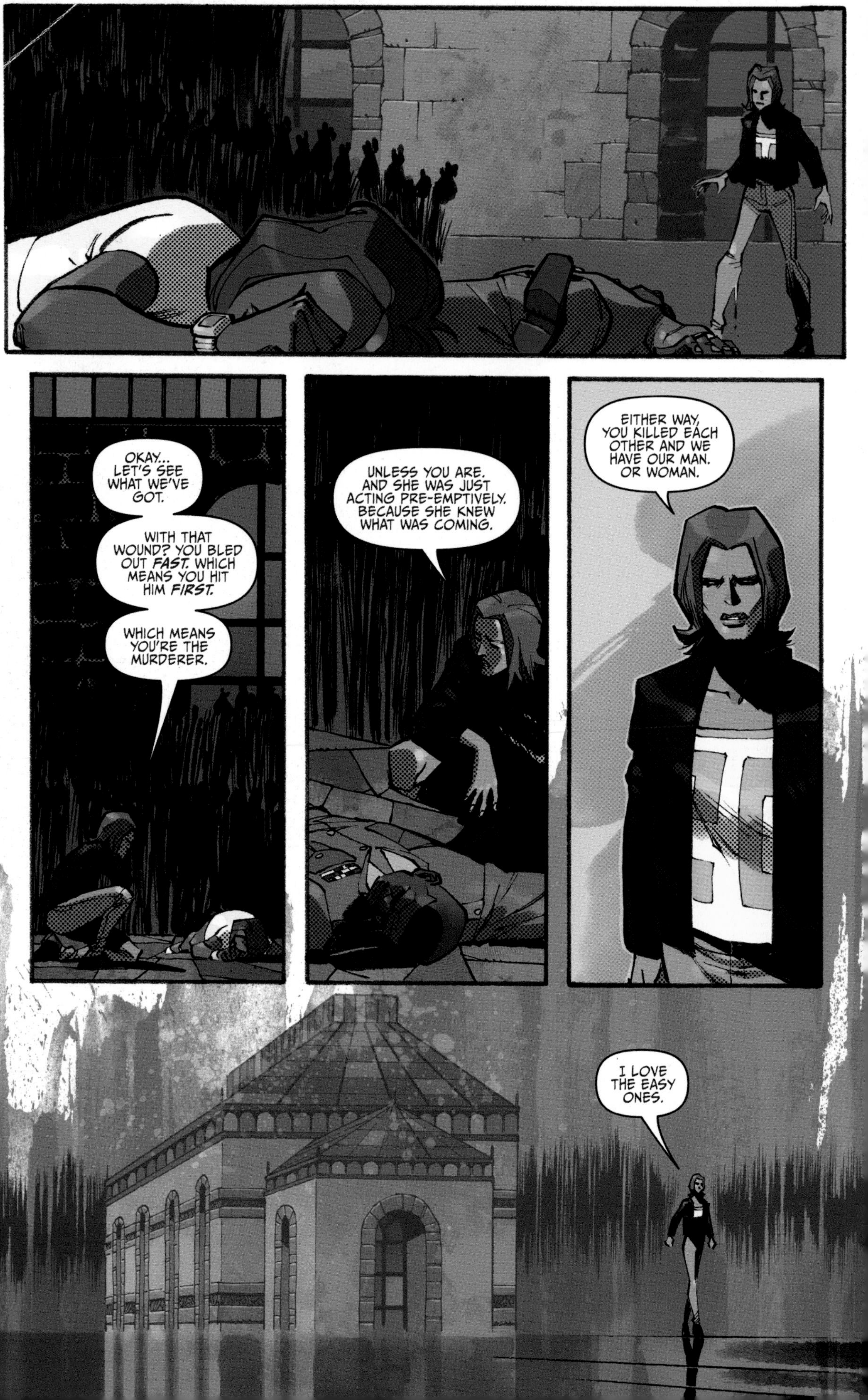
OKAY... LET'S SEE WHAT WE'VE GOT.
WITH THAT WOUND? YOU BLED OUT *FAST.* WHICH MEANS YOU HIT HIM *FIRST.*
WHICH MEANS YOU'RE THE MURDERER.
UNLESS YOU ARE. AND SHE WAS JUST ACTING PRE-EMPTIVELY. BECAUSE SHE KNEW WHAT WAS COMING.
EITHER WAY, YOU KILLED EACH OTHER AND WE HAVE OUR MAN. OR WOMAN.
I LOVE THE EASY ONES.

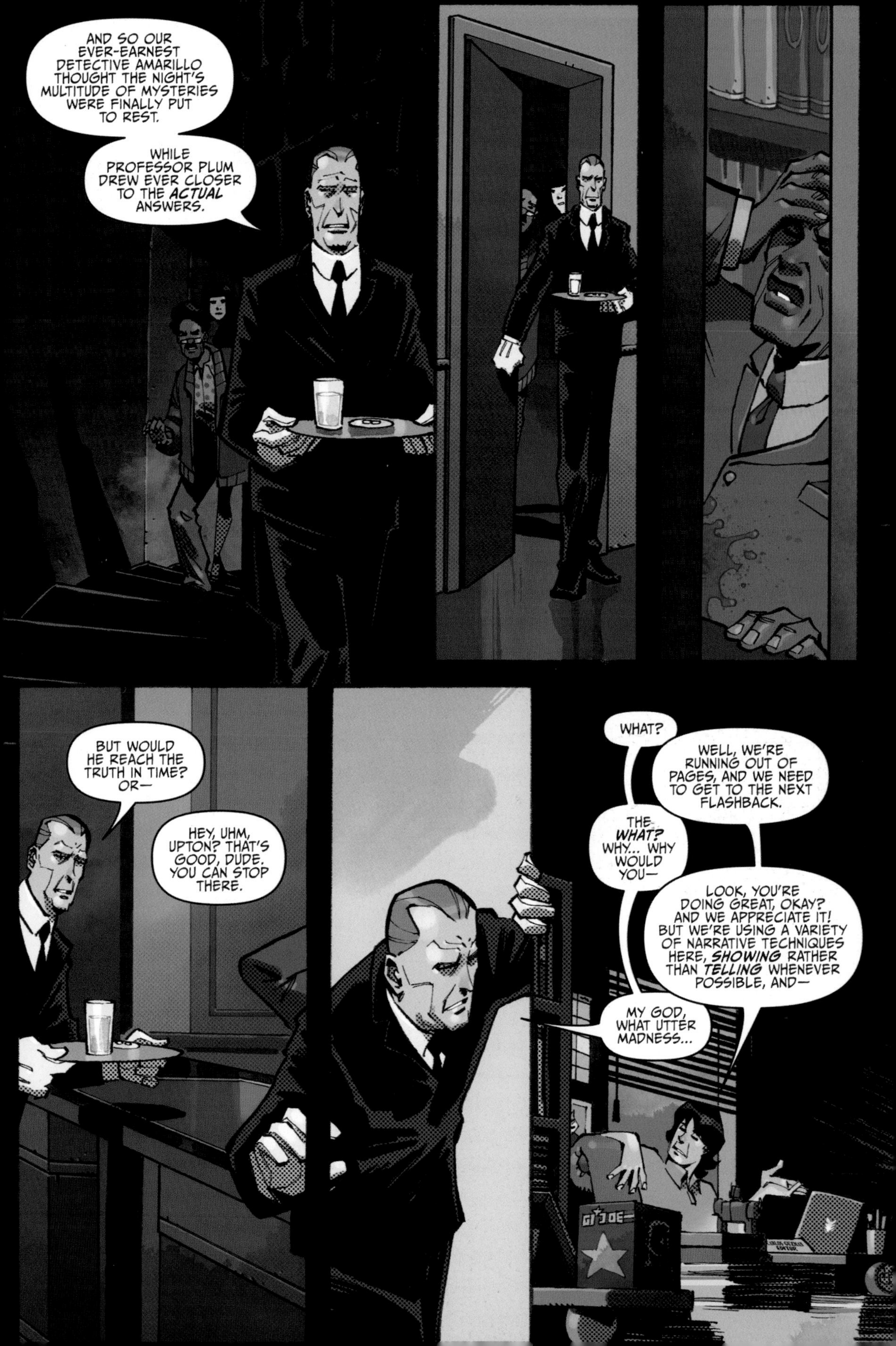
AND SO OUR EVER-EARNEST DETECTIVE AMARILLO THOUGHT THE NIGHT'S MULTITUDE OF MYSTERIES WERE FINALLY PUT TO REST.
WHILE PROFESSOR PLUM DREW EVER CLOSER TO THE *ACTUAL* ANSWERS.
BUT WOULD HE REACH THE TRUTH IN TIME? OR—
HEY, UHM, UPTON? THAT'S GOOD, DUDE. YOU CAN STOP THERE.
WHAT?
WELL, WE'RE RUNNING OUT OF PAGES, AND WE NEED TO GET TO THE NEXT FLASHBACK.
THE *WHAT?* WHY... WHY WOULD YOU—
LOOK, YOU'RE DOING GREAT, OKAY? AND WE APPRECIATE IT! BUT WE'RE USING A VARIETY OF NARRATIVE TECHNIQUES HERE, *SHOWING* RATHER THAN *TELLING* WHENEVER POSSIBLE, AND—
MY GOD, WHAT UTTER MADNESS...

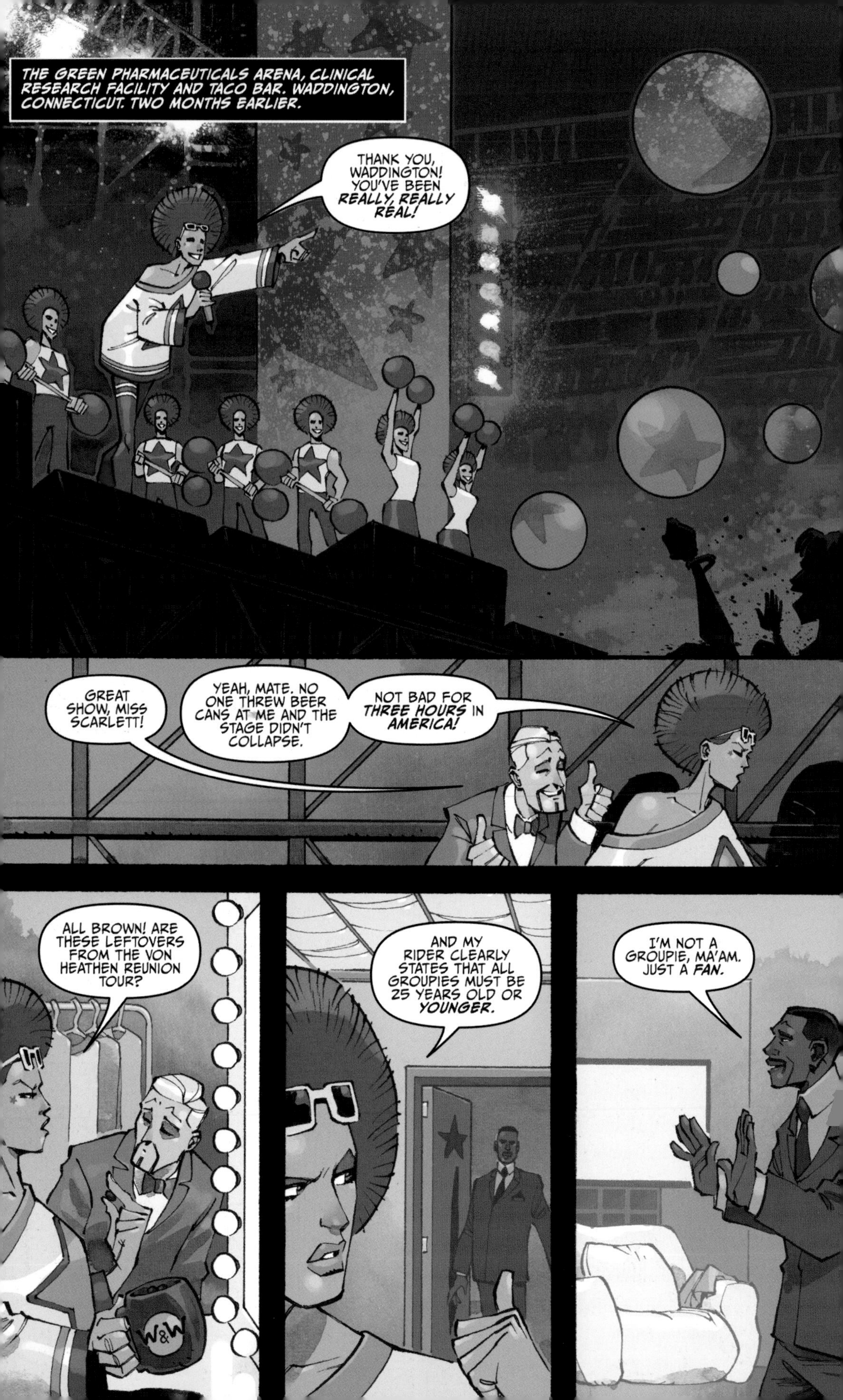
THE GREEN PHARMACEUTICALS ARENA, CLINICAL RESEARCH FACILITY AND TACO BAR. WADDINGTON, CONNECTICUT. TWO MONTHS EARLIER.
THANK YOU, WADDINGTON! YOU'VE BEEN *REALLY, REALLY REAL!*
GREAT SHOW, MISS SCARLETT!
YEAH, MATE. NO ONE THREW BEER CANS AT ME AND THE STAGE DIDN'T COLLAPSE.
NOT BAD FOR *THREE HOURS* IN *AMERICA!*
ALL BROWN! ARE THESE LEFTOVERS FROM THE VON HEATHEN REUNION TOUR?
W&W
AND MY RIDER CLEARLY STATES THAT ALL GROUPIES MUST BE 25 YEARS OLD OR *YOUNGER.*
I'M NOT A GROUPIE, MA'AM. JUST A *FAN.*

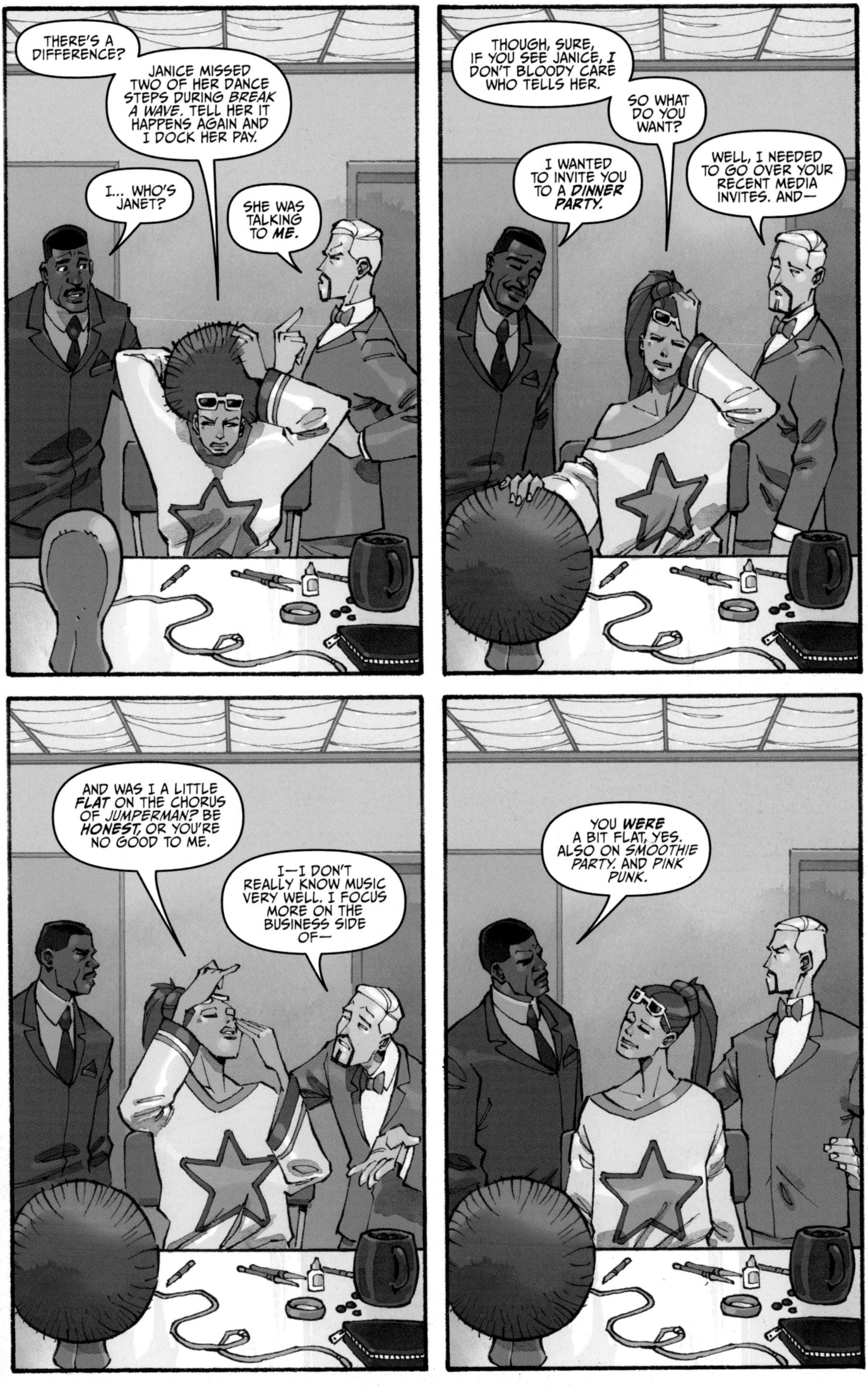
THERE'S A DIFFERENCE?
JANICE MISSED TWO OF HER DANCE STEPS DURING *BREAK A WAVE*. TELL HER IT HAPPENS AGAIN AND I DOCK HER PAY.
I... WHO'S JANET?
SHE WAS TALKING TO **ME.**
THOUGH, SURE, IF YOU SEE JANICE, *I* DON'T BLOODY CARE WHO TELLS HER.
SO WHAT DO YOU WANT?
I WANTED TO INVITE YOU TO A **DINNER PARTY.**
WELL, I NEEDED TO GO OVER YOUR RECENT MEDIA INVITES. AND—
AND WAS I A LITTLE **FLAT** ON THE CHORUS OF *JUMPERMAN?* BE **HONEST,** OR YOU'RE NO GOOD TO ME.
I—I DON'T REALLY KNOW MUSIC VERY WELL. I FOCUS MORE ON THE BUSINESS SIDE OF—
YOU **WERE** A BIT FLAT, YES. ALSO ON *SMOOTHIE PARTY.* AND *PINK PUNK.*

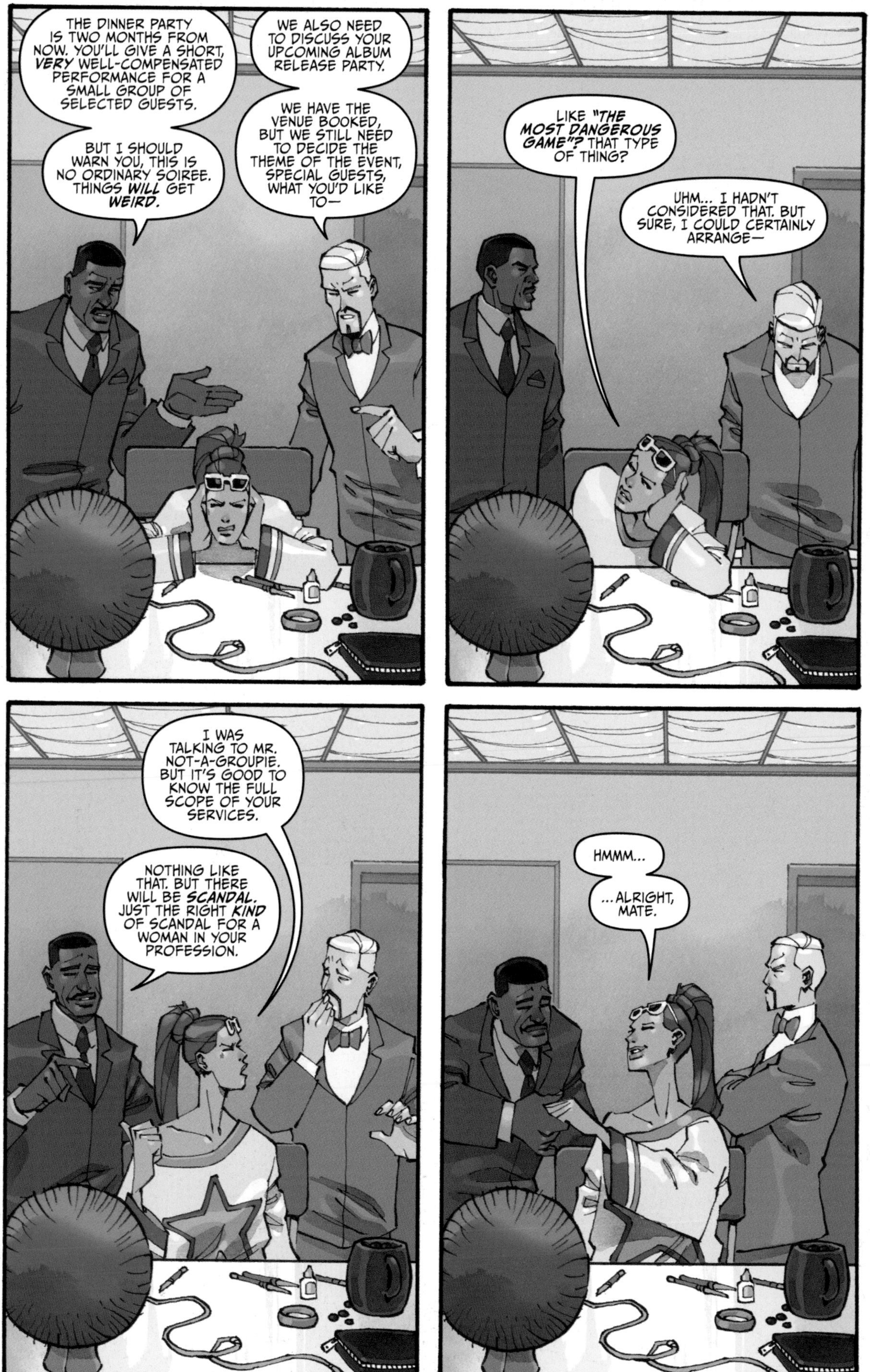
THE DINNER PARTY IS TWO MONTHS FROM NOW. YOU'LL GIVE A SHORT, VERY WELL-COMPENSATED PERFORMANCE FOR A SMALL GROUP OF SELECTED GUESTS.
BUT I SHOULD WARN YOU, THIS IS NO ORDINARY SOIREE. THINGS WILL GET WEIRD.
WE ALSO NEED TO DISCUSS YOUR UPCOMING ALBUM RELEASE PARTY.
WE HAVE THE VENUE BOOKED, BUT WE STILL NEED TO DECIDE THE THEME OF THE EVENT, SPECIAL GUESTS, WHAT YOU'D LIKE TO—
LIKE "THE MOST DANGEROUS GAME"? THAT TYPE OF THING?
UHM... I HADN'T CONSIDERED THAT. BUT SURE, I COULD CERTAINLY ARRANGE—
NOTHING LIKE THAT. BUT THERE WILL BE SCANDAL. JUST THE RIGHT KIND OF SCANDAL FOR A WOMAN IN YOUR PROFESSION.
I WAS TALKING TO MR. NOT-A-GROUPIE. BUT IT'S GOOD TO KNOW THE FULL SCOPE OF YOUR SERVICES.
HMMM...
...ALRIGHT, MATE.

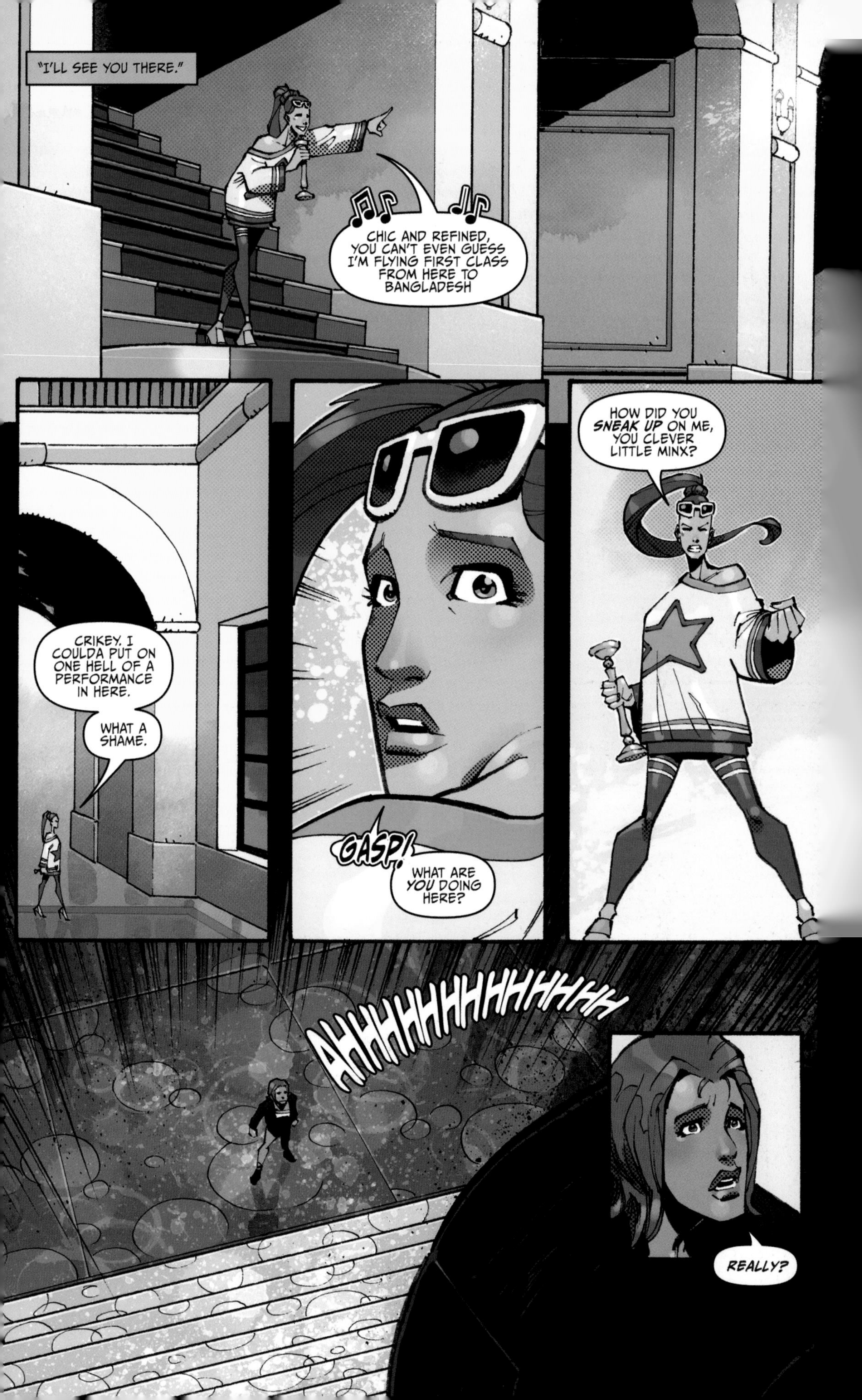
"I'LL SEE YOU THERE."
CHIC AND REFINED, YOU CAN'T EVEN GUESS I'M FLYING FIRST CLASS FROM HERE TO BANGLADESH
CRIKEY. I COULDA PUT ON ONE HELL OF A PERFORMANCE IN HERE.
WHAT A SHAME.
GASP!
WHAT ARE YOU DOING HERE?
HOW DID YOU SNEAK UP ON ME, YOU CLEVER LITTLE MINX?
AHHHHHHHHHHHHH
REALLY?

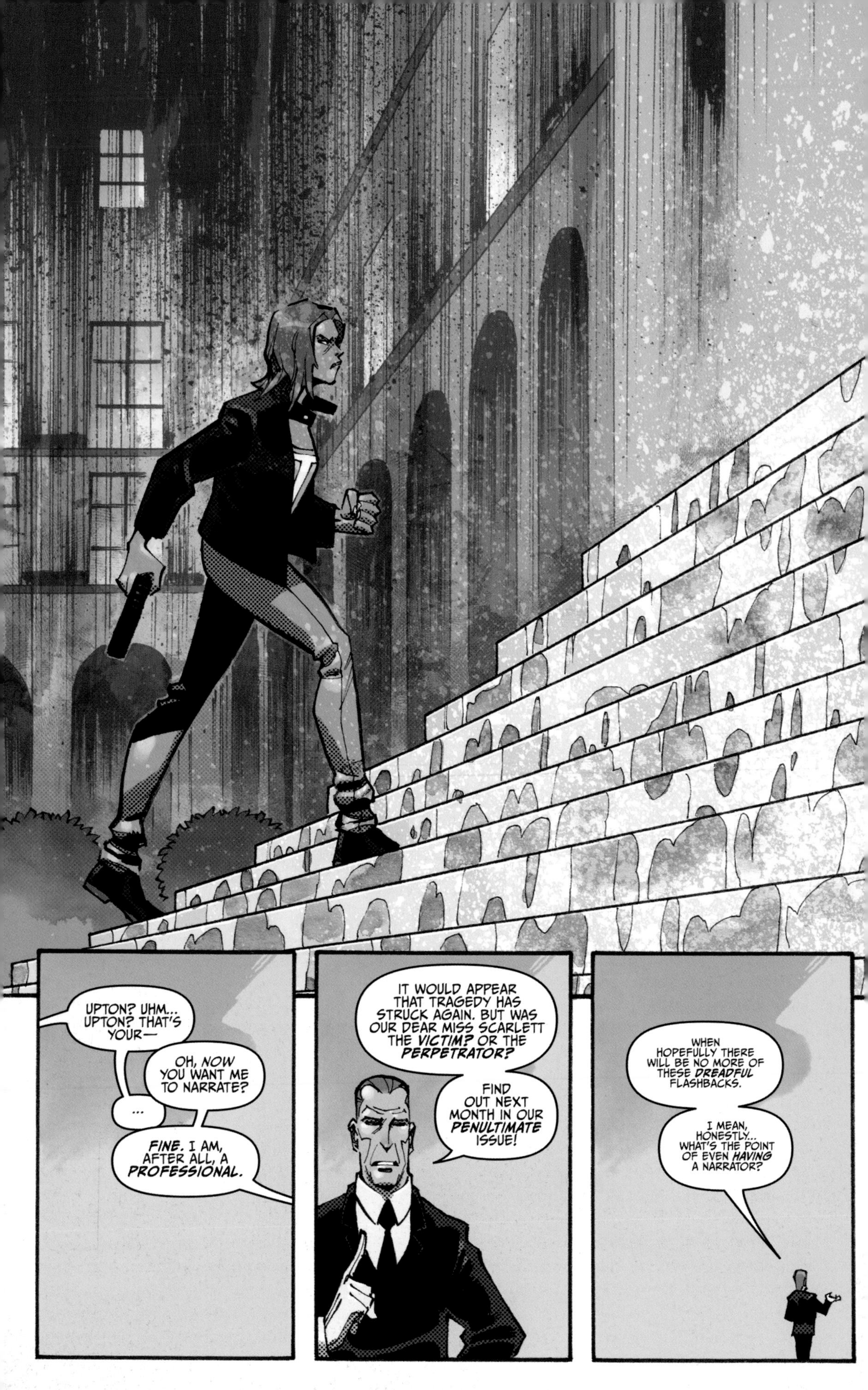
UPTON? UHM... UPTON? THAT'S YOUR—
OH, NOW YOU WANT ME TO NARRATE?
...
FINE. I AM, AFTER ALL, A PROFESSIONAL.
IT WOULD APPEAR THAT TRAGEDY HAS STRUCK AGAIN. BUT WAS OUR DEAR MISS SCARLETT THE VICTIM? OR THE PERPETRATOR?
FIND OUT NEXT MONTH IN OUR PENULTIMATE ISSUE!
WHEN HOPEFULLY THERE WILL BE NO MORE OF THESE DREADFUL FLASHBACKS.
I MEAN, HONESTLY... WHAT'S THE POINT OF EVEN HAVING A NARRATOR?

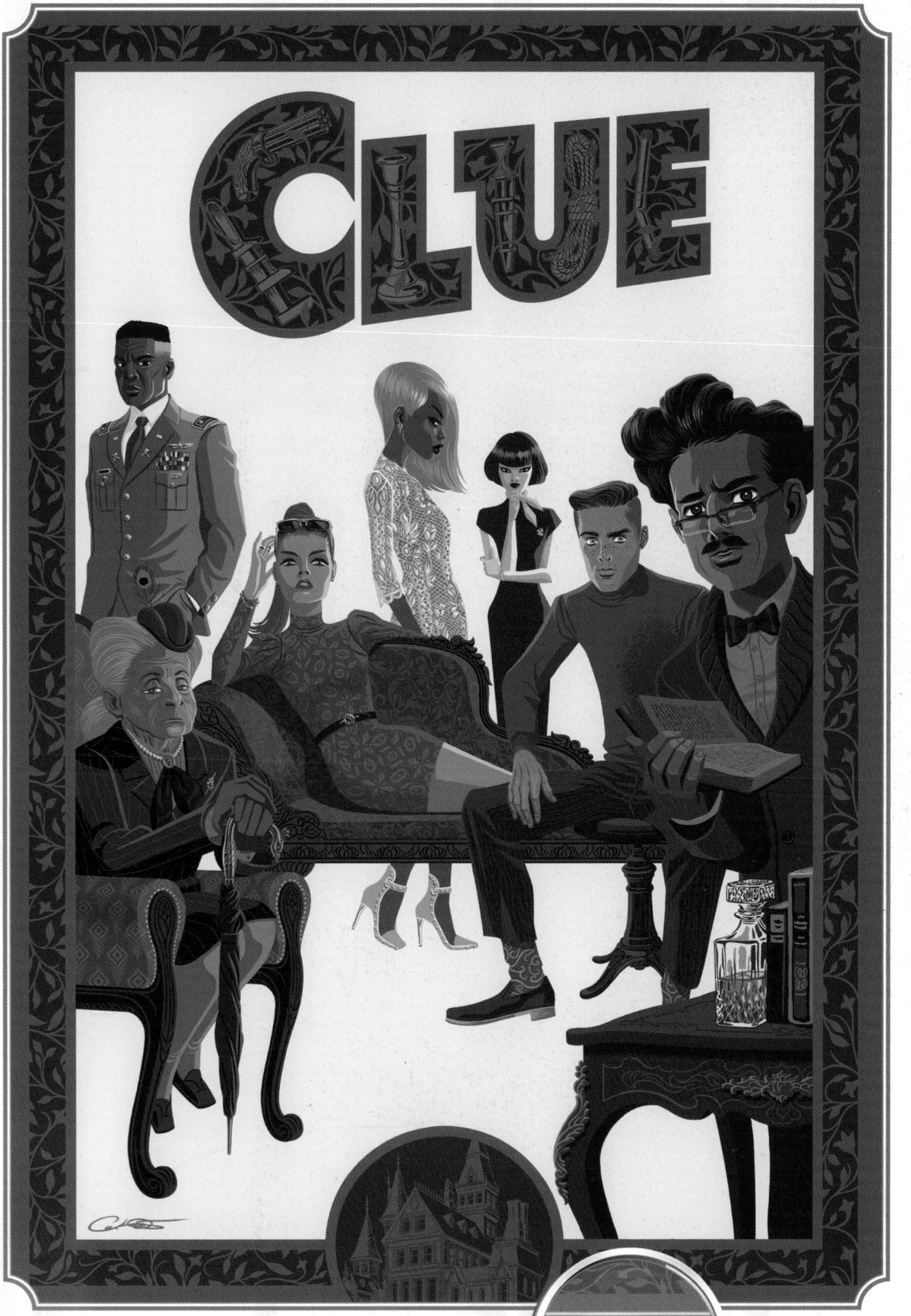
CLUE

COVER ART BY
GEORGE CALTSOUDAS

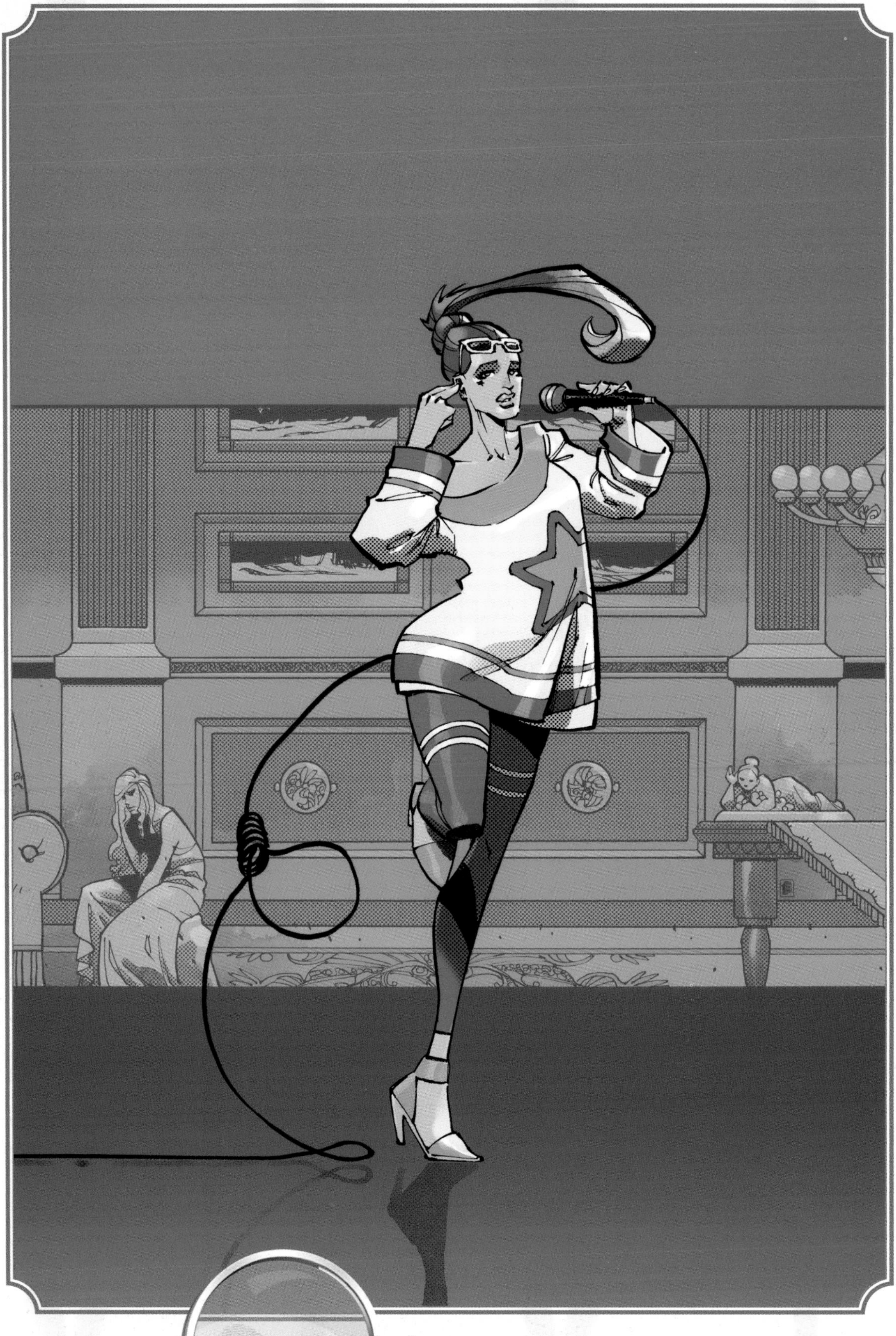

COVER ART BY
NELSON DANIEL

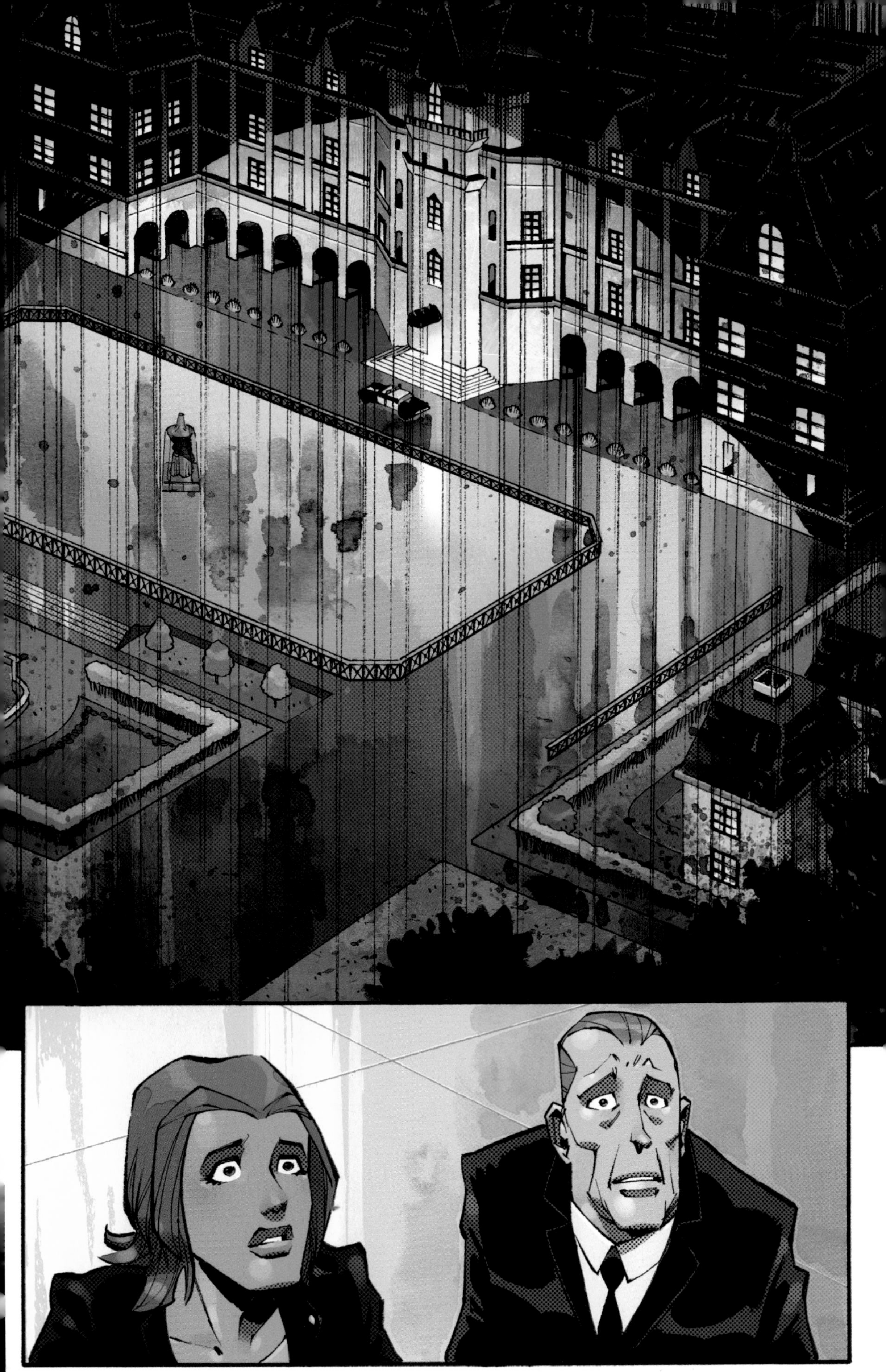

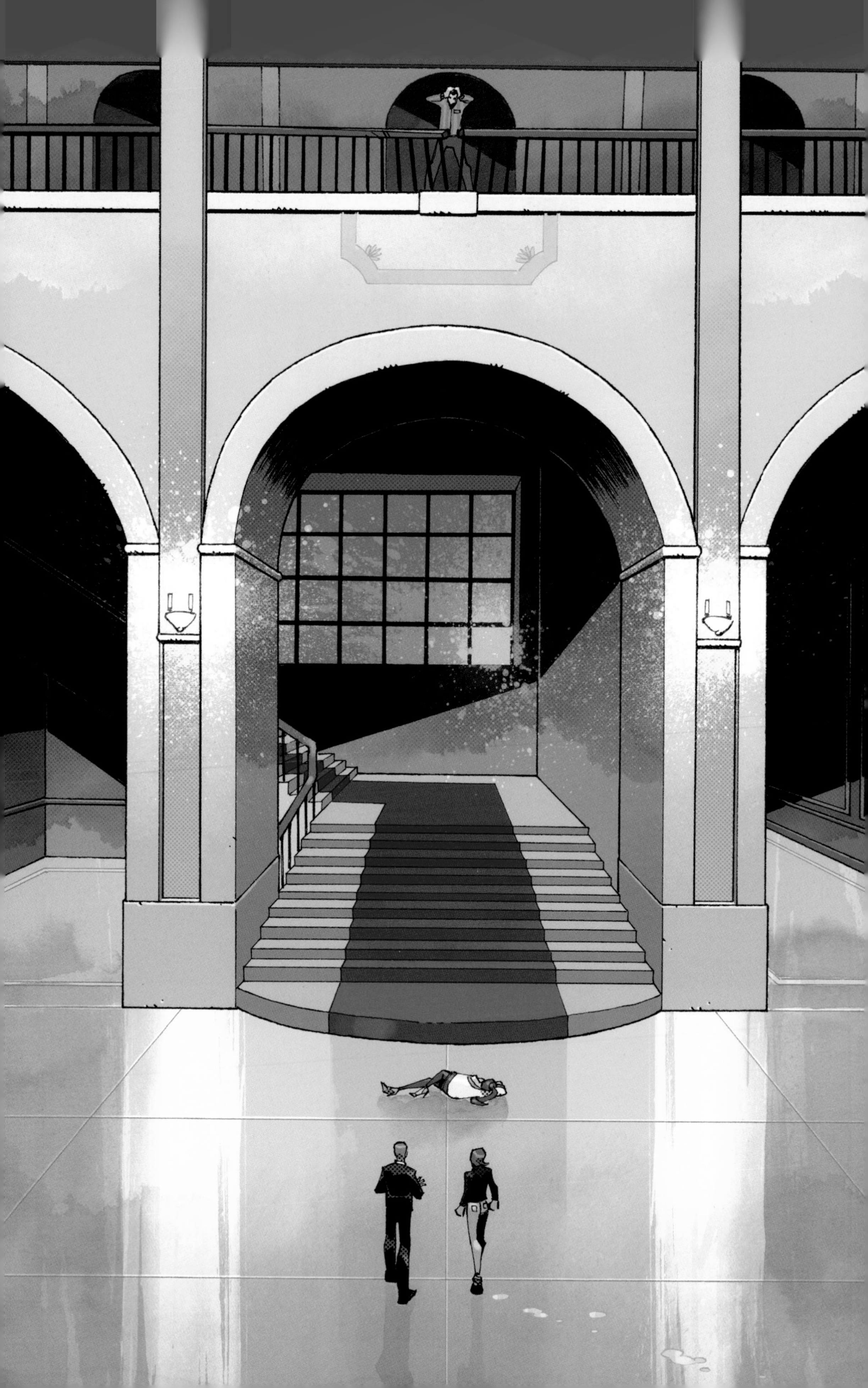

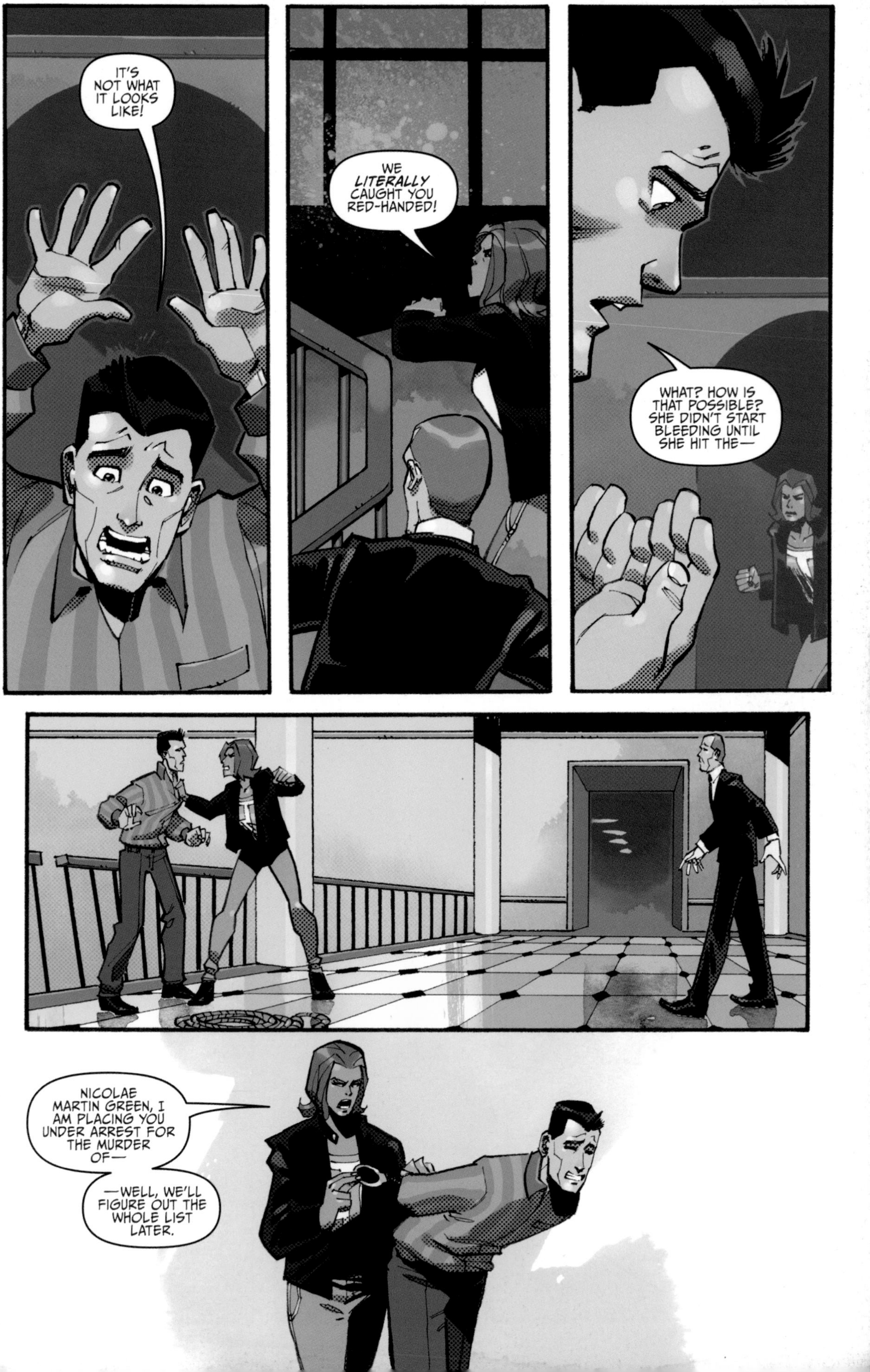
IT'S NOT WHAT IT LOOKS LIKE!
WE *LITERALLY* CAUGHT YOU RED-HANDED!
WHAT? HOW IS THAT POSSIBLE? SHE DIDN'T START BLEEDING UNTIL SHE HIT THE—
NICOLAE MARTIN GREEN, I AM PLACING YOU UNDER ARREST FOR THE MURDER OF—
—WELL, WE'LL FIGURE OUT THE WHOLE LIST LATER.

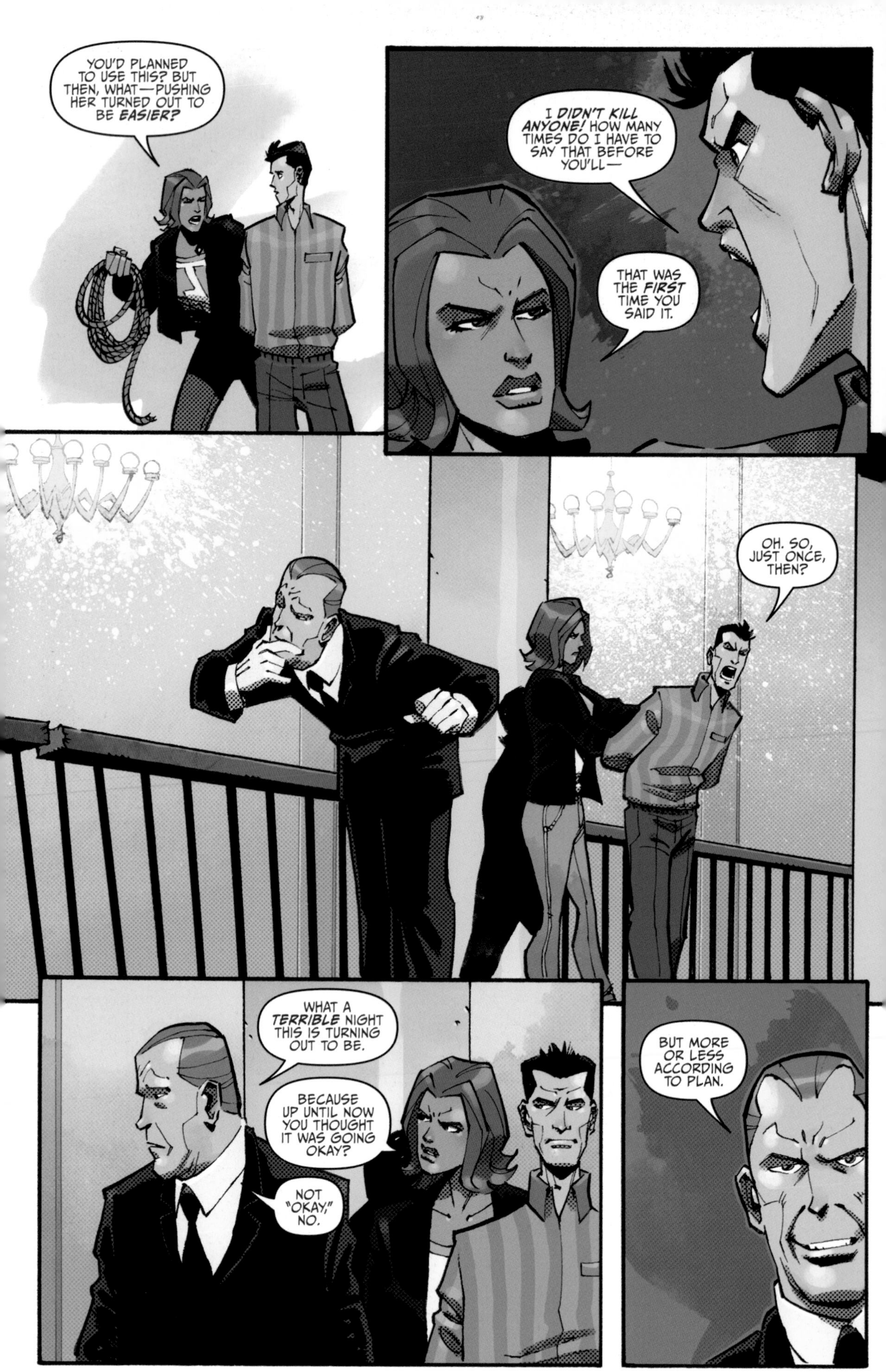
YOU'D PLANNED TO USE THIS? BUT THEN, WHAT—PUSHING HER TURNED OUT TO BE EASIER?
I DIDN'T KILL ANYONE! HOW MANY TIMES DO I HAVE TO SAY THAT BEFORE YOU'LL—
THAT WAS THE FIRST TIME YOU SAID IT.
OH. SO, JUST ONCE, THEN?
WHAT A TERRIBLE NIGHT THIS IS TURNING OUT TO BE.
BECAUSE UP UNTIL NOW YOU THOUGHT IT WAS GOING OKAY?
NOT "OKAY," NO.
BUT MORE OR LESS ACCORDING TO PLAN.

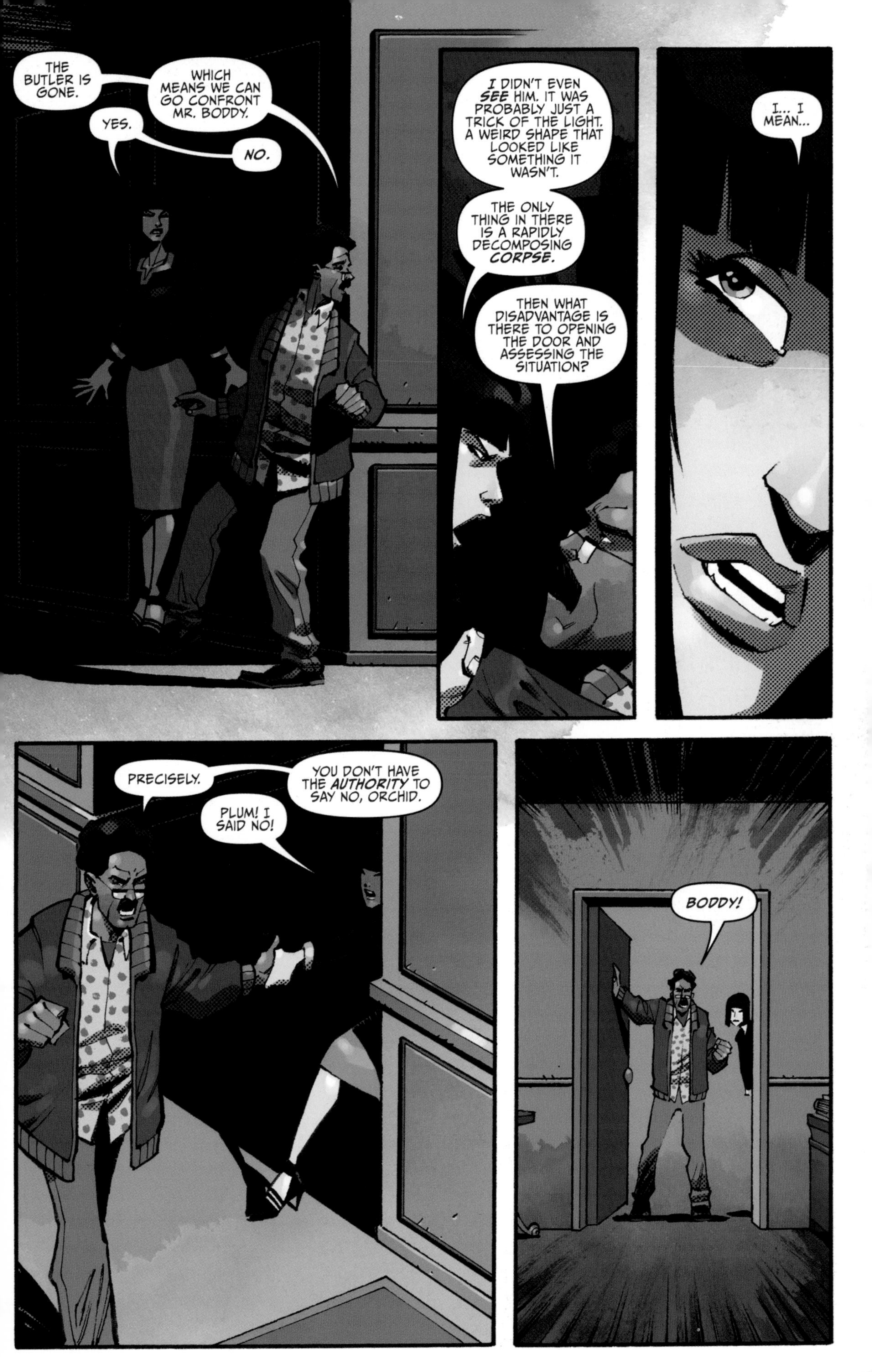
THE BUTLER IS GONE.
WHICH MEANS WE CAN GO CONFRONT MR. BODDY.
YES.
NO.
I DIDN'T EVEN SEE HIM. IT WAS PROBABLY JUST A TRICK OF THE LIGHT. A WEIRD SHAPE THAT LOOKED LIKE SOMETHING IT WASN'T.
THE ONLY THING IN THERE IS A RAPIDLY DECOMPOSING CORPSE.
THEN WHAT DISADVANTAGE IS THERE TO OPENING THE DOOR AND ASSESSING THE SITUATION?
I... I MEAN...
PRECISELY.
YOU DON'T HAVE THE AUTHORITY TO SAY NO, ORCHID.
PLUM! I SAID NO!
BODDY!

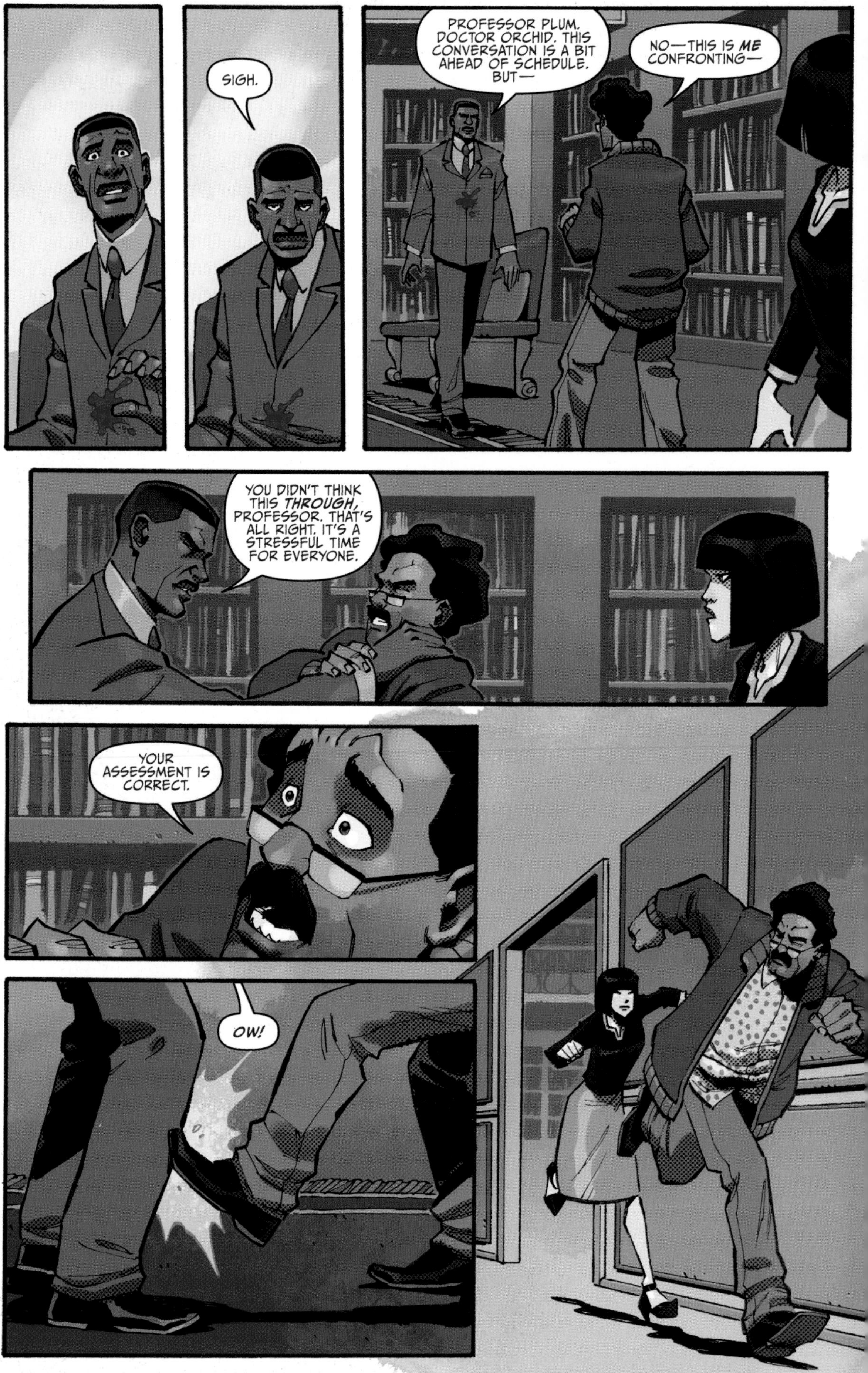
SIGH.
PROFESSOR PLUM. DOCTOR ORCHID. THIS CONVERSATION IS A BIT AHEAD OF SCHEDULE. BUT—
NO—THIS IS *ME* CONFRONTING—
YOU DIDN'T THINK THIS *THROUGH,* PROFESSOR. THAT'S ALL RIGHT. IT'S A STRESSFUL TIME FOR EVERYONE.
YOUR ASSESSMENT IS CORRECT.
OW!

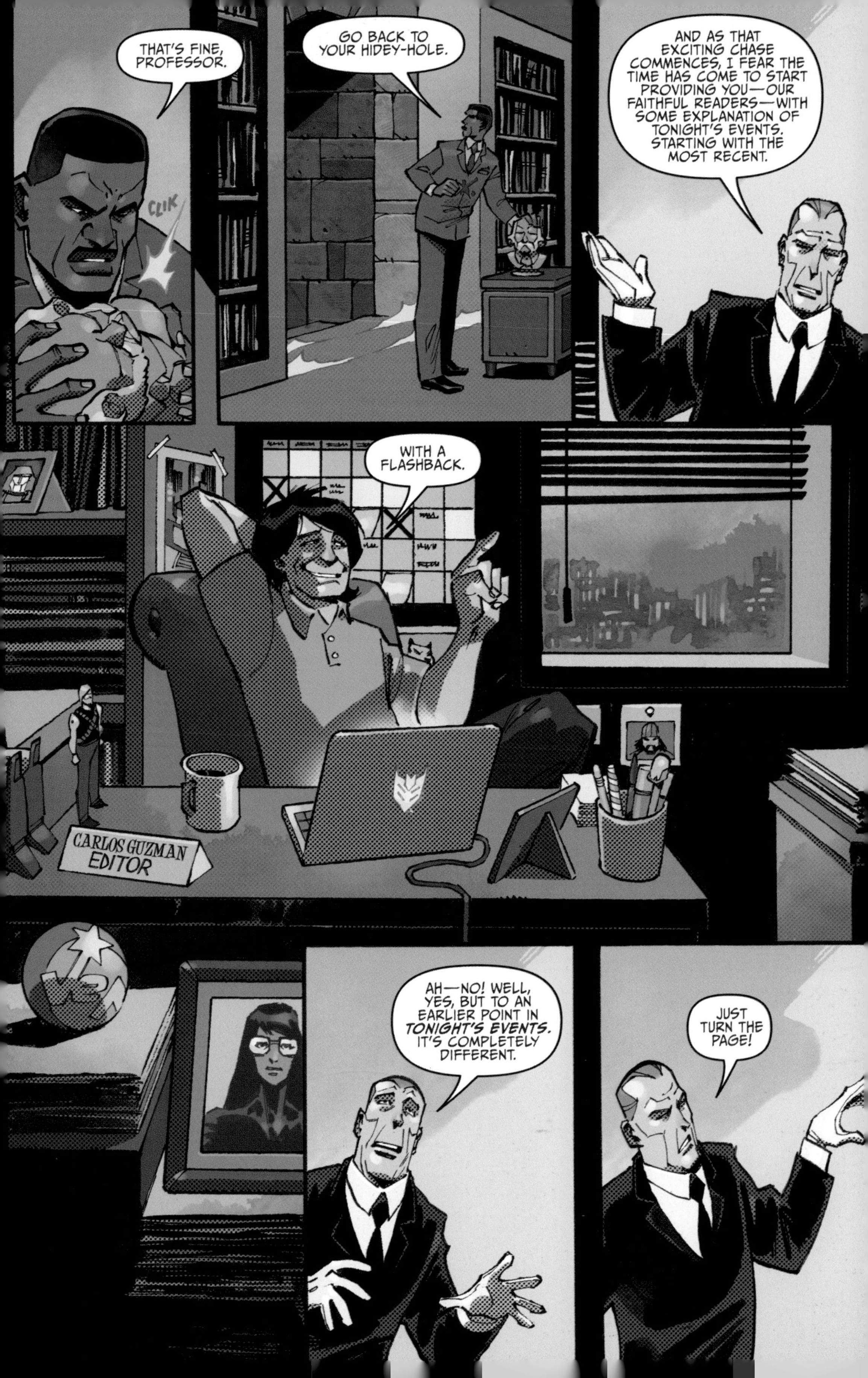
THAT'S FINE, PROFESSOR.
CLIK
GO BACK TO YOUR HIDEY-HOLE.
AND AS THAT EXCITING CHASE COMMENCES, I FEAR THE TIME HAS COME TO START PROVIDING YOU—OUR FAITHFUL READERS—WITH SOME EXPLANATION OF TONIGHT'S EVENTS. STARTING WITH THE MOST RECENT.
WITH A FLASHBACK.
CARLOS GUZMAN
EDITOR
AH—NO! WELL, YES, BUT TO AN EARLIER POINT IN *TONIGHT'S EVENTS*. IT'S COMPLETELY DIFFERENT.
JUST TURN THE PAGE!

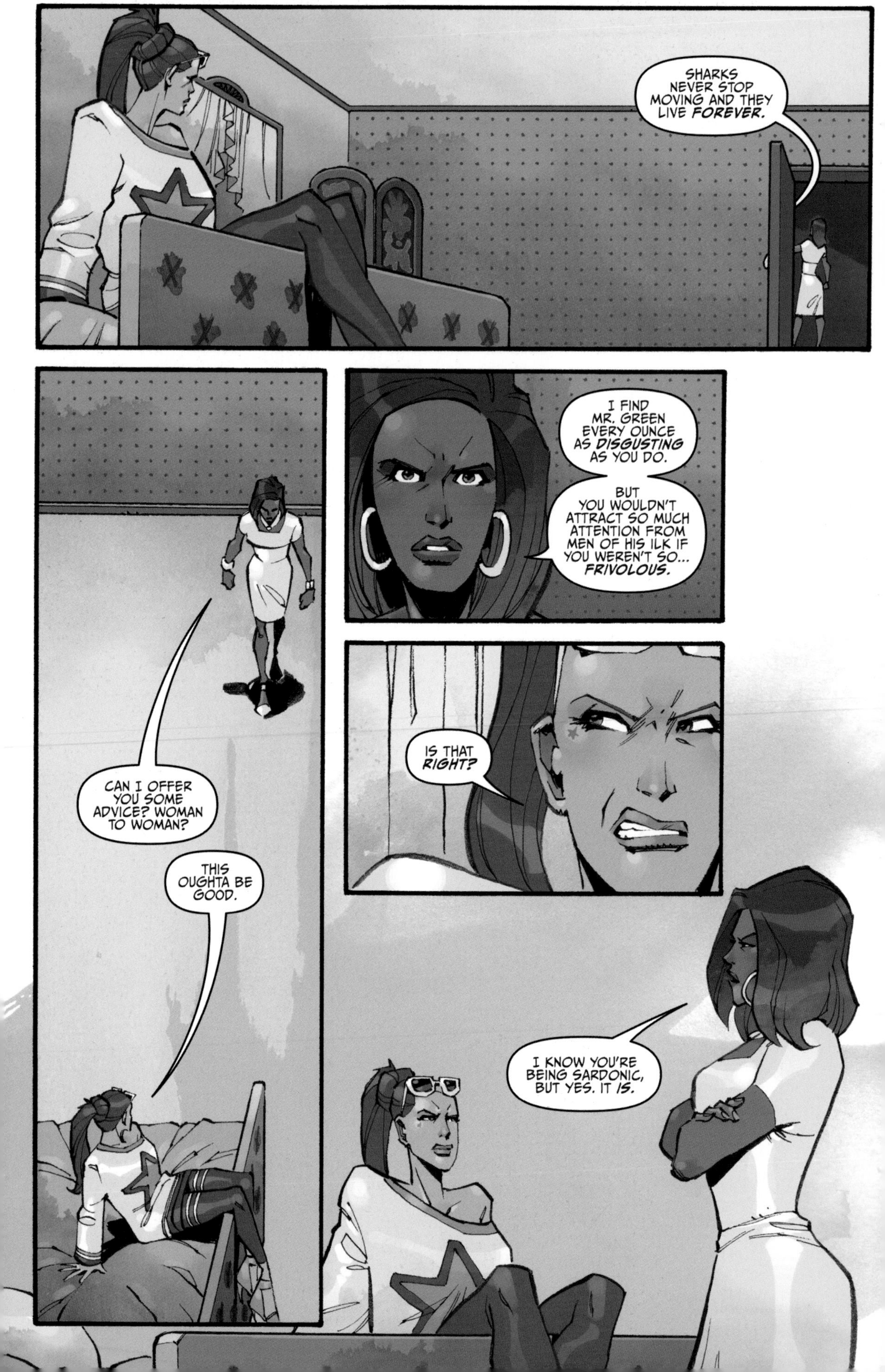

SHARKS NEVER STOP MOVING AND THEY LIVE FOREVER.
I FIND MR. GREEN EVERY OUNCE AS DISGUSTING AS YOU DO.
BUT YOU WOULDN'T ATTRACT SO MUCH ATTENTION FROM MEN OF HIS ILK IF YOU WEREN'T SO... FRIVOLOUS.
IS THAT RIGHT?
CAN I OFFER YOU SOME ADVICE? WOMAN TO WOMAN?
THIS OUGHTA BE GOOD.
I KNOW YOU'RE BEING SARDONIC, BUT YES. IT IS.

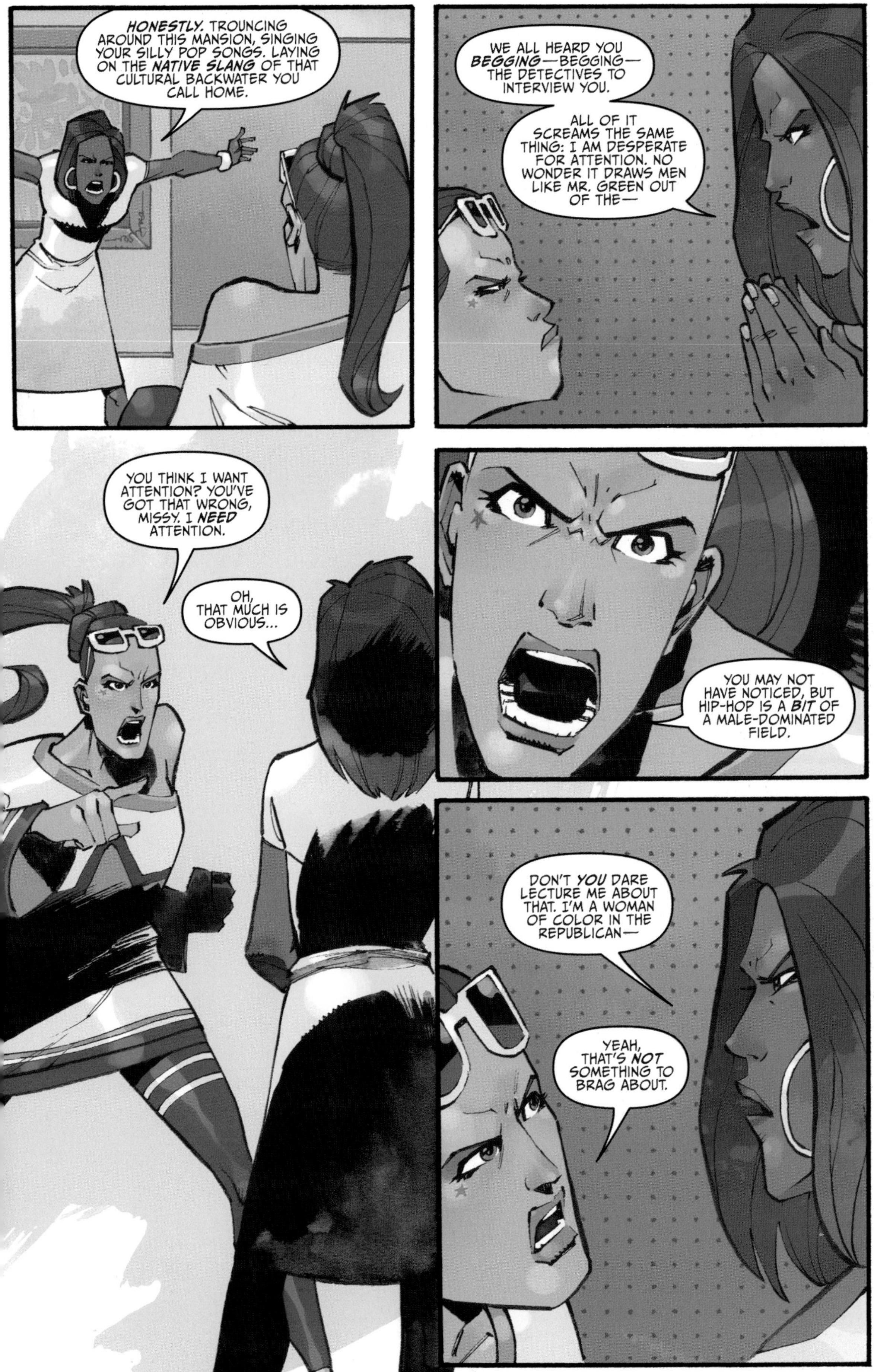
HONESTLY. TROUNCING AROUND THIS MANSION, SINGING YOUR SILLY POP SONGS. LAYING ON THE NATIVE SLANG OF THAT CULTURAL BACKWATER YOU CALL HOME.
WE ALL HEARD YOU BEGGING—BEGGING—THE DETECTIVES TO INTERVIEW YOU.
ALL OF IT SCREAMS THE SAME THING: I AM DESPERATE FOR ATTENTION. NO WONDER IT DRAWS MEN LIKE MR. GREEN OUT OF THE—
YOU THINK I WANT ATTENTION? YOU'VE GOT THAT WRONG, MISSY. I NEED ATTENTION.
OH, THAT MUCH IS OBVIOUS...
YOU MAY NOT HAVE NOTICED, BUT HIP-HOP IS A BIT OF A MALE-DOMINATED FIELD.
DON'T YOU DARE LECTURE ME ABOUT THAT. I'M A WOMAN OF COLOR IN THE REPUBLICAN—
YEAH, THAT'S NOT SOMETHING TO BRAG ABOUT.

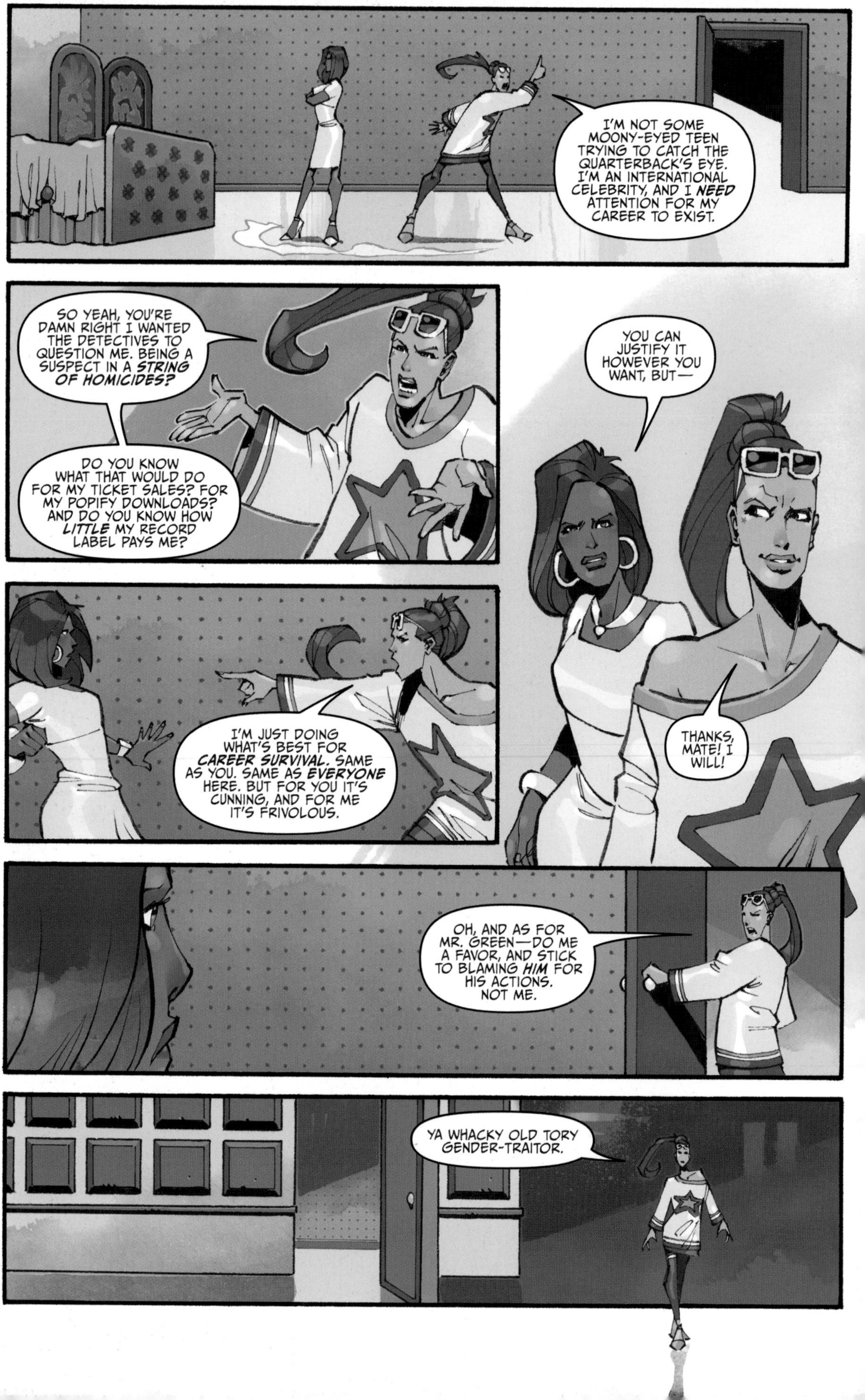
I'M NOT SOME MOONY-EYED TEEN TRYING TO CATCH THE QUARTERBACK'S EYE. I'M AN INTERNATIONAL CELEBRITY, AND I **NEED** ATTENTION FOR MY CAREER TO EXIST.
SO YEAH, YOU'RE DAMN RIGHT I WANTED THE DETECTIVES TO QUESTION ME. BEING A SUSPECT IN A ***STRING OF HOMICIDES?***
DO YOU KNOW WHAT THAT WOULD DO FOR MY TICKET SALES? FOR MY POPIFY DOWNLOADS? AND DO YOU KNOW HOW ***LITTLE*** MY RECORD LABEL PAYS ME?
I'M JUST DOING WHAT'S BEST FOR ***CAREER SURVIVAL.*** SAME AS YOU. SAME AS ***EVERYONE*** HERE. BUT FOR YOU IT'S CUNNING, AND FOR ME IT'S FRIVOLOUS.
YOU CAN JUSTIFY IT HOWEVER YOU WANT, BUT—
THANKS, MATE! I WILL!
OH, AND AS FOR MR. GREEN—DO ME A FAVOR, AND STICK TO BLAMING ***HIM*** FOR HIS ACTIONS. NOT ME.
YA WHACKY OLD TORY GENDER-TRAITOR.

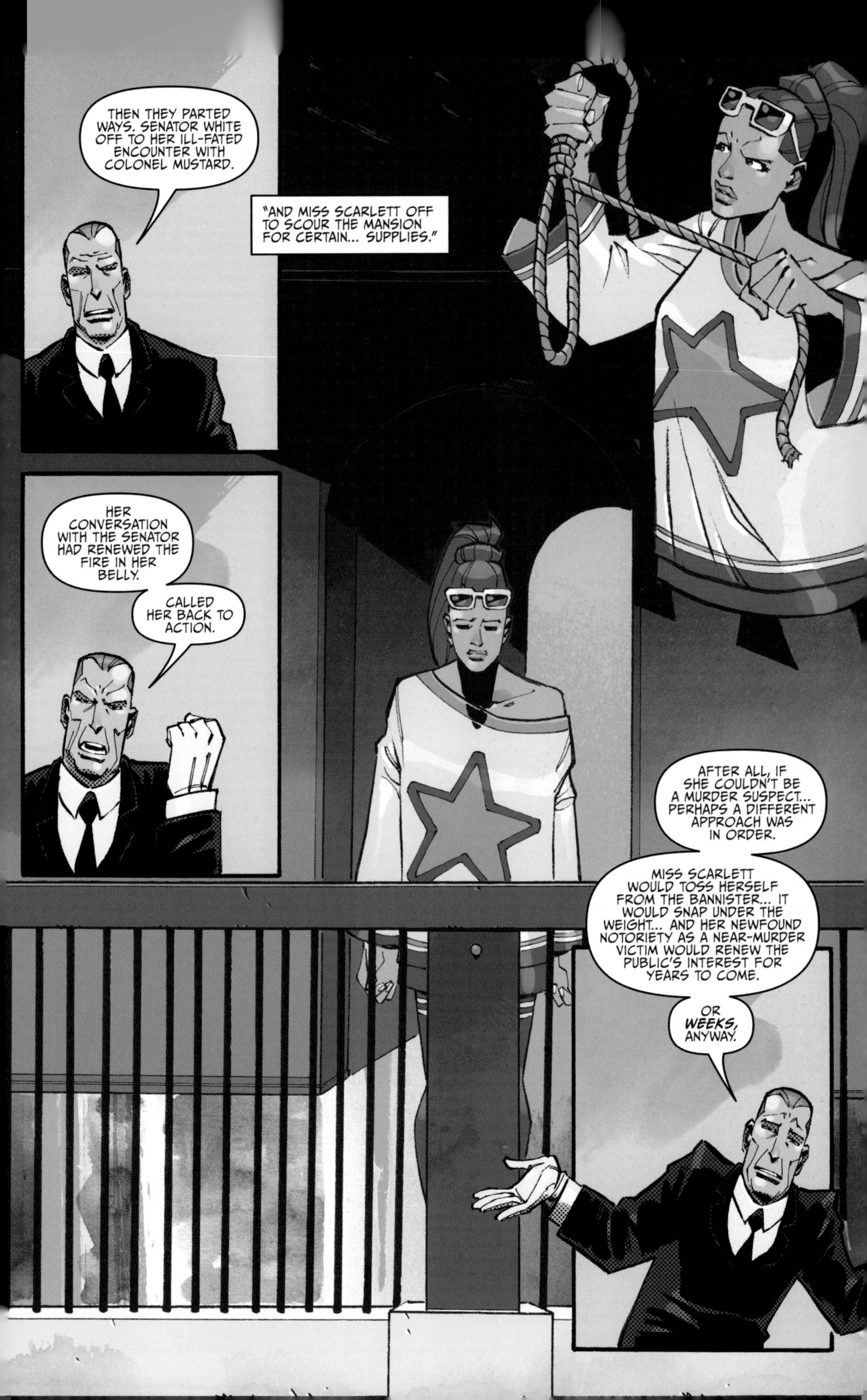
THEN THEY PARTED WAYS. SENATOR WHITE OFF TO HER ILL-FATED ENCOUNTER WITH COLONEL MUSTARD.
"AND MISS SCARLETT OFF TO SCOUR THE MANSION FOR CERTAIN... SUPPLIES."
HER CONVERSATION WITH THE SENATOR HAD RENEWED THE FIRE IN HER BELLY.
CALLED HER BACK TO ACTION.
AFTER ALL, IF SHE COULDN'T BE A MURDER SUSPECT... PERHAPS A DIFFERENT APPROACH WAS IN ORDER.
MISS SCARLETT WOULD TOSS HERSELF FROM THE BANNISTER... IT WOULD SNAP UNDER THE WEIGHT... AND HER NEWFOUND NOTORIETY AS A NEAR-MURDER VICTIM WOULD RENEW THE PUBLIC'S INTEREST FOR YEARS TO COME.
OR *WEEKS*, ANYWAY.

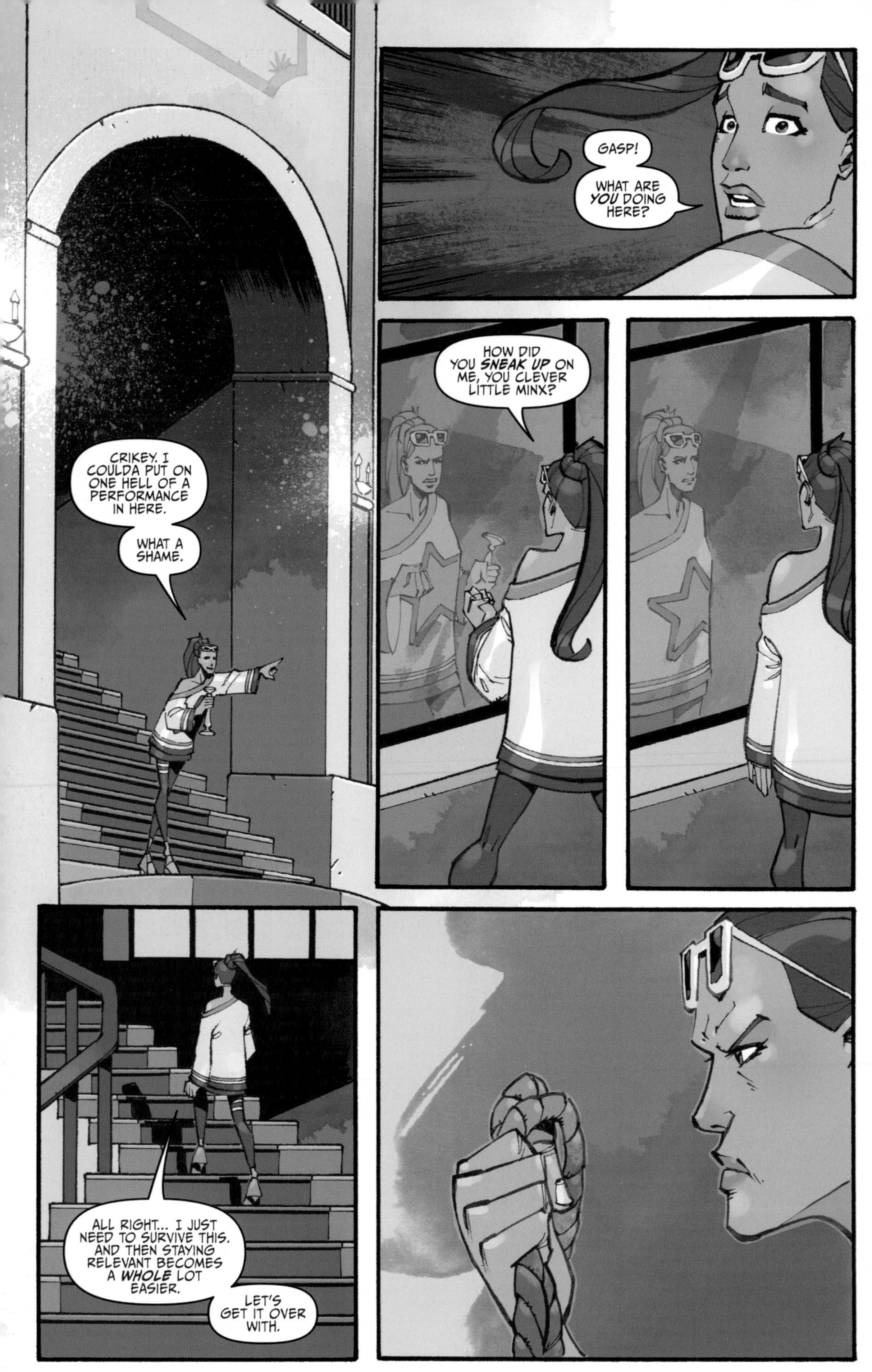
CRIKEY. I COULDA PUT ON ONE HELL OF A PERFORMANCE IN HERE.
WHAT A SHAME.
GASP!
WHAT ARE YOU DOING HERE?
HOW DID YOU SNEAK UP ON ME, YOU CLEVER LITTLE MINX?
ALL RIGHT... I JUST NEED TO SURVIVE THIS. AND THEN STAYING RELEVANT BECOMES A WHOLE LOT EASIER.
LET'S GET IT OVER WITH.

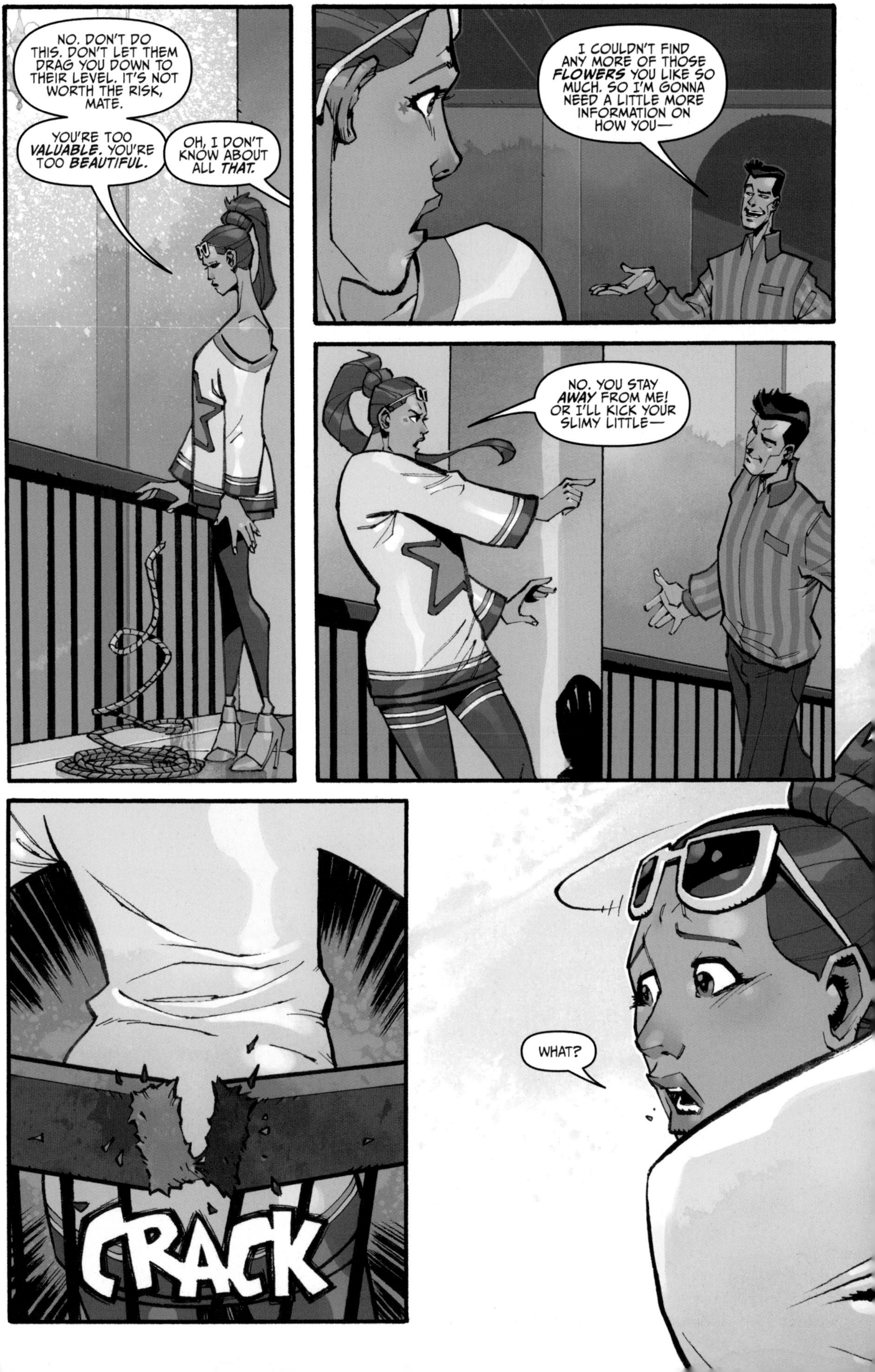
NO. DON'T DO THIS. DON'T LET THEM DRAG YOU DOWN TO THEIR LEVEL. IT'S NOT WORTH THE RISK, MATE.
YOU'RE TOO VALUABLE. YOU'RE TOO BEAUTIFUL.
OH, I DON'T KNOW ABOUT ALL THAT.
I COULDN'T FIND ANY MORE OF THOSE FLOWERS YOU LIKE SO MUCH. SO I'M GONNA NEED A LITTLE MORE INFORMATION ON HOW YOU—
NO. YOU STAY AWAY FROM ME! OR I'LL KICK YOUR SLIMY LITTLE—
CRACK
WHAT?

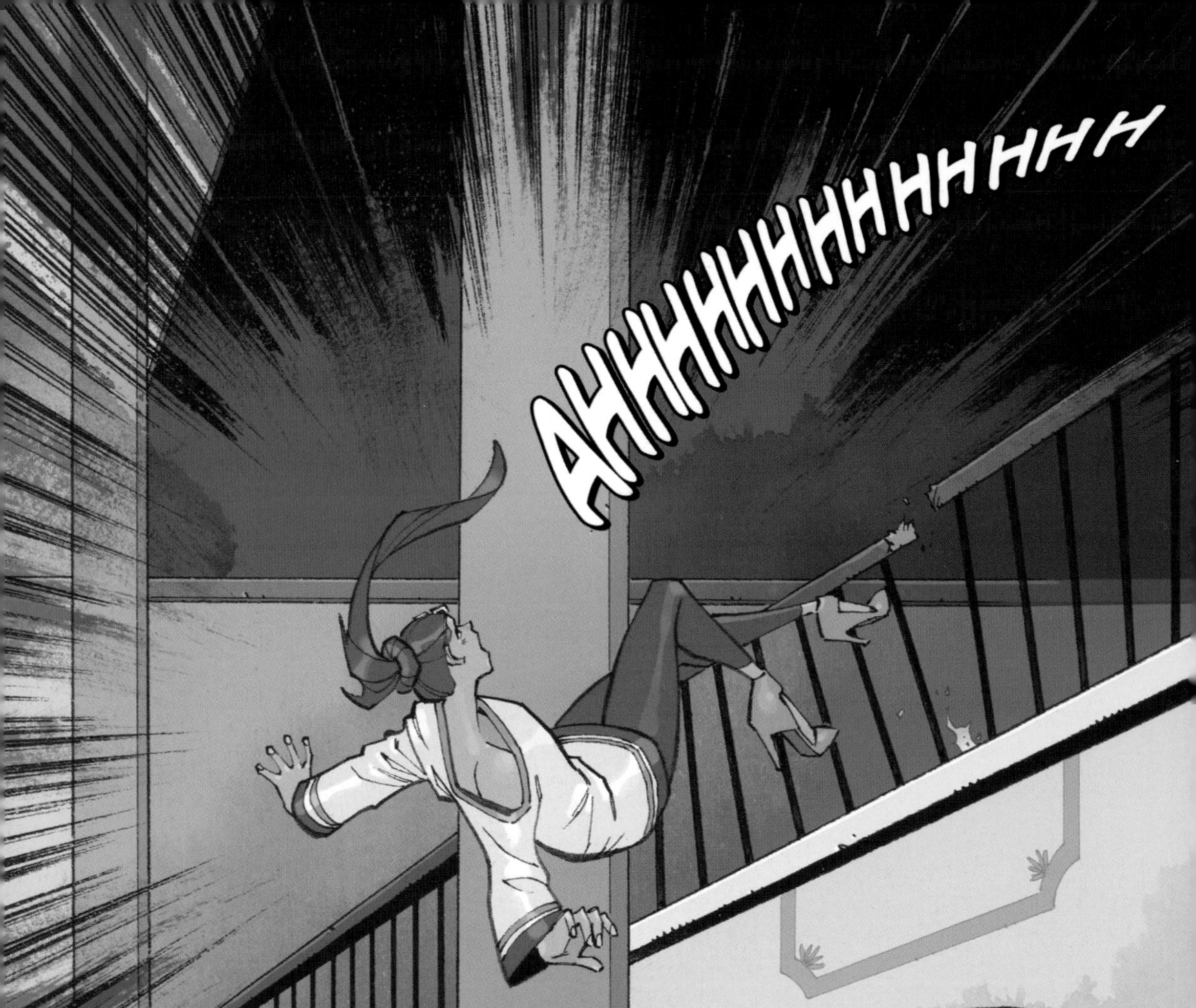
AHHHHHHHHHHHHHHH

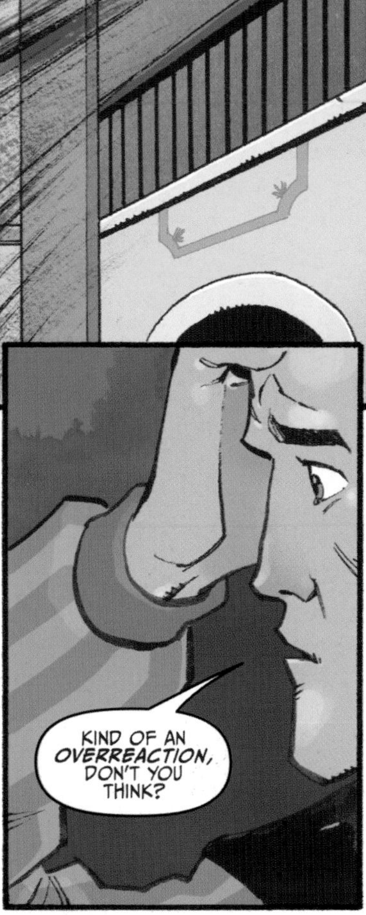
KIND OF AN OVERREACTION, DON'T YOU THINK?

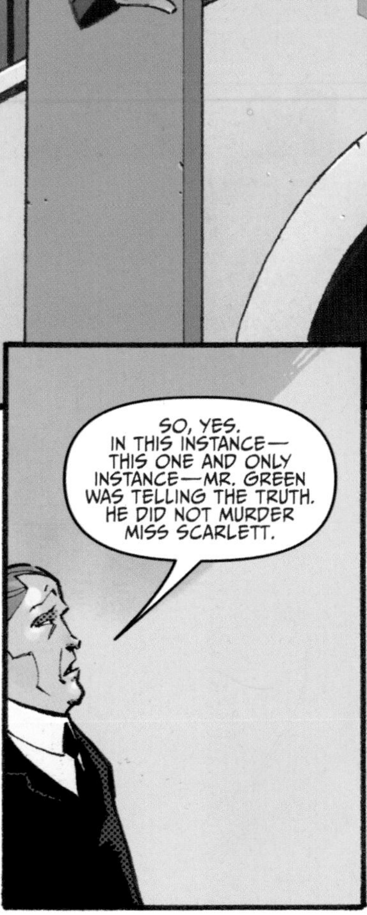
SO, YES. IN THIS INSTANCE—THIS ONE AND ONLY INSTANCE—MR. GREEN WAS TELLING THE TRUTH. HE DID NOT MURDER MISS SCARLETT.

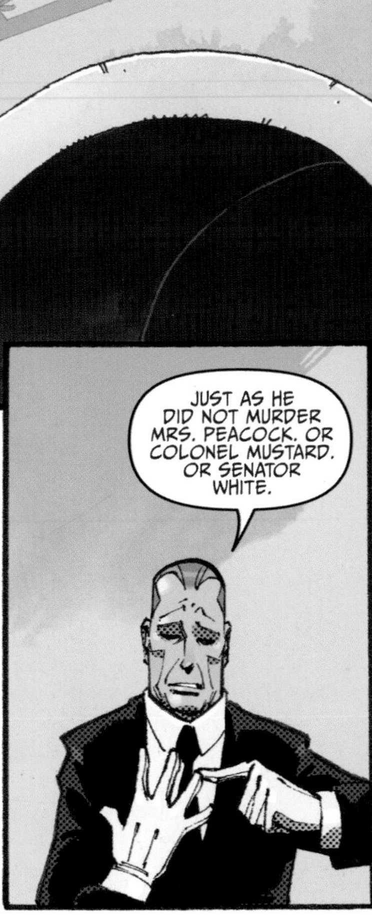
JUST AS HE DID NOT MURDER MRS. PEACOCK. OR COLONEL MUSTARD. OR SENATOR WHITE.

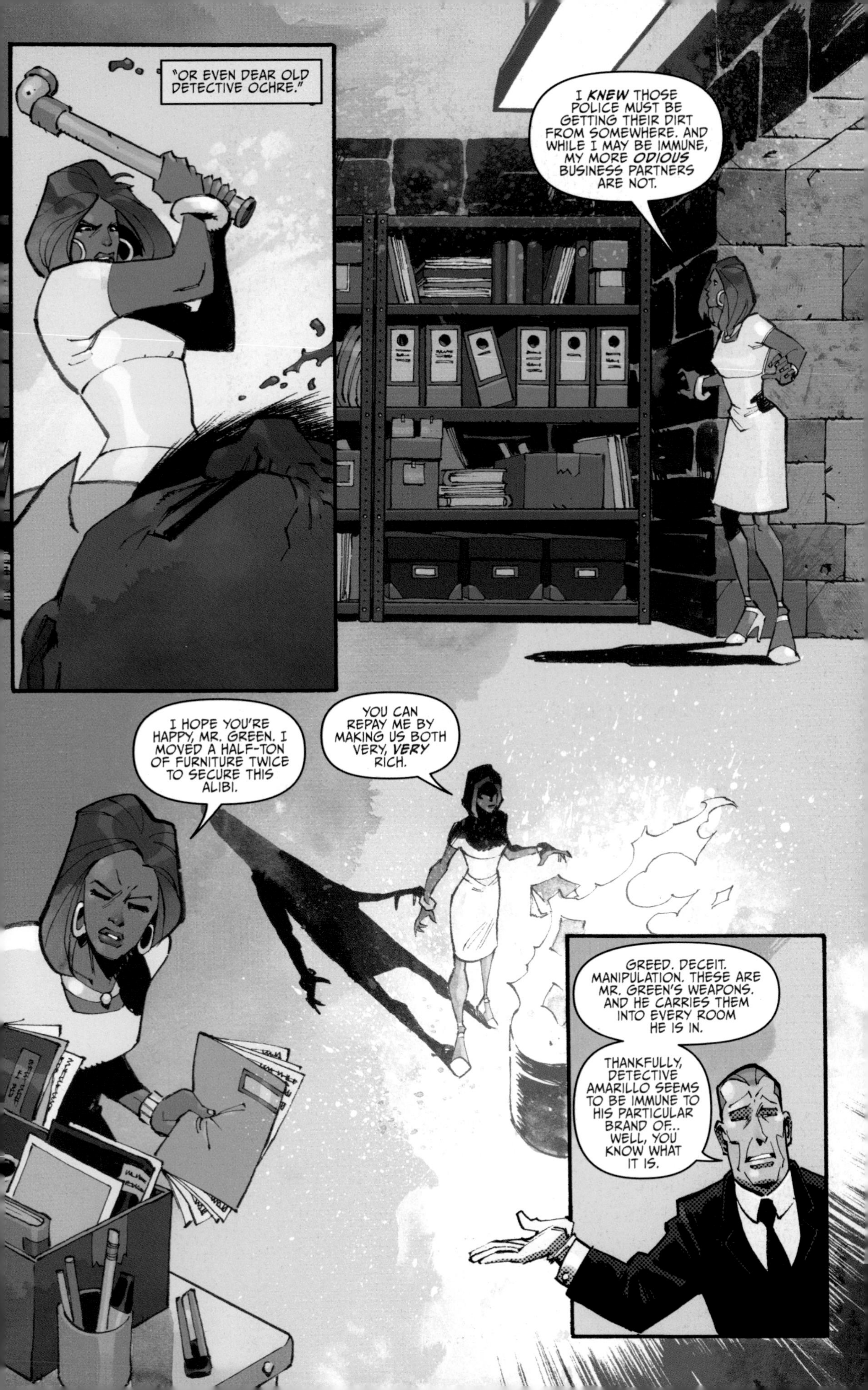
"OR EVEN DEAR OLD DETECTIVE OCHRE."
I KNEW THOSE POLICE MUST BE GETTING THEIR DIRT FROM SOMEWHERE. AND WHILE I MAY BE IMMUNE, MY MORE ODIOUS BUSINESS PARTNERS ARE NOT.
I HOPE YOU'RE HAPPY, MR. GREEN. I MOVED A HALF-TON OF FURNITURE TWICE TO SECURE THIS ALIBI.
YOU CAN REPAY ME BY MAKING US BOTH VERY, VERY RICH.
GREED. DECEIT. MANIPULATION. THESE ARE MR. GREEN'S WEAPONS. AND HE CARRIES THEM INTO EVERY ROOM HE IS IN.
THANKFULLY, DETECTIVE AMARILLO SEEMS TO BE IMMUNE TO HIS PARTICULAR BRAND OF... WELL, YOU KNOW WHAT IT IS.

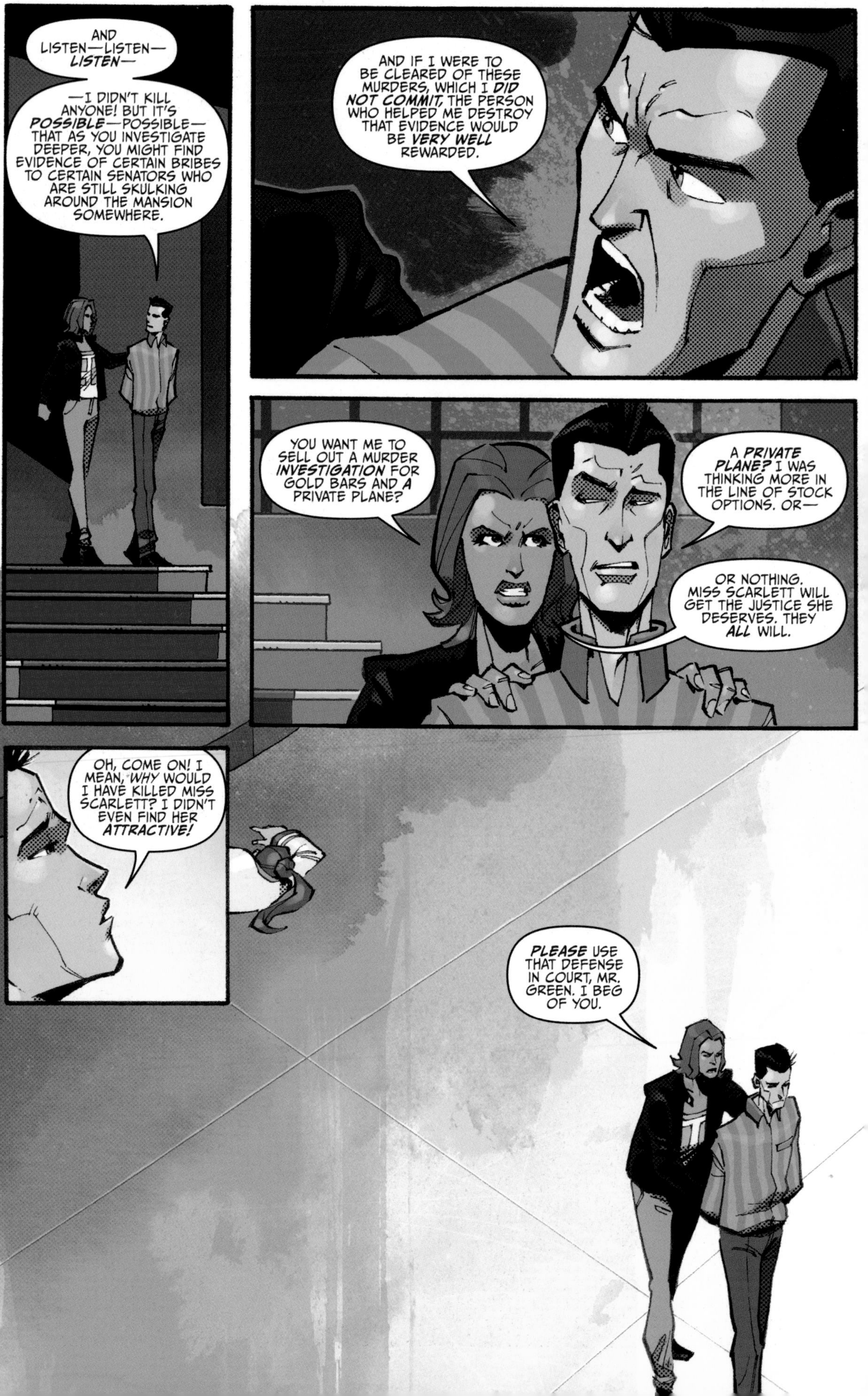
AND LISTEN—LISTEN—LISTEN—
—I DIDN'T KILL ANYONE! BUT IT'S POSSIBLE—POSSIBLE—THAT AS YOU INVESTIGATE DEEPER, YOU MIGHT FIND EVIDENCE OF CERTAIN BRIBES TO CERTAIN SENATORS WHO ARE STILL SKULKING AROUND THE MANSION SOMEWHERE.
AND IF I WERE TO BE CLEARED OF THESE MURDERS, WHICH I DID NOT COMMIT, THE PERSON WHO HELPED ME DESTROY THAT EVIDENCE WOULD BE VERY WELL REWARDED.
YOU WANT ME TO SELL OUT A MURDER INVESTIGATION FOR GOLD BARS AND A PRIVATE PLANE?
A PRIVATE PLANE? I WAS THINKING MORE IN THE LINE OF STOCK OPTIONS. OR—
OR NOTHING. MISS SCARLETT WILL GET THE JUSTICE SHE DESERVES. THEY ALL WILL.
OH, COME ON! I MEAN, WHY WOULD I HAVE KILLED MISS SCARLETT? I DIDN'T EVEN FIND HER ATTRACTIVE!
PLEASE USE THAT DEFENSE IN COURT, MR. GREEN. I BEG OF YOU.

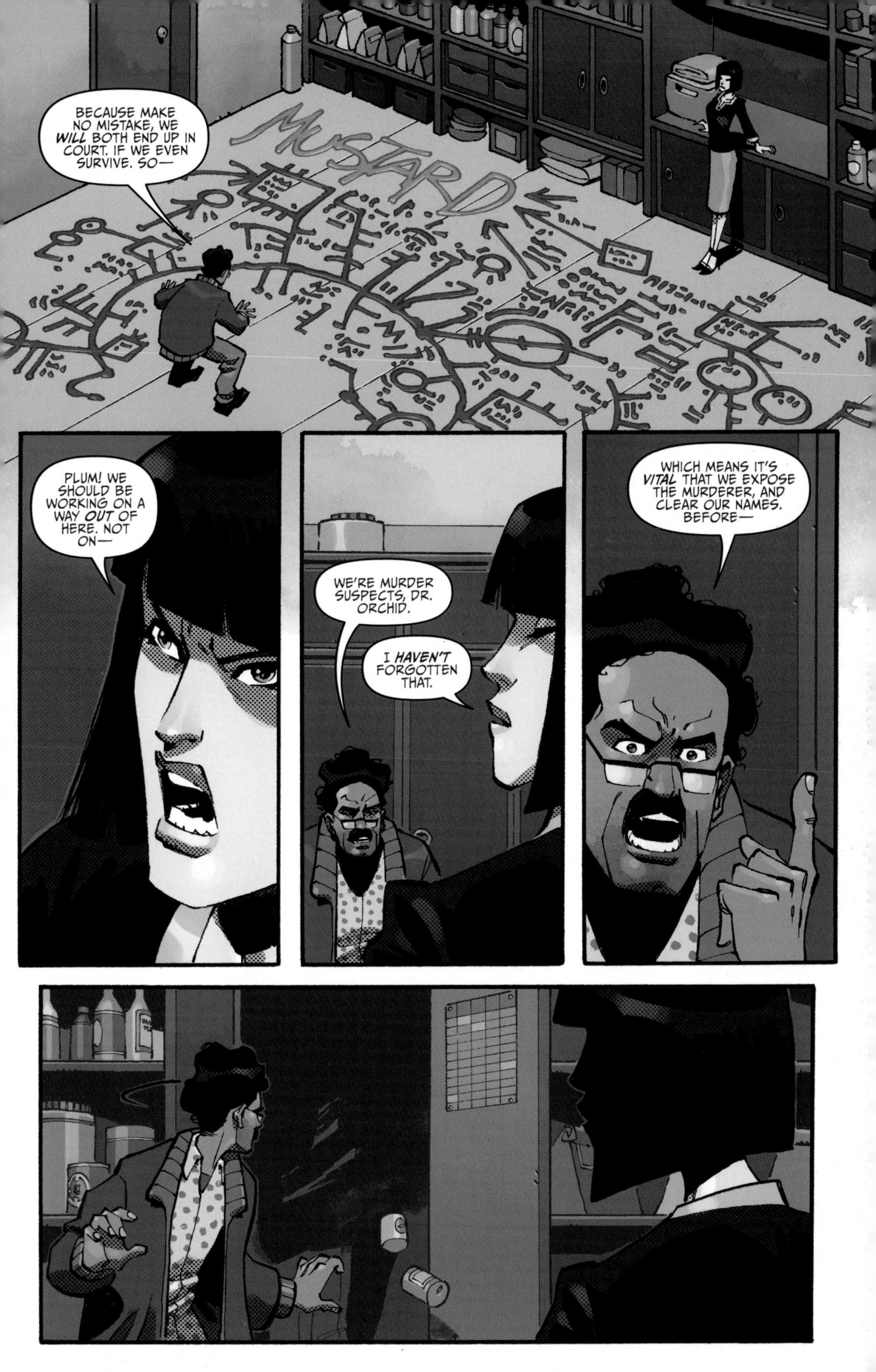
BECAUSE MAKE NO MISTAKE, WE *WILL* BOTH END UP IN COURT. IF WE EVEN SURVIVE. SO—
MUSTARD
PLUM! WE SHOULD BE WORKING ON A WAY *OUT* OF HERE. NOT ON—
WE'RE MURDER SUSPECTS, DR. ORCHID.
I *HAVEN'T* FORGOTTEN THAT.
WHICH MEANS IT'S *VITAL* THAT WE EXPOSE THE MURDERER, AND CLEAR OUR NAMES. BEFORE—

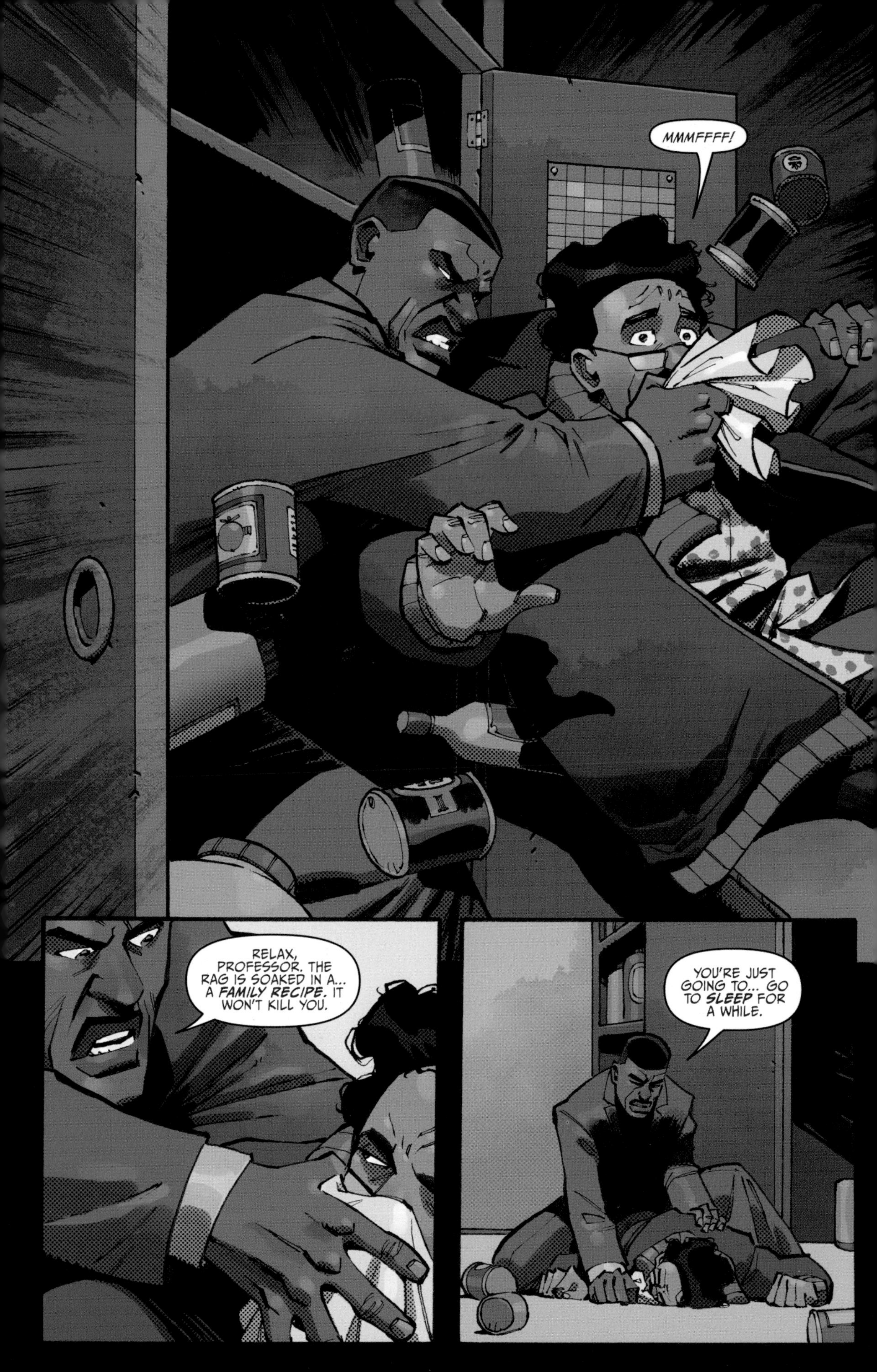
MMMFFFF!
RELAX, PROFESSOR. THE RAG IS SOAKED IN A... A *FAMILY RECIPE.* IT WON'T KILL YOU.
YOU'RE JUST GOING TO... GO TO *SLEEP* FOR A WHILE.

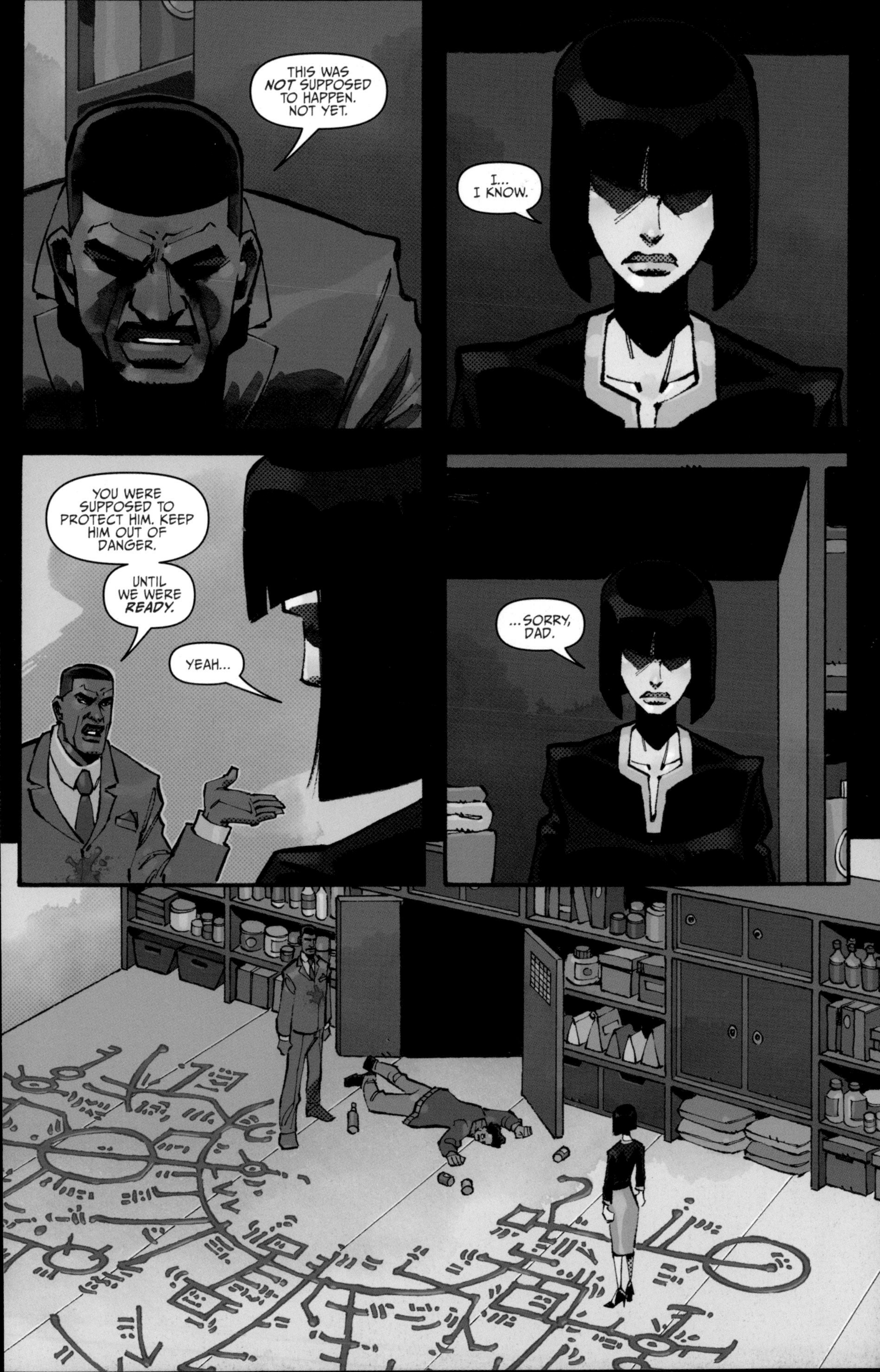
THIS WAS NOT SUPPOSED TO HAPPEN. NOT YET.
I... I KNOW.
YOU WERE SUPPOSED TO PROTECT HIM. KEEP HIM OUT OF DANGER.
UNTIL WE WERE READY.
YEAH...
...SORRY, DAD.

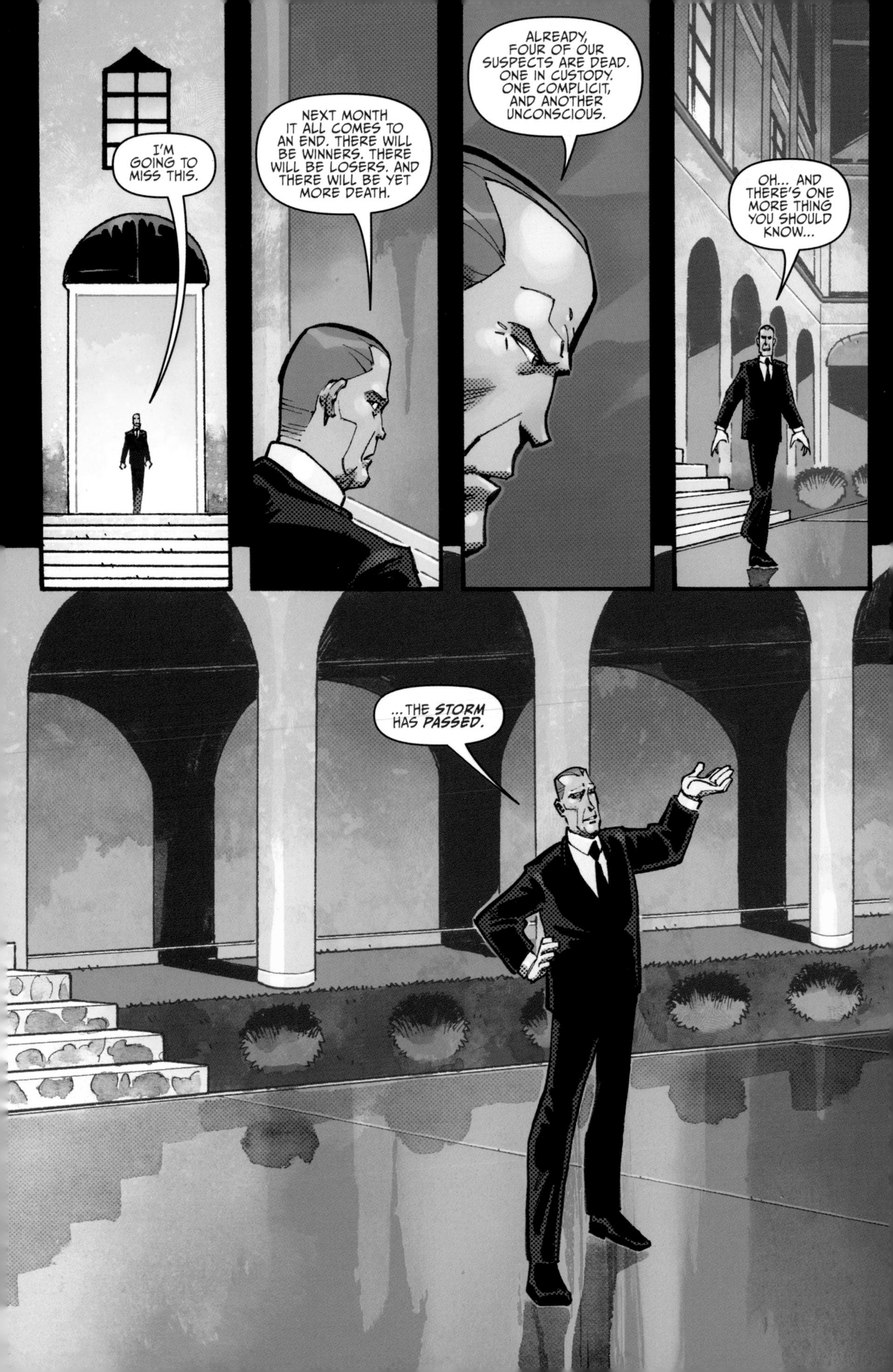
I'M GOING TO MISS THIS.
NEXT MONTH IT ALL COMES TO AN END. THERE WILL BE WINNERS. THERE WILL BE LOSERS. AND THERE WILL BE YET MORE DEATH.
ALREADY, FOUR OF OUR SUSPECTS ARE DEAD. ONE IN CUSTODY. ONE COMPLICIT, AND ANOTHER UNCONSCIOUS.
OH... AND THERE'S ONE MORE THING YOU SHOULD KNOW...
...THE STORM HAS PASSED.

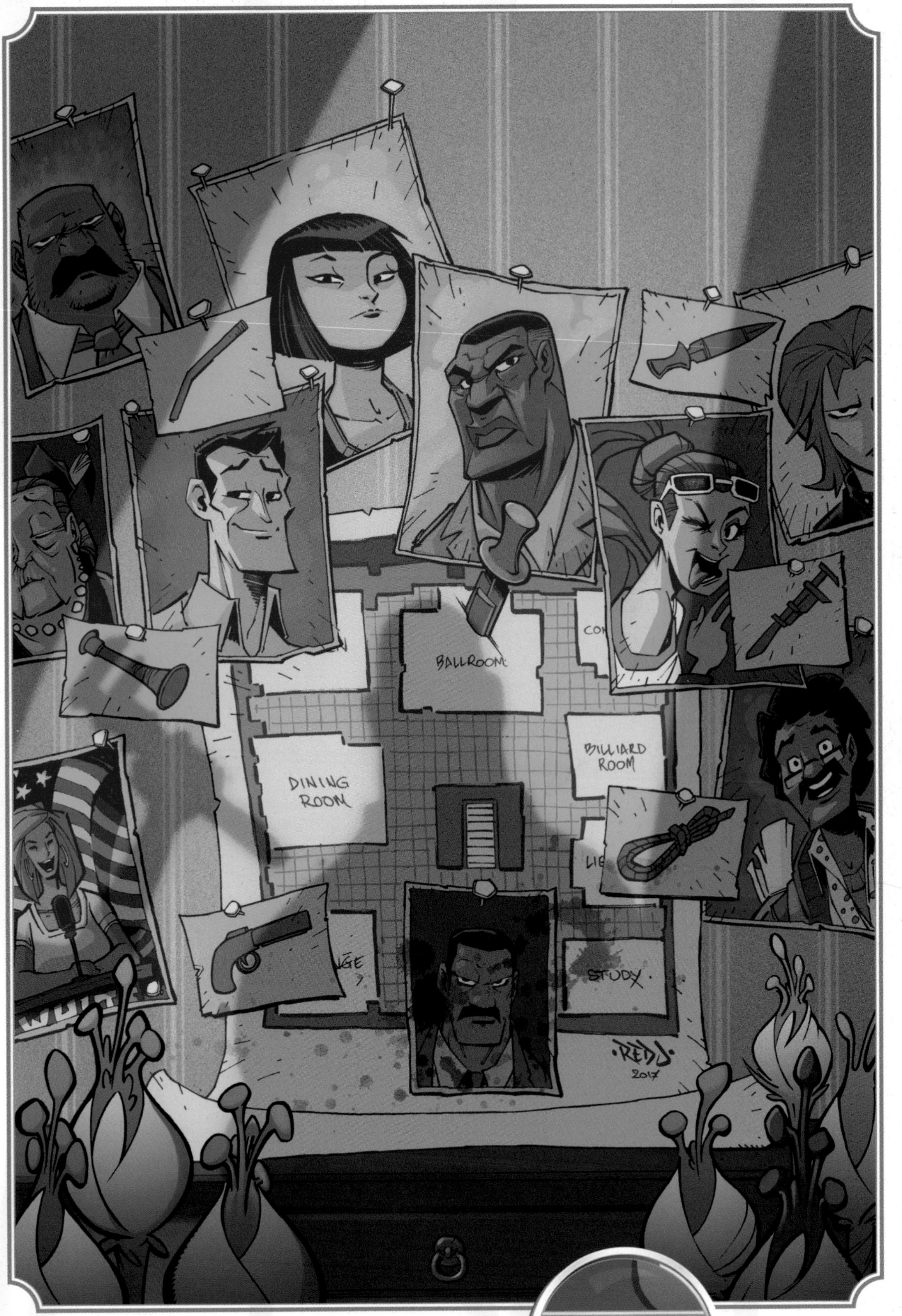
BALLROOM
BILLIARD ROOM
DINING ROOM
STUDY
REDD 2017

COVER ART BY
JON SOMMARIVA

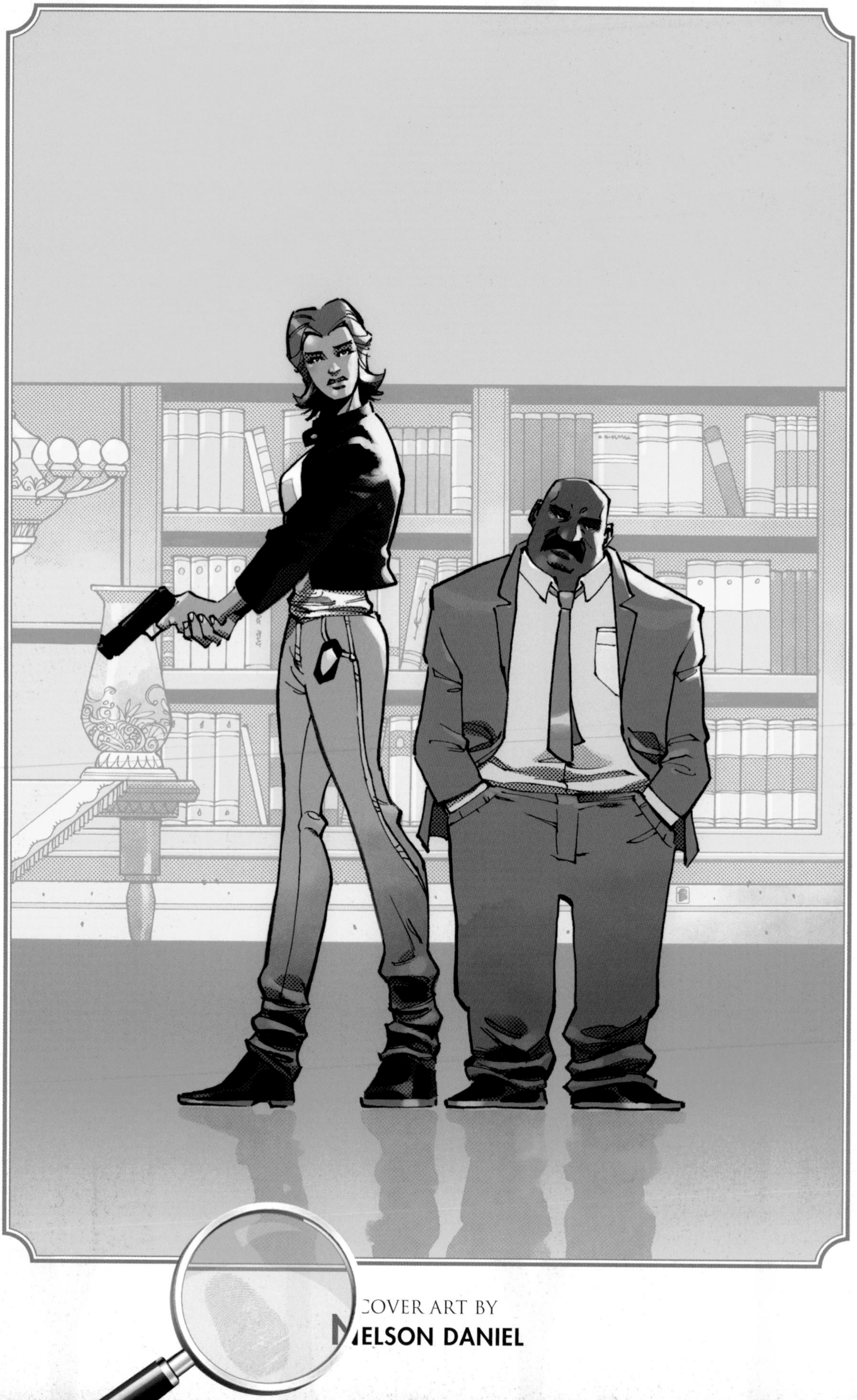

COVER ART BY
NELSON DANIEL

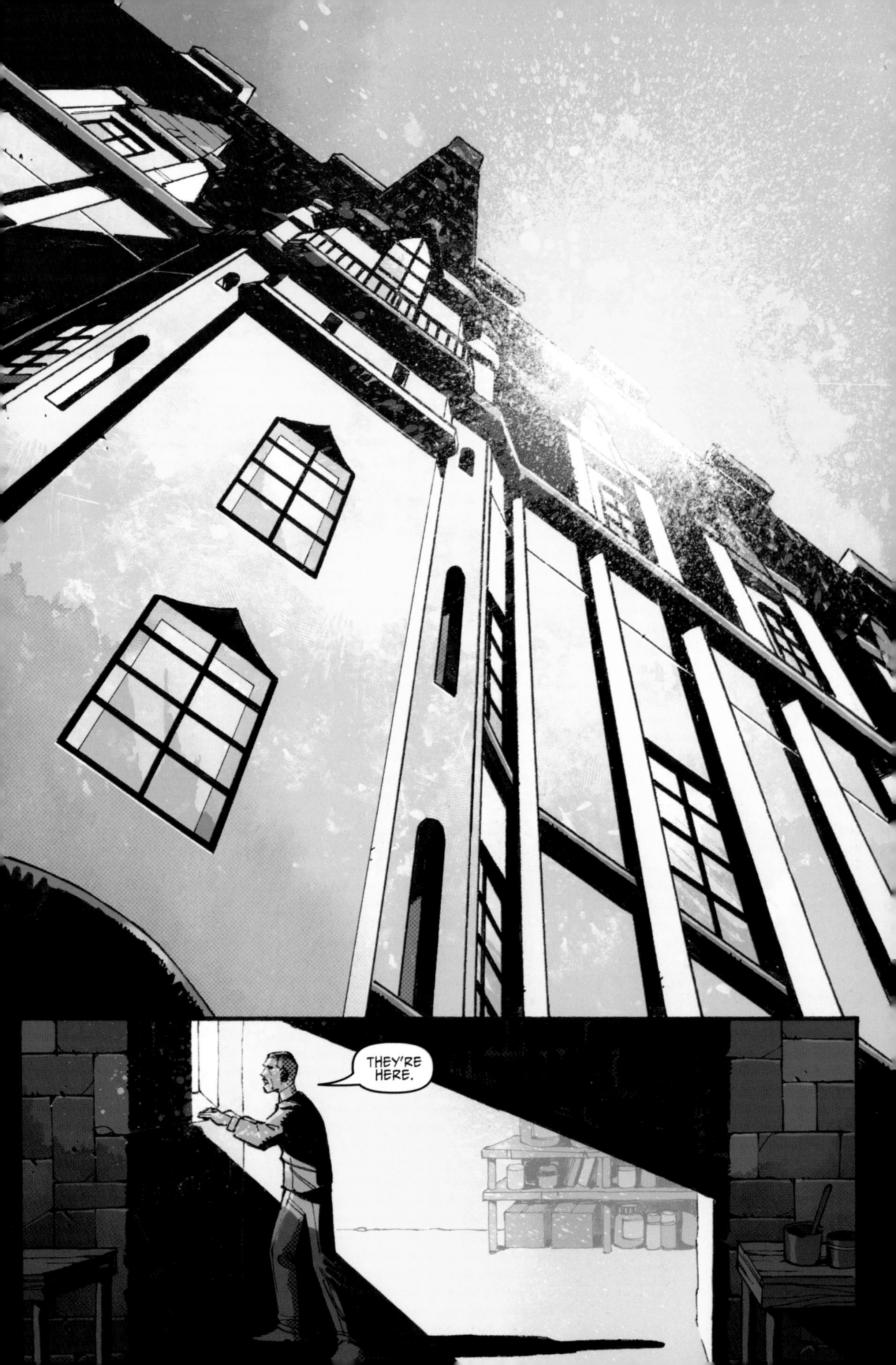
THEY'RE HERE.

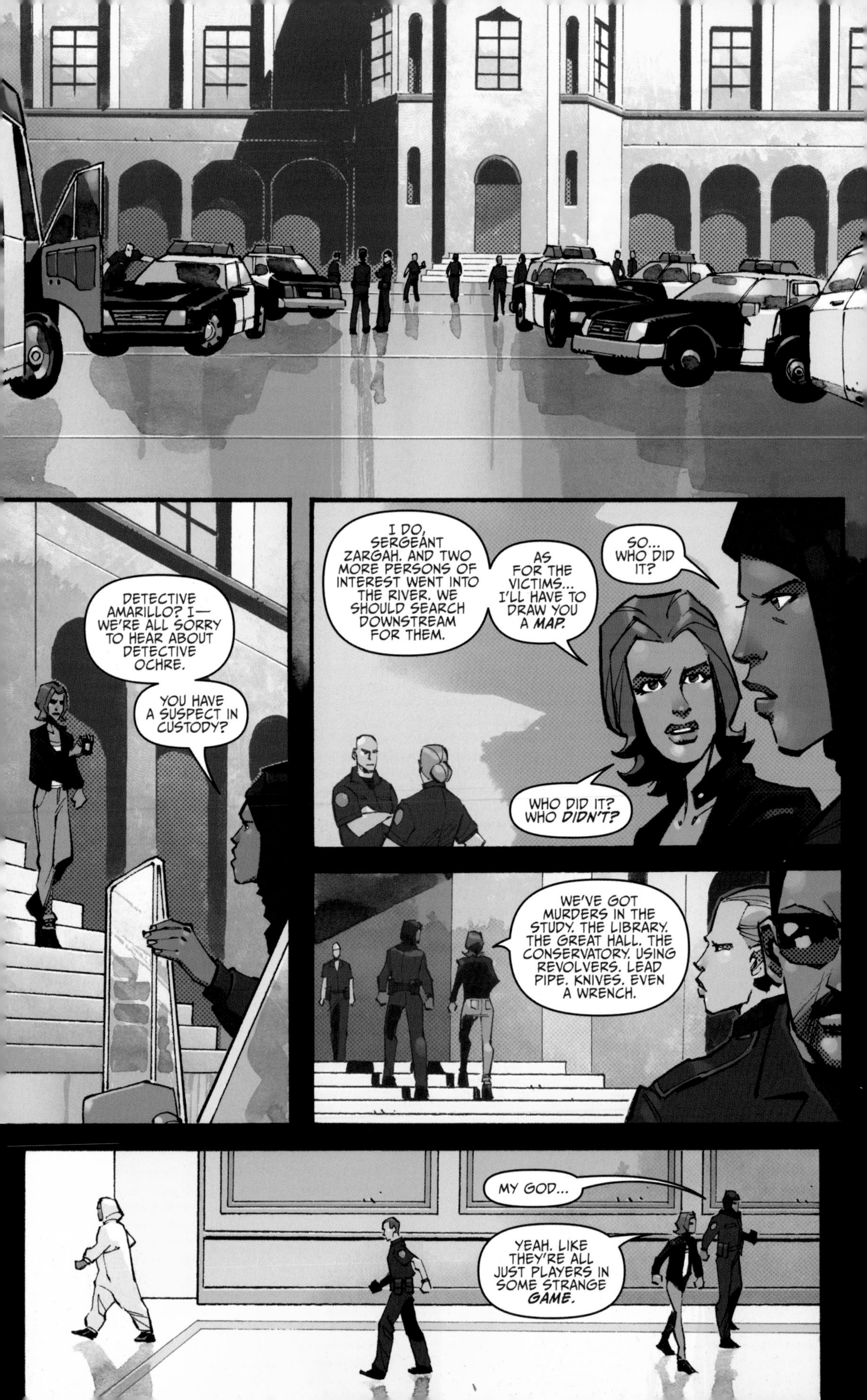
DETECTIVE AMARILLO? I— WE'RE ALL SORRY TO HEAR ABOUT DETECTIVE OCHRE.
YOU HAVE A SUSPECT IN CUSTODY?
I DO, SERGEANT ZARGAH. AND TWO MORE PERSONS OF INTEREST WENT INTO THE RIVER. WE SHOULD SEARCH DOWNSTREAM FOR THEM.
AS FOR THE VICTIMS... I'LL HAVE TO DRAW YOU A *MAP.*
SO... WHO DID IT?
WHO DID IT? WHO *DIDN'T?*
WE'VE GOT MURDERS IN THE STUDY. THE LIBRARY. THE GREAT HALL. THE CONSERVATORY. USING REVOLVERS. LEAD PIPE. KNIVES. EVEN A WRENCH.
MY GOD...
YEAH. LIKE THEY'RE ALL JUST PLAYERS IN SOME STRANGE *GAME.*

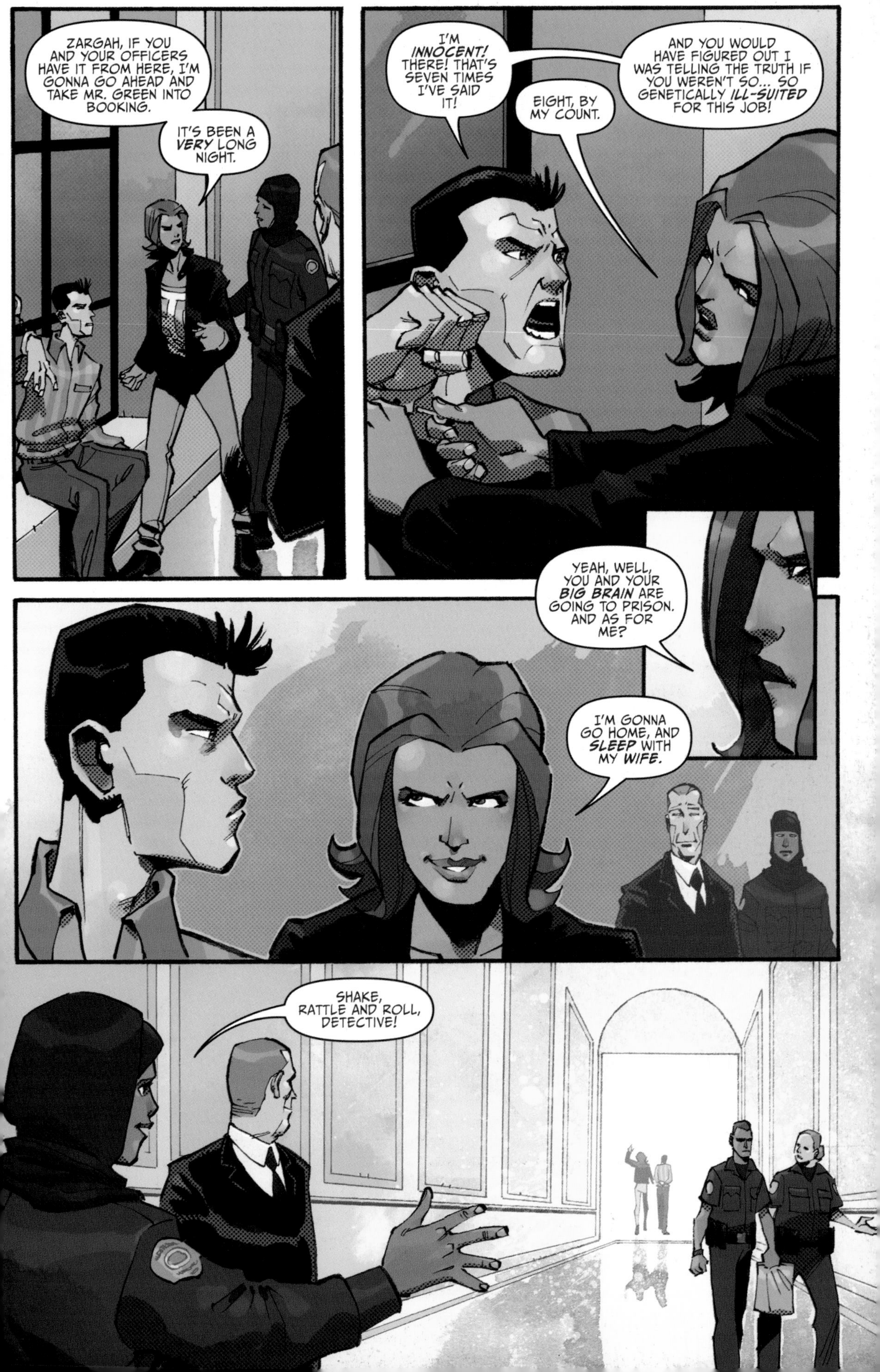
ZARGAH, IF YOU AND YOUR OFFICERS HAVE IT FROM HERE, I'M GONNA GO AHEAD AND TAKE MR. GREEN INTO BOOKING.
IT'S BEEN A VERY LONG NIGHT.
I'M INNOCENT! THERE! THAT'S SEVEN TIMES I'VE SAID IT!
EIGHT, BY MY COUNT.
AND YOU WOULD HAVE FIGURED OUT I WAS TELLING THE TRUTH IF YOU WEREN'T SO... SO GENETICALLY ILL-SUITED FOR THIS JOB!
YEAH, WELL, YOU AND YOUR BIG BRAIN ARE GOING TO PRISON. AND AS FOR ME?
I'M GONNA GO HOME, AND SLEEP WITH MY WIFE.
SHAKE, RATTLE AND ROLL, DETECTIVE!

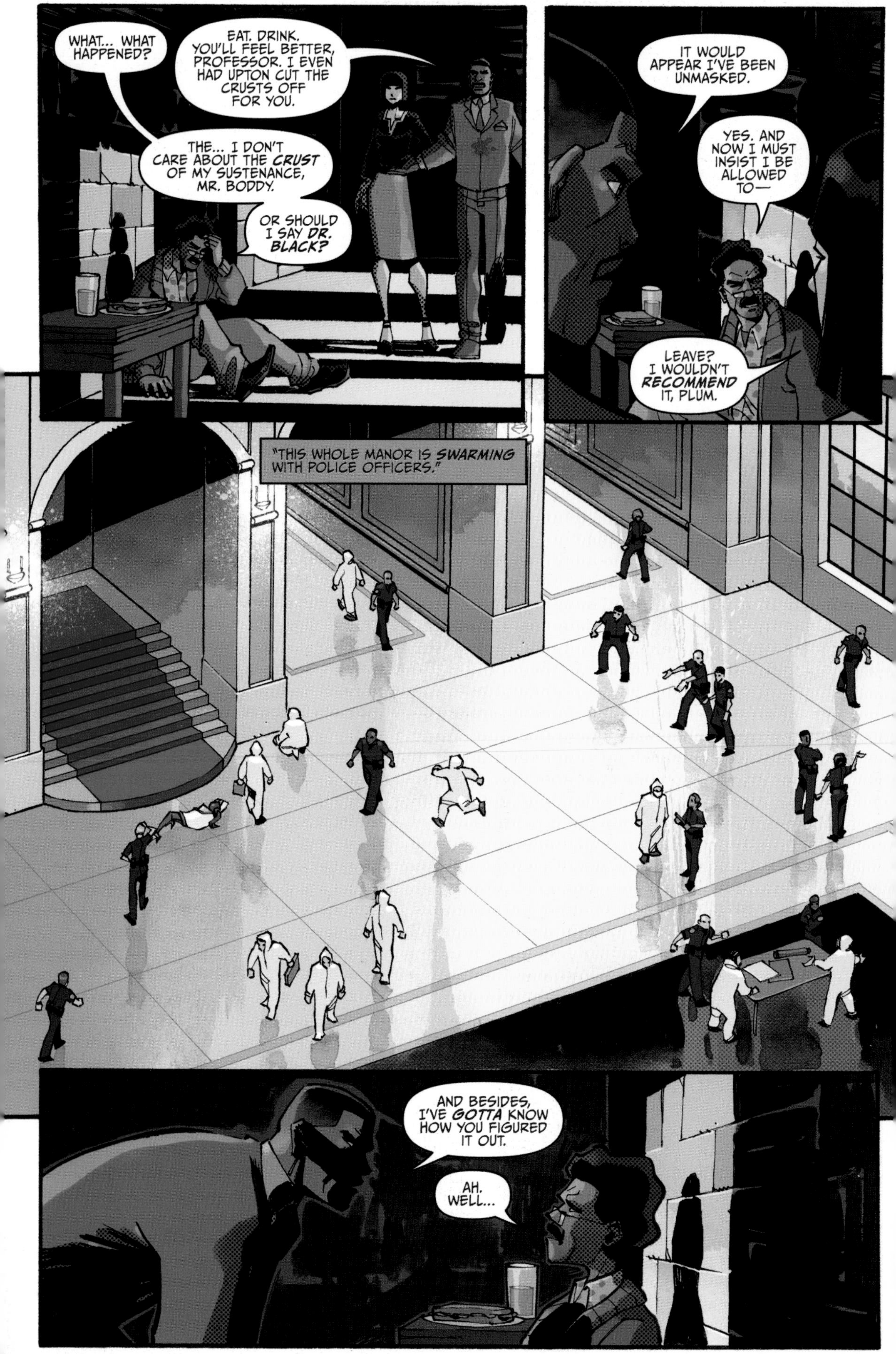
WHAT... WHAT HAPPENED?
EAT. DRINK. YOU'LL FEEL BETTER, PROFESSOR. I EVEN HAD UPTON CUT THE CRUSTS OFF FOR YOU.
THE... I DON'T CARE ABOUT THE CRUST OF MY SUSTENANCE, MR. BODDY.
OR SHOULD I SAY DR. BLACK?
IT WOULD APPEAR I'VE BEEN UNMASKED.
YES. AND NOW I MUST INSIST I BE ALLOWED TO—
LEAVE? I WOULDN'T RECOMMEND IT, PLUM.
"THIS WHOLE MANOR IS SWARMING WITH POLICE OFFICERS."
AND BESIDES, I'VE GOTTA KNOW HOW YOU FIGURED IT OUT.
AH. WELL...

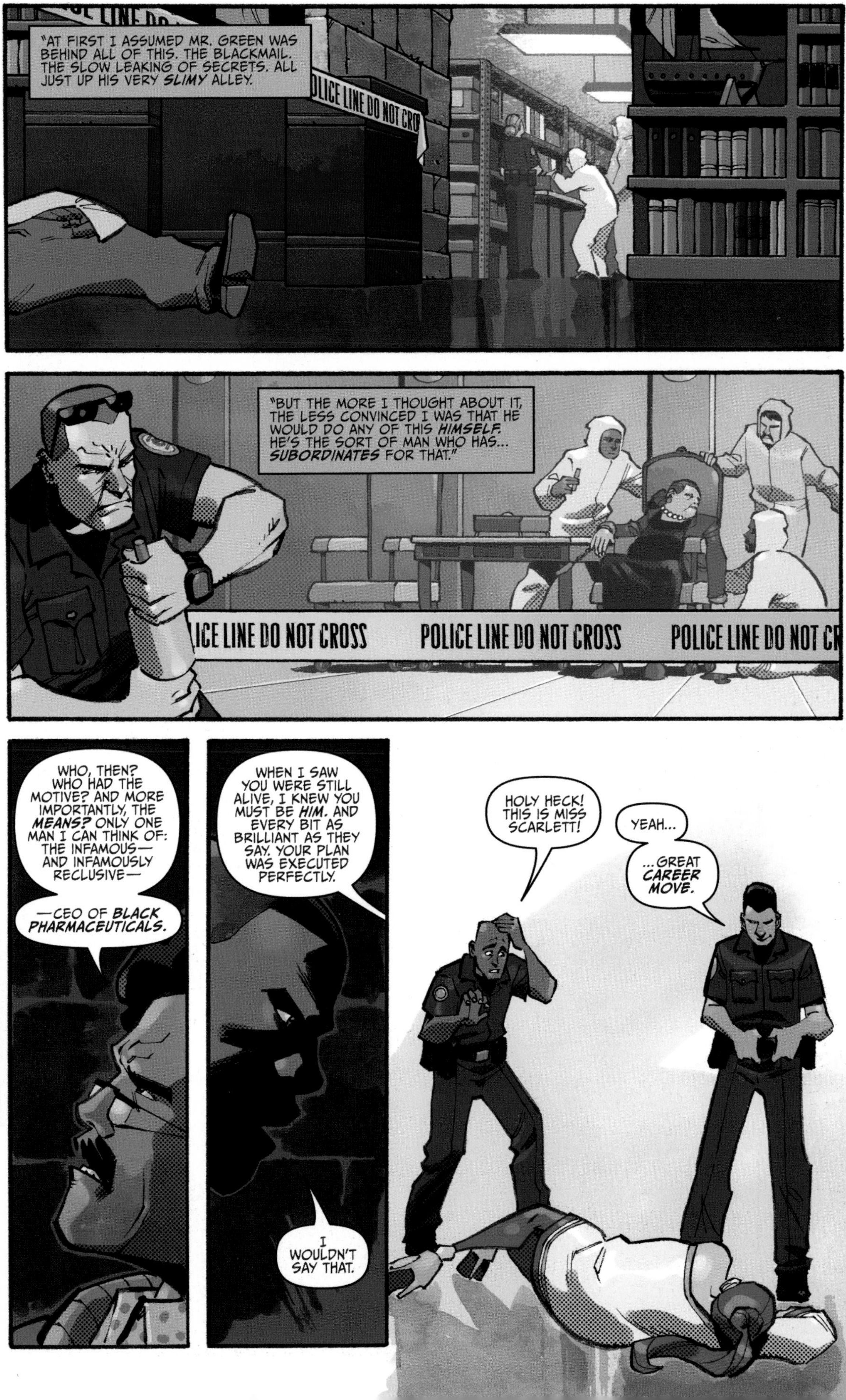
"AT FIRST I ASSUMED MR. GREEN WAS BEHIND ALL OF THIS. THE BLACKMAIL. THE SLOW LEAKING OF SECRETS. ALL JUST UP HIS VERY SLIMY ALLEY.
POLICE LINE DO NOT CROS
"BUT THE MORE I THOUGHT ABOUT IT, THE LESS CONVINCED I WAS THAT HE WOULD DO ANY OF THIS HIMSELF. HE'S THE SORT OF MAN WHO HAS... SUBORDINATES FOR THAT."
LICE LINE DO NOT CROSS
POLICE LINE DO NOT CROSS
POLICE LINE DO NOT C
WHO, THEN? WHO HAD THE MOTIVE? AND MORE IMPORTANTLY, THE MEANS? ONLY ONE MAN I CAN THINK OF: THE INFAMOUS— AND INFAMOUSLY RECLUSIVE—
—CEO OF BLACK PHARMACEUTICALS.
WHEN I SAW YOU WERE STILL ALIVE, I KNEW YOU MUST BE HIM. AND EVERY BIT AS BRILLIANT AS THEY SAY. YOUR PLAN WAS EXECUTED PERFECTLY.
I WOULDN'T SAY THAT.
HOLY HECK! THIS IS MISS SCARLETT!
YEAH...
...GREAT CAREER MOVE.

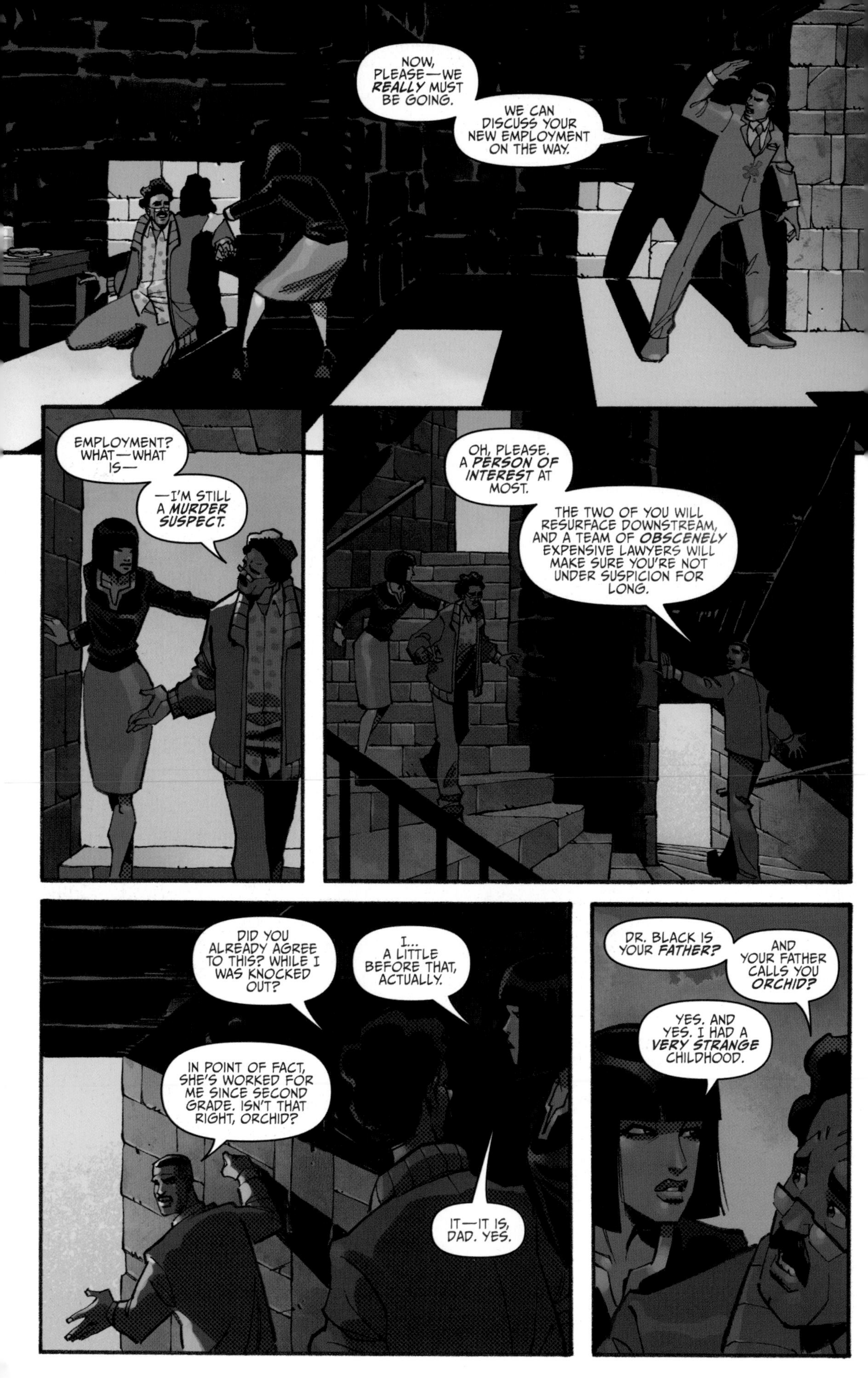
NOW, PLEASE—WE REALLY MUST BE GOING.
WE CAN DISCUSS YOUR NEW EMPLOYMENT ON THE WAY.
EMPLOYMENT? WHAT—WHAT IS—
—I'M STILL A MURDER SUSPECT.
OH, PLEASE. A PERSON OF INTEREST AT MOST.
THE TWO OF YOU WILL RESURFACE DOWNSTREAM, AND A TEAM OF OBSCENELY EXPENSIVE LAWYERS WILL MAKE SURE YOU'RE NOT UNDER SUSPICION FOR LONG.
DID YOU ALREADY AGREE TO THIS? WHILE I WAS KNOCKED OUT?
I... A LITTLE BEFORE THAT, ACTUALLY.
IN POINT OF FACT, SHE'S WORKED FOR ME SINCE SECOND GRADE. ISN'T THAT RIGHT, ORCHID?
IT—IT IS, DAD. YES.
DR. BLACK IS YOUR FATHER?
AND YOUR FATHER CALLS YOU ORCHID?
YES. AND YES. I HAD A VERY STRANGE CHILDHOOD.

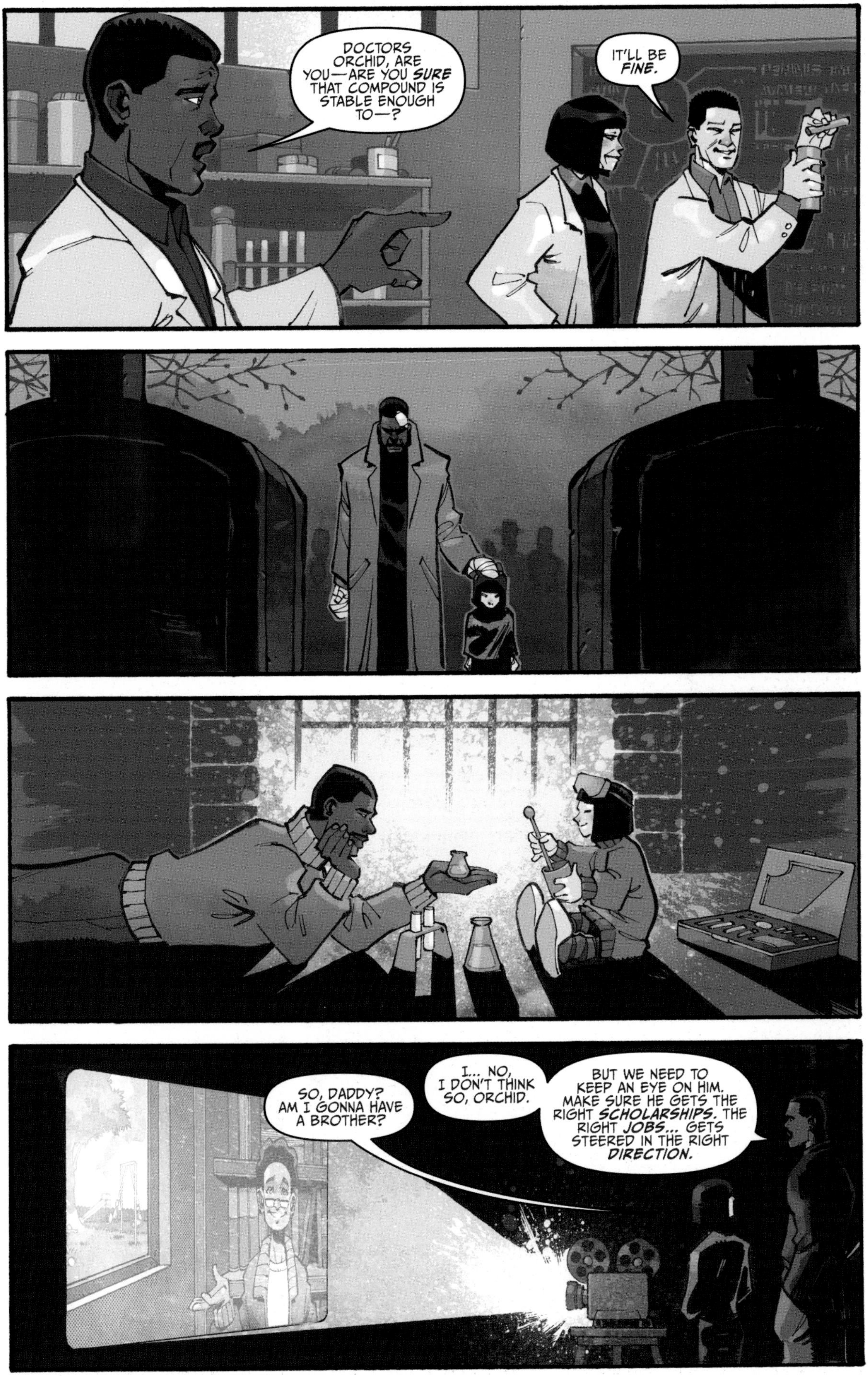
DOCTORS ORCHID, ARE YOU—ARE YOU SURE THAT COMPOUND IS STABLE ENOUGH TO—?
IT'LL BE FINE.
SO, DADDY? AM I GONNA HAVE A BROTHER?
I... NO, I DON'T THINK SO, ORCHID.
BUT WE NEED TO KEEP AN EYE ON HIM. MAKE SURE HE GETS THE RIGHT SCHOLARSHIPS. THE RIGHT JOBS... GETS STEERED IN THE RIGHT DIRECTION.

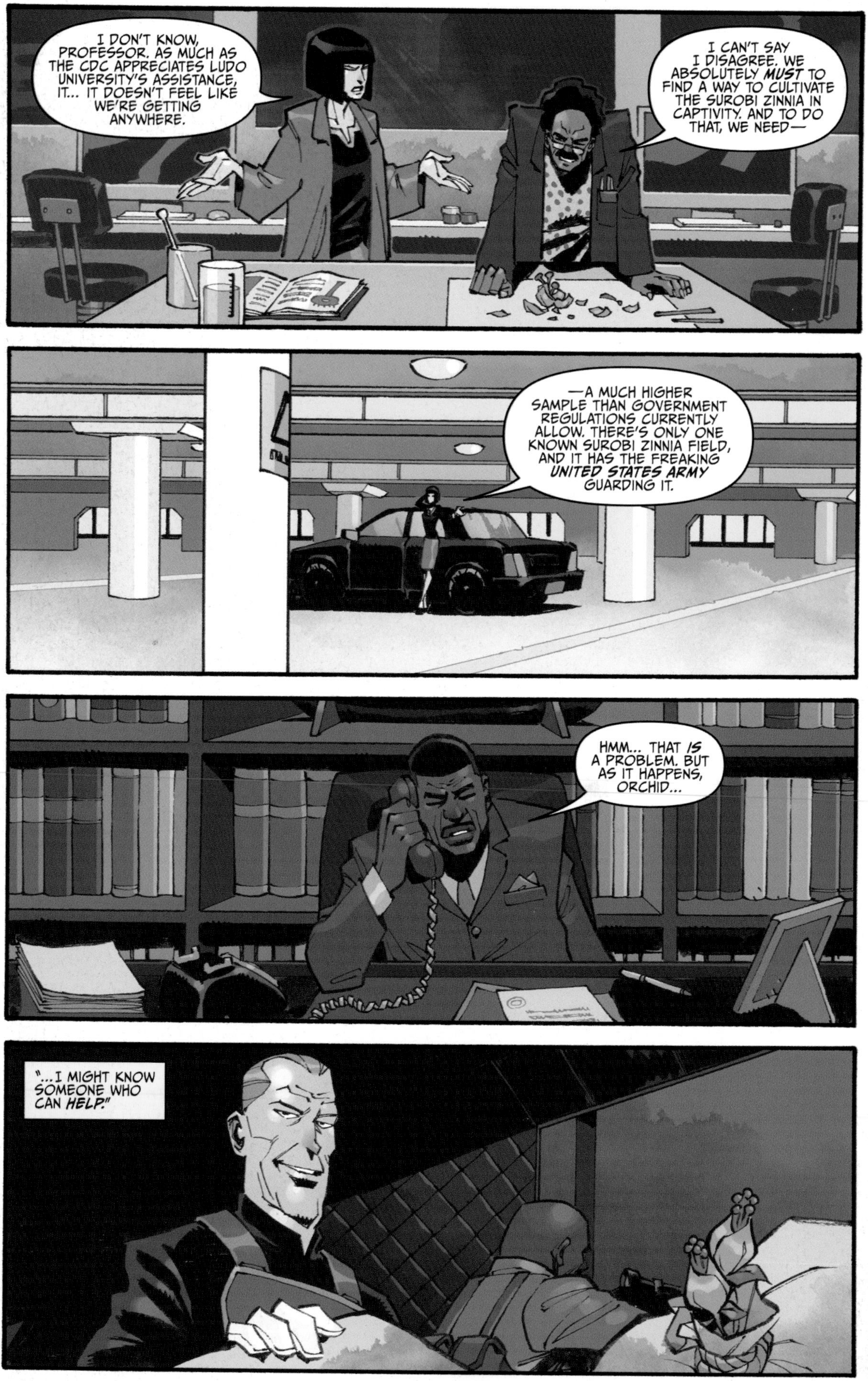
I DON'T KNOW, PROFESSOR. AS MUCH AS THE CDC APPRECIATES LUDO UNIVERSITY'S ASSISTANCE, IT... IT DOESN'T FEEL LIKE WE'RE GETTING ANYWHERE.
I CAN'T SAY I DISAGREE. WE ABSOLUTELY MUST TO FIND A WAY TO CULTIVATE THE SUROBI ZINNIA IN CAPTIVITY. AND TO DO THAT, WE NEED—
—A MUCH HIGHER SAMPLE THAN GOVERNMENT REGULATIONS CURRENTLY ALLOW. THERE'S ONLY ONE KNOWN SUROBI ZINNIA FIELD, AND IT HAS THE FREAKING UNITED STATES ARMY GUARDING IT.
HMM... THAT IS A PROBLEM. BUT AS IT HAPPENS, ORCHID...
"...I MIGHT KNOW SOMEONE WHO CAN HELP."

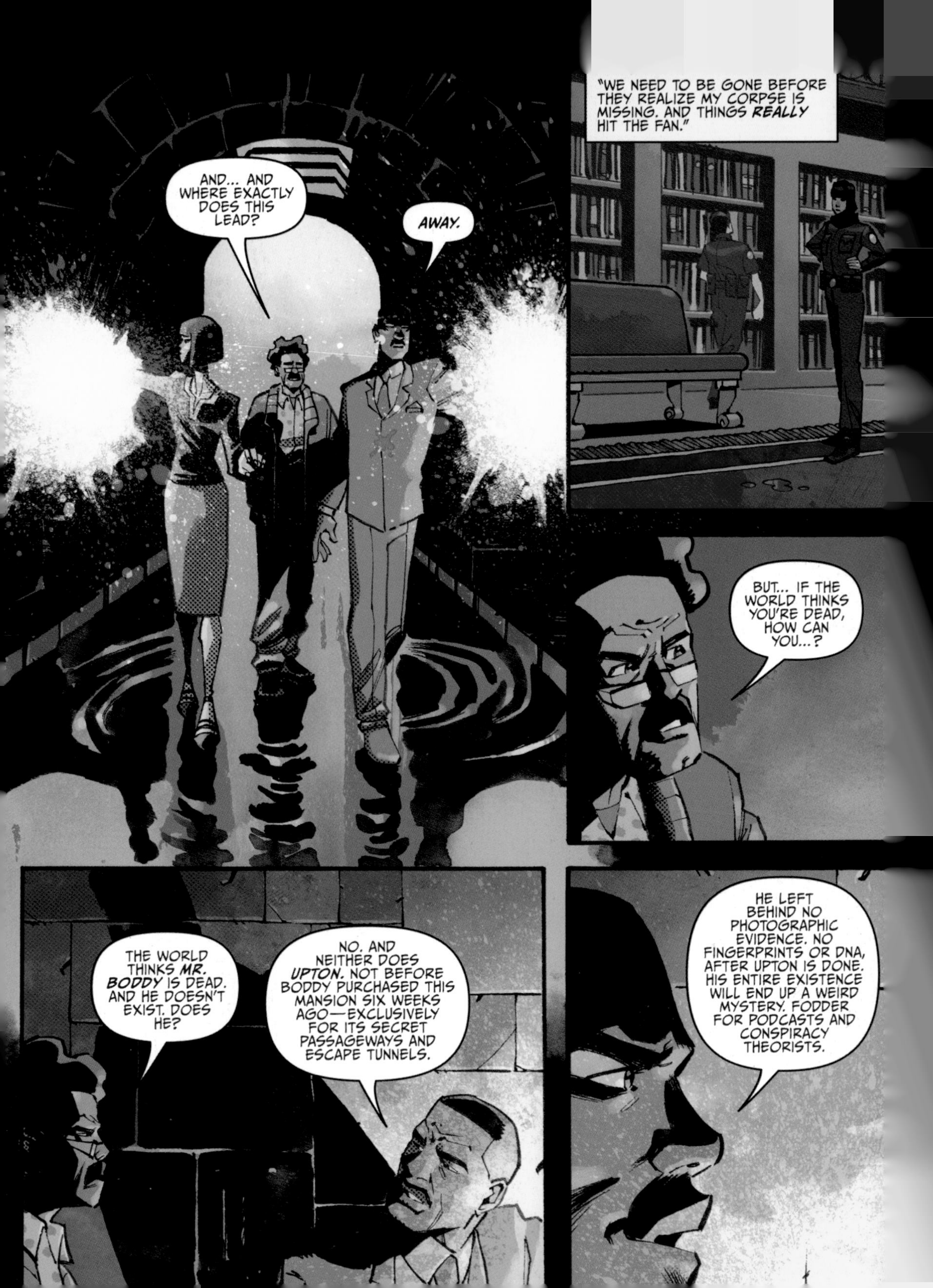
AND... AND WHERE EXACTLY DOES THIS LEAD?
AWAY.
"WE NEED TO BE GONE BEFORE THEY REALIZE MY CORPSE IS MISSING. AND THINGS REALLY HIT THE FAN."
BUT... IF THE WORLD THINKS YOU'RE DEAD, HOW CAN YOU...?
THE WORLD THINKS MR. BODDY IS DEAD. AND HE DOESN'T EXIST. DOES HE?
NO. AND NEITHER DOES UPTON. NOT BEFORE BODDY PURCHASED THIS MANSION SIX WEEKS AGO—EXCLUSIVELY FOR ITS SECRET PASSAGEWAYS AND ESCAPE TUNNELS.
HE LEFT BEHIND NO PHOTOGRAPHIC EVIDENCE. NO FINGERPRINTS OR DNA, AFTER UPTON IS DONE. HIS ENTIRE EXISTENCE WILL END UP A WEIRD MYSTERY. FODDER FOR PODCASTS AND CONSPIRACY THEORISTS.

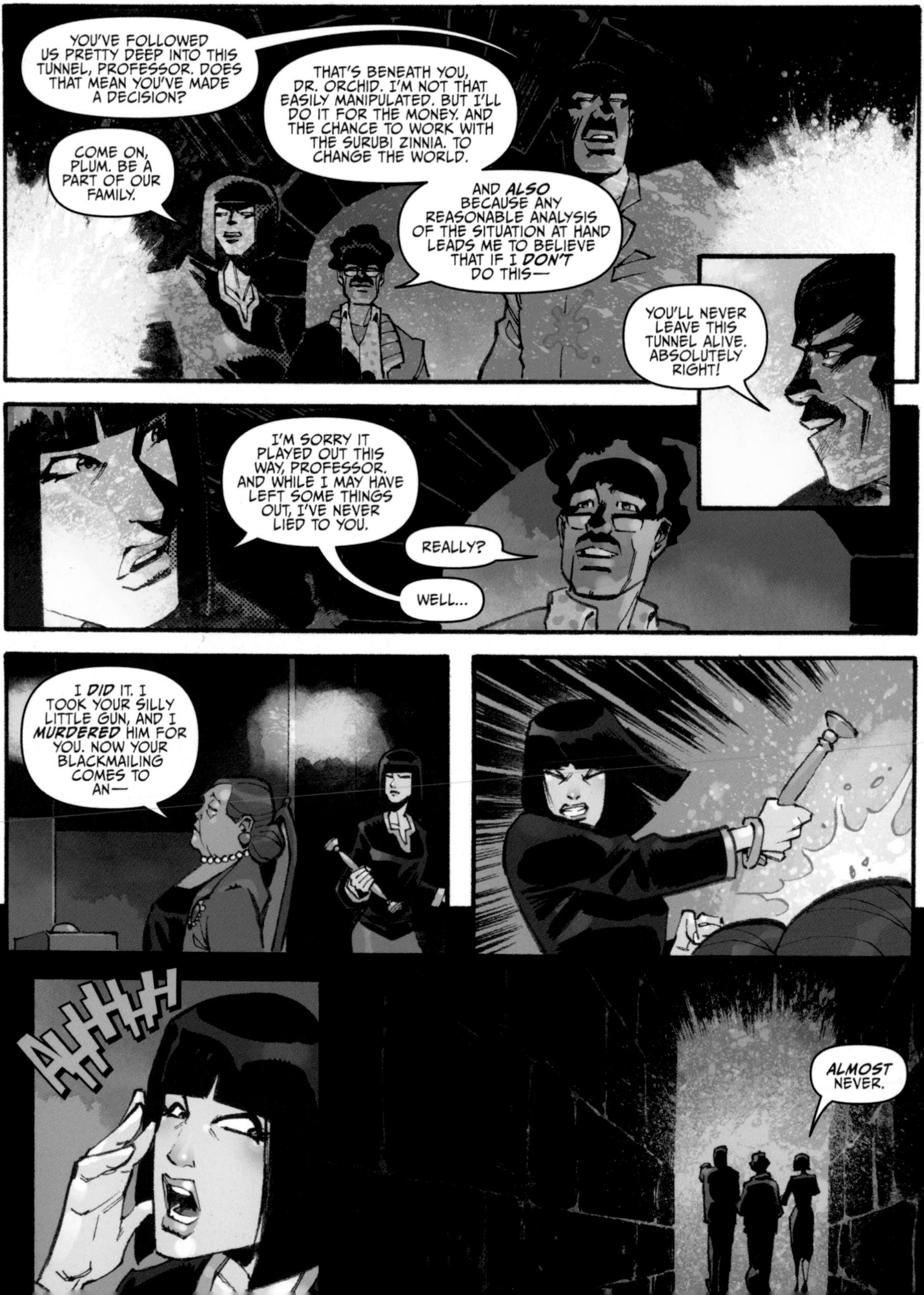

YOU'VE FOLLOWED US PRETTY DEEP INTO THIS TUNNEL, PROFESSOR. DOES THAT MEAN YOU'VE MADE A DECISION?
COME ON, PLUM. BE A PART OF OUR FAMILY.
THAT'S BENEATH YOU, DR. ORCHID. I'M NOT THAT EASILY MANIPULATED. BUT I'LL DO IT FOR THE MONEY. AND THE CHANCE TO WORK WITH THE SURUBI ZINNIA. TO CHANGE THE WORLD.
AND ALSO BECAUSE ANY REASONABLE ANALYSIS OF THE SITUATION AT HAND LEADS ME TO BELIEVE THAT IF I DON'T DO THIS—
YOU'LL NEVER LEAVE THIS TUNNEL ALIVE. ABSOLUTELY RIGHT!
I'M SORRY IT PLAYED OUT THIS WAY, PROFESSOR. AND WHILE I MAY HAVE LEFT SOME THINGS OUT, I'VE NEVER LIED TO YOU.
REALLY?
WELL...
I DID IT. I TOOK YOUR SILLY LITTLE GUN, AND I MURDERED HIM FOR YOU. NOW YOUR BLACKMAILING COMES TO AN—
AHHHH
ALMOST NEVER.

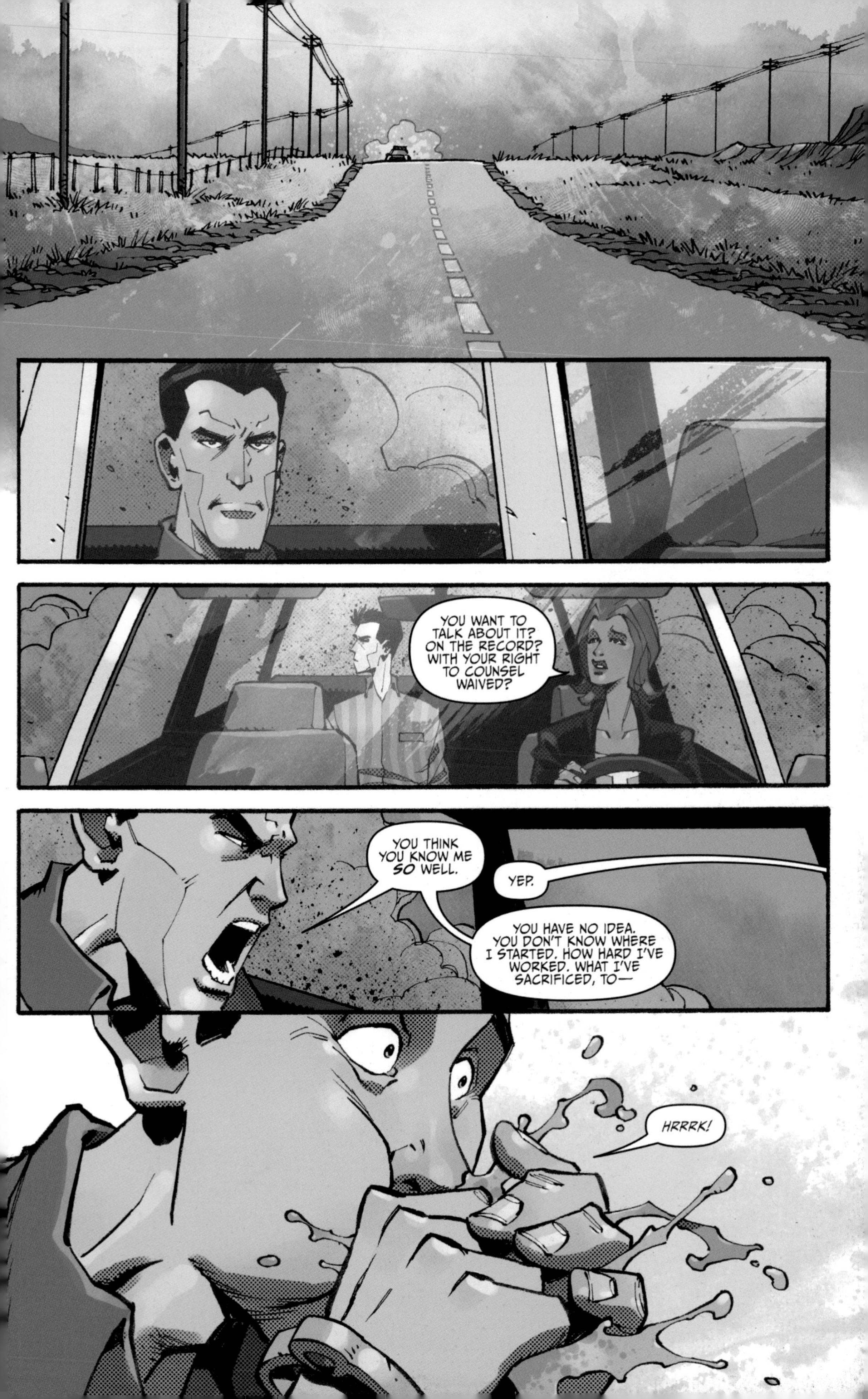
YOU WANT TO TALK ABOUT IT? ON THE RECORD? WITH YOUR RIGHT TO COUNSEL WAIVED?
YOU THINK YOU KNOW ME SO WELL.
YEP.
YOU HAVE NO IDEA. YOU DON'T KNOW WHERE I STARTED. HOW HARD I'VE WORKED. WHAT I'VE SACRIFICED, TO—
HRRRK!

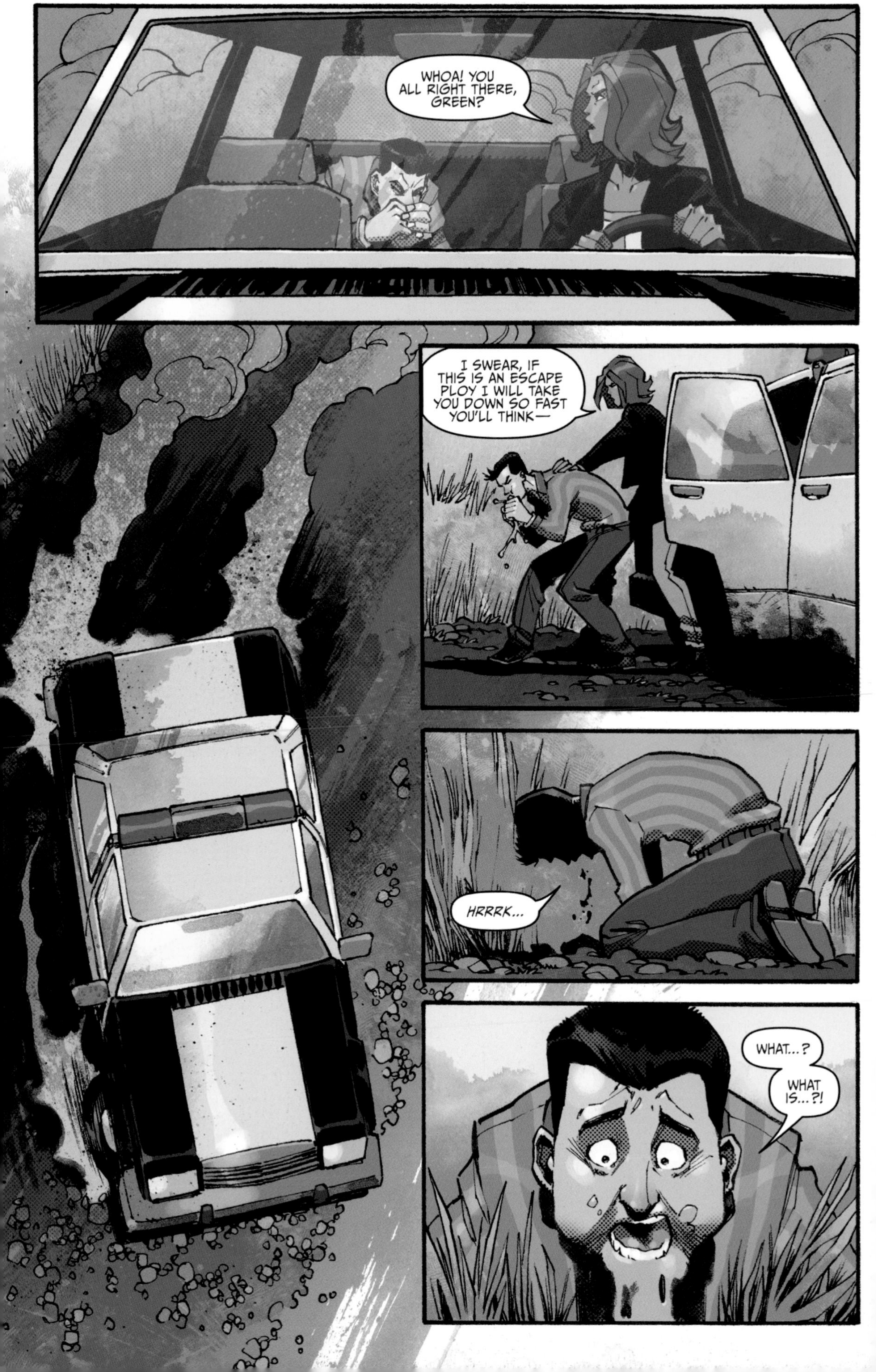
WHOA! YOU ALL RIGHT THERE, GREEN?
I SWEAR, IF THIS IS AN ESCAPE PLOY I WILL TAKE YOU DOWN SO FAST YOU'LL THINK—
HRRRK...
WHAT...?
WHAT IS...?!

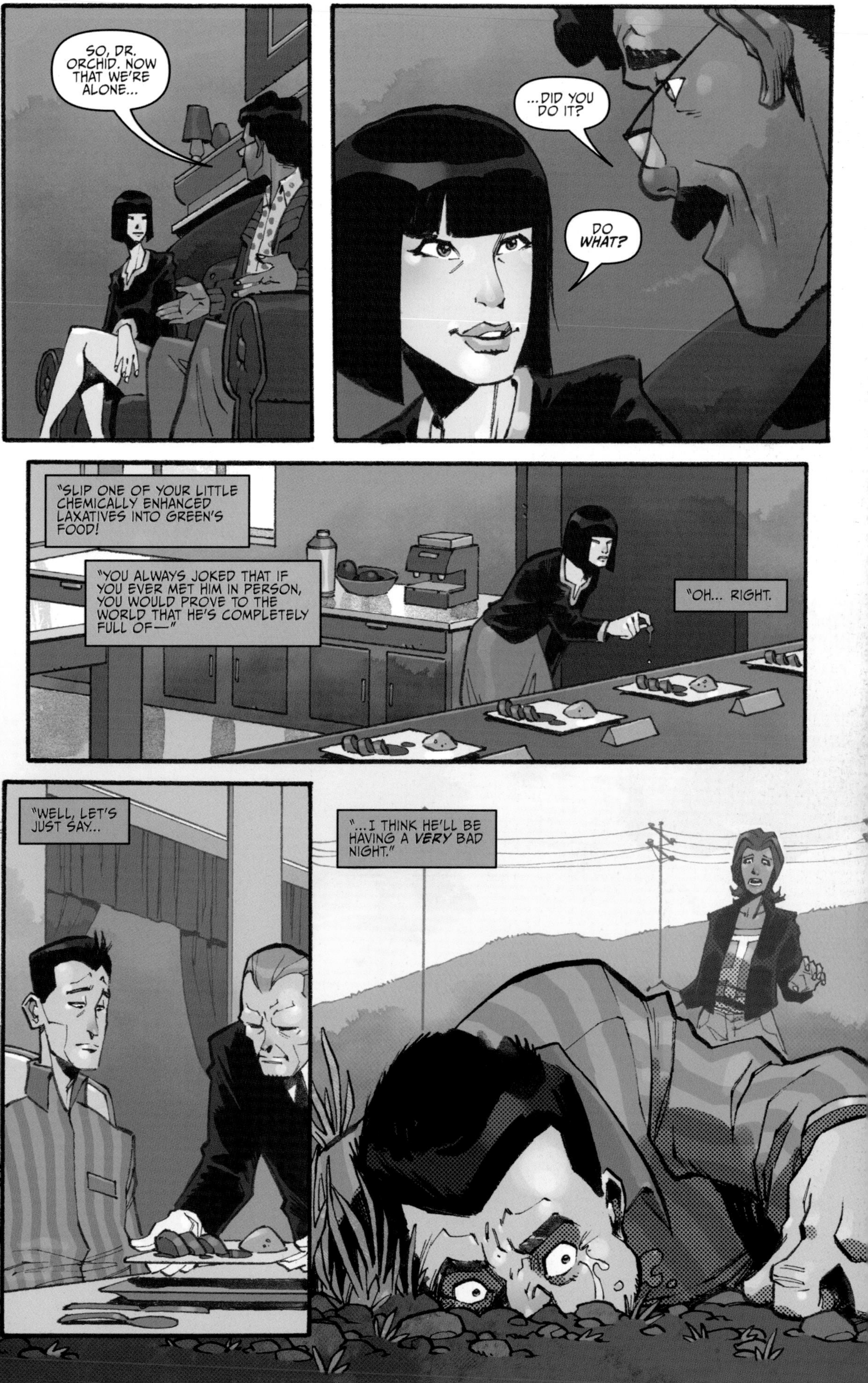
SO, DR. ORCHID. NOW THAT WE'RE ALONE...
...DID YOU DO IT?
DO *WHAT?*
"SLIP ONE OF YOUR LITTLE CHEMICALLY ENHANCED LAXATIVES INTO GREEN'S FOOD!
"YOU ALWAYS JOKED THAT IF YOU EVER MET HIM IN PERSON, YOU WOULD PROVE TO THE WORLD THAT HE'S COMPLETELY FULL OF—"
"OH... RIGHT.
"WELL, LET'S JUST SAY...
"...I THINK HE'LL BE HAVING A *VERY* BAD NIGHT."

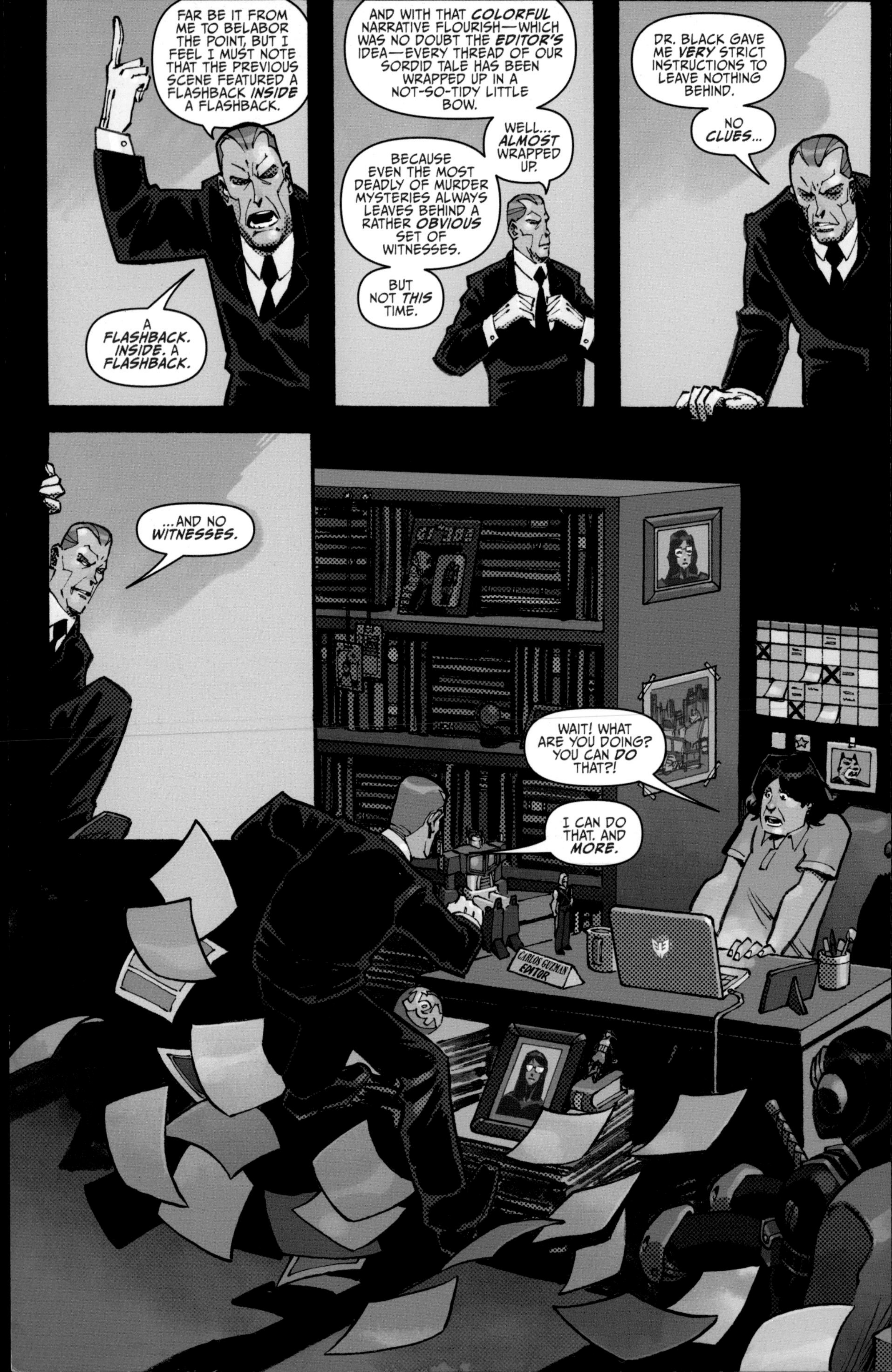
FAR BE IT FROM ME TO BELABOR THE POINT, BUT I FEEL I MUST NOTE THAT THE PREVIOUS SCENE FEATURED A FLASHBACK *INSIDE* A FLASHBACK.
A *FLASHBACK. INSIDE.* A *FLASHBACK.*
AND WITH THAT *COLORFUL* NARRATIVE FLOURISH—WHICH WAS NO DOUBT THE *EDITOR'S* IDEA—EVERY THREAD OF OUR SORDID TALE HAS BEEN WRAPPED UP IN A NOT-SO-TIDY LITTLE BOW.
WELL... *ALMOST* WRAPPED UP.
BECAUSE EVEN THE MOST DEADLY OF MURDER MYSTERIES ALWAYS LEAVES BEHIND A RATHER *OBVIOUS* SET OF WITNESSES.
BUT NOT *THIS* TIME.
DR. BLACK GAVE ME *VERY* STRICT INSTRUCTIONS TO LEAVE NOTHING BEHIND.
NO *CLUES*...
...AND NO *WITNESSES.*
WAIT! WHAT ARE YOU DOING? YOU CAN *DO* THAT?!
I CAN DO THAT. AND *MORE.*
CARLOS GUZMAN
EDITOR

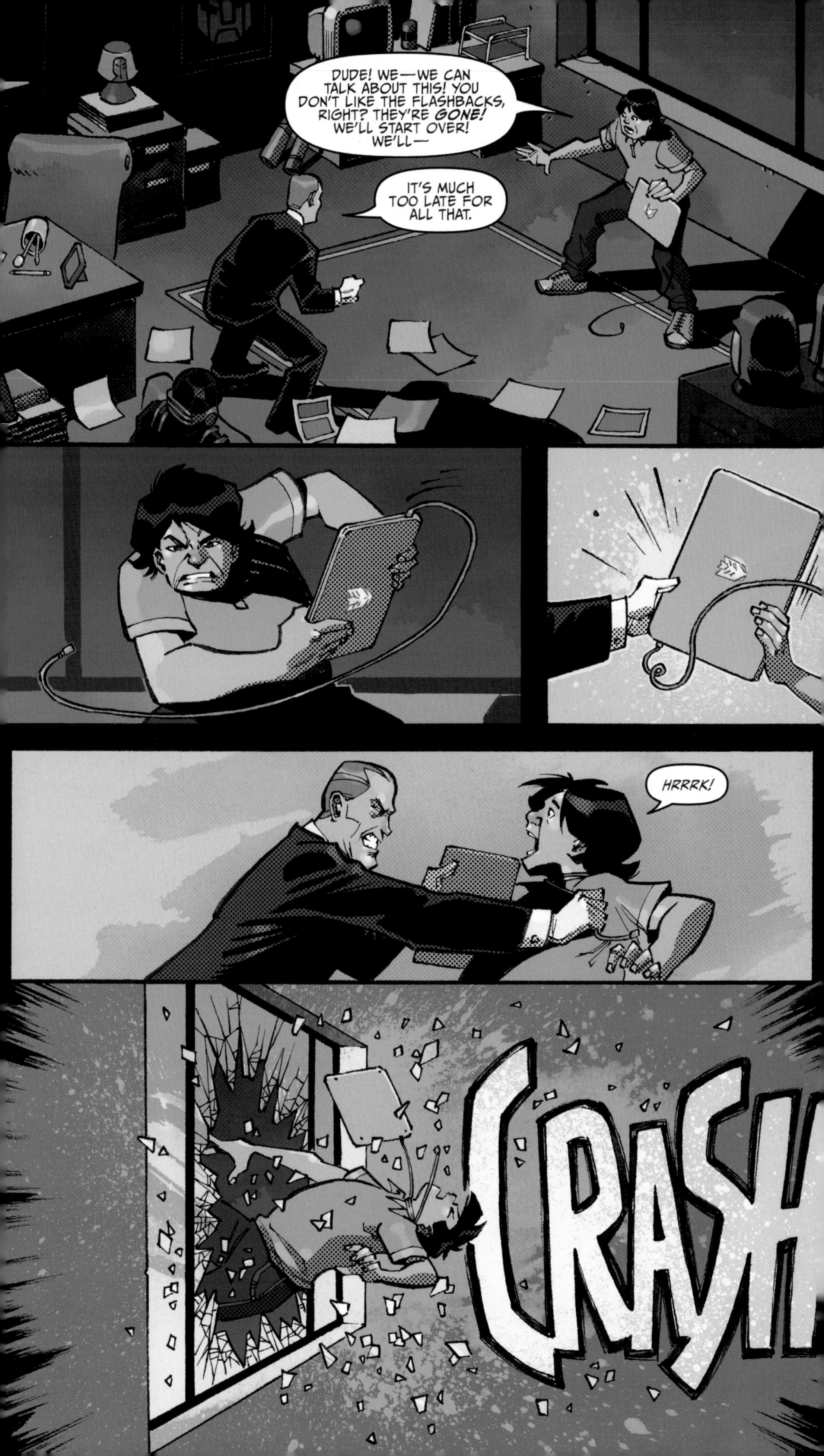
DUDE! WE—WE CAN TALK ABOUT THIS! YOU DON'T LIKE THE FLASHBACKS, RIGHT? THEY'RE *GONE!* WE'LL START OVER! WE'LL—
IT'S MUCH TOO LATE FOR ALL THAT.
HRRRK!
CRASH

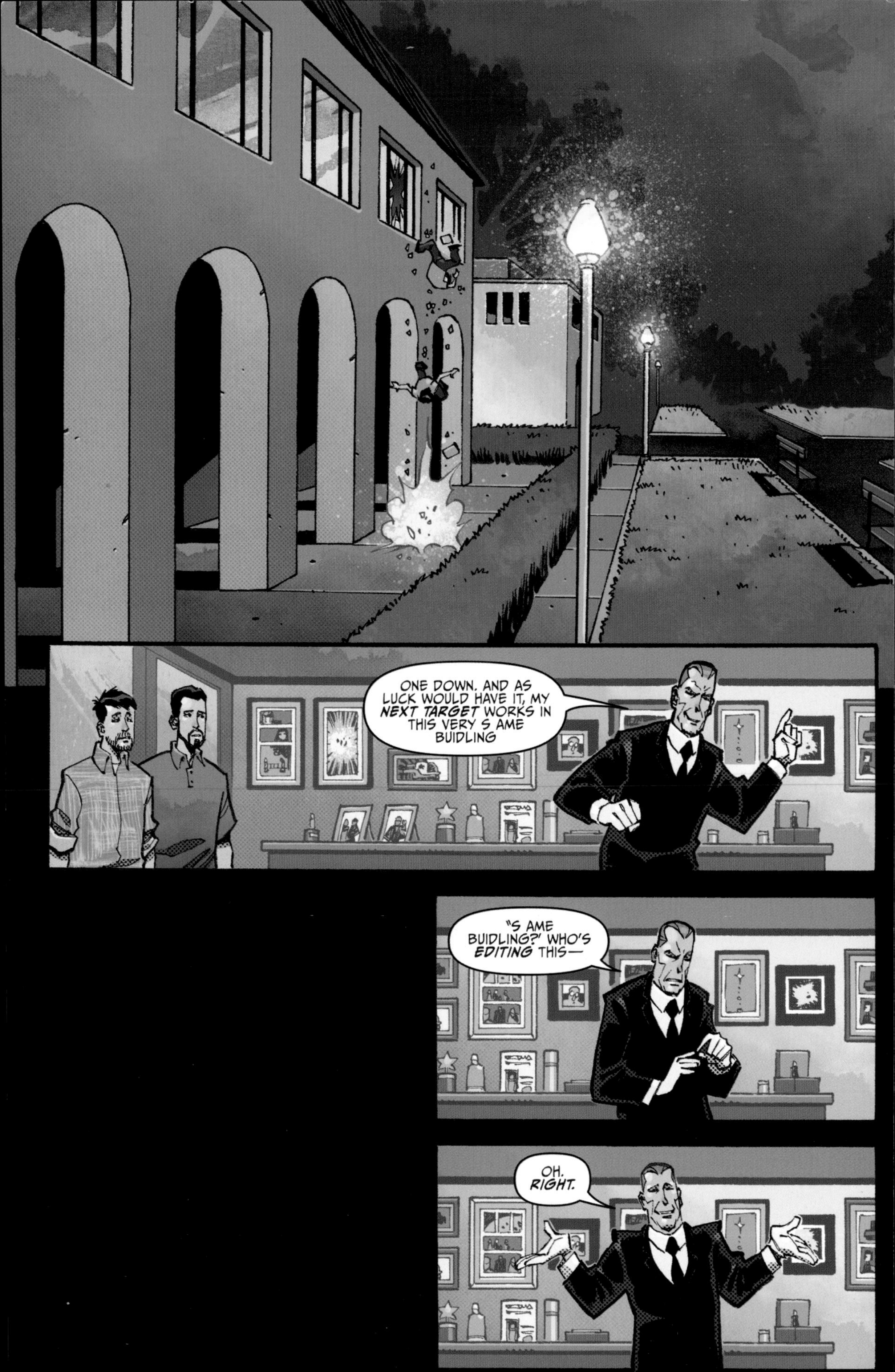
ONE DOWN. AND AS LUCK WOULD HAVE IT, MY NEXT TARGET WORKS IN THIS VERY S AME BUIDLING
"S AME BUIDLING?' WHO'S EDITING THIS—
OH. RIGHT.

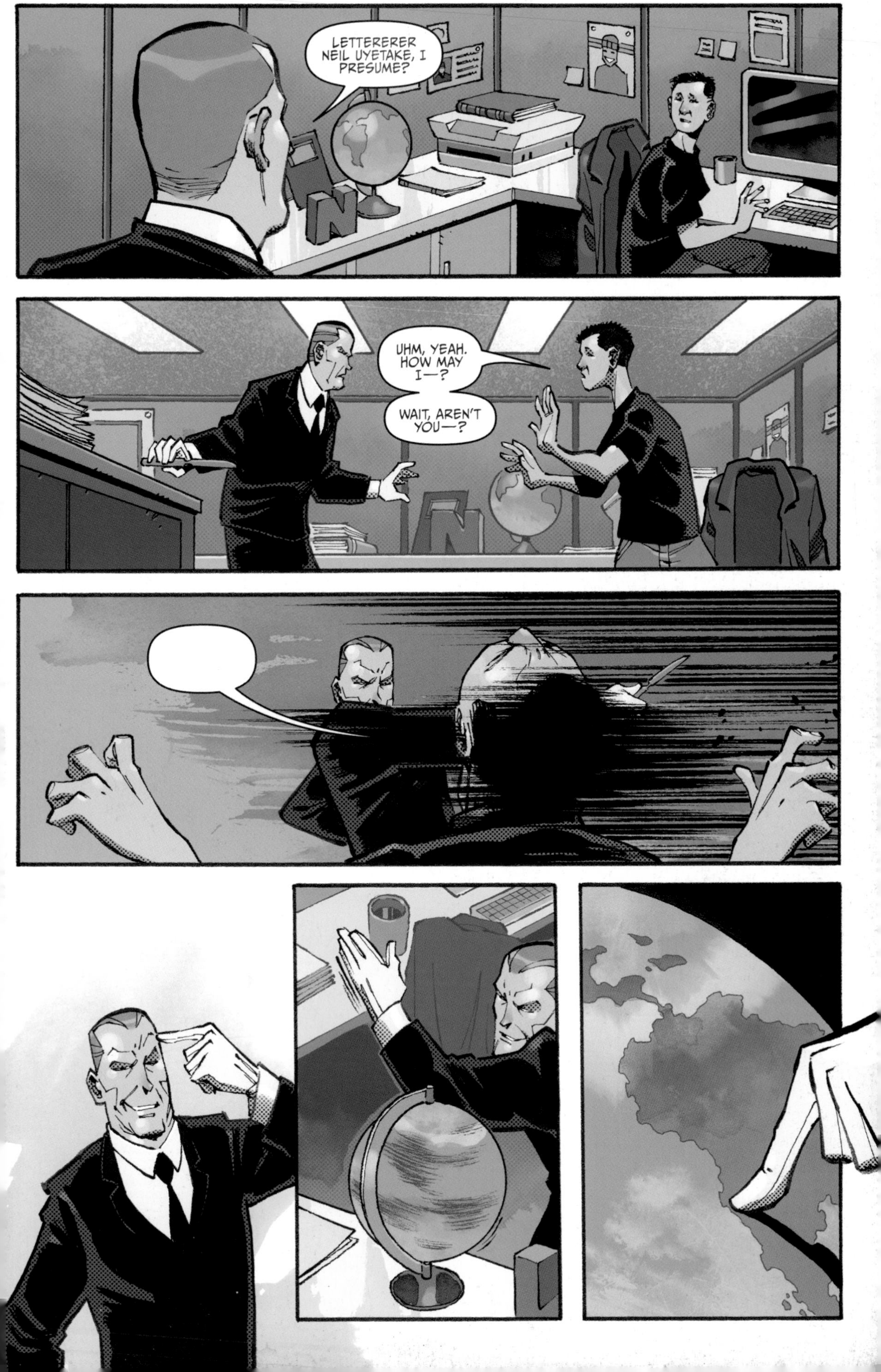
LETTERERER NEIL UYETAKE, I PRESUME?
UHM, YEAH. HOW MAY I—?
WAIT, AREN'T YOU—?

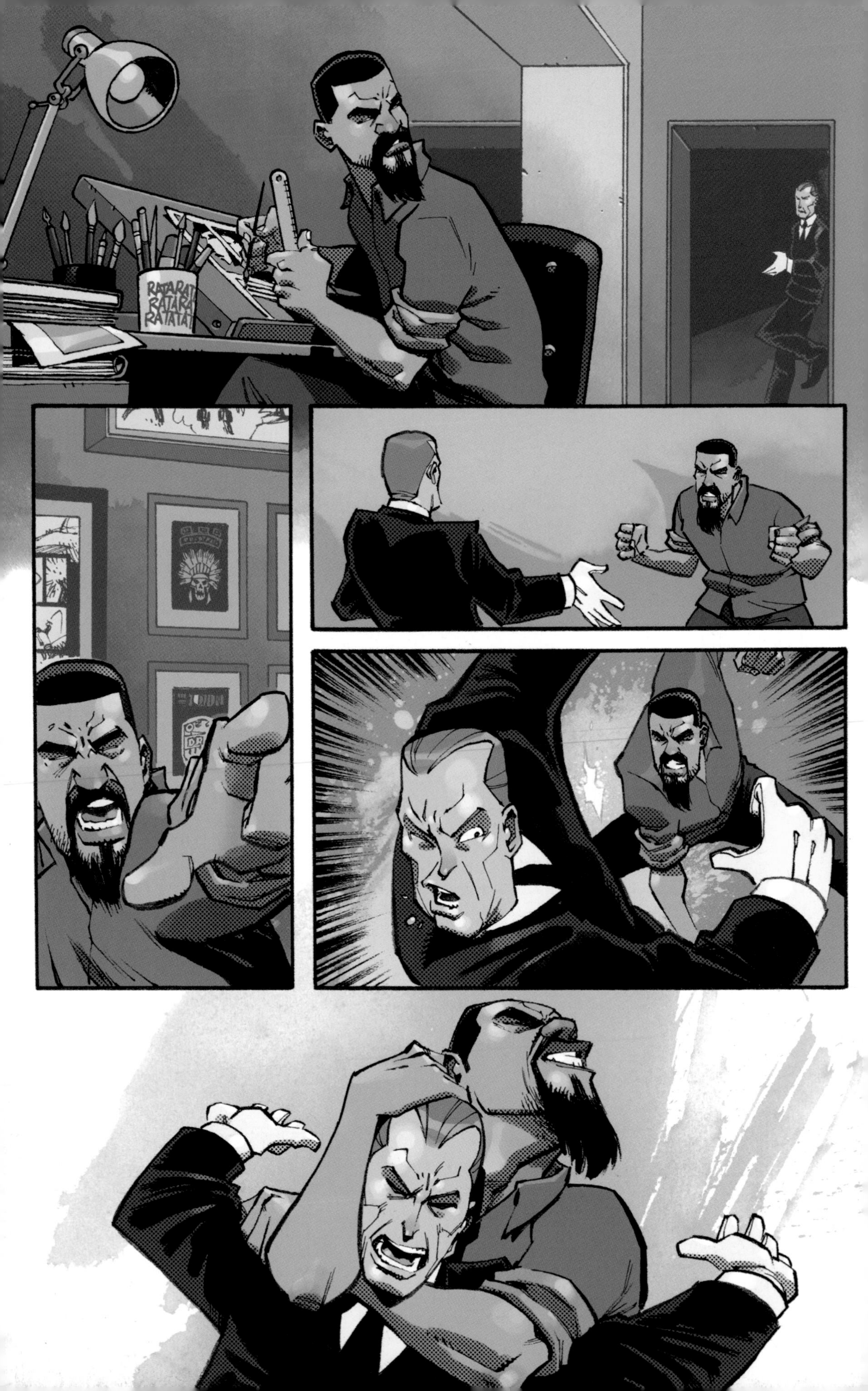

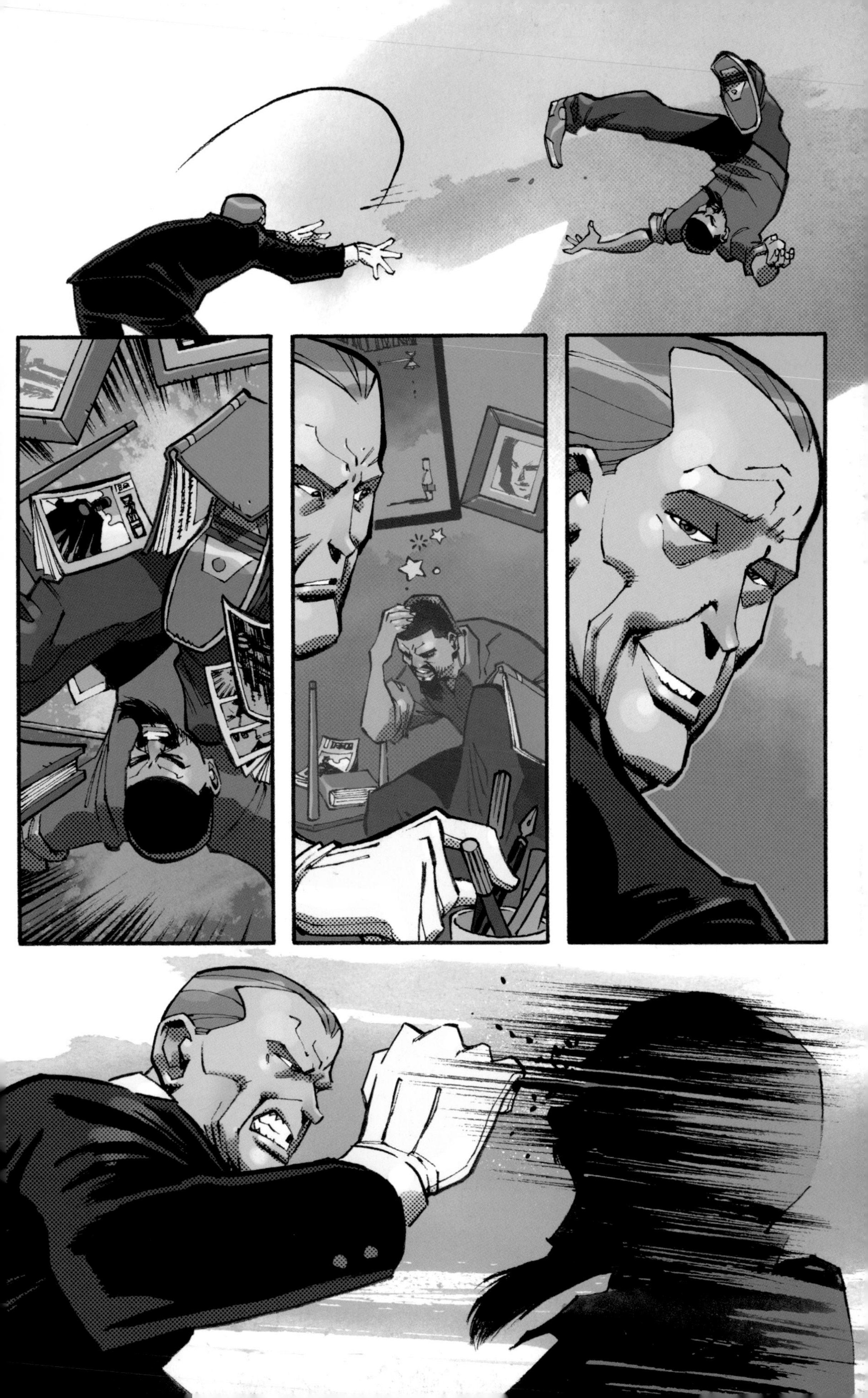

PAGE TWENTY-ONE

PAUL ALLOR, writer of the Clue comic, sits in his living room in Indiana, typing away on his laptop.

PANEL TWO
Allor looks at the screen, confused. Upton stands behind him. Allor doesn't see him yet.

    1. ALLOR: "Paul Allor, writer of the Clue comic, sits in his living room…"

    2. ALLOR: Why would I **write** that?

PANEL THREE
Allor is scrolling through the pages. Behind him, Upton pulls a large book off the shelf.

    3. ALLOR: Why would I write **any** of this?

PANEL FOUR
Allor spins around, as Upton SLAMS the book into his head.

    4. UPTON: It's a **mystery**.

PANEL FIVE
Allor is on the ground. Upton stands above him, holding the book above his head – about to deliver the killing bl

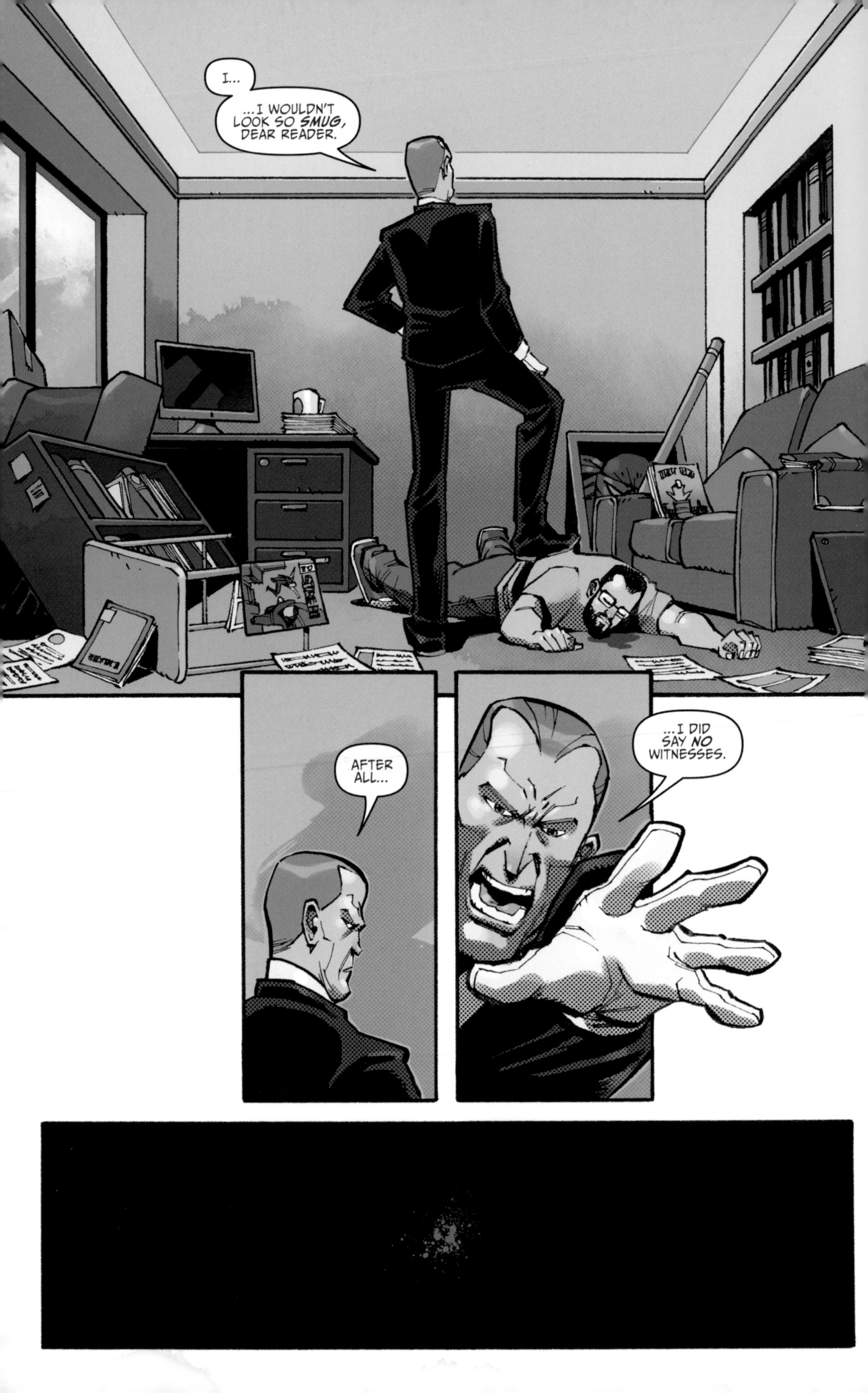
I...
...I WOULDN'T LOOK SO SMUG, DEAR READER.
AFTER ALL...
...I DID SAY NO WITNESSES.

CLUE®

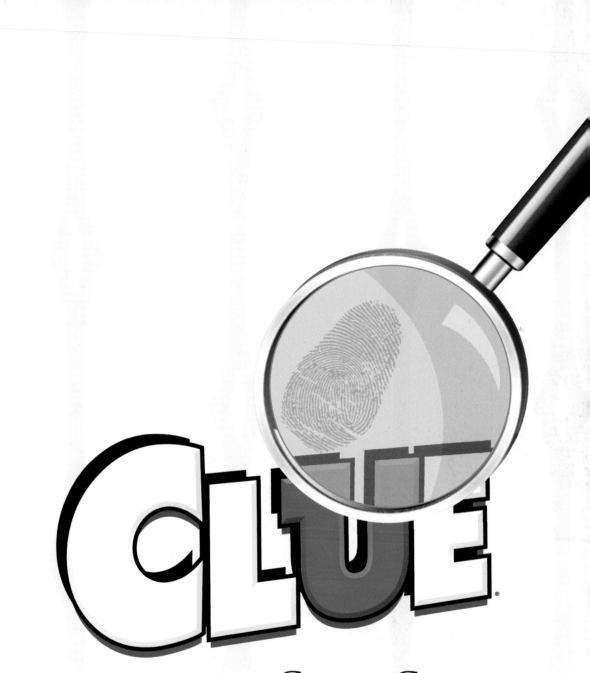

Cover Gallery

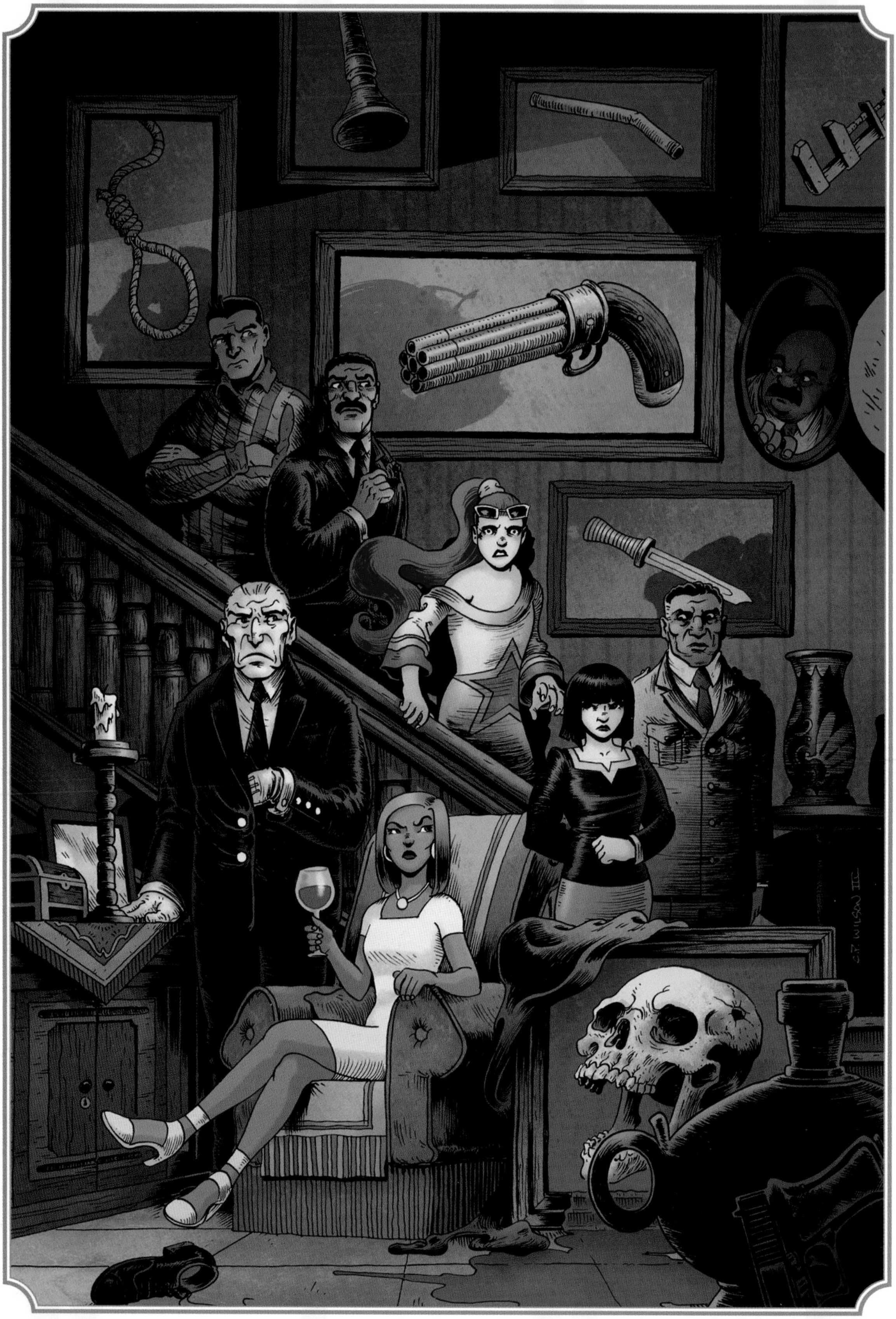

ART BY
CHARLES PAUL WILSON III

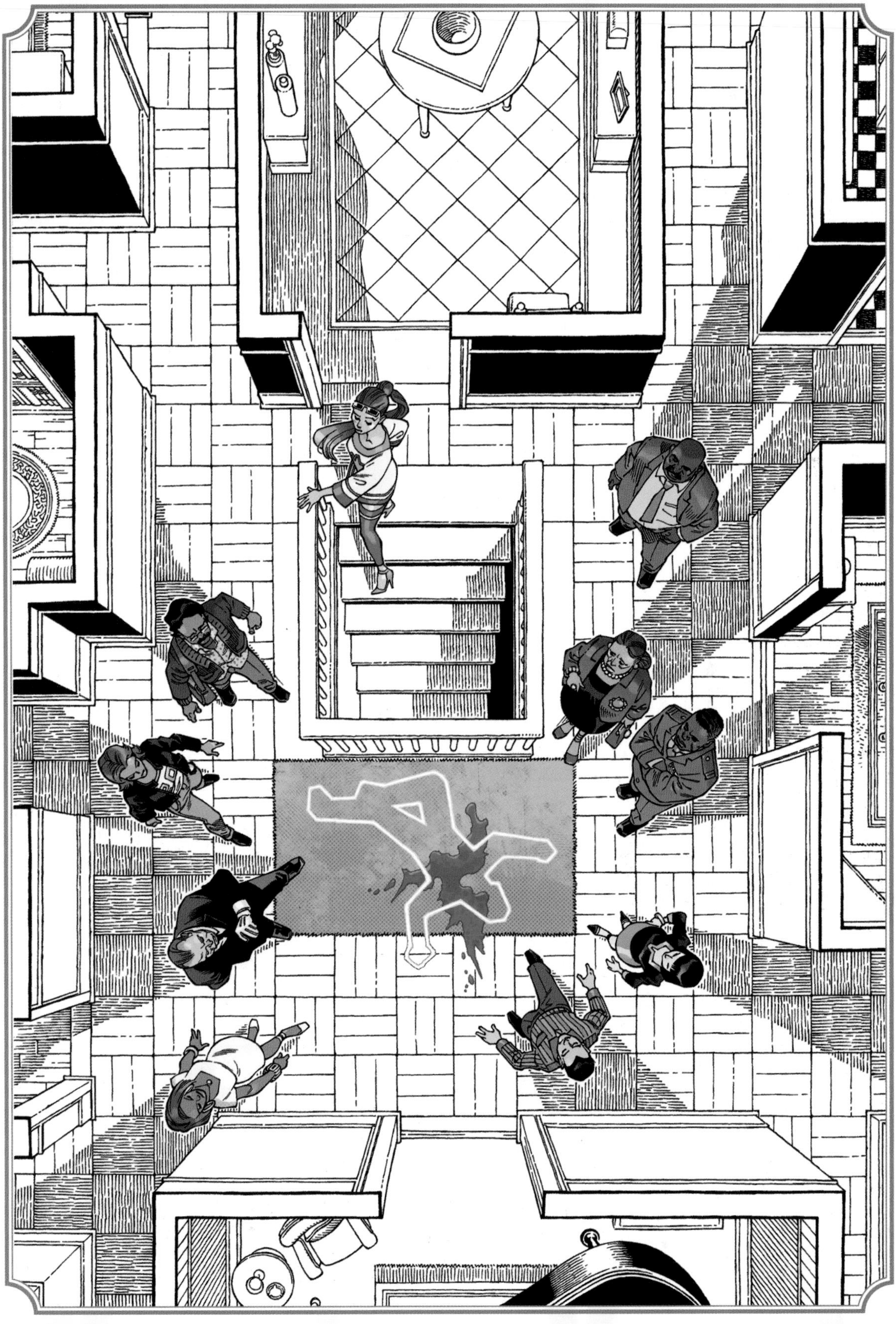

ART BY
GABRIEL RODRIGUEZ

COLORS BY
NELSON DANIEL

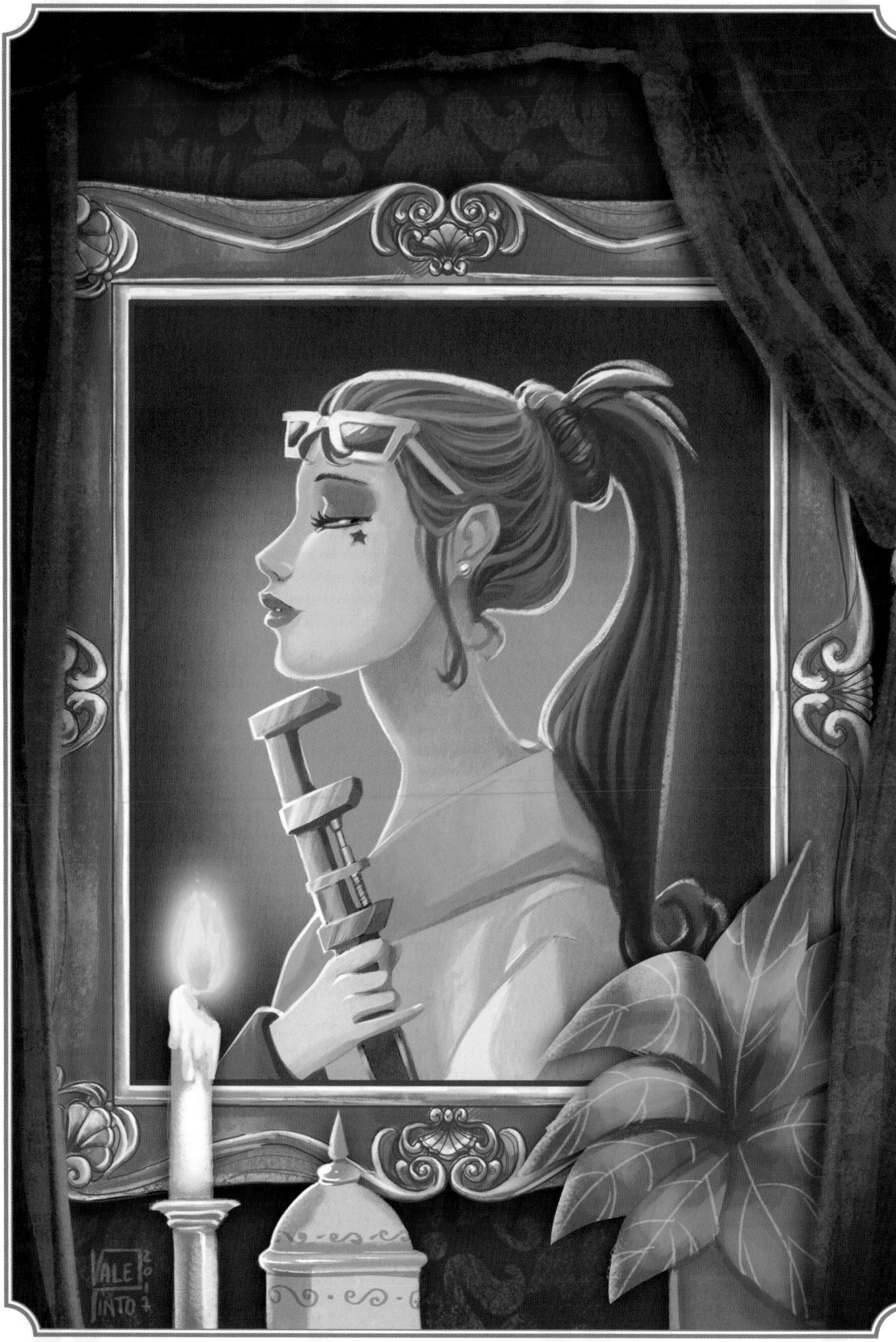
VALE PINTO 2017

ART BY

VALENTINA PINTO

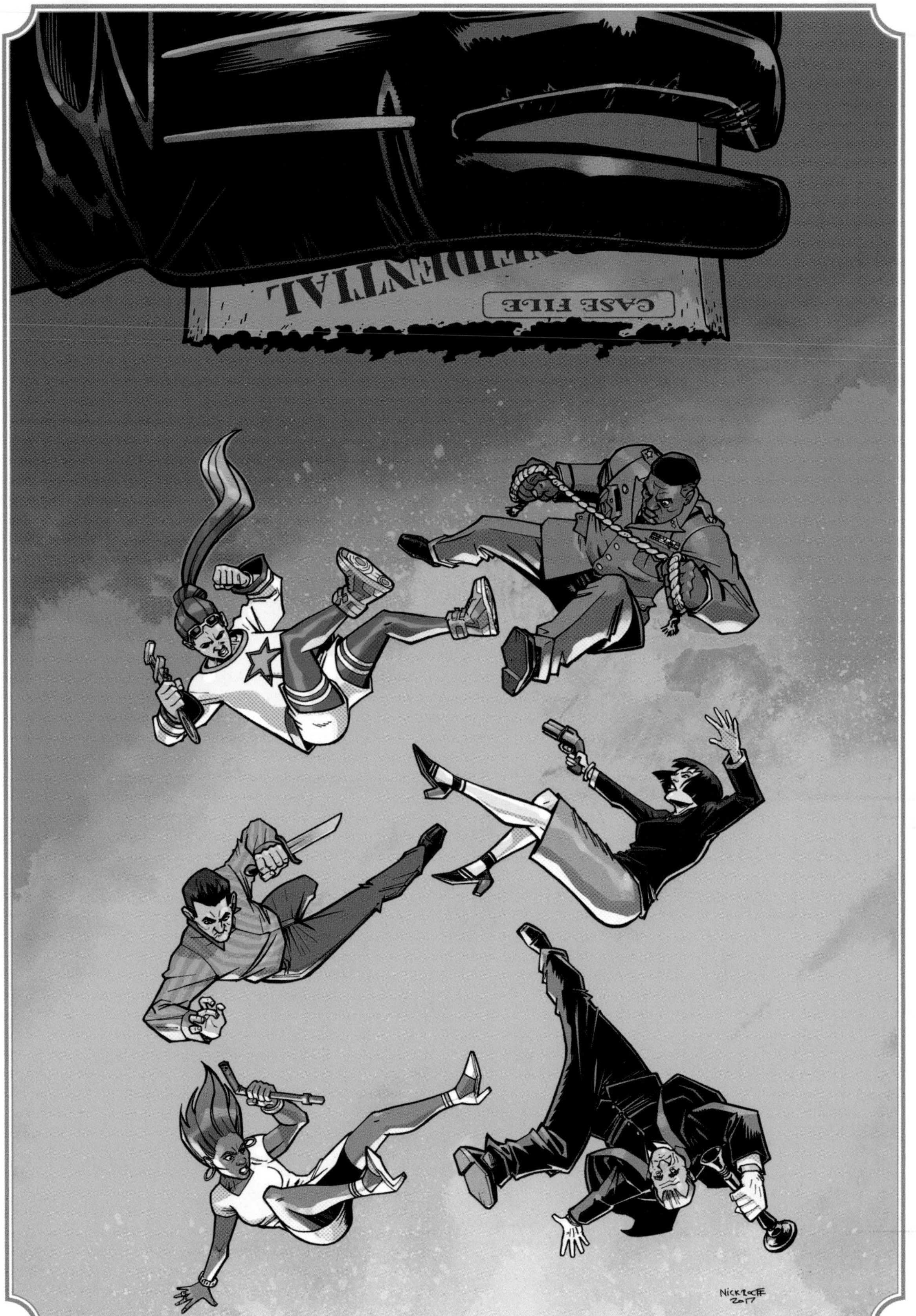
CASE FILE
NICK ROCHE 2017

ART BY
NICK ROCHE

COLORS BY
NELSON DANIEL

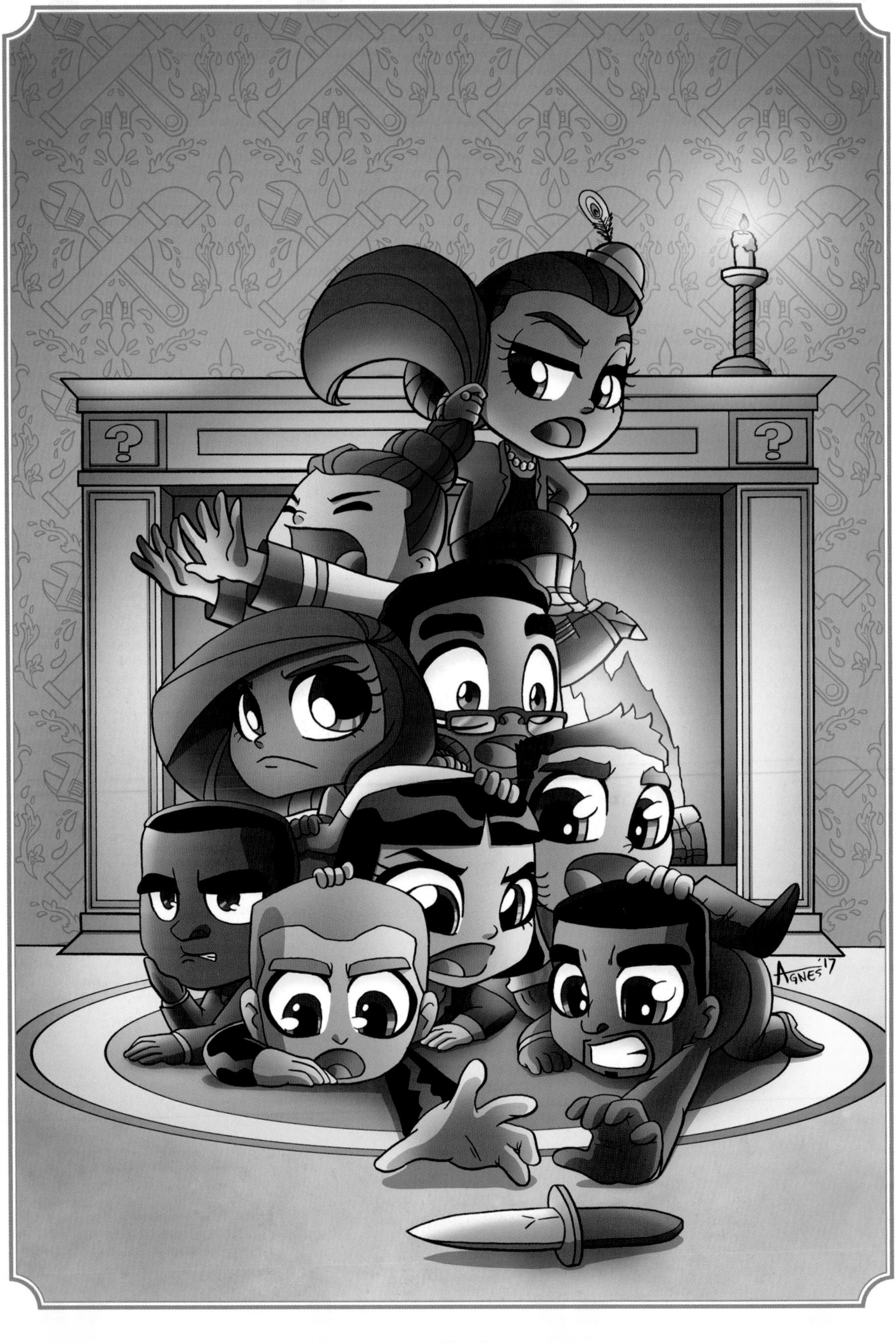
Agnes '17

ART BY
AGNES GARBOWSKA

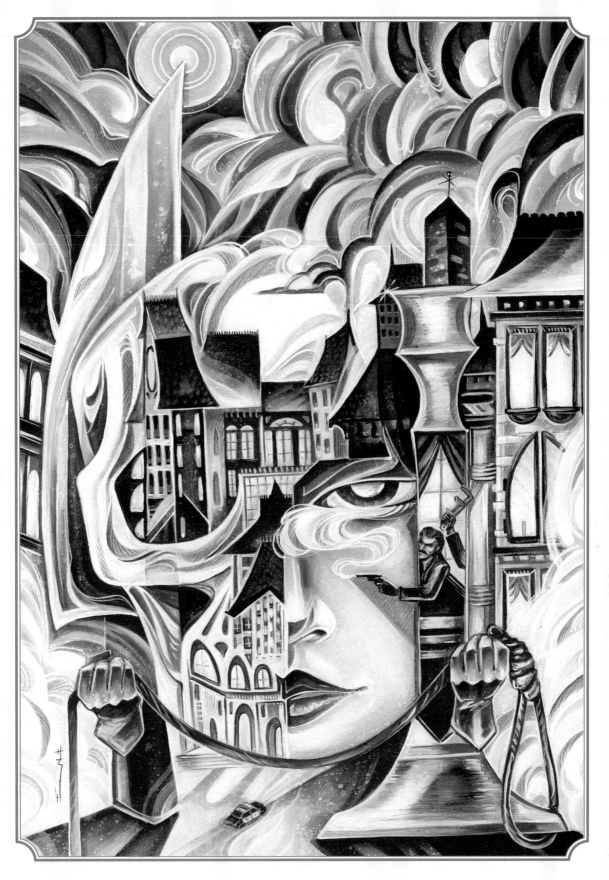

ART BY
SARA RICHARD

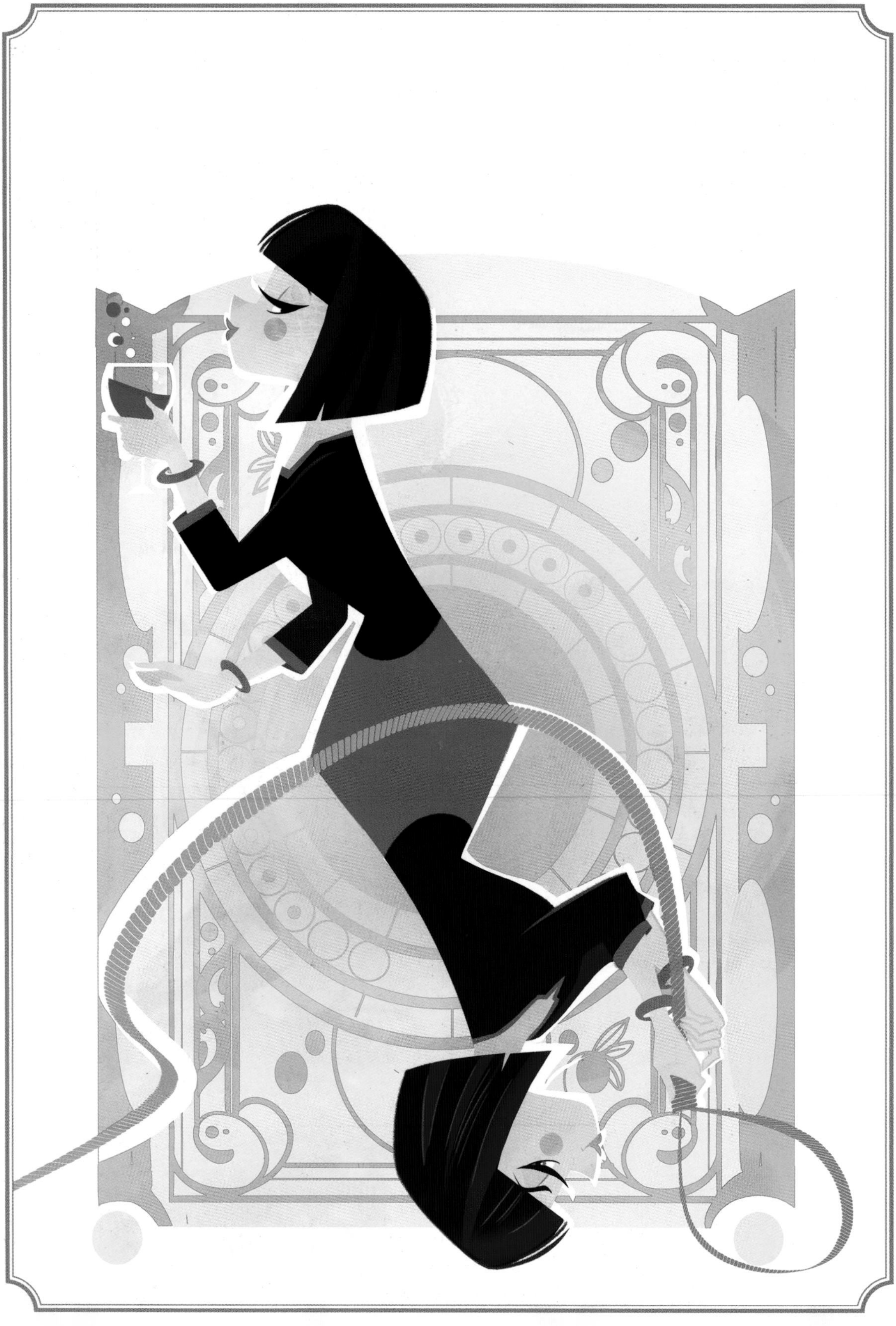

ART BY
NICOLETTA BALDARI

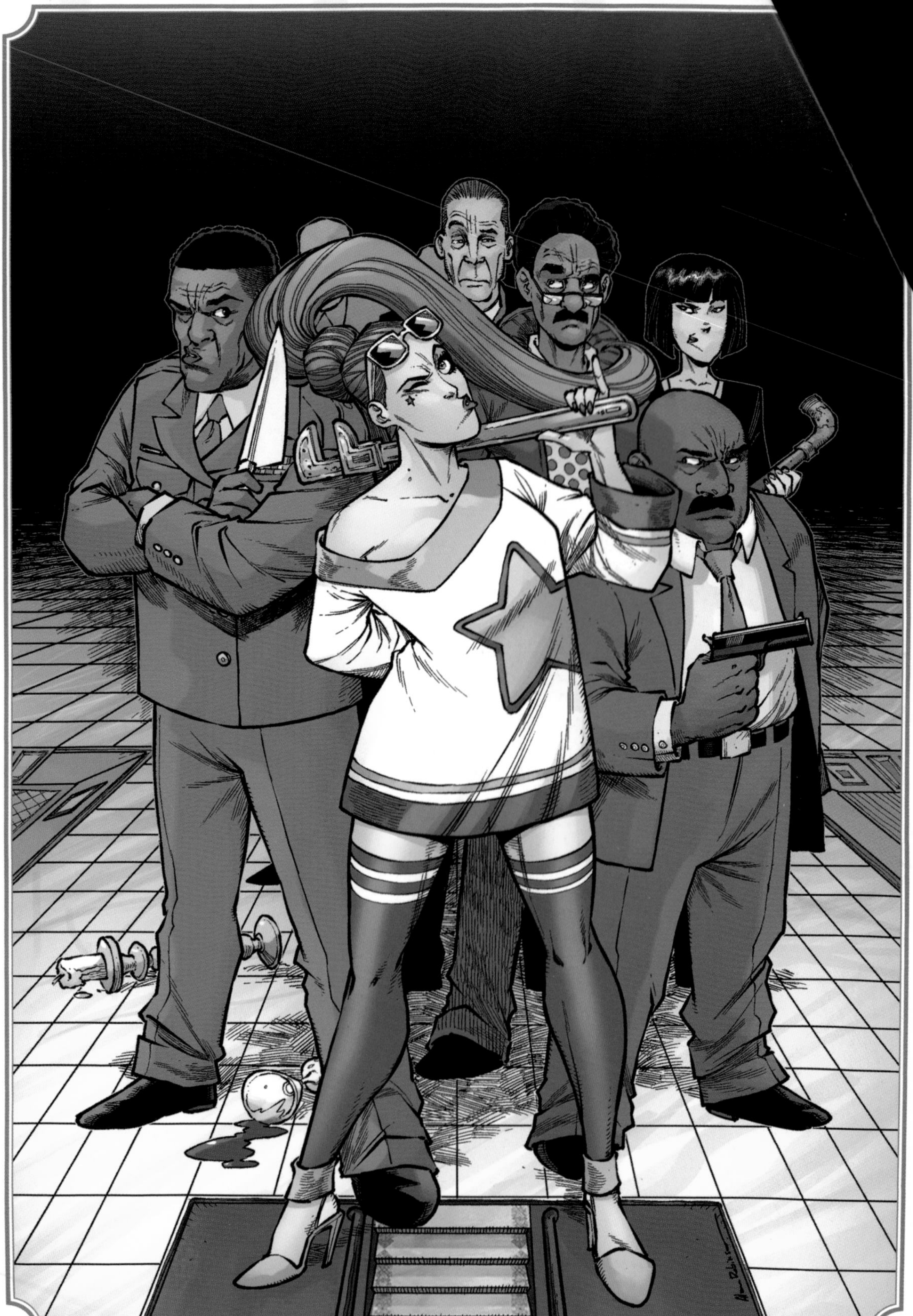

ART BY
ALAN ROBINSON

COLORS BY
JAY FOTOS

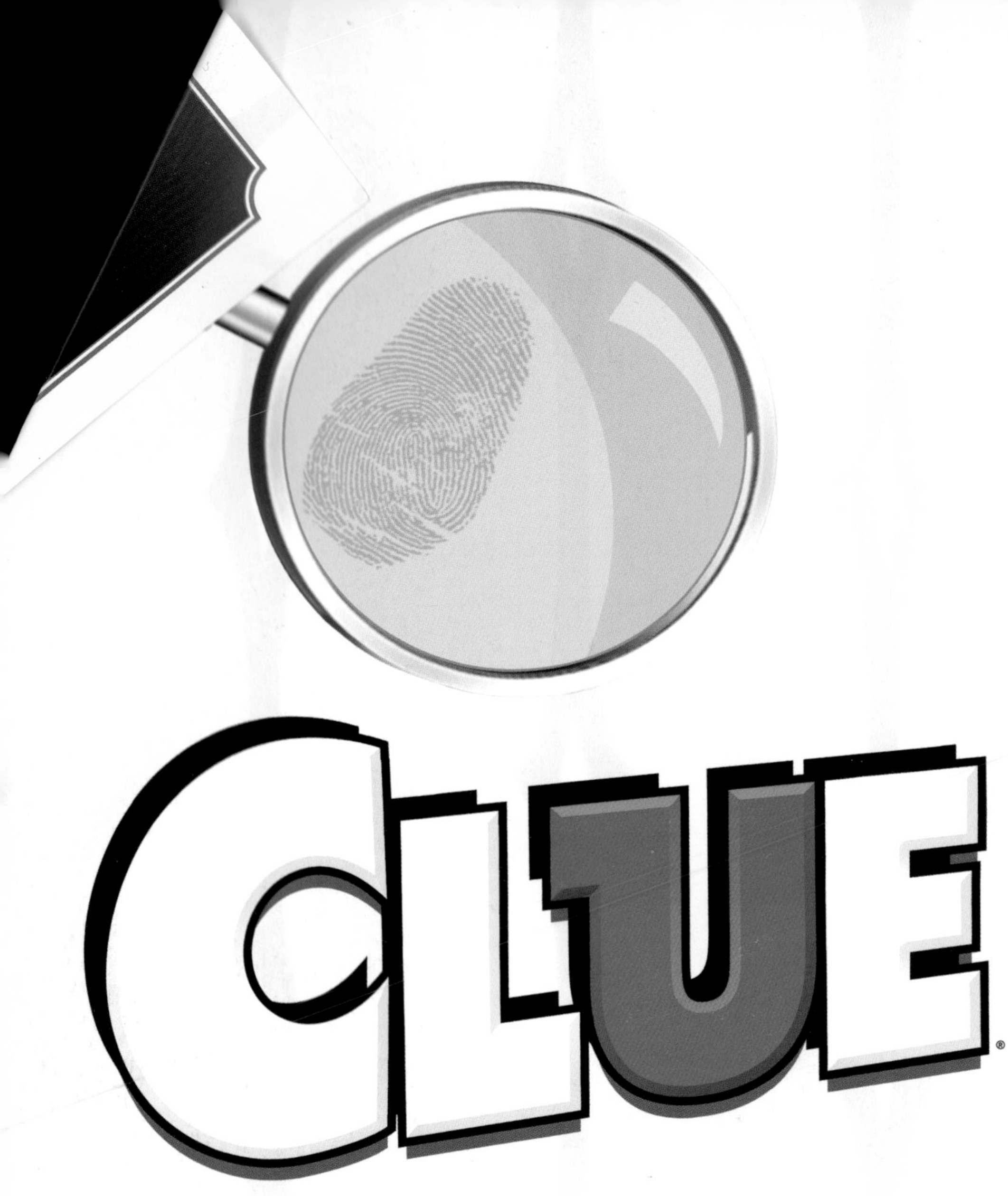

CLUE®